By the Tide
of Humber

Praise for
By the Tide of Humber

'*By the Tide of Humber* is an engrossing novel, which is not afraid to confront moral ambiguities, and speaks authentically of the grimmer side of life – but the quotidian is illuminated by lyrical descriptions of light and water, seascapes and the power of the mighty Humber'
SHENA MACKAY, *prize-winning novelist and short story writer*

'*By the Tide of Humber* totally engrossed me. It explores the difference between swimming pools and open water swimming. The indoor pool experience is a man-made, tamed version where everything is controlled within boundaries. "Wild" swimming is to reconnect with nature, to feel its power and be humbled by the baptism; swimming under the sky, there are no limits.

'The blunt, ordinary lives of Eddie and Lyn are refreshingly authentic. They are solidly built around their jobs, so you can taste the chlorine of the pool and smell the fetid prison air . . . As Lyn's swimming project plaits its way through the narrative, the raw momentum of nature sweeps aside the fragile sandcastles they have built to avoid change'
MOLLY FLETCHER,
swimmer and painter, Hampstead Ladies Pond

'I found *By the Tide of Humber* very enjoyable. It fully encompasses the thoughts and emotions of long-distance swimmers and if I was not "bitten by the bug" already I would be tempted to experience it for myself!'
ALISON STREETER,
'English Channel Queen' and world record holder

'Swimmers in particular will feel the pool, the dock basin and the tidal waters, but you don't need to be a strong swimmer to sense the pull of the Humber estuary. Daphne Glazer's compelling story sets the messy entanglements of day-to-day human life against the uplifting and enduring power of the sea'
JEAN PERRATON, *author of* Swimming against the Stream

'The river Humber is more than an atmospheric backdrop to this tale; it is a powerful presence which runs through past and present, can change lives and is both threatening and potentially liberating . . .

'Lyn commits herself to a long-distance swim in the most treacherous kind of water, a tidal estuary, muddy, windy, and prone to powerful, shifting currents. While the author describes effectively this struggle with a force of nature, she also captures delightfully experiences shared by all open water swimmers'

MARGARET DICKINSON, *director of the film* City Swimmers

'*By the Tide of Humber* is an enjoyable exploration of freedom and restraint, in which Glazer cleverly brings out the emotional extremes of love, hate and frustration with plenty of fast-paced action in and out of the water'

MARK BLEWITT, *long-distance swimmer*

'I could feel for our heroine, Lyn, the moment she first set foot in the open water, the total immersion in the aqautic environment, with all its challenges. Having been in this situation with my own swimming, I could clearly identify with the feelings and thoughts that raced through Lyn's head not just in training, but in the Humber swim itself'

DR JULIE BRADSHAW MBE,
*seventeen times world record holder,
including a butterfly solo swim of the English Channel*

'I found *By the Tide of Humber* thrilling, and I was absorbed by the way the various themes are intertwined – the hopelessness of people's lives, marriage break-ups, the yearning for emotion and physical passion, and the sheer exhilaration of the swimming scenes, among the best I've read. Daphne Glazer conveys so beautifully a swimmer's style and imagination, and the differing characteristics of the pool, lake, and coastal waters'

CHARLES SPRAWSON,
swimmer and author of
Haunts of the Black Masseur: the Swimmer as Hero

By the Tide of Humber

Daphne Glazer

**Tindal
Street
Press**

First published in September 2007
by Tindal Street Press Ltd
217 The Custard Factory, Gibb Street, Birmingham, B9 4AA
www.tindalstreet.co.uk

A CIP catalogue reference for this book is available
from the British Library

ISBN: 978 0 9551 384 5 4

Typeset by Country Setting, Kingsdown, Kent
Printed and bound in Great Britain by Clays Ltd, St Ives PLC

For Peter

Contents

Had we but world enough, and time,
This coyness, lady, were no crime.
We would sit down and think which way
To walk, and pass our long love's day;
Thou by the Indian Ganges' side
Shouldst rubies find; I by the tide
Of Humber would complain. I would
Love you ten years before the Flood . . .

But at my back I always hear
Time's winged chariot hurrying near;
And yonder all before us lie
Deserts of vast eternity . . .

Now let us roll all our strength, and all
Our sweetness, up into one ball;
And tear our pleasures with rough strife
Thorough the iron gates of life.
Thus, though we cannot make our sun
Stand still, yet we will make him run.

From 'To His Coy Mistress'
by Andrew Marvell

I

The Iron Gates of Life

I

Lyn stood for a moment poised, staring over the shimmering length, and then she raised her arms and dived. She was in the lift of her body, soaring and gliding into the water to emerge halfway down the pool.

After the long morning patrolling the bath side the shock of the water on her skin intoxicated her. She'd forgotten the magic of it and the powerful rhythm of the crawl. The winter sun formed amoeba squiggles on the turquoise tiles at the bottom of the pool, and she became a dolphin sliding and frolicking in the golden twirls. Outside, frost lay on the ground in scurfy patches and the sun held no real warmth and yet here you could make believe you were in some tropical paradise; that surf bounded on white beaches and palm fronds clashed together in a breeze.

In turning to coast back down the pool, she looked across at the high chair and met Andy's eyes – he was obviously astonished and mouthed something at her, which she refused to pick up. He couldn't believe that she, a fellow lifeguard, would actually swim in her lunch break. He would never dream of doing anything like that himself.

She'd become no better than Andy, she told herself, a lifeguard who only swam during staff training. She'd hear veteran lifeguard Wes worrying about whether he'd be able to pass the fitness test. Keeping up to speed was growing increasingly difficult for him. If you never trained, you'd not have the go or the speed to rescue someone. Though it wasn't as if this return to swimming was arduous – no, it surprised her how exhilarating it felt. Once you became absorbed in the patterns of your stroke, you forgot everything else. All the petty irritations of annoying swimmers faded away. You concentrated on the whispering of your breath, the flipping of your feet, and the curving of your arms as they urged you forward.

'We never see *you* in the water, Lyn,' a regular called to her when she reached the shallow end. 'You making New Year's resolutions in advance?'

'You'll have to wait and see,' she said, grinning across at the man.

She hadn't intended to swim today – it had somehow happened. The idea had come to her as she plodded round the pool feeling listless. The last day in December was always so cold and colourless . . . you'd survived Christmas but January had to be got through. She'd been wishing she could do something exciting – anything to lever her out of the same routine: wake with the alarm, shower, cornflakes, bike to work, vacuum gyms, patrol the pool, muck out the showers and hose them down. Just the whole lifeless churning over and over of those familiar activities.

Opening her locker to look for the sandwiches she'd put there that morning, her gaze had fallen on her swimsuit and goggles – she always kept them there. And it had occurred to her that she could change the day. Even being in the water and not on the poolside meant you looked at the world from a new perspective, and just that made a difference. You saw the glassy ripple before you, and above you the sunlight glancing off the panes. When rain lashed down outside it set up a subterranean percussion which was magnified under the arc of the roof. Spending time in the water also gave the day an almost exotic and energizing flavour and for a while prevented your thoughts grinding over in the usual depressive grooves: how you couldn't change anything; how you were stuck, always wishing things were different. Nobody knew what had really happened, and she couldn't tell anyone. She'd always been secretive – it was just the way she'd been from being a little kid – only this was so much worse.

Having her emotional life elsewhere sealed her off from everybody about her. At work she had to concentrate on what she was doing, but her other life would keep edging its way back, nudging into her head; a rippling in her vision turning into a migraine that could only get worse. The aimlessness of public holidays and off-duty times was deadly – though Christmas Day hadn't been as bad as she'd expected.

Aunty Mags had tried to pinion her with the usual 'I can't understand why a lovely girl like you can't get a nice lad . . . there are a few about, you know . . .'

It was always the same – but she'd forestalled Aunty Mags by handing her a massive gin and lime and telling her to look after her dad, Mags's brother, in the front room. Her dad always let them know how he found Christmas testing on his nerves and Lyn reckoned it was because he couldn't pay his daily visit to his local. Got up in his best Fair Isle and black polyester trousers, he had the air of someone trying on garments in a big department store – all his movements were rigid and tense, embarrassed-seeming. It was as if he'd lost his ballast and drifted about picking things up, putting them down, and staring out of the window. But once he'd dispatched several cans of super-strength lager, he loosened up a bit. Lyn was fairly sure he'd not enjoyed having his ears punished by his sister's Elvis warbles.

Dad and Aunty Mags safely installed with booze and fags in her front room, Lyn had been free to start on the turkey and the trimmings. She was the family's only cook. Dad opened tins and packets for his meals. Aunty Mags ordered takeaways, ate at the pub or was treated by some boyfriend.

At the sight of the bronzed turkey surrounded by crisp golden potatoes, and the table laid out with a fancy cloth and scarlet crackers, Dad and Aunty Mags broke out in rumbles of praise. Their pleasure buoyed her up. But later, once they'd lurched out to their taxi and it had coughed away, she'd had to prop open the back door to rid the house of smoke, and gloom had closed in on her like a choking fog. Nothing was ever going to change. Her life was slipping away while she waited . . . Here she was, no longer young. The end of the year had snooped up and now it was lying in wait. The baths crowd were all going out to celebrate on the thirty-first. Andy had wanted her to join them – but she'd refused the invitation.

And this was the last day of the old year. Maybe that was why she'd had the sudden urge to do something unexpected, why she'd had her lunchtime swim. After that swim the rest of the day improved. She was still in the luxury of her limbs scything through the water, of the light patterns weaving over the tiles. Now and then she'd see quivers darting along the surface. Looking down from the chair at the swimmers, she could feel the soft cushion of the water holding her and she glided down the black lines of tiles as though smoothing a path; she became so absorbed in the sensation that she had to drag her concentration back to work.

At home that night she looked at the kitchen calendar – a snow scene in the Alps and below it all the days scored out with single black lines. Part of her daily routine was to mark off each day at bedtime, as though she was anticipating an important event. But this was her life she was striking off and she'd most likely be doing the same for the next twenty years, waiting for release. Such a stretch of time made her head reel.

With a mug of coffee she settled to watch the New Year in on telly. At ten Andy rang. 'Come out with us, Lyn babes.'

Music and voices hit her ear and she struggled to make herself say no, no she didn't feel like going out. She didn't want to be alone at home seeing in the New Year while everyone else was celebrating, but if she joined them she'd find her secret life jostling against the world of the baths people and she'd be locked in a conflict that exhausted her. She was bound to feel guilty later. Andy tried a few more times to persuade her but she was adamant.

At midnight she stood at the back door staring out, with a glass of lager in her hand. Fireworks shot pink and gold whirls and silver spears through the petrol-blue sky. Catherine wheels fountained and crackers banged. Ships in the harbour and out on the North Sea wailed, and gouts of music sprayed from passing cars. On the telly they were playing 'Auld Lang Syne' and she felt the tears pressing behind her eyes and, shivering, she went back indoors and snapped off the TV. She'd go up to bed – this afternoon it had been fine; swimming had changed everything just for a while. And it was a new year . . . perhaps this new year would surprise her. Goose pimples prickled on her arms and as she mounted the stairs she could still trace the night-time drama that she'd felt on the doorstep – the blazing golds and silvers, the scarlet and pink and behind them the awful longing; a yearning she couldn't put a name on.

2

With an effort Eddie shot the lock on pad 25 and expected to meet Smithson's sardonic gaze. Smithson was on extended visits from a dispersal prison and wasn't allowed to mix with the other cons. He was of a different order from them – a big boy and he knew it.

Eddie wanted to collect Smithson's food tray but what he saw drove out any thought of it. What the hell was this? His saliva turned bitter and his heart hammered. He wanted to vomit. Smithson was dangling from the window bars. He'd strung himself up by his sheets and his face was trapped in bluish metallic pallor. Behind him lowered a pale January afternoon.

A pigeon keened and woo-hooed on the windowsill, and feet banged on the metal stair treads heading down to the ones, as the inmates were unlocked to make their way out for an afternoon in the workshops. *Move, act*, he commanded himself; *get a grip!* He got on his radio and spoke to control, asked for the ligature knife and someone from the hospital to assist.

He was alone in the cell with Smithson. He must be dead – but what if he wasn't? Eddie fought an urge to rush out of the cell; he had to force himself to approach Smithson's well-muscled body. Somehow he would have to shift the strain off Smithson's neck. He tried to take the man's weight on his shoulder and chest, slide an arm round him.

If Smithson could be resuscitated, he had to act at once. For God's sake, let them hurry! No way could he place his mouth on Smithson's – what if Smithson was a drug user . . . who knew what he might be carrying? This place was full of HIV, Aids, Hep C; you were aware of disease all the time. Whenever a man had a nosebleed or started cutting his arms, you reached for the plastic gloves. Contamination was in the air.

His hand brushed Smithson's neck, and the skin was cold to the touch. Eddie's chest filled with splinters of ice. He couldn't find a pulse. Oh, let them be quick! Why did Smithson have to do this now, and on his landing? If he must, he could have topped himself in his dispersal nick. This was his fault – a man had killed himself. He ought to have made an effort to get to know Smithson – though he'd only been on visits; there hadn't been time. Just an excuse – he ought to have known. But how could you tell what someone might do?

Eddie's head whirled. At least he didn't have Smithson looking at him – the back of the man's head was against his chest and that probing stare would fix on whoever entered the cell next.

In an attempt to ground himself, he studied Smithson's hair. It was black but flecked with grey and the follicles crowded together: coarse, thick, hair – not the sort of hair you would expect on a man of his age. You'd be prepared for a bald spot perhaps, or some thinning. This hair would keep sprouting even when Smithson was in his coffin. Eddie could smell it and feel it tickling his cheeks. God almighty, let them send somebody.

The pad contained better stuff than you saw in other cons' pads in this nick – a Grundig radio; a pile of paperbacks – crime probably; the usual roll-on deodorant; an orange; a writing pad; a Parker biro. A big framed photograph stood on the locker beside two piles of letters.

Eddie's arms ached. He stared at the picture. This must be Smithson's girlfriend. She looked a lot younger than he did – but then the kinds of girls who visited men in prison were a breed apart. They came clopping into the visits room on their dagger-heeled stilettos, wearing stretch denims that accentuated every ripple in their flesh, or minis that skipped on their buttocks. Bet your life they'd be carrying smack or dope or phets – stuffed into mouths, vaginas even.

He'd have topped himself because of her, bound to have – she'd have found someone else or just decided she was fed up with being on her own – though she looked like someone who wouldn't be alone for long. She was a blonde with a big smiling mouth and widely spaced eyes. Looking across at her helped Eddie hold on.

Then he heard the crack of shoes on the landing, and they arrived with the knife and took over, placing the body on the bed. Charlie, a medical officer, felt Smithson's wrist and shone a light in his eyes.

Bri wanted to know if anyone had opened a 2052 on Smithson. No, nobody had suspected he might self-harm; besides, he was only on visits. Suicides like this didn't look good for the prison. The SO frowned and stared at them without speaking.

Later in the day, when the panic had subsided, Eddie ran into Mal, the landing officer on the threes.

'Well, one down, six hundred and odd to go,' Mal said, and grinned. Eddie tried to grin back.

Bri, the SO, called out from his office, 'Ed, in here a minute.'

Eddie stood in the doorway and looked across at Bri. 'You all right, Ed?' he asked.

'Sure, Bri,' Eddie said, his head throbbing.

At teatime he quit the prison and made for the staff mess with Mal. In the road the wind blasted from the estuary.

Car headlights stained the early gloom. Eddie felt the coldness of the wind on his cheeks and was thankful. The prison always seemed to be airless on the fours, even in winter – in summer the heat stifled. The electric fans set high up in the roof only scooped the burning air and flung it back. Heat hung under the roof panes on the coldest days.

They stood at the serving hatch watching the kitchen staff plopping beef-and-carrot pie on to the white plates and wedging hillocks of mashed potatoes beside it.

Eddie took a seat opposite Mal. He looked at his plate and grimaced. 'They always seem to give you too much.'

'Go on, you're a growing lad!' Mal slid up mashed potato with the side of his fork. 'Get stuck in.'

Eddie didn't listen as Mal embarked on a lengthy story about that fucking SO Brian always giving him the crap jobs. This metamorphosed into how the cons got him down – particularly that gobshite, Bainton – nothing was ever simple with him, he was always pestering for something. 'Does my fucking head in – I could strangle the lot of 'em. They never learn.'

Eddie was in the moment of opening up Smithson's pad and staring at the dense shape hanging before the window. He saw the photograph on the locker, the face smiling out. Smithson obviously meant to kill himself – he wasn't crying out for help, like the YPs slitting their arms and later fingering the dull red bracelets so lovingly. No, he had made sure.

The only other dead person Eddie had seen was his maternal grandfather. He'd stood beside his mother in the chapel of rest and gazed into the coffin. He was amazed that Grandad Simpkin's face was blank of all the scribbles he used to notice on it – just as though it was a magic writing pad and the metal bar had been drawn down, erasing everything written there.

His thoughts wound back to the YPs. For two years he'd worked on the YP wing, and he hadn't liked it. The cutting disturbed him.

'I feel better when I cut,' they told him. 'Cutting takes my anger away.'

'What about a pint when we knock off?' Mal said.

Eddie forced himself to concentrate on his friend. 'Yes, that's what I need.' He pushed the remnants of the beef pie to the side of his plate.

They walked back from the mess in the wind. Lorries bounced past on the rutted road, making for the ferry terminal or the BP chemical works at Saltend. At night the oil terminal fizzed with white lights and the air stuck in your lungs. Once there'd been a chemical leak. Men in the exercise yard had looked up and seen a pink cloud swooping over the city. They'd chuntered on about germ warfare and biological weapons.

The red brick fortress dominated the area, like a Gothic palace for the containment of undesirables. People on buses peered across, hoping for a glimpse of criminals and clanking chains. Eddie knew that feeling. As a young lad he used to crane his neck to see what lay beyond the high perimeter wall. But of course he never saw anything, which only increased his longing to penetrate the mysteries.

He remembered his mother warning him as they returned on the bus from a shopping expedition to buy some new shoes: 'You'll go in there if you're a bad lad, so you'd better behave.'

In the shoe shop, something of a tussle had taken place.

'They look crap,' he'd said, puckering up his face at the sight of the boring black lace-ups.

Mam had believed, and still did, in the strictly utilitarian. Things must 'last'. He on the other hand had always been dazzled by style. At that stage he wanted Docs, heavy, conker-brown Docs with lots of lacing. With wear the leather would soften and wrinkle to take the shape of his feet. He grimaced fit to crack his face and wouldn't speak when the assistant tried to find out if the shoes fitted.

On the way home he sat in his nerdy navy anorak, swung his legs and scuffed his shoes on the metal box thing under the seat. The hateful new shoes rested in a plastic bag on his mother's knee. He could just imagine what Whitey and Skelly would say when they saw them.

Mam didn't understand how things worked, how you needed to fit in and be one of the boys, not some nice little kid with his hair smooth and parted at the side; a kid who smiled at grown-ups and was polite, never swore or got into bother.

Funny how after all these years of seeing the fortress from a distance, he should learn to know it as well as his own house. Once you were on D Wing, you saw the tiers of cells rising up and it was like being in a Victorian swimming bath and looking up at the high glassed-in roof and the balconies running round above the changing cabins. When he'd told his parents he was thinking of a career in the Prison Service, they'd been very keen – it was secure, he'd have a good pension. Security was what mattered. But none of them had known then what an uncertain security it was.

At last: eight-fifteen, and Eddie was in the car park with Mal.

'The Minerva?'

'Yes,' Eddie said. He loved it down there by the old pier.

Eddie arrived first and stood watching the water for a while as it weaselled and rocked. Lamplight turned its writhing into pythons or giant water snakes.

'I'm drooling for this,' Mal said, coming up behind him. 'Been waiting for it all day.'

'Yes, but remember you're driving.'

'Sure.'

'You don't want to end up on the other side of the door.' Eddie thought, listening to himself, that he sounded exactly like his mother. It'd always been: 'Do be careful, Eddie, you never know what's just round the corner . . . Don't go out with wet hair, you'll get your death . . . Don't drive too fast . . .'

He'd caught the habit himself – caution, deliberateness and restraint – only he sensed he could react quite differently but wouldn't let himself: he drove with the brakes on. Both his parents shared the same traits. They planned and waited; but perhaps they too chafed at those self-imposed restraints. Sometimes, though, he felt scared of what he might do. Perhaps working in a prison didn't help either – you saw everywhere the result of undisciplined emotion.

Mal made for the bar and Eddie found a table by the coal fire, aware that they were being stared at. People assumed that they were two policemen. Their white shirts and dark trousers indicated a uniform. They looked away, mumbled something to one another and frowned. Mal reappeared with two pint glasses. Eddie shed his coat and let himself drift in the music from the speakers on the wall.

'You can't beat this.' He delighted in the creamy brown head on the beer and stared at it in a moment of anticipation and then sipped. Feeling the froth on his upper lip, he licked it off and wiped his mouth with the back of his hand. 'Perfect – ta, mate.'

'Yes, I could sink six of these before I start.'

'So could I, but I shan't – going to make this last. Though if I don't move on, Sharon won't be best pleased. She doesn't like it if she thinks I've been having a bevvy on the way home.'

'No, they don't – Sal's always sure I'm up to something.' Mal paused. 'Well, she's not wrong, is she!'

He barked with laughter. Angie was about half Mal's age, a blond colleague, with a pert, vivacious air. Eddie knew the affair had been lurching along for several months. Mal's wife was very much a mother and absorbed by their three children. Eddie liked Sally and felt sorry for her. Mal was the gaudy bantam cock and Sally his plain pale wife.

Sometimes they'd have nights out as a foursome and Sally would complain half humorously about how she never saw Mal. Eddie would have to come in with platitudinous stuff: 'Well, that's the downside of being married to a prison officer.' And Mal would squeeze Sally's hand and say: 'Haven't I got the best wife in the world?'

But Eddie couldn't help liking Mal. For one thing, they were woven together by their work – it was always us and them. You knew you had to be able to count on your colleagues. You developed an extra something between you.

'Now then,' Mal started up, 'what do you do if you find an inmate hanging in his cell? If he swings towards you, nick him for assault. If he swings away from you, nick him for trying to abscond.' He expected Eddie to laugh, but Eddie was speechless. He saw again the body suspended from the window bars. An unknown man had died, somebody's son, father, lover.

3

At three a.m. Lyn had been sure that she was not alone in the house. She'd lain still and listened, braced for the door to crash open and someone to storm in. Finally she'd got out of bed and tiptoed to the top of the stairs. Nobody was there, though even after she'd searched the house she'd felt fearful and dared not switch off the lamp.

Since the night when they had taken Max, she'd slept badly – waking in the early hours, rigid with terror. Now the broken nights weren't so regular but they still disturbed her.

She told herself to stop dwelling on the past and act the smooth blonde she tried so hard to be. A bowl of cornflakes and two sugars in her tea stiffened her resolve. She smoothed on sand-coloured eyeshadow, three coats of mascara and her pink lippy in such a natural way that no one could detect them.

Once she was on her bike and cycling down the long terrace of brick houses, the scariness of the night began to recede. Even at six-thirty the air was warm – bruisers in suits with handguns had no place here.

She left the terrace behind and cut across a main road and down an avenue of big semi-detached houses. The jade billows of the sycamore trees floated over the road and threw splattery shadows. In front of her she saw the fish women on the Victorian fountain. Their white upper bodies tilted backwards as they raised conch shells to their lips, and their pale green tails curved up behind them. The mermaids had always fascinated her and on this July morning the sight of them was calming. She saw herself as a small girl standing beside Aunty Mags, staring up at their impassive faces and, later, pestering to be taken back to visit them, fantasizing that they could slither down from their pedestal and flap away to the estuary to dive and frolic.

At the main road she halted, then cycled across into the park. Ducks snoozed on the grass or paddled on the ink-coloured pond, where gobs of bread floated in a scum. The panes in the conservatory were painted white to cut down the glare inside. Young Queen Victoria sat on a throne in a rose garden. She too was white and impassive, like the mermaids, though Lyn remembered the shock of having discovered her one day covered in green paint.

The park stretched wide and empty, but she pedalled as fast as she could because you never knew what might be lying in wait.

Out under the archway and she had only to cross another main road before she arrived in front of the baths, whose turquoise onion dome cut a pattern in the sky.

She slotted the lock on her bike and left it in the racks under the staff-room window. In full view of the street it should be safe, but you couldn't be sure because the phone box on the corner was the druggies' favourite haunt.

She dumped her backpack on the staff-room table and took off her denim jacket.

'It's hot in here,' Ben puffed, 'and fucking Early Birds.'

'No need to swear.'

'You all right, Lyn? You seem a bit edgy.'

'It's just this place and the thought of six whole weeks of kids fighting and splitting your eardrums.'

'Too right. I've got the pool cover off – do you want to do the gym? Andy's doing the vapour.'

Lyn nodded. She would sooner have watched the blue cover wind back on its reel to leave the pool open and shining. Instead she had to scurry off to the gym, switch on the machines, empty the bins and vacuum.

'I'll give you a hand,' Ben said. She knew he'd been watching her face.

'Ta.' She headed off to the gym, which meant making a detour into the pool area, up a flight of steps on to the balcony and entering the space immediately above it.

The pool was a shimmering oblong and she glanced at it, wishing she could plunge in and feel the coolness on her body.

It came to her as she climbed, how strange this place was. You entered it first thing in the morning and often didn't leave until evening, eight hours later, and nothing else seemed to exist. It was like some bubble, suspended above the earth. The days swooned by, hermetically sealed in with the stifling heat and the bodies.

In one way it made everything else appear unreal – she was glad of that. When she'd got the phone call six months ago saying Max was dead, this place had helped her through it. Though at other times the boring sameness of patrolling the pool, alternating with periods sitting high up on the chair, had meant she couldn't escape the horror churning round and round in her head. There were moments when she imagined Max still shut away in prison and she played with the idea that a letter from him would land on the hall carpet. She'd battled with guilt because that January, just before his death, she'd felt so fed up with the changeless life she was leading while he would be in prison all those years . . . When the news came, it almost seemed she'd willed his death, and that alarmed and disconcerted her. You couldn't just pretend it hadn't happened. His disappearing had destroyed her fantasy life, her secret world, leaving her with a hollow core.

She held the vacuum cleaner nozzle in her hand, cleaned out bits of fluff and twines of hair and threw them in a bin, working it under and round the machines. But she wasn't really present.

Right at the start he'd said to her: 'I'd better tell you straight, I'm no good. Never have been, never will be.' Any sensible person would have withdrawn at that point. Only she hadn't, couldn't. She couldn't because he'd intrigued her with his size and his stories.

She'd met him in a club. He wore a gold Rolex, had grey cheeks and a dangerous aura, and when he smiled a gold filling glinted in a back tooth.

'Hi,' he'd said. 'You're the one I've been waiting for all my life.'

When she'd heard that, she hadn't known what to say. It had cut her right out of her boring routine and set her down in a drama. It meant they skipped the interim period where people exchange chit-chat on their way to reaching deeper things. For a second she did wonder if he was fooling with her and whether she should come out with some jokey reply, but looking at him, she saw that he meant it – or at least appeared to at that moment.

They'd ended up at two a.m. standing on the old pier, gazing out over the estuary. He hadn't touched her but he'd looked, stared. If only he'd say something – being alone with him like this was embarrassing. She'd tried to get him to talk about himself but he evaded direct questions, didn't seem to have any need to speak. He wasn't like someone who did a nine-to-five office job or manual work – he didn't slot in anywhere.

Finally, when she'd felt almost dizzy with the wire of tension he generated, she'd said she ought to be getting back home.

He drove her there in his BMW, took her number, said he'd be away for a few days but would phone her when he got back. She thought he'd be like the rest: men you saw in clubs who swarmed round you in the late-night gloom, but were without stamina somehow – as though later, once you were absent from their field of vision, they lacked the energy to follow up the meeting. All her life she'd wanted to be loved, had found herself involved in lots of unlikely encounters always in the hope of being wanted. Perhaps those flabby men had sensed her neediness and couldn't cope with it. But Max had been different – he played for excess. She could see it now.

She'd told Shelly at the baths about that first meeting, and Shelly had said, 'Wow, a Beemer – he must be in the money; you'll have to keep hold of him.'

But Lyn couldn't explain that although she enjoyed the car's suave interior, she was captivated by something else entirely: here was someone who'd been around the world a bit and had a certain ruthless edge that could take your breath away.

A week strolled by before he phoned. She'd found his message on her mobile when she was on her twenty-minute lunch break and biting into a pasty that Shelly had bought from the bakery near the baths. This message was something she didn't want to share.

All that afternoon when she'd been on pool duty, staring into the water, trying to concentrate on the swimmers, she struggled to suppress her excitement.

She'd had no chance to phone him until evening, when she was back at home. Before she did so, she replayed his voice several times and it made her shiver. She couldn't imagine where the next encounter with him would take her.

He met her in a city-centre bar that evening. They talked this time. He asked her about her life and she explained about never having known her mother, who died when she was a baby, and how being brought up by her father meant that she always felt something was missing. He sipped his whisky, smoked and didn't say anything, just listened. She'd talked compulsively, letting him see below the surface.

'I've always wanted to know about my mother. My dad doesn't mention her. Well, of course it's a long time ago – but he never did anyway. It's as though because she died, she's never existed. Dad doesn't like to be serious and won't answer my questions.'

When she thought about it, her father seemed far more comfortable with jokes – he joked people out of depressive thoughts by adopting an ironic stance, making them smile instead.

As Lyn worked the vacuum cleaner over the floor, she pulled those hours spent with Max into focus. If she analysed what took place, she heard her own voice talking – rarely his. He remained hidden. She knew that he'd been married, had grown-up kids, partners at various times. You only had to study his face, the way he moved, the assurance in his shoulders and thighs, to know that there must have been a lot of women.

4

'Eddie, where've you been? I'm desperate. For goodness sake, they're on their own – I can't leave this . . .' Sharon was doing something elaborate with goats cheese and her face was fretted with tension.

'Oh, sorry, didn't realize we were entertaining.'

'I did tell you – Barry and Di and Nigel and Marie.'

'Right.' They were two couples Sharon had met at the PTA.

'Where on earth were you?' she tried again. 'Emma's been waiting for you to go up and say goodnight. She thought you'd never come.'

'A bit late finishing, that's all.' He dared not mention anything about having had a drink and he never talked at home about the prison. But tonight he'd needed that drink – there'd been a near-fatal suicide bid. Opening the pad door and seeing the chalky-faced man on the bed had jerked him back all those months to when he'd found Smithson, hanging.

'Get changed, Ed, only do be quick – they're stranded in there waiting.' She had her head bent and was flurrying about with pans. She couldn't stop worrying about things not being right. She was the same with Emma, frightened to death that something might happen to her . . . but that all came from the miscarriages. She'd never got over the losses. They hung like a curse over their lives.

'Oh, do hurry up, Ed. I can't imagine what they must be thinking.'

He heard Emma calling, 'Daddy, Daddy,' and went up to her.

She held up her arms and he bent down and felt her fingers go round his neck. He nuzzled her face, taking in her childhood smell. Her brown velvet eyes sparkled at him and her fringe stuck up where his face had disturbed it.

'Mummy's been in a mood.'

'Yes, I'm late.'

'You're having a party – I'd like to be at it.'

'Well, you can't, because it's your bedtime – and that means night-night.'

'And no story?'

'Sweetie pops, I can't – I'm in the bad books already. Got to get changed.'

She still clung on.

'Come on, Em. Got to go – night-night, sweet dreams.' He loosened her fingers. He knew he must make sure she didn't come downstairs, otherwise Sharon would be upset and accuse him of undermining her authority.

He stood for a moment in the doorway, looking at the sunshine walls and the hot-pink, orange and yellow duvet cover and matching pillowcase. A seal mobile dangled from the ceiling. Drawings were pinned to a noticeboard and a line of teddies squatted on the windowsill, furry legs splayed out before them. A small blue beany bear shared her pillow. The oldest bear of all, a present from Sharon's mother, lay in the crook of Emma's arm. His nose had a bald patch on it and the felt had worn away on his paws.

'Night-night, sleep tight,' he whispered, switching off the light. His mother had always said that to him, while his father had restricted himself to 'Goodnight, little feller.'

Ten minutes later, revived and smelling of aftershave, he sprang downstairs.

Four faces turned at his entrance.

'Hi,' Eddie said. 'Great to see you. Sorry I was late – work, you know.'

'Yes,' Di said, 'that's what Sharon said – she was telling us you work for the Home Office.'

'That's right.' Eddie sensed a hysterical quality in this woman. She had a high-pitched giggle and seemed to be in an internal jitter.

'That sounds very important?' Her eyes were trained on him. She wanted to dig. He wondered how he could divert her, but he was saved momentarily by Sharon saying would they please take their seats at the table.

The dinner table was laid at the other end of the through-lounge. 'We used to live in a nice little house like this before we moved,' Di said in a silken voice, the sort that could confuse because you expected it to say pleasant things – only it didn't. 'It was like this, wasn't it, darling?' Barry nodded. 'Our problem with it was that we didn't have enough space. I mean, you're overlooked all the time. And of course I like a big bathroom. Well, and I mean, the workmanship was shoddy – the plaster started cracking.'

Eddie saw Sharon nodding her head. 'Oh, dear, I do hope ours won't. You're right about it being poky. I'd like to live further out.' He didn't think she could be serious. This was heaven compared with the estate where they'd both grown up. He got a sudden vision of those rows of identical houses of their childhood, medallioned now with satellite dishes. They'd be walking home together from school, holding hands, planning to make their escape – they weren't going to be penned up on the estate with the druggies and doleys for the rest of their lives – and they'd made it.

Eddie felt Di preparing for another stab at interrogation. 'What do you do in the Home Office, then?'

'Actually I'm a prison officer.'

'Wow! That sounds interesting – I bet you see some things.'

'Not really.'

'Do you get the really bad cases?'

She was trying for something bloodthirsty and spectacular, but he dodged her by going out to the kitchen with a stack of plates.

The evening revealed that Barry, whose shoes repelled and fascinated Eddie – they were winkle-pickerish, black, shiny and very knowy – was a bank manager, and Nigel was in computers. Marie worked in a building society and Di was a private secretary. Their children were in the same class as Emma. It transpired that Barry golfed with Nigel. Eddie couldn't imagine that Di and Marie had much in common apart from school runs and babysitting rotas.

Mid-bite into some *Domestic Goddess* confection, just as he was at the height of savouring the sweet puffiness of the cream and the scrunch of the cherries between his teeth, Marie started.

'Do you feel that you've been doing a prison sentence, Eddie?' And she gave a little laugh.

'Not really,' he said, and defended himself with a smile.

They were both distracted by Sharon saying they wanted the best possible school for Emma – that after all she was their only child.

'Did you not want any more kids, then?' Di quizzed.

'Well, we're very lucky to have Emma,' Sharon said, and there was a pained silence.

At midnight he stood rinsing plates and tureens at the sink prior to stacking them in the dishwasher, while Sharon put any leftover food in plastic containers and slid them into the fridge.

'Eddie, look at all the bits in that.' She held out a tureen. 'I always find myself having to clean up after you.'

'Okay, Shaz, but we don't have to make a fetish out of it.'

'If you weren't so slapdash, I wouldn't have to worry.'

'Do you really like that lot tonight? That Marie is majorly freaky.'

'They're nice people, Eddie, and we need friends like them.'

'What, like Di? She's got a bit of a neck telling us that this house is poky.'

'But it is, Eddie. She wasn't criticizing.'

'You could have fooled me. We haven't been here five minutes and already you're thinking it's not good enough.'

He didn't like the atmosphere gathering around them. Sharon kept her head down and continued inspecting the plates. She'd go into a deep sulk now. He knew the sequence. Acid indigestion burned in his chest. Why the hell had he said anything? But if she became determined to keep up with Di & Co., he didn't know how they'd cope. They'd already got a whacking great mortgage. They needed to talk about it, but Sharon had taken serious offence. Without another word she left the kitchen and a while later he heard the hissing of the toilet and the click of the bedroom door.

After he'd set the burglar alarm and turned off the lights, he mounted the stairs, almost too tired to bother. His stomach gurgled with uneasiness. The whole day had unsettled him. He took his time whirring the electric toothbrush over the surfaces of his teeth.

She'd switched off the bedside lamp and turned on her side facing the window. All he could make out was the shape of her body under the duvet. He stumbled over his shoes and cursed. She'd taken care to keep herself well away from him and he spread out into the cool space in the bed, expecting to fall asleep immediately.

But two hours later he was still wide awake. Sharon's averted face challenged him. She couldn't stand criticism, he knew that – for heaven's sake, they'd been together forever. He ought not to have spoken out. At fourteen this intense girl with her glossy black hair caught back in a ribbon had been so vivacious, he couldn't stop touching her. Sometimes he'd look at Emma and glimpse Sharon as she'd once been. Without noticing it, they'd left that eager youthful world behind. They'd been adults wanting to move on. Time to have a baby – only it hadn't happened. That was when her eyes became dull and speculative.

The first time she got pregnant, for two months everything had been ecstatic. He'd rushed home with treats for her: a downy peach oozing juice, a box of handmade chocolates, a clutch of women's magazines. He'd done his best with the cooking. But then came the griping pains in the night, and the bleeding. He'd held her in his arms afterwards, rocked her like a baby as she cried.

Their twenties were eaten up by hospital visits and more despair. 'It doesn't matter,' he'd told her. 'We've got each other – we don't *have* to have a baby.' She'd just looked at him with blank eyes. 'Look,' he'd said, 'let's leave the baby business. Let's stop trying; it's making you too upset.' That hadn't been any good either. Oh, yes, Sharon got on with her life, only she became obsessively nipped into herself, always scurrying after details, working obsessively at her job, the cleaning, whatever she undertook. But she hadn't talked about it, never had.

Why was he dwelling on all this now? Surely Di's remark about the house ought not to have caused all these memories. He was getting neurotic. But Sharon hadn't always been like this, had she? She'd be fine in the morning. It took time, he knew that. But it seemed to be getting worse . . . If only she wouldn't shut him out. He lay on his back gazing at the ceiling. He must stop this, or tomorrow he'd be useless.

Without warning he was back all those months in Smithson's cell, staring across at the body sagging before the window bars. That day he'd seen a dead man, somebody who'd died of grief. Was it grief? The smell of Smithson's body returned to him. Sweat broke out under Eddie's armpits and a fever burned in his chest. The girl must have got used now to the idea of Smithson's death. He saw her face too, the joy in the smile. That smile had helped him hold on until the officer arrived with the ligature knife. Smithson's life and hers had only grazed his, but now his head was full of them. Why wouldn't the pictures fade?

5

The Early Bird session was about to start. Lyn took up her position on the poolside. Ben climbed up on to the chair.

Through the swing doors banged the first regulars, lugging sports bags. Now they fiddled with the lockers or found plastic boxes to contain their clothes and headed for the poolside cubicles. They were creatures of habit – same lockers, same cubicles, same time . . . A heavy ginger chap invariably lumbered to the cubicles facing the door. Two women made for adjoining cubicles by the entrance.

Splash! The first ones plunged in and executed a clumsy crawl up the pool. A black Adonis dived in and his crawl incised the water, hardly causing a ripple.

In minutes the pool rocked with lines of swimmers. These were people on their way into work and this was their prelude to a day spent before computer screens or classes. Nobody talked. The only sound was water splashing on tiling.

Lyn wished she were out at Filey or Scarborough, walking down the beach towards the sea, anticipating the shock of the waves on her ankles and the rush into it, the hysteria of freezing water on hot flesh – and then the swim out, striking towards the horizon. She loved the buoyancy of sea swimming, the roughness and freedom. Far out in the bay she'd lie on her back and stare up at the sky and the turning of the clouds, and she always regretted having to swim back to shore.

The Early Birds soon clattered out with their backpacks and sports bags and then for half an hour the blue expanse lay empty, twitching, with sunlight forming twirls on the tiles.

Ben shot off to check the gym. Andy swung across the foyer. 'Hiya,' he said, catching Lyn's eye. 'Having a coffee?'

She realized he wanted to tell her something. 'Mm,' she said.

Andy pressed the code for the door and they slipped into the staff room. She plugged in the kettle.

'I've left her.'

Lyn looked up from dropping a heaped teaspoon of coffee powder into Andy's mug.

'Was it awful?'

'Yer,' he said. 'I feel gutted.'

'Well, why did you, then?'

'She's always on at me.'

'What about your kids?'

'I'll have to see 'em at weekends – only I'll be working most likely anyway.'

Andy's legs curved with muscle and he waggled his shoulders when he walked. The young girls giggled and called out to capture his attention and he had intense conversations with women in Lycra swimsuits who lounged at the shallow end, leaning on the side of the pool, staring up at him and cooing like doves.

The baths were a place where temptation moseyed its way into everything. All day long people pushed through the swing doors, stomped round the poolside, or pattered in, heads down, muffled in fleeces and anoraks. Minutes later they emerged, pared down: men with a beer gut you didn't expect; or a body that made you gasp with its taut buttocks, muscular shoulders, small waist; pervy lads with beauty spots tattooed on their faces, lads whose bodies had a scrawny nimbleness – bodies that other people didn't see, not ever. At the Over 45s old men trundled in; their bellies rode before them and their legs were stick thin. But they were sweet, the Over 45s – they wanted to joke and talk about their heart attacks and rheumatism, and tell stories of the past. Yet there was still a glint in these old boys' eyes.

'You can't stay married in here,' Andy said, stirring four teaspoons of sugar into his coffee. 'Nah, you can't. You don't need to go to clubs to pick up lasses, they're here all the time dying for it.'

Lyn sat listening, fingers round the mug. She was doing an Aunty Mags, who always said, 'Men like to talk. When they talk, they feel they've had a good time.' But Lyn found that most men didn't talk about important things. She was prepared to listen to Andy because his outpourings both appalled and intrigued her.

He looked as though he might cry. Lyn didn't know what to say.

'I don't know why I do this fucking job. The pay's crap. The conditions are worse than they were ten years ago.'

Time up. He swallowed his coffee, jammed the mug down near the kettle and turned to her. 'Coming?'

'Just about.' She had to leave her coffee – there wasn't even time for a drink in the breaks.

She was on the chair now. Regulars drifted in. Max pushed his way back into Lyn's thoughts. He'd never been a regular figure at her house – he came and went, disappearing on business for days, but she'd believed in him. Or was it that she didn't want to know the truth, that she'd been too gullible? Whenever he'd turned up, they went clubbing or pubbing and spent hours in bed, sending out for takeaways. He'd tell her stories – he'd been all over the world, knew parts of Africa, India, had lived in

Thailand; talked of tropical nights and white beaches, seas where unsuspecting businessmen had their heads nipped off by sharks. His tales of juju and magic still filled her head. On the rare occasions when he did mention his beginnings she'd discovered he'd never known his father and had left home at fifteen to seek his fortune. He'd cast a spell over her with his sureness.

Once they flew to the Canary Islands for a week, where they drank champagne every night. She'd returned to work honey-skinned and sore between her legs. By the time he'd departed, she was wrung out, squeezed dry. She'd liked it, of course she had, but his fast way of living exhausted her. He grabbed at life, drained it, pulped it out, laughed and moved on.

The night they'd come for him, he'd just returned from a spell away. He carried about him the aura of foreign parts, a scented denseness. She hadn't expected him and was on the sofa watching telly. She hadn't heard the front door open and then his hands covered her eyes and she let out a strangled shriek. She took fright easily, always had, and since that night it had grown worse.

Straight up to the bedroom they'd stumbled, falling against each other, toppling like drunken people, laughing. He'd made love to her as though she was the only woman he'd ever touched. There was a roughness in it, an intensity that frightened her – almost as though he wanted to cancel her out.

And afterwards they'd slept with a breeze wafting in from the street smelling of dust and late-night life. Somewhere in the early hours – it must have been two or three – the door was battered down. Max was wide awake and out of bed, into his boxer shorts, and struggling to get his legs into his trousers, when she'd heard feet pounding up the narrow stairs. Three big men burst into the room and trained guns on Max and her.

'Okay, mate,' one of the men said, when Max made to put on his shirt, 'leave the rest.'

They'd whipped out handcuffs and tried to snap them on his wrists, but Max eeled his way out of their grasp. He wrestled with them, lurching and banging in the little room, while she sat up in bed, the duvet clutched to her naked body, heart thumping in her throat, a scream stuck in her gullet. She shivered at the memory of those guns – small, black, lethal – objects she'd previously seen only in films. They would surely shoot him – but instead one of the men hit Max across the head with his pistol, and he slumped to the floor. Then they'd forced the handcuffs on him.

Nobody uttered a word as they left, pushing Max before them. Down below in the street she'd heard car doors slam and an engine roar off into the night as she fought for breath and tried to slow the galloping of her heart.

Three hours later she'd got up for work and didn't wash the stickiness from between her thighs, because she would lose his smell. Even then she knew that he'd never be hers again. It was a death. The horror and the loneliness squeezed her chest tight.

All day her head had spun and she'd seemed to be separated by a thick plate-glass screen from the swimmers and the pool and the other lifeguards.

First he was on remand and she could rarely manage to see him, but after they finally sentenced him to twenty years for drug running and money laundering, she'd taken a day off work to travel up to visit him at Full Sutton.

Four hours on train and bus to get there and it was hidden away in the country, a modern building like a giant superstore but enclosed by a perimeter wall. When she stood before the bulletproof screen with the prison officer scowling at her, and was told to produce her visiting order and surrender up her mobile, she found herself passing

from nervousness to anger and exasperation, which deepened when she had to take off her jacket and shoes and
place them, along with her bag, on the revolving belt to be
scrutinized. By the time they got to the body search, she
felt like a criminal.

In the visits room she'd not known what to talk about.
Max sat facing her, looking very pale. Near them other
couples chatted at tables, and children, barked at by har-
assed mothers, scampered to and fro. They held hands
across the table and didn't speak.

All the way back on the train she'd gone over the
meeting, how he looked, what they said to each other,
covering every detail of that day, working it through,
examining it. The country flowed by outside the window:
low-lying fields rolling to the skyline, drains, motorboats
bobbing on a stripe of black water. The train stopped at
small stations where plastic tulips and fuchsias dangled
from hanging baskets.

Near home, when the train began to run beside the
estuary, she stared out at mudflats that gleamed like the
skin of herrings, grey banded with silver. Seabirds boated
and balanced on one leg, peering before them. The water
rippled away to Lincolnshire – such a strange surprise of
water. She sat gazing at it, drawn into the swilling of the
waves. A buoy swung in the currents. Lincolnshire crouched
in a haze like the Promised Land, then what must be fac-
tories loomed up and she knew it was an illusion. But the
water, all that water, was calling to her.

She'd made that journey many times. Then he told her
he'd applied to be moved to a prison near home for a
week so that he could have visits from her.

At the end of that week of extended visits, he'd come
out with it.

'Lyn,' he'd said, 'I don't think we should go on – I mean,
you'll want kids . . . Before I'm out of here, I'll be an old

man. See what I mean? I don't want you wasting your life.'

He'd said those things before, and she'd argued against them, but this time she faced him across the table, knowing that he was right. The previous week Andy, Ben and Wes had taken her out on the town to celebrate her thirty-second birthday, and she'd drunk too many Castaways and vodkas and when Andy kissed her, pressing his tongue between her lips, she saw danger coming. She was thirty-two and her body didn't want to be celibate. She decided she must tell Max – only when it came to it, and he was there before her, she couldn't say yes, he was right. He'd offered her a way out, released her, but she was incapable of taking it.

'It's all right,' she'd said. 'It doesn't matter. Don't worry, we'll manage.'

On the way home and all that night she'd thought she'd never stop crying. They were like two birds, each in a separate cage, able to see each other but never to mate.

Towards midday, with the air temperature about thirty-six degrees, Lyn, on duty with Shelly, noticed a man come striding in. He was quite good-looking in a clean-cut way and going slightly grey. She took no further notice of him until he dived into the pool and began plunging down the length with a brutal crawl. Girls swerved aside as he reached the shallow end. Returning up the pool doing the breaststroke, he cut a swathe through knots of students. Some flinched from the force of his kick as he rose up out of the water and swept down again.

'Lyn,' said Pat, a regular, 'you should tell him. He's just kicked my foot. I'll have a massive bruise on it. He doesn't care as long as he gets his swim.' The woman's friend nodded in agreement.

The chuntering increased, and a group of women stared

after the man. 'He's not been getting any,' somebody said, and gave a hoarse laugh.

'Yes,' Lyn said, 'he's very inconsiderate.' She wished one of the men was on duty instead of Shelly – because she was only a youngster, Lyn would have to be the one to accost him. She waited. The man plunged back down the pool. He wore a black Speedo cap and goggles. When he reached the shallow end once more, Lyn slipped down from the chair and called out to him.

He halted, about to power back up the pool. 'Oh . . . yes?' He pulled off his goggles and stood up, seeming to come out of a trance.

Lyn met his eyes. 'You're in a crowded pool and you aren't taking any account of other swimmers,' she said, blushing. 'And you keep kicking people.'

'I'm really sorry,' he said. 'I just got carried away.' He seemed unsure what to do. Then he swam back up the pool, hauled himself on to the side with one thrust of his arms and disappeared into the showers.

Did I do wrong to snarl at him? Lyn wondered. But he had been inconsiderate, swimming like that.

In a ten-minute break from poolside duties, Lyn drank a can of Coke and sat in the staff room gazing out at the street.

Andy made himself a mug of coffee. 'I don't care how hot it is, I need my caffeine fix,' he insisted.

'I had to tell this bloke off.'

'You should have got me. I'd have settled him.'

'He was actually okay once I'd told him.' What could he have been thinking about? She let herself drift in speculation and jumped when she heard Andy addressing her.

'You in, Lyn? Want to have a drink tonight?'

Lyn knew this could be tricky. Andy couldn't be trusted and the role of consoler could easily lead to other things, but it might be better than another night in on her own.

'Okay, perhaps for half an hour. I've got to go round to my aunty's at some point, though.'

Shelly's eyes were on Andy. She and Andy used to have sessions in corners when the baths were closed. Lyn once walked into the vapour area and was faced with Andy's muscular buttocks pumping up and down while Shelly yowled with pleasure.

6

When the inmates had fetched their trays and were locked up once more, Eddie joined Mal and some fellow officers bound for the pub to celebrate Brad Kershaw's retirement.

They strode up the road in their white shirts, their key chains sparkling against their navy trousers. Lorries careering by on their way to the oil terminal stirred up a whirl of dusty air. They received long appraisals from other pedestrians.

'Why wasn't we at Scarborough?' someone said.

'Costa Brava, you mean.'

'Not fucking likely – it'd be hotter than this.'

'Back garden, then.'

'Well, we're not, fellers, so you have to grin and bear it,' Mal said.

The pub was cooler and the smell of stale beer and ground-out cigs hit their nostrils as they entered. Inside, the lights glared in a brown gloom and Eddie had the sensation of stepping back into a pub like his dad used to drink in.

A couple of officers, already ensconced with pints in their hands, chatted. In their midst was Brad, whose face resembled a white paper bag that had been screwed up and smoothed out again. He twinkled through his glasses at the newcomers.

'Hiya, guys. Good of you to come.'

'We're really only here for the free nosh,' Mal chortled.

'Well, it's through there – go when you're ready.'

Brad, wearing a polo shirt and grey flannels, stood out among the uniformed men. Mal handed Eddie a pint and Eddie sat down at a table on the edge of the group and looked across at Brad Kershaw. He'd spent most of his working life in the Prison Service and ended up as an SO. Eddie felt sorry he was retiring – he'd always liked him.

'So what will you be doing, then, Brad?' someone asked. 'You'll be jetting about all over and we'll be sweating away here.'

'My garden, I expect – not thought about it much yet. It'll seem a bit strange. I mean, I'll miss you lads.'

Eddie was upset to notice the regret in his voice and the way he seemed vulnerable and unsure, somehow shrunken, without his uniform, as if he'd lost his bearings and his identity. As an SO he'd be patrolling the wing, keeping everything under control with abrasive humour.

'No foreign trips, then, Brad?'

'Maybe – nothing settled yet.'

After a while they percolated into the next room, where trays of anaemic sandwiches and fatty sausage rolls waited.

Eddie picked up a paper plate and surveyed the sandwiches. The beef poking through the edges of the white bread looked like shoe leather, so he plumped for ham, and egg mayonnaise. Mal heaped his plate with sausage rolls and greasy, yellowish drumsticks.

'It'll be funny driving past and not coming in,' Brad told Mal. Eddie, listening, realized he'd heard the cons speak with the same regret when they were leaving the prison.

'What, do you think you'll miss it?' Mal asked.

'It's what you're used to.'

'Well, I wish I was you,' Mal said.

'Actually, the wife's got me wallpapering.'

'You should show her who's boss, Brad.'

Eddie looked at his watch. 'Best be making tracks,' he said to Mal.

'Yer – I could just sit here all afternoon.'

Before he left, along with half a dozen or so colleagues, Eddie went up to Brad to wish him all the best. 'I hope you do well,' Brad said, grasping Eddie's hand. 'You deserve to – you're a good officer, lad. I'd like to see you get made up. You should have before. I was mad when they passed you over. Drop by and see us – you know where we live. I'll miss the lot of you.' Eddie saw tears in the older man's eyes and had to look away. He could feel his own throat tightening.

Mid-afternoon a buzzer shrilled on Eddie's landing and he went to answer. It'd be some nerd messing about. Williams, forehead gleaming with sweat, sat on his bed, face crinkled in agitation.

'Mr Holmes, I don't know . . .'

Eddie looked into Williams' pad, noticed the photos on the locker, and he was back again all those months with the body hanging before the window. He suppressed a shudder. 'What's the matter, then?' he asked.

'I'm real worried about my partner.' He indicated the photographs.

'Oh, yes – how's that?'

The heat in the pad brought Eddie out in a burst of sweating. The cons, he reflected, seemed to get themselves into extraordinary situations, difficulties that normal people would never imagine possible.

'She's like on Prozac – well, it's like after what happened.' Williams, sitting there, his elbows on his thighs, his head supported by his hands, was some monolithic statue to grief.

'How do you mean?'

'This feller kept annoying her, right – going to the house and she was scared stiff – so I had to do something, didn't I? Hit him with a baseball bat, didn't I? His skull smashed, like an egg it was. I never meant to kill him, right – it just happened.'

'I see.'

'Well, like now she's pregnant – and she's that scared, she won't come out of the house.'

'Have you spoken to her on the phone?'

'Yes, but she's crying all the time.'

Eddie tried to dream up a solution. Williams sat before him, tears dripping down his face. He was on remand – God only knew what would happen when he got sentenced.

'Have you written to her?' No, Williams hadn't. 'Write her a letter, tell her you love her and you're thinking about her all the time. I'll get the chaplain to come and see you.'

Today he was on earlies, so he'd be able to pick Emma up and take her for the first of the swimming lessons Sharon had arranged. Emma was fearful of water, and unlike all her friends had never learned to swim. He'd promised Sharon he'd see that she learned.

He picked Emma up from school and they called home, collected her swimsuit and towel and drove to the baths.

'I'm a bit scared, Daddy,' she said, and he found himself reassuring her, telling her she'd enjoy it. He gave her hand a squeeze and grinned at her.

As they pushed through the swing doors, Eddie was shocked to see the young blond lifeguard from the previous week watching him. He knew she'd been right to tick him off . . . but there was that feeling too of having seen her before.

Parents had already sat down on the chairs arranged in an alcove by the window facing the main road.

Emma trotted off to the cubicles on the poolside to

change. Eddie took a seat with the other parents, watching as the woman gathered the kids round her and got them to sit on the side, kicking their legs in the water. Soon they giggled and splashed, sending up a fountain. Even Emma smiled and waggled her feet.

The woman's blond hair was fastened back in a pony-tail. She wore tracky bottoms and a white T-shirt. He sneaked glances at her face – she wasn't as pretty as she appeared in the photo; suppose he'd made a mistake and this was someone else completely? After all, it was months ago that Smithson topped himself. But he was sure he was right. He was certain too that she'd recognized him, be-cause when she'd seen him arriving, she'd averted her face.

Smithson and this woman – what could the pull have been? Smithson was a big brute so women would have been drawn to him. He was powerful, probably good at sex . . . Eddie caught himself in this thought at the very moment when the woman glanced across. He could feel himself blushing.

He looked at her in profile, and yes, she was quite plain, almost severe. In the photo she was smiling in an ecstatic sort of way.

The lesson was over before he'd realized it, and the kids went to get dry and change back into their clothes. Emma, looking bashful, scurried off with them.

Some of the parents approached the woman, and he watched her greeting them. He remained seated, waiting for Emma, and speculated on her age – probably twenty-eight to thirty, certainly not more – at any rate, about ten years younger than himself.

'It was good,' Emma said once they were in the car on the way home, 'not scary at all.'

'Well, that's brilliant. I think you did really well and I'm proud of you.'

'I'm really, really, really hungry now, though, Daddy.'

'We'll have beans on toast and egg for tea, okay? Or I can make you my special French toast with oodles of ketchup?'

'Yummy!'

Sharon wasn't home yet. She worked flexitime and it often happened that she left for work just as he arrived home. Even when she was supposed to be home, she often stayed late finishing something because she said she couldn't afford to delegate. She'd always return white-faced and twitchy.

Eddie moved about in the kitchen, careful to wipe up every splodge he made on the gleaming surfaces.

Emma told him about Miss Perry at school and how Natasha got told off for talking and rude boys said the f-word and Miss Perry got very mad.

Eddie let her run on and pretended to be listening, but he drifted into a scene between the girl and Smithson – perhaps she'd sent him a Dear John or told him in the visits room that it was over. Every day of the week such scenes happened – if somebody got an awful sentence, it was the only thing to do, the best way to avoid cracking up in the long run. He fell to imagining what it must be like not to know what your wife was getting up to – the dwelling on details, the stills of her with someone else, all passing before your eyes when you were banged up. But this was part of their punishment; what happened when they broke the law – no two ways about it. And he mustn't let himself stray into that territory. He didn't want to identify with them; that way you'd find some of the things you saw in prison intolerable.

When Sharon came home, Eddie drove over to see his mum and dad.

'Your dad's in his greenhouse,' his mum said after she'd kissed him. 'You're looking a bit tired, love.'

'Well, it's been hot at work. Okay, I'll go and have a

look at him,' Eddie said. He glimpsed his dad's flat cap through the glass as he walked down the garden path. Nemesia, snapdragons and African marigolds bloomed in the flower-beds and were edged by alyssum and lobelia. Everything was laid out with geometric precision and not a single weed had escaped his dad's fingers.

Inside the greenhouse, Eddie sniffed the fragrance of tomato plants. They twined up canes held there by little pieces of wire. Scarlet globes hung from their stalks. His dad, watering can in hand, let its contents gush into the terracotta pots.

'They soon get dried up on a day like it's been. How are you, son?'

'Fine,' Eddie said. Sun through glass – he was back in the prison on the fours, peering up at the whited-out panes, way above the arms of the ceiling fans as they scudded hot air about. He lost the sensation as he concentrated on the plants growing in careful seed boxes on the benches.

'What about that, then?' his dad said, indicating an orchid. Its two blooms appeared enamelled, in their glossy brilliance. A frilly petal, spotted like a thrush's breast, curved towards him. Eddie stared at the brown mouth and the frilled paler interior.

'Amazing.'

'Aye – been flowering for weeks. And look at my toms!'

'Fantastic – they smell marvellous.'

'I'll take you some off for Sharon and Emma.'

The hoot of a train sounded and Eddie watched his dad automatically glancing at his watch.

His dad was exact about everything – a railway man all his life, he was punctilious about timing. Dinner was at one o'clock sharp no matter what happened; tea at six o'clock. If you said you'd be there at a certain time, then you must arrive on the dot.

'Hmm – that's the seven-fifteen,' he muttered. Eddie realized that his dad would never escape the tyranny of the trains. He remembered being in town shopping with his mother when he was little and as they queued for a bus out to their estate, she began to panic. 'I'll never get your dad's tea on in time . . .' At ten to six they entered the house and she stumbled into the kitchen and began flurrying away at the cooker. He'd been instructed to lay the table. That was the evening she scalded herself and had to be taken to casualty at the Infirmary.

Inside, over a cup of tea, his mum and dad quizzed him about Sharon and Emma. They'd always liked Sharon, his dad particularly, because they could see that she intended to get on. Eddie tried to keep his dad off the subject of vandalism and drug abuse, because once launched, he talked incessantly about needles on the streets of the estate. Eddie never wanted to live on a council estate again. It was where ninety-nine per cent of the cons were from – that was the life they knew and Eddie wanted no part of it. The prison wasn't mentioned: he never brought it up and they never asked.

When he arrived home with the tomatoes, Sharon was sitting in the warm dusk on the patio sipping white wine and chatting to Di, who was wearing shorts and a low-cut top. Eddie tried to keep his gaze fixed on Di's face.

'Hiya,' Di said, flapping her eyelashes at him.

'Hi. Do I get some of that?'

'Get yourself a glass, Ed,' Sharon said, 'and a chair.' She smiled, and he wondered what had put her in such good humour.

Sitting out there, relaxing in a basket chair, he found a strange pathos in the voices of children playing out in the gardens; neighbours holding barbecues. They were all caught there in a brief moment of harmony – midsummer and this pale dusk would hardly darken.

Sharon's voice sliced through his fragment of contemplation. 'Emma's asleep, no need to go up. We've been round to Di's, Eddie, to look at their conservatory. They've had it built on to the back of the house. It would be ideal for us – she's given us all the particulars. Look at this – this is your one, isn't it, Di?' Di nodded.

Eddie found a brochure in his hands and sighed. Sharon looked animated.

'Fantastic,' he said, though he was really thinking about the swimming teacher's face.

7

Emerging from the baths into the dusty evening sunlight, Lyn wondered about the swimmer who'd brought his daughter for lessons. He'd looked a loving dad as he'd come in with the child hanging on to his hand, but she still thought of him as an aggressive type . . .

She was on her way to see Aunty Mags, who lived a few streets away in one of the terraces. She knew the house's feel, its smell; it meant Aunty Mags – and it was her second home.

Lyn rang the doorbell. Aunty Mags had recently had a double-glazed porch fitted – her window frames were gleaming white plastic and the brass handle on the new front door dazzled, as did the stained-glass Elvis window.

'Hiya, love,' Aunty Mags said, padding up in white puffball slippers. 'I've got the kettle on, but you might like a nip of something stronger – what about a drop of gin with a dash of lemon?'

'Cool,' Lyn said, grinning as she slipped off her trainers in the hall.

'Go in, get sat down, then.'

Aunty Mags sashayed in with the drinks. 'What's new?' she asked as she let herself drop into an armchair. She was a vision in white jeans and a sleeveless pink top squiggled with a diamanté heart. Her upper arms jiggled as she raised her glass in a toast. 'Bottoms up!' she said. She posed the puffballs and looked at Lyn. 'You need perking up a bit. A makeover, that's what you could do with – you know, like them women on telly do.'

Lyn waited for Aunty Mags to remember she'd asked her a question.

'So how are you then, love?'

'All right – everything's just the same. I'm having to watch that Andy, though.' Aunty Mags liked to know anything about relationships and MEN.

'That lad at the baths?' Aunty Mags's eyes brightened.

'Well, I had a drink with him.'

'So what's wrong with that?'

'He's married and he's got all these kids and he's had loads of girls – can't seem to keep it in his trousers.'

'You can give a dog like him a miss, then – unless that's what you're up for. But you're worth better. How's your dad?'

'I've not been round since last week.'

Aunty Mags slipped a CD into her gleaming mini stereo. 'Just listen to this.' Elvis crooning 'Are you Lonesome To-night?' sprang into the room while Aunty Mags leaned back in her chair and hummed along, letting herself swoon into the past. Lyn slugged her drink back and had to stifle an urge to laugh.

'You should have seen me when I was young – I was having a clear-out the other day and came across all this old stuff – I'll show you. Really had fun then, not like now. Still . . .'

Lyn let the gin slither round in her mouth, while 'Teddy Bear' blitzed her eardrums. She could just hear her aunt mousing up the stairs. With Aunty everything had to be carpeted, mostly in cream or white.

Aunty Mags tottered in with a bulging carrier bag. 'Just look here.' She emptied the contents out on to the coffee table and flopped down beside Lyn. 'That's me and you when you were about six – and there's your dad.'

Lyn saw a thin, pale-faced kid with blond plaits, holding her aunt's hand and staring into the camera. Aunty Mags wore shorts and beamed widely. Her dad had a dark, handsome look and scowled.

'Jim wasn't a bad looker when he was young,' Aunty Mags mused, looking at her brother. 'He's got worse as he's got older.'

'Have you got any of my mum?'

'Yes, they're here somewhere. You'll have seen them before.'

'Sure, but I've forgotten.'

'Oh, look – that's when we had that weekend camping at Youlgreave, remember? There's Rick – I was with him at the time.'

Lyn examined a photograph of herself in a swimsuit at about fifteen or sixteen. Her aunt had an arm round Lyn's waist, while she herself was being hugged by a chap with eel-coloured hair.

'I thought Rick looked like Elvis – that's why I fell for him,' Mags said. 'Of course, he was a swine as it turned out, but he did have a certain something.'

That weekend had been blazing hot. They'd camped in a field running down to a dark pool. Being in the open and lying in the grass had excited Lyn, and everything had smelled of earthy dryness.

Nearby, a group of men occupied two bell tents. They'd dive into the pool and come up at intervals shaking water from their hair, then lie sunning on Lilos. Lyn watched them, aware that they were staring at her. She couldn't help stealing glances at their high, tight buttocks, where their wet trunks crinkled.

While Aunty Mags and Rick wrestled and guffawed in the tent that Lyn shared with Aunty Mags, Lyn ran down to the pool and dived in, although she'd been warned not to. She was unprepared for the intense chill of the water –

it made her gasp when it touched her hot flesh. She swam into the centre and kept going. Then the water rocked and a man began to draw level with her. He shouted something, which she pretended not to hear. She recognized him at once as one of those who had stared at her.

'You want to go back,' he'd said. 'It's dangerous to stay in here long. A kid drowned here last week – the farmer told me.'

She'd had to turn round and swim back then. But, even though she was quaking inside, she'd felt the urge to show them all that she couldn't be scared off.

They swam side by side and she enjoyed the sensation of the cold water sliding down her body. The pleasure hinted at scariness: she was aware of the tingling in her legs, and her breath seemed shallow. She thought of giant weeds with roots way beneath her in the mud that could entwine themselves about her limbs and drag her under.

'You're a strong swimmer,' he said when they reached the bank and climbed out, 'but it's too risky.'

The water gleaming on his flesh was like a film of oil all over him. The shock of him standing close to her made her pulse bob.

'It's an old lead mine,' he told her, 'just about bottomless.'

Her head dizzied with the idea of all that dense dark volume stretching to infinity – not out but down, into claustrophobic regions of blackness. But at the same time she'd had an urge to test herself against it, go beyond her fear . . .

Lyn was in the feel of that day – the excitement and terror overlaid with languor. She'd been hovering on the verge of knowing but was too young to let herself explore it, and so had to back away. An idea had come to her out there of swimming into somewhere unknown and wild, away from tamed pools. It flickered back now in the memory of that lost afternoon. Why couldn't she make a long outdoor swim?

Aunty Mags peered at another photograph. 'Oh look – that's your mam.'

Lyn picked up a black-and-white box-camera photo of a woman shielding her eyes against the sun. She was on a beach and the sea stretched into the distance. Her smile was self-conscious.

'I think I took that picture of Elaine. She'd just started going with your dad then.'

Lyn couldn't stop gazing at the picture of this unknown woman – she was just a person on a beach smiling: nothing indicated that they had any connection. She struggled to see a likeness in the woman's face. Had she got her mother's eyes? Her hair? Her figure?

'What was my mum like, Aunty Mags?'

'How do you mean, love?'

'I mean, am I like her or anything?'

Aunty Mags swigged her drink and narrowed her eyes. 'You're more after our side,' she said. 'She was real slim, a bit too slim, and quiet . . . yes, real quiet. Didn't talk too much, maybe because she was an orphan – got brought up in the sailors' orphanage. I've told you that before.'

It was clear that Aunty Mags was the one who didn't want to talk, and she unearthed another photograph. 'That's her and your dad – yes, Jim was quite a looker then – must have been on the same day.'

The girl – she didn't really look like a woman and must have been quite a lot younger than Lyn was now – stood on the beach beside a dark man whose upper lip was outlined by a thin moustache. He pulled the girl against him and his arm encircled her waist. He was handsome in a flashy sort of way and looked older than the girl. Lyn found it difficult to believe that he was her father.

She wanted to keep looking at the pictures for a long

time, hoping that she'd understand where she fitted with those two people, but Aunty Mags had already begun to turn up other photographs.

'What did they see in each other?' Lyn asked.

'Who?'

'My mum and dad.'

'*See?* Well, your dad always had a lot of lasses round him, never thought he'd settle down. He was very good-looking – nice hair, you know – and he had a way with him. Lasses loved it. Was a good dancer as well, always at the Locarno.'

'Anyway, why did he choose my mum?'

'Oh, yer – that's where he used to meet 'em – I'd go with him. Your mam? Well, your mam was like pretty in her own way, like – nice enough figure but too thin maybe.'

Lyn tried to reinvent this handsome creature. Instead, she could only see a bald-headed man whose veiny cheeks blazed with alcohol; and her mother, the slender orphan, wrenched at her heart.

Just then the phone in the hall began to trill and Aunty Mags padded out to answer, leaving Lyn free to delve into the heap of photographs and papers. She found many cuttings from local newspapers of herself after winning swimming awards and trophies at school and at the swimming club. There were phrases like 'amazing young swimmer' and 'talented newcomer' and 'she will go far'. She stared at them – all that seemed such a long time ago. At school, swimming was the only thing she could ever do – she simply couldn't concentrate, just wasn't interested in school work or even other sports. The school reports invariably said, 'More effort needed; could do well but doesn't try.' But swimming was different.

She only came to life when she was in the changing room at the leisure centre, preparing for the training session. The ozoney smell gave her a jittery feeling in her middle – but above all it was the baths, the way you took off your clothes, became someone else, almost like shedding a skin. Here she could shine. She wasn't a sinker or a bobber on the surface; she belonged in the water. Seeing water always came with a shock of surprise. Now, working in the baths environment, she had forgotten how it used to be, and remembering set her nerves trembling. Why hadn't she tried a really big swim, not just flogging up and down in the safety of a piss-easy pool?

In the hall Aunty Mags tittered. Lyn continued leafing through the cuttings until a smaller, much older one slipped out from a bundle. She picked it up, intending to thrust it back with the others, but then her eye caught the headline and she began to read. 'The inquest on the woman's naked body found in the Humber and identified as that of Mrs Elaine Newton, 22, has recorded today that she took her own life while the balance of her mind was disturbed.'

A freezing wave engulfed her and she leaned back, staring unseeing before her. So this was the mystery, this was why nobody would tell her anything about her mother. Aunty Mags and Nana had brushed it off with, 'Well, love, she died just after you were born.' But why? Why? Shrugs, grave faces and then a quick shift to divert her. Sports days and other kids: 'My mam's coming to see us. You can bring your mam.' Only she couldn't because she hadn't got one.

In other people's houses wedding photos stood on the TV sets in silver frames, but not in Dad's. He didn't go for photographs.

'But Dad, what did my mum die of?'

'Doctor didn't say – don't go getting morbid. Here's a quid; go and get some chocs.'

So they knew all the time. It had been a conspiracy. Everybody had decided to keep it from her, pretend it wasn't important – her mother's death shrunk to a yellowing newspaper cutting shoved in a bag with a heap of old photos. She was sinking into a deep dark pool. *Don't panic*, she instructed the sick jangling sensation in her middle. You'll not find out if you let it sweep you away.

Aunty Mags returned smiling. 'I've got a toyboy, you know – Lee. He's going to take me to the races at Donny. He's a lovely lad – you have to catch 'em while they're young. When they get old it's all heart attacks and dead wives.'

'Aunty Mags?'

'Yes, love – want another drink?'

'Please.' Lyn had a longing to get insanely drunk. She didn't want to think any more.

Aunty Mags brought in the gin bottle and poured both of them a hefty measure.

'Aunty Mags, look. I found this.'

'Oh, yes.' Aunty Mags took the cutting from Lyn, made a performance of finding her reading glasses and then glanced down at it. 'Poor Elaine.'

'You've lied to me. Whenever I've asked I've been fobbed off. All my life I've wanted to know about my mum and nobody's ever told me.'

'They wouldn't want to upset you, love.' Aunty Mags's face turned blotchy pink.

'Upset? What do you think this is? How do you think I feel? This is worse – this keeping quiet. I should have known. She was my mother, part of me – I ought to have been told all about it. Why did she kill herself?' Lyn felt her heart rattling against her ribcage and her skin growing clammy. She wanted to throw up. 'What is it that's being covered up? You have to tell me.'

'Nobody really knew, love.'

'Look, I've been lied to too much. I can't believe anything any more. Don't tell me she just walked into the Humber?'

'That's right – at night.'

'Oh, God . . . What on earth did my dad do?'

'What could he do?'

'But he must have wondered why. You can't just let your wife go and drown herself in the middle of the night. If it was me I'd have had to know – I couldn't bear not knowing. This is terrible. Didn't he care?' Lyn couldn't stop the tears draining down her cheeks and on to her hands.

Aunty Mags looked shocked. 'Course he did, love.'

Lyn, fighting to drive back her tears, took a long swig of gin and lemon. The words 'Woman's naked body found in Humber' repeated over and over in her head. *This isn't some unknown person, this is the one who gave birth to me . . . my mother, my flesh and blood.* She could see the woman, her mother, wading out. She could feel the deadening chill of the water. Once with school they'd been taken to London on a trip and they'd visited an art gallery where she'd seen a picture of a girl tangled in a lush mat of water-weeds floating down a river. Lyn had stood a long time before the picture. She'd wanted to know who the woman was. None of the others seemed bothered.

'Lyn, love, it was a long time ago and it doesn't help to dwell on it,' Aunty Mags said.

'Why does everyone want to pretend this never happened?'

Aunty Mags began stuffing the photos back in the bag. 'Try not to be upset, love. We were saving you.'

'Saving! What, saving me from the truth?'

Lyn sank her drink. Her head whizzed as though she'd been on the waltzers, and she couldn't trust herself to speak, nor to look at Aunty Mags, because now she was just part of the conspiracy. What else did she know that she wasn't going to say?

Eventually Aunty Mags telephoned for a pizza, and a while later the doorbell belted out a bar or two of 'Greensleeves' and she went out to answer it.

They sat at the white shiny-topped table and Aunty Mags divided the pizza into segments, crowded with pepperoni and green pepper. She tried to fill any silences with chatter about going to the races and this kid she'd met, while Lyn struggled with nausea and kept seeing that yellowed newspaper article, and its headline: INQUEST ON WOMAN DROWNED IN HUMBER. So devastating, yet it had lain casually thrust between all those photographs, disregarded for years. Terrifying questions. What appalling experience would make a person leave a baby and take her own life? You couldn't forget this, pretend it hadn't happened. Nana, her dad, Aunty Mags, all were guilty of deception. People she had relied on throughout her life could no longer be trusted.

8

Eddie battled with a blinding headache as he unlocked pad doors. He braced himself for bodies swinging from the window bars and was relieved to see the inmates lumbering off to the workshops.

Once the wing was quiet Eddie began checking the cells along the fours, searching for anything unusual. Recently an officer doing a daily routine check on D Wing fours had discovered that two YPs had battered their way into plaster and brick to make a massive hole, through which the lads might have plunged to their death in the yard below.

'It would have served the little fuckers right if they had,' Mal had snarled at the time.

None of these cons would really want to escape, though, Eddie thought, as he peered at the bars and tested them. His main job here was to nose out drug stashes or weapons that they could use on one another.

He was still checking the cells when an alarm shrieked. Eddie shot into action; he locked the pad and was off, pounding down the stairs to the ones with a posse of officers. His blood surged, his head cleared. Weird how only at such times did he feel he was part of the others, united against the cons.

A fight had broken out between some wing cleaners, and everyone not at work and not banged up had joined in. One kid was getting a battering and Eddie dragged a toughie off his back and tripped him. The combatants, mostly druggies, hadn't the muscle to withstand the officers and in no time the ringleaders were being carted off to the seg yelling abuse.

An asthmatic silence returned to the wing. Eddie climbed back up to the fours, thinking how you could never allow yourself to relax for a minute because anything could happen: someone could kick off at any time.

He glanced at his watch. Eleven-thirty already – time to unlock for exercise.

Saunders, a con who often talked with Eddie, told him once that now whenever he was on the out in the town, wandering about, he felt nervous somehow. He didn't quite know why, but he thought it might be to do with being fastened up for long stretches – you knew every curve of the walls, the stairways; you were enclosed – even in the yard you were hemmed in by electrified fences, gates and walls. You were used to looking up at the stronghold all around you and couldn't adjust to the unfamiliarity of open spaces.

He descended the staircase in the wake of the cons, pausing in amazement at the sight of a face he knew. Whitey – Wayne White from school. His face hadn't changed all that much, only grown thinner with the addict's greyish pallor. Instead of being tough and stringy he'd become fragile, sick-looking, and derelict. Like the others, Whitey was on his way out to exercise.

They came face to face in the stairwell and Eddie didn't quite know what to do. Wayne's face pulled into a smile. 'Hiya, Eddie,' he said. 'How you doin'?' It was just as though he'd last met him a week ago. Eddie was aware of Mal standing nearby, listening and looking surprised at this level of intimacy.

'Oh, fine,' Eddie said, embarrassed, and moved away so

that Wayne had no option but to follow the other inmates out.

'Do you know that merchant, Ed?' Mal asked. 'Looks like he'll not last long.'

'Just a kid I was at school with.'

The idea that Mal could see the hand of mortality on Whitey's shoulder chilled Eddie. Whitey had been one of the kids who knew where things were at. His level of sophistication had made Eddie feel insecure and childish – he was the first to own a Snorkel Parka. Like Eddie he'd played football for the first team, was selected for the county, played a couple of times but then developed problems with his Achilles tendon and after that he lost interest. Could a damaged Achilles change the entire pattern of a person's life? Eddie wondered. It shocked him to think that the injury might have led to Wayne becoming this stooped, muddy-faced wreck.

Eddie tried to remember what Whitey was supposed to have been doing when he left school, but he couldn't be sure – after all, it was more than half a lifetime ago. In a few weeks he'd be forty. The thought disturbed him. Forty was old – he'd never envisaged himself reaching this great age. Before he realized it, he'd be retiring like Brad. Age stole up on you – it scuttled along and one day it hit and everything was too late.

After work Mal and Eddie dropped in at the Minerva for a quick pint.

While Eddie was at the bar buying drinks, he kept glancing round at the estuary. The sun had turned it into a giant sheet of corrugated metal. It would be magic to be setting out on a trip to some far-flung shore. Sharon had booked a fortnight in an apartment in Spain in August, but their holidays together had a habit of being difficult. By the time they came round he'd have forgotten how treacherous they usually were, but once on holiday he'd realize his stupid mistake.

The glow of the estuary decided him on a run. Sometimes he ran in the lunch hour with a few of the others but today he'd missed out. If he didn't keep up his running he could see himself ending up like Mal with his beer gut, or Benson, dead of a heart attack at forty-two. But it was more than that. He had to get outside after all those hours penned up, absorbing anger and insults and not responding. Sometimes he hated the job. It made him inhumane – though when he heard of one inmate kicking another to death, his head reeled with revulsion. He listened to his colleagues calling the cons scum, and he flinched from going that way too. No, he needed to be out running with his dreams – he dreamed of a new career, something in sport, a trainer, a teacher . . . He'd loved sport at school, been good at athletics and football.

'Can't stay long,' Mal said. 'Can't push it too far. Sal thinks I'm always with you.'

'You'll land me in the shit one of these days,' Eddie said, luxuriating in the cool bitter liquid sliding down his throat. 'If she ever rings Sharon it'll all come out.' He didn't like Mal doing this to Sally; she was a decent woman and the constant lying somehow demeaned Mal.

'She won't – she's not like that. She trusts me.'

'You don't know. If she trusts you, you shouldn't lie, should you?'

'I hope you're not getting on your high horse, mate.'

'No way,' he said. 'It's your business, after all – it's just that I don't want dragging in.'

'You won't be.'

Matter closed. Eddie suspected that Mal wanted to rabbit on at length about the eternal triangle but he couldn't be bothered to listen to Mal's bragging. He longed to be outside in the open, running.

At home, Eddie found Sharon in a good mood.

'I've bought a marble statue. It's not one of those awful plaster things that you see in some gardens – Di and Barry have just bought one. He'll stand on a plinth at the bottom of the garden. The path will need flagging or tiling or something, and we'll position the water feature nearby.'

While she talked on Eddie calculated the cost and the amount of labour he'd have to expend. He followed her out to look. The male figure, genitals discreetly hidden beneath a curly leaf, stood on the patio.

'Very nice,' he said to placate her. 'Only you do realize garden ornaments are the latest objects to be nicked – there's a big market for them. And what's more, the thieves are coming out here.'

As she digested this, he said he was off for a run.

'Ed, you said you'd start on the papering upstairs.'

'Well, I will, but not now. Anyway I want to get round later to mow your mum's back lawn and do a few jobs for her – you told her I'd come tonight.' That seemed to silence her, but she had that ill-done-to look he hated to see: it reminded him too much of those years before Emma's birth . . . the miscarriage years. 'I'll go straight round to your mum's afterwards – be back as soon as I can.'

At a viewing point down by the estuary, he parked up. On the right the Humber Bridge arced above the water. Cars the size of Dinky toys, like the pristine ones he played with as a child, snailed along the bridge. Normally he'd gaze in awe at that bridge and think of the breathtaking feat of its construction, and the engineer's satisfaction at the sight of his handiwork. The span leaped across the water. Viewed from a train you got a different picture of gigantic ribs supporting it, and that thrilled him too. To-night it was the swell of the estuary on which his eyes focused. He let the tension ease out of him as he gazed.

He took off, running by the side of the foreshore. The

smell of water and mud was in his nostrils. Black boulders lined the shore, buzzed over by blue-green flies. A buoy bobbed far out in the current. Away over in Lincolnshire a chimney speared the sky.

As he ran, the breeze off the estuary cooled his cheeks. He heard the thunder of cars on the bridge behind him like the sound of waves drumming on a pebbled shore, and now and then the screams of herring gulls.

From the nearby railway track he felt the vibration of the ground before the train shot into view. It was an old diesel, a short tin box rocking alarmingly as it sped along. He got a brief glimpse of faces staring out at him. A child waved; he waved back.

He kept his gaze steady. He wouldn't think about work. It was all a great cage, a cage that constricted. Running, running, his feet on the snuff-dry path sent up dust – the rhythm formed, but first came the slow burn. His right calf ached, his hamstring threatened to cramp. He forced his concentration into the cramping hamstring and he held his mind on the pain, moving into the centre of it.

On, on he went, panting, pushing, until he flew through the pain and out beyond it.

The evening settled around him. For a while he'd not seen anyone, then he noticed a figure up ahead, a young woman on her own. She was staring out at the water. On his approach, she turned her head and looked at him. And as he gazed at her he realized that he knew this face: the girl in the photo; the swimming teacher.

9

Two evenings after she'd learned the truth about her mother's death, Lyn cycled round to see her dad. She caught him just before he left for the pub. He was a regular there and the barmaids had his bitter lined up on the bar even before he reached it. Lyn knew that any change in his routine was impossible – the pub was his world.

He was finishing his tea of a shop-bought meat pie with a tin of potatoes and peas.

'Hiya, Dad,' she said.

'Cuppa?' he mouthed through cheeks stuffed with potato. He raised the brown pot towards her.

'Go on, then.' She unhooked a mug from a line he'd screwed into the wall.

The tea tasted strong and bitter and she shuddered. She'd been imagining how she could approach this all day, going over and over it, trying out different scenarios. He must know something and she had to break through the stockade of his routines and make him tell her why her mother had drowned herself.

'All right?' her dad asked, finishing off his pie.

'Yes.' She forced herself to speak. 'I was round at Aunty Mags's the other day.'

'Oh, yer – how is she, then?'

'Fine.'

'These pies haven't got any meat in 'em these days. Dead loss – not like they used to be – 's all potato.'

'Right.'

'How's your work, then?'

'Okay. Dad . . .'

'Yer?'

'Aunty Mags showed me some old photographs. And there were some of my mother – and a newspaper cutting about her drowning.'

'Yer?'

'Well, why did she?' Lyn couldn't look at him and she jammed her trembling hands between her thighs.

'Why did she what?'

'Kill herself.' She forced herself to look over at her dad. He'd risen from the table and was lumbering across to the sink, where he sluiced his plate and mug under the running tap.

'I don't know,' he said. 'She just did.'

'But don't you have any idea? You must have noticed something. People don't just do these things out of the blue.' This was a rerun of the scene with Aunty Mags. Her chest burned – she couldn't stand another session of the same denial. A scream stuck in her throat. She wanted to yell at him, make him respond, prise the truth out of his skull.

'No.'

'I should have been told the truth. I've wanted to know all my life. She was your wife and my mother and – doesn't that mean anything to you?' Now she was fighting to hold back her tears.

'What difference would it have made, lass?'

She paused. 'Well, I wanted a settled family like everybody else and not being palmed off all the time on Nana or Aunty Mags – and not having any brothers and sisters . . . and she was my *mother*.'

'Yer, you might have, but I couldn't help that. She died when you were a baby, and whether one way or another it doesn't really matter, does it?'

'I think it does – it matters to me because I'm her daughter.'

She could see that her dad could hardly wait to close the conversation and for her to leave. Perhaps there was nothing more to be said, but she couldn't let it go. 'She must have been depressed – there must have been a cause. I mean, people don't kill themselves for nothing. Didn't you notice? Didn't you try to stop her? Women don't leave a little baby for no reason. It just blows my mind thinking about it – I can't get my head round it.' She thought she might start crying again and she swallowed hard.

'Like I've said, Lyn, she just did, and it won't do any good bringing it all up and getting morbid.'

'Dad, I am not getting morbid. I'm sick of being lied to. But since you don't want to talk, I'll get going.' She went to the sink, poured the stewed tea away and banged the mug down on the draining board, fighting the urge to sling it at the wall. Her dad didn't respond but sat staring at her with an uneasy expression on his face.

'Yer, all right, love. Give us a kiss, then,' he said, exasperated. She could tell that he thought she was having a tantrum. She brushed her lips against his veiny cheek and turned to go.

'You should have trained up properly, Lyn,' he said out of the blue. 'I was watching telly this afternoon and it showed you these swimmers – up and down the pool in a dozen strokes.'

'See you,' Lyn said.

She unfastened her bike and rode off down the road, avoiding speed bumps where she could. Children kicked a ball along the pavement. On impulse she cycled down towards the estuary.

As she rode, she struggled to digest her anger, but her dad's last words tormented her: 'You should have trained up properly.' There she'd been, a teenager with her swimming club. Other kids' parents ran them to competitions, but she was stranded. Nobody thought they should encourage her, and she accepted swimming as a sport she was good at but didn't take seriously. As a lifeguard she could earn a living and Aunty Mags and her dad had considered that sufficient. It was as if she'd always been this quiet girl who did what she was told and didn't create a fuss.

Lyn cycled on, leaving the built-up areas behind. Now she pedalled up a gradient. At last she was up the hill, a cooling breeze on her face. Left she went, down a road between houses set back in huge gardens. No shops up here and no loud noises – this was a smart neighbourhood. Periodically she passed cream Labradors and poodles being walked by people who could afford to look dowdy.

She sped down a green tunnel beneath sycamore branches and, after negotiating twists and turns, reached the estuary, where she locked her bike to a railing. For a while she gazed out over the water, watching the dimpling and swilling. Where would her mother have waded in? Perhaps she couldn't swim – if you could swim, surely your instinct for self-preservation would cause you to strike out.

Suddenly a sliver of sandbank humped up midstream. Deep water alternated with shallow water, making the passage treacherous, unlike the area close by the pier where the ferry used to sail for Lincolnshire. That too was treacherous but for different reasons. Cross-currents could sweep small boats right off course and drive them into open sea.

Tonight the water washed right up to the rim of boulders coated in sage-green weed. Tall grasses fringed the shore in places so that you might expect to see miles of rolling dunes.

Nowadays people didn't walk out into the estuary to kill themselves: they took a leap from the Humber Bridge and sometimes their bodies were never recovered. Lyn gazed back to the left at its sharp outline – only a couple of weeks ago she'd read about the chap, someone her own age, who'd climbed on to the railing and, despite police efforts to restrain him, plunged to his death. That seemed far more violent than simply walking into the water.

Behind her a train whooshed by and mooed into the silence. She turned to stare after it. If you saw the estuary as a visitor, arriving in the city for the first time, you might imagine that here was a seaside resort where you would be able to lounge on sandy beaches, swim and sunbathe. But that wasn't so – this was a tricky, wilful place.

She wandered on further to where the path spread out and moved slightly inland. Lincolnshire, way over on the other side of the estuary, was lost in a faint mist.

Lyn concentrated on the long stretch of water and twitching grasses. She saw her mother stumbling towards the pebbles, watched her wading in, her flesh glimmering and opal in the darkness. From what was she escaping? Did she think about the baby she'd left at home asleep in her cot? Did she falter, or did she walk on with never a backward glance? Of course her actions could have been a plea for help – she might have wanted someone to hear her – only nobody did.

Why do I have to be connected to people who take their own lives? she thought. First my mother, then Max – what does it mean? Always people running away.

Just then she heard a panting behind her and the slide of trainers on pebbles. She swung round to face a runner who'd come upon her unobserved. Panic made her heart bang.

The man pulled up. She took a deep breath.

'Hi,' he said. 'Fancy seeing you here.' His face shone with sweat. 'You're my daughter's swimming teacher, aren't you?'

'Yes,' she said. Of course – he was the man from the baths.

'You just out for a stroll?'

'You could say that,' she said. She didn't intend making polite conversation and so she turned round and was about to excuse herself when he declared he'd call it a day himself and fell into step beside her.

'Emma was really scared of water when she came to you,' he said.

'Oh?'

'But she's come on enormously – in fact, she looks forward to the lessons.'

'Great.'

'Do you swim a lot yourself, then?'

She was surprised by the question. 'Used to,' she said. 'Well, actually I've thought of taking it up again.' She didn't know why she said that; perhaps she was still needled by her dad talking about lost opportunities.

'You mean competitive?'

'Not exactly.'

Silence stretched between them and was filled with the scrunching of their trainers and the slap of water on boulders and the far-off thunder of cars flying over the Humber Bridge.

'Not many women would walk down here alone in the evening,' he said.

'Is that right?' she said, beginning to sense a warning.

'Well, it's pretty isolated.'

'Hardly the Amazon basin – anyway, you're more likely to be attacked in town.'

He laughed. She relaxed a fraction, but avoided looking openly at him, though she'd noticed his muscular legs with their feathering of dark down. He'd be proud of those. He obviously took care of himself – he'd got fantastic teeth and no overhanging gut.

When they came into sight of the bridge viewing area, she breathed out with relief. Now she could mount her bike and be rid of him.

'Here we are,' she said, chancing a glance at his face. He seemed very spruce, and she liked the way he smiled. He didn't have Max's slumberous quality, that coarse-grained, hulking look. This person was formidable in a different way. She glimpsed it in his controlled movements, his questions, as though he expected murderers or deviants of some sort to be wandering about. She knew she was edgy with him because of having seen him in action that day at the baths. People didn't realize how much swimming revealed about their character. When he'd been bombing along with his powerful crawl, she'd thought him aggressive, but after her reprimand, he'd seemed contrite. She knew he was watching her as she unlocked her bike, mounted it and rode off.

How long she might have stayed down by the estuary had he not interrupted her musings, she couldn't guess, but the evening left her dissatisfied – an inner unease was drawing her back there. In her head she carried a picture of the wide expanse of glossy brown water with its fringe of biscuit-coloured grasses and reeds and the scattering of black pebbles. She'd heard that long ago the Lincolnshire coast was attached to the foreshore but the changing tides had eaten away at the land. Had there been no estuary her mother couldn't have drowned herself like she did. 'What-if' thoughts always unsettled her. More disturbing were her efforts to piece together the events of the night her mother died. Could there have been a horrendous row, or had she been suffering from postnatal depression?

That Friday evening after work Lyn cycled off again to the Humber. The fine weather hadn't broken, but the air was stultifying and bundles of cloud obscured the sun. All day at the baths it had been ferociously hot and they'd all been gulping down water from the cooler.

Under the green arch of horse chestnut trees she cycled, following the ribbon of road as it wound down to the foreshore. She swerved round the last bend and up to the viewing point.

For a while she stood gazing at the sweep of the bridge and the motion of the water. She wondered how long it had taken for her mother's body to be found. She'd heard that it might be weeks before a corpse turned up.

The evening she'd first heard how her mother died, she'd asked where her mother was buried. Aunty Mags had told her then that it had been a cremation and they'd scattered her mother's ashes in the Humber because she'd always liked to walk down by the foreshore. Lyn had found that strange.

She set off up the path once more, wandering beside the water. Blackflies buzzed in her face and she wafted them away with her hands. At intervals the ground vibrated as a train rocked by – sometimes the long snake of the London train, at others a stubby diesel, perhaps shooting to York or Sheffield. Her gaze focused on water. It must be quite a few miles across to Lincolnshire. Water usually attracted young kids to play in it, but nobody ever bathed here. Surely they must have done in the past; perhaps they didn't now because of pollution.

As a child she'd never gone near the estuary – it had always been the swimming baths. She remembered Fred, her swimming teacher: she could still see his hands and arms describing the movements of pushing back water – they seemed so sure, so perfectly controlled and yet easy. She'd been swept into the poetry of his crawl, how he covered the pool in five strokes, gliding like some sea creature, scarcely breaking the surface. To watch him butter-flying up the pool was to witness a great bird swooping and soaring. Veils of water flew from his shoulders as he extended his arms and flipped his feet. Even as a small child, the first time she saw him swim she knew that here was something very special – having such a talent set him apart in some way. On hearing he was an Olympic gold-medallist she'd felt the goose pimples rise on her arms, and when he told her she was good, had the makings of a fine swimmer and should go on, her face went hot with pleasure. But it hadn't come to anything. She'd trained, but her heart hadn't been in it. She'd lacked purpose then, any purpose, and seemed to have been mired in aimlessness ever since.

Puzzling over this lack of drive made her walk further than she had before and she was shocked when she heard the runner addressing her.

'Hello. I did wonder if I'd see you up here.'

'You must do quite a bit of running, then?'

'As many times a week as I can squeeze in – it's not far from home and it's quiet – helps me relax.'

'Busy life?'

'Yes, shifts at work, driving my daughter to various lessons – you know how it is.'

'What else does she do apart from swimming?'

'Dance, drama, music.'

'Wow!'

'All the kids round about seem to.'

'We never did anything like that . . . well, except the swimming.'

'Same here.'

He'd fallen into step beside her. They'd reached a flat open stretch; on their right lay a wilderness of scrubby land, on their left the estuary. The water seemed very close and Lyn imagined that in stormy weather or at high tide the ground could become inundated. A crack of thunder shocked her and they both came to a halt. Fat raindrops hit their faces and everywhere smelled of earth and dry-ness. The coolness was a relief.

'You okay in this?' he asked.

'Yes – yes, I'm fine.'

'Mind you, I think we'd better turn round – look!'

The estuary lit up with a crooked flash and another barrage of thunder began to roll.

The rain fell in long straight rods, bouncing on the ground. In the gloom, land and estuary merged into a cobweb-grey mist. She felt a coolness spreading on her skin. Her white T-shirt moulded to her and her jeans clung to her thighs; her hair slapped against her cheeks.

'I've never walked like this in the rain before,' she said, and laughed. 'It's brilliant.'

'Yes,' he said. 'It's not something you get to do.'

'I mean, we're cooped up all the time.'

'Like battery hens,' he said. 'Shall we run in it?'

They pounded along with the rain driving in their faces. The thunder kept up a constant growling, now as though a building were tumbling down and pieces of masonry were crashing to earth. The sky split open with livid forks. Lyn caught water on her tongue and rain spiked her eyelashes. She gave a whoop of elation and sprang across a puddle. He turned briefly to see what she was doing and grinned. They plunged forward, hooting and laughing.

The skeleton of the bridge hove up out of the mist and the lights of cars on it sent orange sprays into the dark-ness. Panting, they reached the deserted viewing area.

'Look,' he said, 'I can stick your bike on the car and drop you off at yours.'

Buoyed up by the sudden strange release of the rain and laughter, she debated whether to offer him a drink.

When they arrived at her door, she asked him in. 'You could have a coffee or I've got some whisky and lager – I always keep the whisky in for my dad.' He opted for coffee, and said he hoped she didn't mind him sitting on her furniture in his wet things.

'Oh, don't worry about that – I just hope you won't get cold.'

She switched the gas fire on to full and fetched a towel, then went into the kitchen to make coffee. It occurred to her that she didn't even know his first name.

'By the way, I'm Eddie,' he said when she reappeared with the tray. 'I know you're Lyn from what Emma's said.'

As he raised the coffee mug to his lips, Lyn noticed that he wore a wedding ring, a thick gold band. She tried not to be aware of his legs and the hair lying close to the flesh. The same down feathered his arms, only it was a shade lighter. His eyes seemed to laugh a lot and she liked the way his mouth turned up at the corners. He scrutinized her too, giving her appraising glances that she refused to acknowledge. We're playing games, she registered, *and he's married.*

'Do you like working at the baths?' he asked.

'It's okay. Anyway, I don't know how to do anything else – I'm not trained.'

'I'm the same,' he said. 'I work for the Home Office.'

Home Office – she didn't know what to make of that, but she gathered he expected her to probe.

'Home Office?'

'The . . . er . . . Prison Service.'

'Oh. Oh, right – you mean you're a prison officer?' She thought of Max. For Max such a person would be a hated screw. 'Screws,' she heard Max's voice saying, 'screws, they're just doing time the same as the cons – must have something wrong with them if they want to do this job.'

She knew he expected her to make a rejoinder but she had nothing else to say to him and wondered why they were sitting here in her front room; and why, down by the estuary, the storm and the brown waves and his laughter and her own had intoxicated her.

Not much later he looked at his watch, shot up from the sofa and said he must be going. She rose at the same time and they remained a few feet apart. When he smiled at her, she had to return his smile. She was disconcerted by his body – challenged by its woody smell, and its compactness.

'Bye, then,' he said on the doorstep. 'Thanks for the coffee.'

'A pleasure.'

He still lingered, and her stomach muscles clenched with anxiety.

'Right, well, I'll be off.'

At last he went. She sensed this wasn't going to be the end of it.

10

Eddie watched Sharon sitting before the dressing table mirror in a black underwired bra and black lace-trimmed briefs, rubbing various potions into her cheeks. He noticed the chubbiness of her hips as they spread on the stool. For a slim woman they were a nice surprise, but she hated them. He had an urge to kiss the back of her neck and run his hands down her spine and caress those fleshy bulges that all the private gym sessions couldn't budge. He placed his fingers on the nape of her neck. She glanced at him through the mirror.

'Ed, if you don't get in the shower and hurry up, we'll be late. Don't forget you've got to fetch the baby-sitter.'

He withdrew his fingers. His fantasy of sliding his hands into her knickers and easing her down on the fluffy white rug shrivelled and died.

'Emma's got to be collected from Sophie's as well.'

With Sharon everything had to run exactly on time – in a way he supposed it was like the regime in his parents' house.

'You couldn't have done that?'

'No, Ed, I couldn't – I've had a lot of paperwork to attend to.'

By this time Sharon's face and neck were a uniformly apricot hue. She was now using tiny plastic-handled implements with foam ends to work a beige-toned shadow over her eyelids. Her face tensed with concentration. He knew he must not interrupt this important ritual.

Defeated, Ed took himself to the shower, trying to rid himself of the girl in the white T-shirt racing through the storm.

Water cascaded over his head and he closed his eyes as it trickled down his face. He was out by the estuary running, and then came the jolt of recognition; of wanting to know. He couldn't divert the conversation to her and Smithson – he couldn't ask baldly: 'How come Smithson had your photo in his pad?' And what if it wasn't really Lyn at all?

'Ed, don't make us late.'

He bit back a furious retort and soon he was driving round to fetch Emma from her friend's.

'Daddy,' Emma said, as soon as she saw him, 'where is it you're going tonight?'

'Just those friends of your mum – Di and Barry.'

'Oh, you mean Harriet's mum and dad.'

'That's right, I'd forgotten.'

'I don't like Harriet very much – she's stuck-up. But she has riding lessons – Dad, do you think I could? It'd be great!'

Eddie hated having to deny her anything – but riding lessons? That would be another expense, and it wasn't only that, there'd be more fetching and carrying and he was sure most of it would fall to him.

'It might be difficult at the moment, Em.'

'But Daddy . . .'

He mustn't say he'd see, because that generally meant he'd capitulated. 'No, I can't promise anything just now – and you're already busy with lots of other lessons.'

But by the time they'd reached home he'd half promised that maybe . . . Emma rushed straight into the house calling, 'Mummy, Mummy, Dad says I can have riding lessons.'

'Oh, yes?' Sharon appeared in a new black dress with spaghetti shoulder straps. Her perfume went before her. 'I don't know anything about this, Ed?'

'Mummy, he said I could.'

'Well, we aren't going to discuss it now – there isn't time. I haven't said yes – I haven't even been consulted, have I, Eddie?'

Eddie was glad to be out of the house and on his way to collect the babysitter, a sixteen-year-old whom Emma liked.

Amy smelled penetratingly of cheap scent and she sat beside Eddie fiddling with her multiple chains as he racked his mind to find a topic of conversation. He asked her about school and she pulled a face and said it was all right and she'd done her GCSEs and they were horrible. Had she got a boyfriend? As soon as he asked, he wished he hadn't, because she might think he'd designs on her.

'Well, there is somebody,' the girl said, now perking up, 'but we've only been going out' – she consulted her watch – 'two weeks, three days and forty-five minutes.' She gave a laugh, smoothed her stretch jeans down and popped her gold cross between her lips.

When Emma reached that age, Eddie knew that he'd live in a constant state of apprehension in case some no-good lad preyed on her. He shuddered in the heat and tried to disguise it with a show of jocularity, glad to be turning into his own drive.

The girl swung her legs out of the car and he was back with Lyn, her wet denim-clad thighs next to his. The baby-sitter was blonde too, and he watched the bounce of her hair as she trotted up to the door, where Emma was waiting on the front step.

'Hi, Amy!' she called and Eddie was pierced by her vulnerability, the way her straight black hair fell almost to her shoulders from the thin white line of her parting. She was so complete, so new, so enthusiastic about life and yet so fragile. He'd thought it from the first moment he saw her in the hospital. As Eddie had watched Emma being born, Sharon pushing her out from between her thighs, he'd sensed that he was glimpsing some essential truth, and he'd cried. At last he and Sharon had got their longed-for baby. Even right up to the last Sharon had been convinced some disaster would intervene to rob her of that moment. He didn't let himself explore it too often in case he wore out the thrill and elation of it.

'Nice to see you, Amy,' Sharon said. 'I've put you some sandwiches in the fridge and you can make drinks. Don't let this one stay up late, will you?'

'No, Sharon,' Amy said.

Eddie kissed Emma goodnight and went out with Sharon into the rosy evening, clutching the two bottles of Australian red wine chosen by Sharon. He knew little about wine, but Sharon had indicated that massive social gaffes could be made over such a matter.

'You shouldn't have put that suit on,' she told Eddie. 'They're bound to be in casual gear.'

Eddie sweated in the navy wool-and-polyester suit. 'Why didn't you tell me before?'

'You dilly-dallied getting ready and then went off before I could say anything.'

'Too late now.'

'It gives the wrong idea.'

'They'll get over it.'

'Ed, you're always so clueless, and we need to make a good impression.'

Eddie saw she'd plunged into a major sulk and her mouth sagged at the corners, giving her that awful injured look. They walked out of the estate, she tapping in her stiletto sandals and he striding ahead so that she had to puff to keep up the pace.

'Can't you slow down?' she said at last.

'You're the one who's been bellyaching about being late.'

'We should have called a cab.'

'It's not far enough for that.' He felt the dampness in his armpits and on his forehead. At the thought of having to cope with one of Sharon's long silences, exhaustion hit him.

They arrived outside the Chapmans' mock Georgian mansion, with its double garage and landscaped front garden of pebbled areas and carefully selected conifers and shrubs. Eddie was red-faced and Sharon complained of a wrenched ankle. She rang the doorbell and Di appeared, her scent blasting the air. Eddie took in a tight scarlet dress (scarlet seemed to be her colour) with a deep V-neck – she was all scarlet from her shiny lips to her stilettos and toenails. She whizzed her mouth past Sharon's ear, grazing Sharon's cheek with her own and reserving the lips-on-lips kiss for him. As soon as Di led them out to the garden, Eddie rubbed the back of his hand across his mouth and discovered a greasy scarlet stain.

On the terrace, ensconced in cane chairs and recliners, and surrounded by earthenware bowls of flowers, were the other guests. Barry, the host, casually attired in pale chinos and an open-necked shirt, rose. Eddie glanced at his feet, curious to see whether he'd still be sporting the geeky shoes. No – this time he wore expensive suede loafers, without socks of course. Barry's fucking geeky shoes and the cons' decrepit prison-issue sand shoes coalesced . . .

'What can I get you, Shaz?' Barry asked, kissing Sharon. So it was 'Shaz' now, Eddie noted.

'A gin and lemon, I should think, please, Barry.'

Eddie got a bottle of lager and found a vacant chair beside Marie, the nunty dresser. He remembered her pursed little mouth and the way she kept tugging at her skirt to make sure her knees were covered. Tonight she was in a floral number that reminded Eddie of something his mother might have worn. She bubbled at him a bit, giving a coy smile and saying, 'So, we meet again.'

'Yes,' he said, unable to come up with anything to ease her coyness along.

'What have you been getting up to, then?' she said as though she expected him to mention something outrageous.

He swallowed a good mouthful of his lager and said, 'Well, I don't get time to do much other than work.'

'Oh, I see – you just look the sort of person who does lots of interesting things.'

He was surprised at this evident attempt at flattery. She seemed too stodgy for anything like that, and he laughed. 'Thanks for the compliment, Marie.'

She turned slightly pink and beamed into her glass.

They had a thorough discussion on their respective offspring's education, but then he found himself sucked into a monologue about Marie's difficult mother and her endless complaints about her grandchildren's diet and lifestyle. He sympathized, nodded. Preferring to listen rather than talk, he'd often find himself hearing confidences. In the past, he'd heard Sharon telling her mother, Delphine, 'Eddie's like a honey pot where women are concerned. I'm always having to shoo them off. Once I see them talking to him I know what's next . . .'

The evening stretched around them, warm and still. The only sounds were their voices and the tinkle of the water feature. The garden fell away below the terrace and was an elaborate pattern of shrubs, pebbled ways and furniture. Di had told Sharon that they'd paid a firm to landscape it. Eddie couldn't help thinking the traditional lawn and herbaceous borders were far more attractive.

'Do you find your job depressing?' Marie asked, just when Eddie was drifting off into his own thoughts.

'Oh, no,' he said. 'It's just what you're used to.'

Di appeared dramatically in the French windows and said would they come and eat.

A cold buffet waited on the dining room table: a salmon on a silver dish, with sprigs of parsley protruding from its mouth; a pink ham sliced off the bone; any number of beany salads in glass bowls, plus salads composed of green things whose names were unknown to him.

He noted the crystal and the linen table napkins (no paper ones here) and was sure Sharon would be monitoring all these for future reference. Special-offer wine glasses from the supermarket would definitely be out.

Marie, whom he now hoped to escape, seemed to be shadowing him. He decided he must relocate so as not to end up beside her on the terrace. He had to abandon his suit jacket and loosen his tie, and even then he felt overheated.

Di, or Barry, had now put on music of a smoochy type intended for dancing. Eddie cut into his ham and glanced about. Snatches of conversation reached him: somebody's holiday in Florida . . . Somebody else had been to Mexico, and everywhere seemed to be fortified and you must only visit carefully mapped-out places, and even then . . . A woman in green described how she'd come upon a burglar in the house mid-afternoon and how she now felt desecrated.

Eddie pondered on the word 'desecrated', unsure whether you could apply it to human beings. Biting into a cherry tomato, he was back by the estuary, walking along the foreshore with the girl, sealed into that world of rain, gusting wind and waves fretting the pebbled shore. He traced the coolness of it on his skin; saw the girl's hair flattened to her skull, the blond darkened, rain on her eyelashes and pearling her cheeks. He was caught in a sweet melancholy and wanted to escape the laughter going on around him. The evening had a raucous, sexy feel; he'd sensed it from the moment they entered the house and thought it related to the impersonal opulence of the décor. The pale leather sofas received you as though in an embrace; your feet sank into the carpets. White lilies lolled in a glass vase and their perfume permeated the house.

He slipped his plate on to a corner of the table and wandered out casually to the terrace. Dusk had fallen, and he let the stillness absorb him.

At that moment he heard footsteps behind him and turned to face Marie.

'Followed you,' she said.

'Yes,' he muttered.

She came in very close to him, closer than he found comfortable – the cons sometimes tried this on to intimidate him and he would bluff it out with them. He didn't step back tonight either.

'I think we're two of a kind,' she said.

Before he had time to respond, her arms wrapped round him and her mouth pressed against his. He tasted lipstick and wine. Part of him was curious to discover what her motive was. She didn't seem like someone who'd go in for quick gropes at parties. Against his will he felt stirrings in his boxers – and was irritated at this automatic reaction.

While they were still entwined he heard the clip of stilettos on pavers and Sharon's voice.

'Yes, I think you've got it fabulous.'

'Glad you like it. Of course, it was Di's idea, not mine.'

'Oh, there you are Ed,' Sharon said, appearing with Barry. 'I wondered where you'd got to.'

'Just taking the air,' he said. Marie twittered on about the beauties of the new garden layout, and Eddie was surprised at her aplomb.

An hour or so later Sharon and Eddie thanked their hosts and set off on the walk home. She was very quiet at first and then out it burst.

'What the hell did you think you were doing?'

'How do you mean?' He tried to sound nonchalant.

'Messing with Marie in the garden.'

'Whatever do you mean?'

'Look, don't make it any worse. I saw you and so did Barry. We had to pretend we hadn't. It was terribly embarrassing. You are so pathetic. What the hell did you think you were doing?'

'Nothing.'

'Nothing! What kind of an answer is that? What if Nigel had come down the garden instead of me? I can't imagine what Barry must think – and what about Marie? I'm surprised she didn't smack your face.'

'As a matter of fact, Marie started it.'

'I know what you're like – you let them pour out their hearts to you and then they can't leave you alone . . . I just wish you'd think about me for a change.'

This was going to run and run, he knew. Sharon had embarked on the list of his wrongdoings and he felt an ache in his guts and a desperation that culminated in indigestion. He'd been backed into a corner from which there was no escape, and assigned the role of villain, and yet he didn't think he was to blame.

'And you,' he bellowed to the silent road, 'are a demanding, bloodsucking bitch.'

'How dare you!' Rage turned her crimson.

She stumbled along, lurching in her sandals, a small, wronged figure. He didn't need to see her mouth to know how her lips would be pressed into a stringy line. Now she'd be lost to him for days.

They didn't speak as they entered the house.

'Has Emma been all right?' Sharon asked Amy, who nodded. Amy was clearly fed up and eager to get home.

'I'll drive you back,' Eddie told the girl.

'You've been drinking,' Sharon said. 'Get her a taxi.'

Eddie took no notice. 'Come, Amy, soon get you back.'

The girl trotted at his side, humming to herself. He dropped her off at her gate and was reluctant to return home. The night was balmy and on a whim he turned the car round and headed for the bridge viewing point.

Once there, he sat in his car gazing out at the black water, spangled with moonlight. He got out and wandered up to a low wall, where he stood listening to the sucking of the waves. The great bridge arced to his right. He wondered whether the girl was still awake, or lying sleepless in her terrace house. If only he knew more about her life. He re-examined the moment of elation as they ran through the storm.

The bubbling in his gut subsided as he watched the ebb and flow of the estuary and became absorbed by the night sounds. A ship out somewhere, perhaps in the North Sea, set up a low wailing.

Reluctantly he returned to his car and drove home. By this time the sky had turned dove grey and birds twittered in the trees. He had wound down the windows and the breeze washed his cheeks.

He parked the car and entered the house as quietly as he could.

'Where on earth have you been?' Sharon demanded, emerging in her dressing gown. It was clear that she'd been lying in wait for him.

'Nowhere,' he said automatically.

'What on earth do you mean, "nowhere"? You've been gone hours – you went to drop Amy off, remember? You *have* taken her home?'

Seeing the idea forming in her head, he stomped off upstairs in disgust. Without bothering to undress, he lay down on the bed in the spare room.

11

After waking from a dream where she soared through water as though on air currents, Lyn knew she had to phone her old swimming teacher. This realization was bound up too with the news about her mother – but she wasn't clear how. Again she found past moments flickering through her mind. She was swimming in that inky, bottomless, fatal pool, feeling the urge to sprint forward through the yellow, spear-shaped leaves bobbing on the surface. The compulsion to swim into uncharted territory goaded her – pushed her towards a journey she had to take.

She made her usual detour so as to cycle by the mermaids on the fountain. They presented their white faces to her as their backs arched down towards the flip of their tails. Skateboarders had stood on and crushed the rim of flowering shrubs below the women, she noticed.

'Hiya, doll,' Andy said when she came into the staff room. 'All ready for the attack?'

She smiled. ''Spect so.'

At ten the kids' free swim started and on a day like this masses of them would swarm in.

'They're fuckin' lunatics, some of them kids.'

The first hour passed with the regulars plodding down the lengths and complaining to one another about the lack of time and space.

Heat built up under the glassed-in roof. Lyn patrolled

the poolside, gazing at the swimmers, who called out to her now and then. She nodded and smiled but she was really wondering what her mother would have looked like if she was alive now – the girl in the photograph gave no inkling of how the middle-aged woman might have been. When she was a child, she used to imagine that she might bump into her mother in the street, and she'd look at the women in supermarkets or pushing prams or with children about her age and choose a mother for herself.

If only she'd been old enough to remember her mother, then she could have challenged Aunty Mags and her dad's amnesia about her. From Aunty Mags she would have expected a different response – she liked to gossip about people and what they got up to – but when Lyn had asked her to describe her mother a shutter had come down.

Ten o'clock – the session was over. The entrance hall reverberated with shouts and battles. *Wham*, the doors banged back and a thrust of children pelted in, clutching Nike bags and plastic carriers, jostling and rushing to reach the changing cabins.

A series of crashes followed as bodies hurled themselves into the water. In seconds the pool vibrated with tadpoley kids; some diving, others doing a splashy crawl, heads and shoulders half out of the water as they waggled from side to side, others stood in the middle of the pool peering about. Shouts rang out and the sound was thrown back from the cavernous walls.

Lyn tried to keep her eyes fixed on the heaving mass of bodies. She was terrified that someone might drown when she was on pool duty: a kid could break another's spine by leaping on it in the water; somebody might get jostled under and panic. If she missed some initial sign a child might die. A series of pictures jammed themselves into her head. She didn't want to see them.

In the afternoon Lyn, sitting on the high chair, watched a large contingent of youths fling back the swing doors and strut in. She felt a flutter of anxiety at their hard, streetwise faces and rough voices.

'That kid hasn't even got trunks on,' Ben remarked, standing beside the chair. 'They've just come in off of the street.'

'They look like trouble,' Lyn said, feeling a throbbing in her temples.

The newcomers took over the deep end and bombed into the water, one after the other, bending and twisting in showy dives. Then they hauled themselves out, preened and started all over again.

The other kids kept near the shallow end, apart from a group diving through one another's legs. These moved up as though they might want to join in, but the deep-end lads didn't take any notice and continued flinging themselves into the water.

Lyn couldn't be sure how it started, but the next moment, both groups had become a frenzied knot of flailing limbs and twisting bodies.

Andy blew his whistle and bellowed. No effect.

'Get out!' Andy shouted. Lyn slid down from the chair. Wes appeared with the baths' manager. Shelly, up on the balcony and about to leave the gym, made no move to come down. Lyn saw her eyes widen with fright and yet she was grinning in a hysterical way.

'Okay – out, now!' Wes joined in. His deeper voice carried more weight.

'Who?' A lad looked up with a complicated, innocent face.

'You lot – the lot of you,' Wes shouted.

They hauled themselves up on to the poolside, taking their time, pulling faces and cursing.

'We've fuckin' done nowt,' one said.

'Just go,' Wes insisted. 'Get your togs on and clear off.'

'It's not us – what about them fuckers?'

'They were all right until you came stirring it.'

'It's not fuckin' fair.'

'I'm not arguing – get out.'

When the baths finally closed, Lyn flopped down in a chair in the staff room. The others did likewise, groaning and sighing. Shelly burst out giggling. 'Oh, shit, what a day – when them kids kicked off, I thought we was in for a riot.'

'Nah, I could have settled that lot,' Andy said.

'Could you hell,' Lyn said, deciding that it was time to burst his bubble.

Wes, who'd been silent so far, launched into a diatribe about kids today having no respect.

Andy suggested they all go for a drink. Lyn was momentarily tempted, but pulled back – there was something else to do and she didn't want to be diverted . . .

'You coming?' Andy wheedled, turning to her. 'Or are you playing hard to get?'

'No – I'm busy.'

'Oh, yer? What's his name?'

'Just keep that out, Romeo!' And she tapped the side of her nose.

'All right, be like that, then, snooty bitch.'

Once on her bike, Lyn tried out what she might say to Fred on the phone. She hadn't seen him for years and he'd never remember who she was – might think she'd got a bit of a cheek.

Riding home through the evening park, thinking of her swimming days, she was catapulted into the past. The park was where she'd hung about after school. First kiss – you never forget that. The boy was two years ahead of her at school. He started with a prim pressing of her lips and then it was kissing with tongues, making her feel wild.

Nobody until that moment had touched the inside of her – up to that point she belonged to herself, and then with this piece of his body, like a mollusc squirming between her lips, everything changed. She didn't like him particularly, but because he had done that, she felt excited ever afterwards when she was near him.

Later, a boy she met swimming took her into some shrubbery at dusk and pushed her hand into his open 501s and told her to rub him while he kissed her – tongues again. She did as he asked because he had the sort of body that made girls stare. When a burst of creamy stuff squirted out of him, smelling like bleach, she cringed with embarrassment and wished she wasn't there. But they never spoke again after that incident and she saw him the following week with a girl whose father drove her to the leisure centre in a new Jag.

She used to hang about with her best mate Sarah and another girl from school and they draped themselves on the swings in the children's play area, or sat on the seats in the rose garden passing a ciggy between them and giggling whenever a group of youths swaggered past.

Bernie was the first one she did it with. Sarah and Fay speculated endlessly about 'doing it', while she listened and said nothing, but in the end she was the one who finally knew what 'it' was all about. Though after it happened, she felt awkward and let down, just as she'd done about the secretions dripping like thick glue down her fingers in the dusky shrubbery. She didn't like Bernie either, but he kept on badgering her to let him so she decided it would be easier if she did – and then she could say she'd got a boyfriend. Only it didn't work out like that.

She cycled home past the straight rows of terraces, past Aunty Mags's house. These unexpected memories had almost driven out her decision to phone, but immediately she entered her own house and dumped her backpack in the narrow hall, she knew she must make that call. If she didn't do it now, then most likely she never would.

First shot must be the phone book – would he be in there? There was his name: F. Conway. Amazing! She took a deep breath and dialled, half hoping he wouldn't be in, or that it was a different person. She let it ring five, six times and was about to replace the receiver when a voice said, 'Hello – who is it?'

'Oh, hi, this is Lyn Newton, I do hope you don't mind me calling you like this, I know it's a bit of a cheek; you won't remember me, but you gave me swimming lessons years ago when I was little. I'm a lifeguard now – I just wondered if I could get some advice from you about swimming?' Lyn paused, out of breath, feeling idiotic.

'All right,' the voice said. 'You can come round here for a chat if you want to.'

There it was – arranged, just like that. He agreed to see her on her afternoon off that week. She went to the fridge, poured herself a glass of orange; wandered about the kitchen sipping it, not knowing what to do. In the front room she pressed the remote and watched a couple of minutes of *Coronation Street* but couldn't concentrate.

The chat was bound to be embarrassing because Fred, too, would ask her what she'd done with her life, why she hadn't trained up properly – just like her dad had done. She was a failure, had frittered her chances away. A failed athlete. Was that what she was, somebody who showed a lot of promise but couldn't deliver? She had won inter-schools competitions and a coach wanted to train her, said she'd go far. So what had happened? She'd just not fol-lowed through.

She could imagine Fred's face. Champions didn't under-stand weakness. He wouldn't take her seriously, because she'd passed up an opportunity, wasted her talent. She'd never thought she was good enough – and she'd known she wasn't prepared to train week in week out. It would have meant no drinking in bars, no clubbing, no late nights out, no boyfriends. So what? Had she gained anything from all those years of bars and boyfriends? From sixteen, fifteen even, to meeting Max, she'd seemed to be numb to everything around her. She'd floated in and out of relationships. Men propositioned her in clubs and, excited by their kisses and the promise of intimacy, she'd spent the night in unknown flats that smelled of frying and air freshener. Sometimes they got repulsively drunk. Sex felt like a detached poking about. One or two, usually older married men, were quite kind and wanted to buy her things, but they seemed dazzled by the fact that she was twenty-five and more years younger than they. Of course they wouldn't have dreamed of leaving their wives for her, and she wouldn't have wanted it – somehow they were too pitted by life and that depressed her. The older men would say, 'Oh, Lyn, you're so innocent.' And she supposed she seemed that way, because she was sliding through life, not really living it.

To shake off these disturbing thoughts, she wheeled her bike out of the house and set off for the estuary.

Several cars were parked at the viewing point. Instead of setting out to walk, she leaned on the wall and gazed at the water. It looked deep at this point and gave off an odour of seaweed and ozone. The sound and smell of the water filled her with yearning: it seemed a wild unfettered world that was calling her, challenging her. Even on a hot evening like this, it would still be cold, icy like the water in the old lead mine at Youlgreave. That water woke her in the night, telling her she must strike out. You could let the currents drag you away, or go with them and struggle on through.

A car drove up, and she heard herself being addressed.

'Hi, Lyn. Just starting or just finishing?'

'Oh, hello. Actually, I just came down here to look at the water.'

He stood beside her, also looking out. She didn't know what to say and kept her eyes fixed on the water. They didn't really know each other. And he was a prison officer: the enemy. Max leaped out of the shadows asking her, 'What sort of cunts want to be locking other people up all day long?' People became their jobs – they couldn't avoid it. The body searches, the cold eyes scrutinizing her from behind bulletproof glass: it was because of Max that she knew of these indignities.

She made no move to initiate a conversation but remained staring out to Lincolnshire.

'What about coming for a walk?'

'All right,' she said – but why the hell couldn't she just say no?

They fell into step, following the same pebbled way they'd taken before. She was curious to discover what he wanted of her, because he must want something – they all did.

'How's the baths?' he asked, and she told him about the free swims and the pitched battles. She expected him to behave like Wes and condemn the ruffians out of hand. But he merely laughed. 'Kids! Better off the street than out doing villainy.'

'So you think we should have to cope with them?' She'd risen to the bait, but he continued to smile at her.

'It's all right – I'm only winding you up.'

'Oh.' She hid her irritation by smiling back.

After they'd been walking for some time, he broke the silence. 'Would you mind if I asked you a question, Lyn?'

'Ask away.'

'Did you know a chap called Smithson?'

Lyn felt as though he'd slapped her across the face. She stiffened with shock but tried to conceal her reaction.

'Why do you ask?'

'That's not an easy question to answer.'

The sky up ahead had taken on a rosy opalescence and the air didn't move. Lyn listened to the pattering of her heart. He'd begun to intrude, venture into a private zone. Since the time when the Special Branch had broken into her bedroom, she'd been on her guard – though maybe that had happened a long time before, the violence in the bedroom merely confirming something she'd already sensed.

'So did you know him, then?'

She wrestled with herself. If she denied it, she was denying Max and that was cowardly, a betrayal. 'Yes,' she said at last. 'And now perhaps you can tell me why you're asking.'

'I saw a photograph in his cell, and when I met you, I realized it must have been of you.'

She shuddered and somehow couldn't bear to know any more.

'I've been wanting to ask you from the first time I saw you.'

She was certain he'd not leave it there, that more questions would follow. 'Why?'

He didn't answer immediately. She concentrated on her left trainer, which rubbed her little toe.

'I don't know,' he said finally.

Now she wanted to prise information from him. What had he been doing in Max's cell? What did he know about Max's death? He must know things she didn't. She waited.

'Was he your boyfriend, then?'

'Yes.'

They carried on walking and she wondered what on earth she was doing with him on this flat, empty stretch. 'Don't you think we ought to turn back now?' she asked.

'Had enough?'

'Yes, I think so – I hadn't really meant to stay down here so long.'

'No, well, I'd just come for a run but then I saw you and I couldn't resist.'

She pretended she hadn't heard the last few words and they began to retrace their steps.

They talked about Emma's swimming lessons and things seemed to be normal and safe, but perversely she hankered after the rapids.

When they reached the viewing point, she smiled at him. 'I've enjoyed the walk,' she said. She was about to unlock her bike when he halted her.

'How about another walk on Friday?' he said. 'Eight-thirty?'

She nodded. 'Okay, well, I'm off. See you.'

Three o'clock and she cycled on her way to visit her old teacher, Fred. If he asked her why she hadn't bothered with her swimming before now, she thought she'd make an excuse and clear off fast.

He met her at the door, looking almost exactly as she remembered, although he was an old man now. His eyes were blue as the summer sea at Scarborough and when he talked his hands moved into a familiar swimming motion and you forgot his age in the surge of vitality springing off him.

She sank into a plush sofa and grinned. 'Don't think I'm silly or anything, will you,' she started, feeling a blush rushing into her cheeks, 'but I wanted to ask you something – get your advice.'

He watched her with his canny blue eyes. 'Right?'

'Well, it's like . . . well, I feel I want to swim the Humber.'

He cracked out laughing. She'd expected a response like this. She knew people would think she was mad. Why would she want to swim the Humber – what was the point? She couldn't explain what this meant to her because she wasn't sure yet herself, only that she, a person who'd never had any direction in her life, had been seized by a compulsion and was now on a quest after something she couldn't name . . .

'I know it might sound crazy, because nobody ever swims it.'

'No – I'm not laughing because I think it's crazy – oh, no. Well, my dad, Arnold, swam it. You see, there used to be a race every year. He won it three times. Look, his shield's there on the wall.'

She followed him to the other end of the through-lounge, where a huge shield hung against a pale wall. On it, surrounding the central design, was a series of small silver shields bearing the names and dates of the winners.

'He swam it for the last time in nineteen thirteen – and because he was the only one to win three times, they presented him with the shield to keep. They didn't have the race again after that because war broke out.'

Fred handed her a photograph, turning beige now, of a group of men, all in full swimming costumes. They appeared oddly formal, staring into the camera lens. He pointed to a man with brawny shoulders and chest. 'That one's my dad.'

Lyn shivered as she stared at the men. Although it belonged to another age, a different generation, they reached out to her. Nineteen thirteen – he'd last swum it as war was about to be declared. Mr Morris had droned on about the First World War in history lessons, only she hadn't listened much except to the bits about the trenches and the rats and all the young men who'd perished. Now the world opened up before her.

'Aye,' Fred was saying, 'he'd quite a history, had my dad, and the swimming here wasn't the end of it. They'd swim from New Holland after the packet had taken 'em there. If you stood on the planking in New Holland, you could see across to the old pier here.'

'Wow!'

'You had to have a boat with you, guiding. If you didn't you could be swept out into the open sea. They'd all leap in together and first one out at the other side got a hot bath, a brown dinner in the Minerva and the trophy. There'd be a great crowd watching, of course.'

'Fantastic – it's amazing!' Lyn thought of the gunmetal water swaying and thumping against the concrete and planking of the pier and caught her breath. How could a swimmer survive in miles and miles of that? It called for superhuman strength. In the swimming baths hardly a ripple disturbed the water's surface – even a host of people bombing forward in the crawl would scarcely churn it up, and there were no Humber tides to drag you off course.

Lyn didn't want to leave Arnold and his story and she hesitated before handing the photo back to Fred. 'Why don't people make the swim today, then?' she asked.

'Be too dangerous – lot of river traffic, and there's the pollution. Estuary's a different place today.'

'So what was it your dad did, Fred? You said he didn't only swim in the Humber.'

'Did you ever think that some things have to happen?' Fred asked after a slight pause. His blue eyes flared at her and the question vibrated into the silence.

'I don't know . . . I'm not sure,' she dithered. The way he'd put the question made the hairs rise on the back of her neck.

'Well, listen to this, then.'

She could tell from his face that whatever she was going to hear would be extraordinary.

'Right, so it's nineteen fourteen and my dad's joined up in the navy. He's down in the engine room stoking and he's sweating cobs, it's that hot, and his dog tag's burning his chest so he takes it off. Decides he'll go up on deck for a breather. He's standing there at the rail when he notices this black thing in the water whizzing towards the ship.

Nobody's about, so he hasn't time to raise the alarm and he just dives overboard. Good job he'd got used to swimming across from New Holland,' Fred said, and laughed.

'Wow!' Lyn said.

'Wait a bit, it gets better. So he's swimming for all he's worth and he hears this bang, looks back, sees flames and debris flying through the air, treads water. The waves are boiling but there's nothing left of the ship. Went down with all hands – torpedoed.'

Lyn could see the churning sea, the black object hurtling towards the ship, Fred's dad, alone, a speck in an ocean, rolling to the edges of the world. In that stretch of open sea, extending relentlessly to infinity, lay a challenge.

'Oh, yes, that's how it went. Right, now remember there was a war on and even if he saw any shipping it could be the enemy. You wonder what he must have thought when he was out there miles from anywhere.'

Fred suspended his story when his wife appeared with tea and chocolate digestives. 'This is Lyn,' Fred said. 'I'm telling her about my dad.'

'Right, love, then I'll leave you to it.'

'He'd been in the sea three days and three nights before a trawler commissioned as a minesweeper saw him. This feller who spotted him floating said, "Eh-up, there's something over yonder, looks like a creature." They didn't know it was a human being because that long in the sea had made him swell up and he was all white and bloated. Anyway, when they'd hauled him on board, they realized it was a man and he was still alive. He couldn't speak or anything and he'd got total amnesia.

'They kept him in the military hospital in Alexandria for weeks. Nobody had any idea who he was. Everybody this side had been mourning a good while. Now, this is where you have to wonder. He's out in Alexandria one afternoon with recuperating troops and all of a sudden this feller yells, "Eh, Arnold! Hello, mate! Fancy seeing you." And without a word of a lie who is it but this kid who'd lived next door and gone to Dock Street Primary with him, shared the same desk. He hugs him and that was how my dad found out who he was and could go home.'

Fred sat back and Lyn saw the tears shining in his eyes. 'Aye, Lyn, he was a brave man, was my dad.' Lyn, opposite him on the sofa, nodded.

When Fred started to speak again and they returned to the present among everyday things, she came back with a shock from a far-off country.

'I see you've got the bug, haven't you?' he said. 'But I've got to warn you . . . it's very tricky out there in the Humber – four currents. You have to know where you're going and what you're up against.'

The old teacher, Lyn realized, was steeped in swimming lore; he belonged to the water, knew it like part of himself.

'Loads have died in it, you know. There were these two bath attendants, they had a wager . . . it was nineteen thirty-nine . . . one of them got drowned because he didn't have a boat guiding. Oh aye, there's a lot never made it.'

Lyn sipped her forgotten tea. Fred was gazing out of the window, and it seemed to her he was staring into a world of fortitude, thinking of the qualities a real swimmer needed.

'A young lass tried a while back. She got halfway but she couldn't go on . . . too slim, no flesh round her heart to protect it.' He turned to look at her and his sea-blue eyes drilled into her. 'Kids today are too soft. We grew up swimming in the drains – Barmston, for one – we were used to river swimming. All you kids know is heated pools. It's the cold that does for you. Looking back, I wonder we didn't get poisoned. There'd be dead dogs, rats in there, prams, mattresses. The hot water from the leccy station killed the fish. We'd dive from Barmston Bridge – aye, it was a bit rash, was that.'

Lyn didn't know what to say and studied her hands. 'Anyway,' she found herself blurting out, 'I do want to try.'

'You'll have to be determined. What you need is a bit more of an aggressive streak – you have to psych yourself up . . . takes a lot of training and willpower too.'

Lyn sat motionless, trying to see herself as this new, powerful person who would strike out undaunted into wild seas.

'If you're serious, this fellow might be able to help you. He's a long-distance swimmer – I taught him when he was a kid.' He jotted a name and a phone number down for her.

As she stood on the doorstep, Fred smiled at her. 'I remember you as a lass – you were a plucky little bugger, but if you swim it, this'll really show what you're made of. Keep in touch, let me know how it's going.' He gave her a long straight glance that seemed to weigh her up. Lyn had the strange feeling that he was conferring an honour on her and she knew she couldn't let him down by messing the long-distance swimmer about. 'Bye then, Lyn, and good luck,' he said, resting his hand on her shoulder for a moment.

She suddenly wanted to cry. 'Thanks ever so. You've really given me something to aim for, and I'm going to get there.'

Riding back across the city, she imagined the great metallic mass of water stretching away into the distance and the lone figure battling on through the waves without a destination and with no hope of rescue. Would she be like that girl who got halfway and was then defeated by the weakness of her own body? How could you face the idea that you weren't ever going to be strong enough, that all the training couldn't help you conquer it? Perhaps this was a fool's dream and she was kidding herself, asking for trouble. People would think her a complete idiot and she wouldn't blame them. But by not going on now she wouldn't just be copping out, she'd be showing Fred what a pathetic creature she was.

Instead of cycling home, she took a diversion that brought her down to the estuary. It was now past six o'clock and the viewing area was deserted. She dismounted and stood there, as she'd done so often recently, staring at the water. Was it friend or enemy? Her mother had been swallowed up by those waves; they had closed over her in the darkness and she had been swept away. Would she, her drowned mother's daughter, be strong enough to battle through to what lay beyond?

Lyn wandered up the track, choosing a place where the pebbles had given way to sandy mud. When she was sure she was completely alone, she took off her trainers and walked to the water's edge. She felt the mud squeezing between her toes and then the sharpness of the water. The chill echoed through her. She ventured further in until the water was beyond her ankles. She stood there with wavelets splashing about her legs. Why not wade in – why not know what it must have felt like for her mother? It would have been dark – she was moving into blackness, cold sliding up her limbs like a paralysis. Did she close her eyes or keep stumbling on, staring into the distance as the water devoured her?

But it might not have been like that – Aunty Mags said her mother's favourite walk had been down by the estuary; maybe she wanted to be taken by the tides, saw them as somehow benign. There was, after all, in the ebbing and flowing a certain constancy.

12

Night gave you a long time to think. Tonight when he started the shift at eight p.m., Eddie wished he could be down by the estuary setting off on a run. On long summer evenings like this it seemed a particular punishment to be locked up inside and quite alone, the only officer on the wing.

He started his half-hourly patrol of the landings. At first he could hear the twittering of radios behind doors and voices talking to one another and the shouts of lads bellowing through their windows to mates on other landings. Sometimes somebody sang. Arguments battered back and forth, and men cursed. He heard his feet plodding along the landings.

A con shouted at him, 'Boss, got a light?'

'Sorry, can't open you up – haven't got a key.'

'That's not much fuckin' good.' Then a volley of abuse.

He reached the end of the landing and pegged the night clock. As he mounted the stairs to the twos, he heard another voice screaming at him.

'Gov, me padmate's sick.'

'What is it?' Eddie shouted through the door. He pulled back the observation flap and peered into the cell.

'He's sick.'

'I haven't got any keys – can't unlock you. You'll have to manage until morning.'

They could trick you by getting you to open up and then overpower you. It was security first – it had to be. But what if the other kid really was ill? Suppose he died? He'd be in deep shit if the man was seriously ill.

A buzzer went up on the fours and a light flashed on the wall. He mounted the staircase. The night light was on and the landing almost in darkness. He felt a trickling of dread tensing his neck and shoulders. All sounds were magnified. The wing took on a different aura. It appeared empty now, abandoned, just a monstrous cavern, or a ship adrift in the middle of an ocean – but then you listened to the night sounds, and you knew that behind these lines of doors human beings lay sleeping. You could sense the secrets hidden on this wing. The place rustled with information withheld. Pad 24. He flicked back the observation shutter.

'What's the matter?'

'I'm going to top myself,' the voice said. It was Brown. An attention-seeker of the first order, he was always making such statements.

'Well, what do you want me to do about it?' Eddie shouted. 'You know I can't open you up.'

'Well, I am.'

'Okay, go ahead – only don't make a noise about it.'

Perhaps Brown really would this time and if he did that'd be the end. This job, Eddie thought, was about decisions – you had to make decisions all the time and there was nothing to indicate what the right ones might be.

Between the half-hourly checks Eddie installed himself in the office and tried to get the court lists ready for the next day.

Time for supper. While he was microwaving his baked potato and tuna and boiling up the kettle, his thoughts turned to Lyn and Smithson. When she said she'd been Smithson's girl, he'd not known how to respond. He'd wanted to ask: 'Did you live with him? Love him? Where did you meet? Was it really the sex? Was it that good?' Gross. He was embarrassing himself by thinking it. He had no right to pry, it wasn't his business. Dead Smithson had dragged him into a place of ambiguities. Here he was, thoughts of this girl filling his head – this girl, a swimming teacher and a gangster's moll.

He squeezed the tea bag against the side of his mug and hoicked it out, slinging it into the bin.

Why did he, of all the officers in the prison, have to be the one to find Smithson's body? He'd been waking in the middle of the night, thinking of Smithson, his heaviness, his thick grey hair. He remembered the tickle of that hair on his cheek, the tingling horror in the pit of his stomach.

Lately a recurrent dream disturbed him too. He was locked in a cell – at first he didn't realize it, but then he dragged at the metal handle and understood he was captive. He'd wake up shouting and scare Sharon.

Sharon seemed happier. He'd papered their bedroom and promised to do the spare room; he'd taken her out and bought her a posh handbag. She'd been vivacious, how she used to be years ago, before the miscarriages had taken the light out of the marriage. 'You're not so bad sometimes,' she'd said, and smiled.

He could swallow his own dissatisfaction once Sharon was pleased, but that couldn't quell an inner tension. Tonight, driving through the city on his way to work, it came on him again – he didn't want to be fastened up all night, seeing nobody until morning. If he were out by the estuary running, it would be all right – he wouldn't be constantly hemmed in. Smithson, for God's sake, was free, anarchic; he'd lived how he wanted. But had he? Perhaps he was just being romantic. Of course Smithson hadn't been free – he was locked into a circle, caged, just as these poor druggie bastards were behind their doors.

At three-fifteen a buzzer went. He climbed up to the twos. 'Boss, can you give me something?' Eddie realized it was Wayne White, his old school friend.

'I've no keys – sorry.'

'Ed,' Wayne said, 'it's you?'

'Yes, that's right.'

'Can you get us something?'

'Believe me, I would if I could.'

'I can't sleep.' The voice reached Ed through the door, grating and miserable. 'Can't stop thinking about my lad. He's up in court.'

'Oh, yes?'

'Smack. He's only sixteen – been robbing to pay for his habit. Haven't seen him since he was two.'

Eddie couldn't hear Wayne properly but he could guess at what he was saying. His mumbled monologue started on another tack. 'I done nowt with me life – wasted it.'

Listening to the awful pathos of the voice behind the door, Eddie had a vision of Whitey, as he'd known him then, the tearaway bad boy always up to something outrageous. In those days he made you gasp because he'd do anything.

'Drugs make you selfish – you don't care.'

'Yes,' Eddie said, at a loss as to how he could escape from being pinned to the door by Whitey's sorrows. 'Look, Whitey, I've got to get on – I'm sorry.'

He returned to the office, remembering fragments: Whitey climbing into the garden of an old boy who lived in a detached house a walk away from the estate. Eddie, proud of the chance to be part of Whitey's gang, had dropped over the high wall after Whitey. The old boy shot out, bellowing, and chased them round and round. Only a long time afterwards did Eddie understand that the man hadn't wanted to catch them, merely to scare them.

Memories of Whitey and far-off boyhood triggered thoughts of the dreaded four-oh, now drawing ever nearer and which Eddie was sure Sharon would insist on celebrating in an ostentatious and expensive way. Barry of the nerdish shoes and Di would be bound to feature, Di encouraging Sharon to spend. Sitting alone in the office with the huge silent crate surrounding him, he could empathize with Whitey's lament for a wasted life. If he were really old like his dad, he could reduce his vision to the tomato plants and chrysanthemums he nurtured in the greenhouse. Their shoots would give him pleasure – no need to look further. There was no point in thinking about escapes, though, because he'd be spending more time at work, not less, and he'd have to sign up for more overtime to pay for Emma's riding lessons and the conservatory that Sharon was determined to have.

'Frankly, Eddie, these houses are like little boxes, and a conservatory will shoot the value up no end. You can see that, can't you?'

Their life seemed to be governed by Di and Barry. They knew what were 'must-haves' – which houses, cars, furniture . . . Sharon modelled herself on them. He sometimes had the impression that these two leaders of taste and style were ghostly presences in their house. They thought the light shone out of Sharon. Di nattered on the phone with her for hours and he'd heard her saying, 'You're just like the sister I never had . . .'

As he sat staring at the paperwork he'd done earlier and the glass-fronted cabinets where tools were locked away, he experienced a surge of irritation: the midlife crisis – it must be that. He'd be all right; it'd be fine in the long run. But in the long run he'd be pensioned off like Brad and it'd be wallpapering forevermore and an ache in your gut because you didn't know what to do with yourself. You'd not see the other guys any more, your co-workers, the fellow sufferers, the ones doing time along with the cons – you'd be outside, not penned in, but locked out with all that space around you, the weeks no longer divided into early and late shifts. With every new debt he was being pinned more securely into the job. He'd gone into it in the first place because he'd wanted to marry Sharon and be able to support a family . . . but now, now he'd have days when he loathed this life – since finding Smithson his nerves had felt exposed.

He'd dodge the discomfort of these thoughts by making a list of things to do:

Mow Delphine's lawn, put up two shelves and fix a bracket; repair back fence;

Integral fire alarm for Dad;

Lower kitchen shelves for Mum (without Dad knowing: 'Your dad thinks we're all giants and I have to get the steps to reach anything.').

He must pay Delphine a visit: his shift pattern had prevented him over the past few weeks. Right from the off he'd loved Delphine – she was how Sharon might have been, somebody soft and lively, with a sense of humour, who didn't build up grudges. After the death of his father-in-law, he'd tried to support her by doing the jobs she couldn't manage. She'd prepare treats for him, like a golden sponge cake so light it dissolved on the tongue. 'For my favourite son-in-law,' she'd say. 'You've been my lifeline.'

He could go on Friday – on Friday Lyn might fail to turn up, because she didn't like him – or . . . or what? This meeting was playing with fire and he didn't care. He wanted to let it happen, whatever it was, go into it and not draw back.

13

Whatever she was doing, Fred's story stayed with her. She saw again that inscrutable sea with the man beyond hope or despair battling in it. And then there was Fred, who carried the sea with him, and who didn't tell her things directly but let her see that he believed in her.

As a counterpoint to all this was Friday – Eddie – and if Friday evening turned out to be wet, then she'd have an excuse not to cycle out to the viewing point.

All day at work Lyn sweated and wondered. Andy pressed her to go for a drink when they knocked off, but she told him she'd promised to visit Aunty Mags (her usual excuse – from the way she talked, he must imagine that Aunty Mags was very infirm and not some girly old swinger). Why couldn't she come on afterwards? he said, but she shook her head.

Rain threatened, but although clouds kept rolling over the sun and the light turned pewter-coloured and electric, she set off on her ride out to the foreshore. She hadn't told anybody about this meeting, but she'd always been secretive so this was no change. She wasn't sure what was happening here, though. Perhaps this wouldn't turn into a relationship but just something she could treat casually and forget. After all, he was a married man and a prison officer, and both these set him off limits.

He wasn't there. She felt relief at first and then disappointment. Perhaps he'd forgotten – the invitation was thrown out so easily that he might not have meant it.

After ten minutes of staring at the water, she locked her bike and set off up the track. She became engrossed in watching the pattern of waves frilling along the boulders and the boating of the seabirds.

Fred had told her that a man and his son swam the span of the Humber Bridge at the time of its opening. From its appearance this could be a different river from the one at the old pier head down by the marina. There the currents were sinuous and you could sense the pull of the North Sea, the thrashing monster force that could devour a vessel in minutes. Ahead you could catch sight of ships gliding in the hazy distance. The ferry to Amsterdam sailed from a point higher up the estuary. She remembered one crazy weekend spent with Max, when they sailed out on that ferry and she stood on deck watching the waves as they spumed and leaped at Spurn Point. Later they crammed their plates with giant prawns, slices of ham and turkey and potato salad from a massive buffet, and caught glimpses of the sea through the portholes, and the land slipping away. They drank in the bar and danced on the sliding floor until two a.m. At six-thirty she awoke sticky and queasy from too many vodkas. The ferry tilted and she listened to the throb and creak from down below and she wondered if the cars had come adrift and whether they'd slide to one side and cause the ferry to go hiccuping to the ocean bed.

The past moved away from her as she stared at the estuary and noticed how the sandbanks lent the water a tawny shadow in places. A strip of mud met the waves and was marked with the runnels of water draining off the land. She gazed at the mud, remembering how her feet had sunk into it just a couple of weeks ago and she had sensed that in no time she could have been sucked down to her knees. A shudder caught her and her skin felt icy.

Since the conversation with Fred she'd been locked in indecision. The long-distance swimmer's number was still in her purse but she'd not phoned him. If she did, it would mean she was committed and she didn't know whether she was capable of such commitment. Swimming the Humber wouldn't be like a few miles in the pool. She thought for the umpteenth time of Fred's dad floating for three days and nights alone in the sea.

As she walked she wrestled with her fears: loneliness, drawing attention to herself and then appearing stupid, letting herself down, striking out and not making it. She knew there was a flakiness in her, a fragility she could disguise, but now she was being swept away and felt cut adrift with nothing firm to anchor her, her life drifting about her like weed in strong currents. That was what must have happened to her mother: she'd been washed away to her death on a tide of despair.

What have I ever done that I've been proud of? she asked herself. She couldn't think of anything.

Eddie not turning up was a disappointment. She'd liked his smile, how he seemed genuinely interested in what she had to say and didn't simply want to talk about himself. And he was natural, easy to be with. It would have been interesting to know more about him. She tried to shrug it off, tell herself it didn't matter, though it was just one more dent in her self-esteem.

But another voice insisted: Fred thinks you're plucky; he wouldn't have told you about his dad if he hadn't thought you needed to know that story.

So what had he been telling her? The story was about endurance. His dad had gone beyond that point where actions were curtailed by fear. Out there alone in the sea his father must have found peace, because when you had to face what you dreaded, there was nothing else to terrify you – maybe then you'd feel exhilaration. That was something you couldn't know in advance – she would have to find out.

It came on her like a gust of rage: she'd show them, show her dad, show all those hopeless men who'd let her down, and she'd make Fred proud of her. She'd phone the long-distance swimmer and see what he'd got to say.

14

Friday. He'd see Lyn. The evening beckoned. If only the shift would end. He ran into Mal on the wing.

'She's found out,' Mal said.

'Who has?'

'Sal, of course.'

Eddie was halfway down the stairs and kept going, intent on escaping Mal.

'Well, you might take some interest,' Mal snapped.

Why the hell did Mal have to capture him just as he'd hoped to get away fast?

'Coming to the pub after?'

Eddie realized this was a test of friendship. He ought to say immediately that of course he would, no matter whatever else he might have planned, because Mal needed him. Eddie couldn't dodge this one.

'All right,' he said, 'but I can only stay for a half – I've got to get back, I promised Sharon.'

Mal stomped off and Eddie heard him bawling at a prisoner.

The cons trooped back from the workshops and climbed up to their pads. Whitey saw Eddie and grinned; Eddie nodded back. Whitey still had the addict's pallor but had put on some weight since his arrival in prison.

Eddie watched Whitey's back as he mounted the stairs. The defeated hunch of his shoulders disturbed him.

At last he was on his way to the Minerva. He parked his car and felt the wind off the estuary cooling his cheeks. He walked out to the end of the pier and stood for a moment watching the rollicking waves. On the horizon a ship slipped away towards the mouth of the Humber.

'Come on,' he heard Mal bellowing. 'What're you doing?' Eddie registered that Mal was too old to have a diamond stud in his ear, it was at odds with his pink face and his big untidy look.

'Just having a look at the water.'

'Thinking about jumping in, then?'

Once in the pub they made for their usual corner by the window. Eddie chose a seat facing the view over the estuary; Mal had his back to it.

Drinks before them on the table, they sat in silence for a while and then Mal burst into his story.

'Sal saw this email from Angie – she must have known I was up to something. Since then she's been like a bloodhound. Won't stop. Says it's over, she's had enough. She'll take the kids – she's not moving, I should get out.'

He was talking as though Sal had let him down and the whole thing was her fault and not his. Mal's words came back to him: 'It's all right for you, good old honest Joe. You've never been tempted, got a wife in a million.' What did Mal know? He didn't want to go there.

The tale rumbled on and there was no stopping the onrush. Eddie's job was to listen, but he could scarcely take in what Mal said because his whole attention was focused on the need to escape.

An hour later, Eddie finally extricated himself. Mal remained seated, pint before him, staring into space.

The journey home took aeons. He wanted to be there immediately but had to endure the waits at the level-crossing gates, or at red lights. Everything crawled. He drummed his fingers on the steering wheel, hummed along to Radio 2 and tried to tame his impatience. He could already see himself parking the car in the drive, striding in, changing and exiting. 'Just off for a quick run,' he'd announce to Sharon. She wouldn't take much notice. His pulse zoomed – he felt like an athlete waiting for the starter's gun. The evening glowed around him. He took in the knots of young people on the pavements, the drift of the clouds, the iridescence, and he moved into a tantalizing unknown world.

Arriving home he bumped down. He noticed with irritation that Sharon's car wasn't in the garage, but parked before the garage door, so he had to leave his car behind it. Why hadn't she bothered to put her car away? Better not refer to it; he couldn't afford to get her into a bad mood, it could jeopardize his plans.

Forcing a smile, he let himself in. Sharon met him in the hall, looking ultra-smart in her black business suit. Her face was knotted with tension.

'Where on earth have you been? What took you so long?'

'Problems at work.'

'I've left you a ham salad under plates in the fridge. We've had ours. Remember Emma's got to be at her lesson in half an hour.'

'Where are you off to, then?'

'Eddie, you never listen – I tell you my schedule and you don't take anything in. You know I said I've a meeting at work. Can you see to Emma? When she gets back from her class, she can stay up another hour and then it's bedtime.'

Sharon opened the front door. 'You're blocking my car, Eddie, you'll have to get yours moved.'

He retraced his steps, backed into the road and watched her swan into her car and away.

Emma waited for him at the door, eager and beaming. This evening was her great love, the dance and drama class.

'They're going to pick dancers for the musical tonight, Daddy. Do you think I'll get a part?'

'That'd be nice, Em,' he said. He hadn't got Lyn's number, so he couldn't ring her and let her know he'd not be able to make it. Driving to her house was out, because he'd got Emma with him and must get her to her class.

While the lesson was in progress, he sat in the old church, which had been turned into a miniature theatre. No natural light permeated it and so in there it was always late evening. The darkness suggested a play about to start.

Eddie had looked forward to this evening, invested it with so much intensity that he hadn't been aware of anything else. Nor had he dared to imagine where it might lead. She might at this very moment be waiting for him, and now he wouldn't see her and she'd think he'd stood her up.

When Emma rushed up, face dimpling with smiles, he had to force himself to look animated.

'Guess what?' she said, and her eyes sparkled at him.

'You didn't get picked.'

'Guess again!'

'You're fed up and wouldn't want to be in their silly old play.'

'Shall I tell you, then?' She twiddled round on one toe, spreading out her arms, her cheeks pink with pleasure.

'Go on, then.'

'I'm in the chorus.'

'Well done, Em – brilliant. Shall we go and have a special treat to celebrate?'

'Wowee!' She jumped up and down and her hair flapped out at the sides.

He took her to a café and bought her an ice in a tall glass with fruit in the bottom, a twirl of cream on top and a stick of chocolate.

He watched her eating it and licking the corners of her mouth with dainty precision like a little cat. The sight of her delight helped him to swallow his disappointment.

But already he'd begun to wonder what he should do next, and the force of his longing seemed enough to sweep all obstacles aside.

15

It started like a normal day at the baths: Lyn patrolled the side and Andy sat on the chair frowning. Through the big window Lyn glimpsed buses crawling along the road outside, another life bumbling along out there.

The usuals were in: the man with his plastic bag, which he left in the changing cabin (against pool rules), eased himself down the steps and started his routine of breaststroke one way, followed by a backstroke the other. His arms scooped the water and were inclined to whap anyone in the vicinity in the eye. The rheumatic lady plied her dogged crawl, and the black Adonis flew up and down the pool.

A father brought two children under five into the adjoining small pool, fooled around with them for a while and left them. Lyn saw him dive into the big pool and felt apprehensive. He shouldn't leave these kids alone in the pool – they weren't old enough; it was against the rules. Andy didn't seem to be paying any attention. She moved round the poolside to keep an eye on the small pool. The boy kicked water at his sister, who started to grizzle.

'Er, excuse me,' she called to the man, who'd paused at the shallow end.

'Yer?'

'I don't think your children should be on their own.'

'What you getting at?' He paused, red-faced, and stared at her.

'Well, the boy's upsetting the little girl.'

'Oh.' He turned, looked over at the small pool and yelled in the direction of his kids, then swam away. Lyn continued to keep her eyes on the children.

She still hadn't phoned the long-distance swimmer and she kept telling herself that she'd been too busy – it was the hours, the unsociable shifts. She'd have phoned if she'd had more time. The trouble with patrolling the pool-side or sitting on the chair was that your thoughts capered away. She glanced across at Andy and she could see he was off somewhere in his head – she could guess where. The children needed her full attention, but she was distracted from watching them by a swimmer in the main pool finning along underwater. He'd just completed his second length. He should stop that, she thought. Why the hell didn't he pack it in? She could see him lying face-down, his elbows and hands hidden.

'What's he doing?' she asked the father of the kids, who had just swum up.

'Tying his trunks,' the man said. He obviously thought she meant to say something more about his children.

'Just touch him with your foot.'

The man scowled but obeyed. The swimmer didn't move. Shocked, the guy reached down and began hauling him up to the side, where Lyn crouched down and slid her hands under his armpits. She had to shout for Andy, who leaped down from the chair. Together they laid the swimmer by the pool. He was pale as milk, blue eyes wide open. Lyn's heart pounded. She knew what she had to do and she knelt down by him, nipped his nostrils together with her right hand and started mouth-to-mouth resuscitation, something she'd only ever done on models. Nothing happened. No flutter in his chest, nothing. Again she tried. Nothing.

'Here, Lyn, I'll have a go,' Andy said.

'No, you have to keep at it to make it work.' She

breathed in, trying to force her energy into him, willing him to live. Her fingers pinching his flesh were slippery with sweat. All of her glowed. *You must*, she made her breath and her fingers tell him. On the fourth attempt the lad blinked, struggled into a sitting position and coughed up blood. She sat back on her heels, exhausted.

Two ambulance men pushed through the swing doors with a stretcher and lifted the youth on to it. At this point Lyn began to tremble. She looked around and saw the swimmers waiting in anxious groups. It was the end of the session, thank goodness, and they dispersed to the changing cabins muttering to one another.

'You all right?' Andy asked. 'Your face is real pasty.'

'I'm fine.' But she wasn't; everything inside her felt weak and jangling.

After work they all trooped down to the pub. 'I thought that kid was a fucking goner,' Andy said. 'I didn't think you'd get him back.' He looked at Lyn. 'I was going to push you out of the way.'

'I did get him back, didn't I? Anyway, what makes you think you could have done any better?' Lyn looked across at him, irritated, and could see him trying – and failing – to come up with a clever remark.

'That kid should have had more sense than doing those two lengths underwater,' he said at last.

Andy and Ben bumbled off to the bar to fetch the drinks and Lyn stared out of the window at a group of lads playing chicken in the middle of the road. Exhaustion made her feel drunk before she'd even touched her drink. She couldn't rid herself of the white face with its dead eyes and the feel of this unknown person's skin. The tension of exerting every particle of energy in her own body to revive this inert mass wouldn't leave her.

'I'll have to be getting off,' she said.

'You've not been here five minutes, Lyn,' Andy said.

'No, sorry, got to go.'

She walked back to the baths and unlocked her bike. In the road the lads catcalled and whistled, but she ignored them. It was too late to take the short cut through the park.

No sooner had she arrived home than the doorbell chimed. She couldn't make out the figure behind the fancy glass and was afraid. *Stop it*, she told herself. On the doorstep she faced the prison officer.

'Oh, hi,' she said, taken aback but relieved too.

'Hi, Lyn, I came to apologize – something cropped up. Didn't have your phone number or anything.'

'Right.' She stood at the door, looking at him, wondering what to say.

'I'm really, really sorry. I've come to ask you if we can make a proper date.'

'Oh, well.' She realized she ought to ask him in. It was rude to keep him hanging about on the doorstep. 'Come in a minute, then.' That sounded sufficiently frosty.

He stood in the front room clutching his car keys. 'Sit down,' she said.

'When do you get off?'

'It depends,' she said.

He asked her about Tuesday or Thursday afternoon. She said she thought she could maybe arrange her shift. He'd pick her up from her house; they could have a drive out into the country. It wasn't until he was about to leave that he asked for her phone number.

When he'd gone, she sat considering what she'd done. Whatever it was between him and her had moved on. This would not be a chance meeting down by the foreshore but a planned arrangement, an understanding. And he was married . . . warning lights flickered before her eyes and she shivered.

She was back with the inert body of the white-faced youth, saw herself kneeling beside him, hesitating and then clamping her mouth on his, fighting to bring him back. Then another picture superimposed itself over this one.

She was eight or nine, taken to the baths by Miss Sanders with the rest of the class. All the way there she and two other girls had planned how after swimming they'd try to dodge into the goodies shop across the road before Miss Sanders marshalled them on to the coach back to school. Only it hadn't worked out like that. Rachel Spurling, a dumpy girl with plaits, began to thrash around in the water. Miss Sanders didn't notice because she was flirting with the lifeguard. Everybody thought Rachel was fooling about, but Lyn didn't. At first she'd been too embarrassed to shout out, but then she'd screamed. The lifeguard had jumped into the water and hauled Rachel out. That was the first time Lyn ever saw mouth-to-mouth being done. Miss Sanders had ordered them out of the water and into the changing cabins. Later, they all made for the coach as fast as they could, chattering and giggling with hysteria, and Rachel was taken to casualty.

On that day all those years ago a moment of delay had almost cost Rachel her life. The lad at the baths could have died too because she and Andy hesitated . . . She trembled again as she had done after the ambulance men arrived. Messing around, indecision – these could be fatal.

Without thinking she scrabbled in her purse for the swimmer's number and she dialled. A woman's voice answered. 'You want Dave – just a minute.'

'Dave Jamieson here. What can I do for you?'

Lyn stammered out her request, not daring to say she was aiming to swim the Humber. Long-distance swimming, she said, and he told her about a club in Grimsby and how he went there and she could have a lift if she wanted.

Before she'd realized it, they'd arranged that he'd drive her there next week, Wednesday. 'I go twice a week myself –

Wednesday evening and Sunday morning. Are you used to swimming outdoors?'

'No,' she said.

'Oh, well, you'll be in for a shock – a lot of them can't stand the open water.'

His voice sounded breezy but matter-of-fact. He'd probably think her a fool, that she'd not have the stamina.

After replacing the receiver, she sat in her front room half listening to Galaxy 105 and half focused on the tumbling amazement inside her. She had made things start to happen. Scared and elated, she leaped out of her chair and embarked on a cleaning routine. The roar of the vacuum cleaner cut down the radio voices. She scrubbed the nozzle over the beige carpet (one of Aunty Mags's cast-offs) and then made for the stairs, her most hated task apart from cleaning windows. The vacuum flex wasn't long enough to reach the top steps and she had to unplug it after lugging the cylinder up to the landing. It annoyed her because she liked to whiz through things and be done with them. Everything was in a jumble and behind the frenzy was the moment on the poolside leaning over the youth and knowing that this was for real, this wasn't a plastic dummy but somebody whose life depended on her getting it right. It was so easy to panic and cause someone's death, to let yourself be defeated by terror. But he hadn't died – it was all right.

The sun shone and a breeze kept the clouds moving. All morning at work Lyn had felt tangles of excitement sparking along her nerves. Arriving home at lunchtime she'd only just changed into a pair of jeans and a pink striped top when the doorbell rang.

'All set?' Eddie asked.

'Just about.' She scuffled a few items into a small backpack and they were off.

'Lovely day,' he said.

'Yes – don't think it'll rain.'

'Been praying it wouldn't.'

They both laughed. She felt odd sitting beside him in his car – after all, he was a virtual stranger.

'I thought we'd have a drive out to Spurn. Would you like that?'

'Cool – I've never been there.'

He seemed surprised. Of course he didn't know what it had been like being shunted back and forth between Aunty Mags and Nana and sometimes her dad. If home was at Dad's, nothing much ever happened because Dad wanted to get to the pub. He didn't 'do' holidays. She was able to play out with the kids round about, stay up late, watch videos and stuff herself with crisps and chocolate. Aunty Mags did take her places, but not often and not to anywhere remote or interesting and they were invariably accompanied by one of Aunty Mags's dodgy boyfriends.

They slipped along through the city centre up Freetown Way, and as they crossed the blue bridge that could lift to admit shipping, Lyn gazed at the thin trickle of the River Hull, where barges lay beached on banks of glistening mud. Water was a magic thread linking every part of the city.

After the oblique right turn at some traffic lights they were soon driving down a long straight road. On the left Lyn watched the red brick prison looming up. She suppressed a shudder and the skin on her back and arms turned clammy in the heat. Max died there. Max never got to walk by the estuary with the wind on his cheeks. Chilling to remember how she'd gone there to see him that last time, not realizing he must have arranged to be brought there to say goodbye.

'My place of work,' Eddie said, nodding as they passed. Lyn didn't speak. Everything was too edgy, too sensitive – she couldn't bear to know the details, the truth.

The mood passed as they left the spikes and convolutions of the oil terminal behind.

Now they ran through flat farming country with bendy roads that disappeared in the hedgerows high with cow parsley and long grass. The clouds rolled above the plain, drifting in the blueness. A dark line of hedges trimmed flat on top was thrown against the wide cobalt wash on the skyline, and before it stretched a field of mown grass.

They passed villages with white-walled houses decorated with hanging baskets; an old church, a war memorial, a village square. Then a right turn and the sign said 'Spurn'.

They bumped along more winding roads and always the low fields and the clouds bunching and rolling down the horizon. Lyn had the feeling they were driving to a secret land, and she was gripped by suspense.

At Kilnsea they saw a sign for the Blue Bell Heritage Project and teas. After Eddie had parked, they walked up the road to where it ended and found the sea crashing on a long expanse of pale brown beach studded with grey and maroon pebbles. A rim of dried-out bladderwrack showed the high-tide mark.

Lyn stood, caught in the ultramarine of the sky, which paled on the horizon, and the beige sea turning to azure. She watched the water rearing up on great chunks of concrete and metal, fizzing and spitting. The silence was broken by the pounding of the waves.

Part of a building had tumbled from the cliff top and hanks of plastic-coated cabling protruded obscenely. The long spit of sand stretched into the distance and was lost in a haze. Ice-white foam glossed the waves into a blinding brilliance. A couple with a dog were way down the beach; otherwise the rolling expanse was deserted. The wildness in the wind off the sea tugged at her, and she sensed its savagery. This was the cold, relentless North Sea, not some warm south coast paddling pool. You could soon be swept under such waves. The terror of them was thrilling. The sight of so much irresistible power fascinated her.

'Wow,' she said, finding her voice after a long silence. They'd been clambering over concrete blocks, remnants of former sea defences. 'My grandad got drowned in the North Sea, went down on a trawler. When I look at this I can see why my dad wasn't allowed to go to sea. Seems Nana put her foot down.'

'Yes,' he said, 'it was one hell of a way to make a living.'

They stood for a while in silence, staring out, and then he suggested tea and she nodded. They retraced their steps to the tearoom and sat at a pine bench eating egg mayonnaise sandwiches and drinking tea. 'This beats work,' he said, and grinned.

'It's great,' she said, meeting his gaze. She'd not really dared to stare at him before. His eyes were the colour of the shingle on the beach. As she sat opposite him, she let herself be absorbed by him. He ate firmly, taking care to keep his mouth closed. She couldn't bear men who chewed with their mouths half open.

The feeling of waiting as the day unfolded dizzied her and threw her into a jokey routine. She listened to herself skidding along, kidding him as she often did the punters at the pool. ('Oh, so it's the mile today, is it, Joe?' she'd say to an old boy who flapped along for a couple of lengths punctuated by lengthy chats with the lifeguards.) He listened and smiled. She liked his quizzical look, the way even the silences between them were friendly. Though as they sat there, she could feel the energy darting off him.

Soon they were back in the car and Eddie drove down a path so narrow two cars couldn't pass each other – not that they met any traffic on this afternoon.

Abruptly on the right a salt marsh opened up. Long flat expanses of mud were spotted here and there with viridian pads of vegetation. Knots of birds stood peering before them on one leg, or perched in the mud.

'Sandpipers,' Eddie said.

'You'll be an expert on birds,' she said, and gave a dirty laugh. He shot her a sly look and smiled, but didn't follow that up.

The road wound on. In places speed was reduced to ten miles an hour and the tarmac gave way to a washboard surface. Ahead of them the abandoned black-and-white lighthouse poked up, and out in the water stood another striped tower. Here the road stopped and beyond it was a sign saying 'Private'; behind this were a line of coastguard houses and a bridge leading to an installation set on stilts out in the estuary. On this side of the peninsula, a sandy beach strewn with pebbles bordered the undulating waters of the Humber Mouth.

'This is so odd,' Lyn said, staring ahead of her at the sheet of water. 'I mean, this place has two faces – there's the savage North Sea side and here, where the estuary looks so smooth. It'll be going all the way to Lincolnshire.'

'Don't get carried away,' he said. 'That's not as tame as it seems.'

'Well, at least it's not banging away like the North Sea, is it?'

'It's the currents at this side.'

She didn't want to hear about any difficulties, so when he suggested they strike out to the left, she followed him.

He was ahead of her as they scrambled up a track leading through a thick undergrowth of thorny plants. Hidden in the middle of the sea buckthorn lurked wartime concrete bunkers. Up there the heat was solid and no breeze stirred. Unseen breakers crashing on shingle formed a lulling background music. Lyn paused, mesmerized by the strange atmosphere, and stared around. Before her was a bush of blazing butter-yellow gorse. Swallows zipped about, swooping and pirouetting. The air smelled salty and of wild herbs.

He'd turned and come back. 'All right?'

'Yes, great – just looking at things.'

'Let me give you a heave up.' He got hold of her hand and she stumbled into him, coming up against his body. His T-shirt was damp and she smelled his skin, aftershave and something herby. They were both laughing.

'You only did that so you could touch me.'

'Course I did – and now I want to touch you a bit more.'

Pressed against him, she felt a rush of dampness drench her pants. They were up so close she could see every pit in his cheeks and the jimpy corners of his mouth. Seeing the texture of his skin as though magnified seemed impossibly intimate and overwhelming. Then he kissed her, and she was in the sensation of his tongue forcing into the soft places of her mouth. Their mouths twisted together and the pressure sent slivers of electricity down between her legs. Sun on flesh, on herbs and all this wanting – a terrible urgency, a need – and she was back in her bedroom with the police cracking open the door and dragging Max away. She hadn't been with anybody since Max, and he'd set a seal on her.

Eddie's erection pressed against her thighs. His right hand had begun to touch the front of her T-shirt, and her breasts felt so sensitive she could scarcely bear it. But Max was leaping out of bed, dragging on his trousers. The room was full of lurching men and muffled curses, panting.

'What's the matter?'

'Nothing.'

'But there is – you're shaking.'

They turned now and she saw the North Sea below them washing on a beach scrawled with a tidemark of bladderwrack and scattered with small white whelk shells and pastel-coloured pebbles. The waves thrashed in, brown against the blue sky, booming and crashing and swooping up the beach as they devoured it.

Four huge vessels were anchored out in the bay. The sea fanned out in a great arc, and the ships seemed unbelievably close.

Where the sea buckthorn ended, the dunes started and their feet sank into the dry slithery sand spiked with marram grass.

'Wow, look at that!' she said, struggling out of the moment in the seclusion of the buckthorn hollow. She ran towards the sea, infected by the spuming and threshing.

He caught her up, seized her hand and they raced to the water's edge, where they had to leap back to avoid a sudden wave.

They took off their trainers and wandered along the damp sand. The feel of his fingers sent surges of excitement up her arm. A warm wind blew in their faces and the beach floated before them empty and open.

After a while they sat down on the sand. 'Why were you shaking up there?' he asked.

'Lots of things,' she said.

She fixed her gaze on the repetitive bounding and swilling of the waves, imagining how it would feel to be in there, diving through the glossy heights and swooping up the other side in the slack troughs. Fred's dad swimming hour after hour, stranded in such a vast expanse, floated into her head. Fred and his story never seemed far away. She couldn't get over the way a person could keep on without hope of being rescued. What could have kept him battling on when others would have let themselves drown in despair? Fred had asked her whether she thought things were preordained. Just thinking of it challenged her, brought the mystery closer.

Abruptly she got up and wandered back down to where the waves were breaking. She wanted to test the temperature.

The chill of the water shocked her. Even on a hot day the cold stung; echoes of the foreshore but without the darker undertones. She let it wash up her calves, wetting her rolled-up jeans, and then she skipped back. Whenever she turned, she found him watching her. After a while she returned to him and flopped down in the sand.

'I wanted to see how cold it is.'

'Why, thinking of a swim?'

'Yes, but not today.'

He reached out and put his arm round her and again they kissed, overbalancing in the sand, so that he was looking down into her face. His mouth was pressing her nipples through the T-shirt when they heard voices and he rolled away from her. A middle-aged couple passed, debating something in clever voices.

'You're making me too excited, Lyn.'

'Well, we'd better cool it.'

They started to walk along the beach once more, now towards the east side and the estuary, along past the coastguard station. The lighthouse reared up and Lyn looked across the water, straining her eyes to see what lay in the distance – that must be Lincolnshire and there before them was the Humber Mouth.

That strange radiant afternoon caught her in its magnetic current, and had she brought her swimsuit she would have plunged in. She stared at its shining ripples and the shadows of shipping and the grey tracery of distant crane arms.

'It's awful to think,' she said, 'that one day this will all be washed away. I want it always to be here.'

'I know,' he said. 'I expect it'll vanish quite soon.'

He glanced at his watch, and she guessed he'd be thinking of his family.

'Where does your wife think you are?' she asked, although they'd never spoken of his wife before.

'She won't know,' he said finally.

'Right. I just wondered.'

'I know what you must think. But I'm not like that.'

'Like what?'

'I'm not having it off with all and sundry.'

'You don't need to justify yourself to me.'

'Lyn, I'd hate it if you thought me a slippery bastard.'

She didn't answer.

They drove back with the windows wound down, and Lyn stared out at the salt flats, the pecking seabirds, and the swathes of pinkish-mauve sea rocket. The landscape was drenched in amber light. Her body was molten. She noticed the dark hairs on his forearms and backs of his hands. His smoke-grey hair had been blown by the wind into spines, which she would have liked to touch, but didn't.

She felt strange to be arriving back in the city after those hours in the air booming with waves and threaded with seabird calls and dancing swallows.

He dropped her at her house. He wanted to make another date, but she put him off.

'Let's take it easy,' she said.

16

In a dream of Lyn Eddie drove home. Sharon had taken Emma to London for the day on a shopping spree. He would fetch them from the station at six o'clock. He had enough time to shower, change, make a mug of tea and sit in the garden for a few minutes, but he couldn't bear the inactivity and instead paced to and fro, mug in hand.

He was still in the afternoon out on the point with the girl. He could feel the shape of her breasts, their heat penetrating his fingers, the softness of her mouth, its taste, the mound between her legs under the tight jeans. Right there on the headland he would have wanted to enter her, on her back among the flowers. He would slide his hands down her naked body. There would be a pearl of sweat in the little runnel beneath her nostrils, nestled in the V of her upper lip. He would lick it away, lick her breasts, running his tongue round her nipples. He loved it when she told him something and for a fraction of a second her blue eyes looked directly at him but then flicked away as though she was overwhelmed with shyness.

What had she felt for Smithson? Did she still think about him? If he made love to her once, he thought he would be able to break down the barrier of silence between them, be rid of Smithson.

Sharon couldn't feature in all this – she seemed to have drifted off to the side somewhere. Instead the day was filled with the girl. He wanted to be with her, watch her face, the fall of her long blond hair, the way she absently wound a strand round her fingers and mused. When she laughed and paddled in the waves he loved her. She seemed to take him to a place he had forgotten, where you could react spontaneously to the sight of sand and sea, paddling, just being alive.

He glanced round the garden at the carefully tended borders, the newly acquired piece of statuary, the strip of weed-free lawn. How much effort had gone into the up-keep of all this and the house itself. He'd still got some more decorating to do in order to pacify Sharon. Not that she'd stop there – oh, no. She had her heart set on another house, a better property. Onwards and upwards. If only they'd never met Di and Barry.

Lyn had shied away from making another date. Perhaps that meant she didn't want to be involved, thought him a chancer and didn't intend meeting him again. He couldn't pester her – it wouldn't be right. He must be realistic: he was married, had a daughter whom he adored; he had a duty to Sharon – they'd been together forever. He'd noth-ing to offer – why should he expect Lyn to be interested? She'd only be the loser if she involved herself with him. He must accept that perhaps it was not meant to be between them.

Downhearted, he backed his car out down the drive. He had a headache, wished he'd taken some Ibuprofen but realized that if he delayed any longer, he'd be late and Sharon would be upset.

The train had just arrived and the passengers were bumbling through the barrier into the station forecourt. He hurried forward in time to hug Emma.

'Daddy, Daddy, look what I've bought.'

She pushed a collection of plastic bags at him. With her pocket money she'd chosen some hair clips covered with tiny pink hearts, a scarlet bead necklace and a pencil case decorated with pink and orange patterns.

'Fantastic!' he said.

'Look, and Mummy bought me three new tops and a skirt and some shoes and we had our lunch in a really cool café.'

'Great,' he said, trying to sound sufficiently enthusiastic.

Sharon clutched several plastic bags bearing expensive logos and looked quite animated.

'Had a good day?' he asked.

'Mm, nice.'

He told her how hot it was in the prison. She thought he'd been at work all day.

'Poor Daddy. You should have come with us,' Emma said.

'Your dad had to work,' Sharon said, and Eddie, holding Emma's hand and seeing her face turned up towards him, wrestled with a sick feeling. He shouldn't be lying – it was wrong; it wasn't fair to Sharon, to Emma . . . he was being a bastard and a hypocrite.

'Next time,' he said.

They bought a Chinese takeaway on the way home and Sharon fetched out a bottle of red wine. She seemed to be trying to be friendly. He wondered what had made her iciness thaw and decided she must have spent a lot of money. After a major shopping spree she tended to be in a good mood and sometimes almost apologetic. When she shopped she did it with concentration, meticulously, just as she did everything else.

He drank several glasses of wine while they sat at the kitchen table eating their meal and Emma prattled away to Sharon. He had such a longing to see Lyn again that it hurt, and an awful emptiness yawned, which he disguised by smiling and nodding and appearing to keep in touch with their chat. He tried to be glad that Sharon seemed happy. Perhaps it would all be fine . . . they'd been through so much together. He recalled her hand on him in the night. 'Ed, Ed, I'm bleeding.' After the loss he'd held her, seeing the wound in her face. But the closeness seeped away with that blood, to be replaced by flintiness – you couldn't reach her. She was all of a piece and, well . . . The night when her mother rang to say her dad had died of a heart attack, she reeled as though from a stunning blow. Her dad had been a good bloke and she'd been the love of his life. 'We'll get over this,' he'd said, holding her, but that time she didn't cry.

Later he sat in the lounge with Emma watching a DVD of *Fly Away Home*. Emma leaned forward, eyes wide with concentration as she stared at the TV screen. He could hear Lyn's voice and her pleasure as she watched the swallows and sandpipers. The little girl saving the wild-goose eggs and the creatures hatching out made him want to cry. They were all linked with the afternoon out on Spurn Point, with that feeling of yearning and wonder. It had been as though he was seeing the wild beauty for the first time, and its poignancy left him intoxicated.

With perfect timing, Sharon appeared three-quarters of the way through the film, sashaying around in a filmy dress with ruffles at the neck plunging to a deep V. Scarlet poppies bloomed against an impressionistic blue and mauve background, giving the effect of a herbaceous border. She did look remarkably vivid.

'Oh, Mum! We're watching,' Emma squawked as Eddie paused the DVD.

'Well,' she said, spinning round, 'what do you think, Ed?'

'Great,' he said.

'Do you really like it?'

'Yes.'

'You don't sound too enthusiastic.'

'Oh, I am! Yes – brilliant.'

'Mummeee – can we go on?'

'Do you really think it suits me?'

'Absolutely.'

'I was wondering if it wasn't a bit short.'

'Well, I suppose you are showing plenty of leg.'

'I just knew you didn't like it. I should have known.'

'But Sharon, I do – I think it's brilliant.'

'No, you don't.'

'Mummy, we're watching!'

'Emma, this is serious. I can't take it back now. Anyway, *I* like it. I should never have asked you. You never care how I look. I could be wearing any old thing and you wouldn't notice.'

'Sharon, that isn't true.' Eddie became aware of Emma, who had fallen silent, and whose eyes were big and watchful. He knew she hated it when the rows started. Sharon had stalked out and he heard her stilettos tapping across the hall floor. She'd hide herself in silence. He sighed, but let himself slip back into the magic of the afternoon.

17

Wednesday evening, and all day at work Lyn had found it difficult to concentrate because she was going to meet the long-distance swimmer. His voice had given nothing away. She'd been waiting outside her front door ten minutes before the appointed time and twenty minutes earlier had started peeking out of the front-room window at regular intervals in case the car drew up. When he did arrive, she was almost surprised.

He bounced out of his car as though on elastic and bounded towards her with his hand outstretched, seizing hers in a hearty businessman's handshake, only perhaps a tad more vigorous. Will I have any bones left in my hand? she wondered, careful not to wince in case this was a test of stamina.

'Dave Jamieson, pleased to meet you.'

'Oh, hi.'

'Lyn, isn't it? Get in.' He opened the passenger door for her, whipped round to the driver's door, and sprang in behind the wheel all in one swift sequence of movements. 'Wagons roll! Good evening for the dock. So – you're up for a spot of swimming?' He controlled the car with a finger of his left hand. His right arm was propped on the open window.

'Yes – well, I just thought it might be. I thought, like . . .'

'What's wrong with the swimming baths, then?'

Lyn was thrown off balance. Dave wasn't remotely like Fred; for one thing, Dave was middle-aged and Fred was much older. But it was more than merely an age difference. Dave seemed jocular, a jokey, blokeish sort, whereas with Fred there'd be long spaces and rustling seas – a weirdness, as though he knew things you'd no idea of.

'I just feel I want to swim the Humber.' Let him enjoy being clever about that.

He brayed with laughter. 'A tall order.'

'I know.'

'You don't – just wait until you've immersed yourself in the dock, then you'll know whether you're still keen.' He turned his pouchy face towards her, grinning.

'Right.' She didn't want to give him the satisfaction of showing any reaction – did he think she would start whining before she'd even got in the water?

'A lot of 'em think they can. They get down there, and as soon as they're in the water, they've had enough and they're straight out – never see 'em again.'

'You aren't exactly advertising for it.' She gave him what she hoped was a mocking smile.

'I don't want you to get a shock.'

She stifled an urge to snap at him. So what? So what if she should find she couldn't do it, which she might? He needn't make such a great thing of it even before she'd tried.

He had a brief, familiar exchange with the toll collector at the bridge before they drove on. He'd be a man's man – you could tell from the way he and the toll collector billed and cooed at each other; the sort who played rugby and liked steamy changing rooms. His wife would be one of those really girly women.

Lyn stared down at the brownish-blue expanse of water that rippled its way to Lincolnshire. She glimpsed the foreshore, a thin edge of sand and pebbles away on the right.

Up there somewhere her mother would have waded out into the currents. Sunlight slithered over the estuary, turning it into a gleaming mass. On this evening you might just think it beautiful, innocent, but it wasn't – it was devious, treacherous.

'Why did you swim the estuary, then?' she asked.

'Humber Mouth. I've always swum. It's just what I've been doing all my life.'

'But there must be something?'

'Must there be?' She caught him scrutinizing her with amusement. A thing like an echo sounded again. She'd heard it at home before he arrived and it was as though a mountainous wave came howling before her, rearing up, and her eardrums vibrated with the weight of the water. She turned to face him, smiling still, but tracing its echo in her head.

'Well, I mean, it's not the sort of thing everybody wants to do, is it?'

'Exactly. That's why I got my question in first.'

She sat silent for a while. Now they'd left the bridge behind and the road stretched into Lincolnshire, low-lying fields on either side of a dual carriageway. The early evening sun glanced off the cars flashing towards the Humber Bridge.

'Perhaps it's just because I want to see what it's like. Anyway, when there's water, I always want to go in it.' She almost said, 'Push myself to the limit for the first time, see what I'll find.' But she didn't think he'd understand, though Fred did. Fred knew what this was.

'Yes – well, it's like why do some people climb mountains. Who can say? Some folk will always think you're loopy anyway.'

He moved into swimming tales, swims he'd done in lakes and waterways. He made it sound as though open-water swimmers were a race apart. She sat, tense and absorbed, listening. Just as they entered Grimsby he said, 'Oh, be prepared – swimmers aren't prudes. We'll all be changing together in the same hut, same room. Nobody bothers. In some places folk wander about naked – no big deal. There used to be this old bloke when we were swimming Windermere – you'd see him striding around bollock-naked. One of the women once protested and he came back, "It's only a load of half-inch washers welded together." He was a grand bloke.'

As he parked up, Lyn suddenly wished she were back at home, or in fact anywhere but here. She couldn't imagine why she'd taken this on. But Fred's voice whispered to her: 'You were a plucky little bugger . . . this'll show what you're made of.' Yes it would. Inside her she carried the horror of walking through that black mud and feeling the chill of the water as it rose. She seemed to become that desperate woman advancing ever deeper. Her head whirled, her palms sweated, she could scarcely attend to Dave's cheerful voice.

'Whatever you do, when you're coming for training in the dock, don't have a skinful the night before. You drown fast in the docks, you know – it's not like the baths.'

She kept on walking beside him while the tumbling and panicking racked her. It would be nothing like the baths, it would prey on her and make her nerves blaze and throb. But when she'd plunged into the lead mine in Youlgreave she hadn't faltered – it was other people who'd pulled her back. She'd not been freaked out by the endless volume beneath her, or the thoughts of cramp or the octopus ropes of twining plants that could drag her under. Before she'd settled into the lifeguard job, when she still might have trained, she hadn't been frightened then – as a kid she'd run into the sea at Withernsea. No, this fearfulness had come on her later, this feeling of having given up. But it didn't have to control her – she could fight it now.

'You've no need to worry, though, because they've got the boat out for you – look over there. He'll keep an eye open for you, they always do it for new ones. He'll have a word with you when you're ready to get in.'

The boat. Yes, the boat could save her, but she didn't want it to be like that. Let her sink rather than face the embarrassment of it.

He led her through a snicket to a hut, beyond which lay the dock. She stared over at it and shivered while he unlocked the hut. Lyn paused before the door, fighting an impulse to flee – she couldn't, she wouldn't. Fred would have been in the water without thinking. She looked about, smiled, kept quiet as she wrestled with surges of jitteriness, but kept moving, acted as though this were a big adventure, an easy-going way to spend the evening. She must jam down the seesawing horror in her guts, so nobody would guess.

Stumbling after Dave, she went into the hut. Two other big chaps followed her in. She didn't catch their names when Dave introduced them. All she took in was their rough-hewn brawn and muscle and huge shoulders. She could see how they came to be long-distance swimmers. By concentrating on them, smiling, keeping herself focused on physical details, she tried to stop herself panicking. But just the sight of them worried her – if it took this kind of bulk, how was she going to manage it?

'There's only a cold shower,' Dave announced, 'but it'll still get the crap off afterwards.'

'Yes,' she muttered. She went on nodding and grinning while she shed her tracky bottoms and her pants and eeled into her swimsuit, trying not to expose her crotch – not that anybody looked. While they gossiped about a mutual acquaintance, jagged fragments detached themselves from the past, from dreams, and stabbed her.

'All set?' Dave asked. 'Just take your time – you'll probably not do much today. Go easy.'

She fought an urge to back down, say she wasn't up for it. She could just stay behind until they came back. For a couple of seconds she hesitated, and then she heard voices and didn't want to be found cowering in the hut. To explain why she didn't want to swim in the dock would be more difficult than going through with it. She turned the handle and came face to face with another hefty chap.

'Sorry,' she said, and edged out past him. Nothing for it now – there was no way out. She saw the men away on the other side of the dock moving rhythmically through the dark water. Two swimmers wandered up behind her, chatting. She didn't turn round but advanced down a greasy wooden slipway towards the water. At this point the man in the boat chugged across.

'Nick,' he said. 'You're Lyn. Your first time?' She nodded. 'Right now you should be fine – just keep near me and any problems, call out and I'll have you out in a jiff.'

'Thanks,' she said. The guy was obviously waiting for her to get into the water. No escape. The chill struck up her legs, hit her stomach and chest and her breathing stuttered. All of her went rigid with shock and her heart pattered. *I'm weak*, she thought. I can't do this, I haven't got the stamina. I'll show myself up, and the man will see what a fool I am.

She trod water for a few seconds, struggling to get a grip, but still couldn't bear to immerse her face. Fred had told her that a person's face – under the eyes – was particularly sensitive to cold. The coldness swiped at her like a hard slap. She struck out, webbing her fingers against the icy water. Looking down through her goggles into the depths, she could see nothing, only volumes of blackness, no guiding lines like the rows of coloured tiles in the pool. Panic started in her solar plexus and echoed in her chest like discordant music. Anything could lurk down there in that blackness – dead creatures, the skeletons of birds, rusting mattresses, flotsam tipped into the dock to rot; cargoes dropped from long-broken-up vessels. And coating everything would be black mud, smooth as melted chocolate. Last week the newspaper described how a man and his daughter were stranded out on a beach, sinking into mud as the tide raced in. The little girl was drowned.

Nick in the boat waved at her. 'All right?' he shouted.

She tried to grin back. 'Okay,' she mouthed, and made herself kick out in breaststroke, now daring to dip her face into the water. Concentrating on her stroke and the glide of her body, she moved forward. As she swam, she tried to avoid dwelling on the coldness and strangeness of everything, but she still felt breathless and terrified. Dave was right – it was totally different from swimming in a pool. The pool was intended for swimmers, the dock for ships, huge ships. Its size dwarfed – you felt you were a cork bobbing on an ocean. But this was nothing compared with swimming in the estuary and the North Sea. This was just the first stretch of open water to overcome.

She swam back to the jetty, her skin red and stinging with cold. If only she could get out at this point, but she daren't because she'd lose face in front of everyone. She'd have to try another circuit. According to Dave, the aim was to build up distance by swimming half-mile circuits.

After a while her body seemed set in a permanent tingling and she felt if she didn't get out she'd die. Unable to stand it any longer, she climbed out and waved farewell to the boatman, who stuck his thumb up and bellowed, 'Great!' Stumbling up the slipway, her limbs juddered and pimpled and locked in a shaky spasm. She rushed into the hut and under the shower. Even the cold water straight from the mains didn't seem half as icy as the water in the dock.

The shower sloughed off bits of weed and fragments of wood and sooty particles clinging to her skin. She was so cold, she didn't care who saw her dragging off her swimsuit – all she wanted was to peel the freezing Lycra off her body. Still shaking, teeth rattling like marbles in a glass jar, she pulled on her tracky bottoms, T-shirt, sweat-shirt and fleece top. By this time Dave and some of the other men had come back.

All the way home in the car she shivered.

'So – copping out now?' Dave asked. His tone sounded sardonic, as if he expected her to give up. He assumed she hadn't the strength – whereas he had the experience, the staying power – and that rankled. He'd already told her about the 'Young Turks' in gold goggles and caps, diving straight into the water and bumping along madly for a mile or so. 'Oh, you reel 'em in after forty-five minutes – they're used to blasting up and down the pools, can't pace themselves. A quick bang and they're finished.'

Lyn stared out unseeing at the Lincolnshire plains. She didn't intend to let him get away with this. 'Oh, no,' she said, smiling but with a tightening of her lips, 'you've not seen the back of me yet.'

'Pleased to hear it – there's a long way to go, though.'

Irritating bastard, she thought. 'You don't need to tell me,' she said. 'I think I get the idea.'

'You up for Sunday, then?' he asked as he dropped her outside her house, almost as though he still expected her to change her mind.

'You bet.' She gave him a big smile. '*Insufferable geek*,' she muttered as she stabbed her key into the door. The memory of that first moment in the icy water made her heart pound.

Straight upstairs she leaped, dumped her gear outside the bathroom door and she was into the shower. What a relief to relax under the hot jets. She massaged the green shower gel all over her skin, wanting to be rid of every trace of the dock. Vaguely through the sishing of the water, she could hear her phone ringing.

Since she'd parted from Eddie, he hadn't been in touch. Well, she had told him to cool off, after all – but perversely the fact that he hadn't even tried to contact her niggled. Could he be the one ringing? But she wouldn't hurry. She'd take her time, dry off, put on her towelling robe and see about a bowl of vegetable soup and some buttered toast and whatever she could find in the fridge.

But she couldn't help herself. She had to check, and she was dismayed to see that the caller had been Aunty Mags.

18

Eddie, arriving home from his shift and an unwanted visit to the pub with Mal, found Sharon and Emma out, so he changed into his running gear and set off.

His head still rang with Mal's voice droning on about what a cow Sal was and how he ought to have married Mand, the previous girl and mother of his first child. Sal was determined to prevent him ever seeing his kids. But this, Eddie saw, was what happened when you broke up a family.

The air was chill, much cooler than in the past days, and felt almost autumnal. People complained and muttered about the hole in the ozone layer and the cooling down of the Gulf Stream, not things he'd ever got excited about – though even Emma pressed them to take their empty bottles and jars to the bottle banks because they'd been learning about the environment at school. Of course Sharon said it was too much of a work-up to be lugging stuff to bottle banks and never mind what teacher said. They'd managed to survive so far without it, and it hadn't killed them yet. Remembering that argument hurtled him back into all the other accusations: how he was always too busy helping everybody else, and what about his own family? How he was slapdash in certain respects . . . The ghosts of a thousand quarrels chuntered back and forth in his head.

So preoccupied was he with his moilings that he didn't notice the figure ahead until he had almost reached it.

'Hi,' he said, coming to a halt, still panting. 'Didn't realize –'

'I jogged up here myself,' Lyn said. 'Was just about to come back.'

'I see. How have you been?' he asked, now letting himself look at her face.

'Fine.'

He thought there would never be another opportunity like they'd had out at Spurn. Should he say he'd walk back with her, or would she think he was taking advantage?

'So you're going back, are you?'

'Yes,' she said. 'I reckon I've had enough.'

'Perhaps I'll pack in now myself,' he said.

They had the wind in their faces. The estuary had turned dark brown, almost purple in places, and clouds swung across the sky.

'Looks like a downpour soon,' Eddie said. 'Want to put your bike on the roof rack? I can drop you back at your place.'

He expected her to refuse, but she didn't and they jogged together back down the track. They made for his car just as the first splatter of rain hit them.

No sooner had Eddie turned on the ignition than he felt her looking at him. 'Are you going to tell me about Max, then?' she asked.

He hadn't expected this and didn't know how to respond. 'What is there to tell?' he said, keeping his gaze fixed on the road ahead.

'But you said you saw my photograph in Max's cell.'

'Did I?'

'Yes, you did – you said you recognized me from it.'

'Yes.'

'Why don't you want to tell me?'

'Lyn, there isn't anything to know.'

She sat in silence awhile, a silence he found unnerving.

They pulled up outside Lyn's house. He got out of the car and lifted down her bike and was already back in the driver's seat when she bent down and looked through the open window at him. 'Do you want to come in?'

'Yes – that would be nice.' He kept his voice flat and tried to play it very cool.

While she was in the kitchen he sat on her sofa staring about him. In that small room there was a TV, a music centre, a sofa, two armchairs, two spider plants and some pink geraniums in pots on the windowsill, and very little else. He liked the pale colours, the cream and beige and the warmth of terracotta touches. It was a young room, he thought – it didn't have all the expensive knick-knackery that the rooms of older people acquired. He compared it with his own home. Of course the décor was usually Sharon's choice. In their house everything had to be brand-new – no second-hand furniture, no making do.

'Here,' she said. 'I know you drink it from the bottle.'

'That's right.'

The talk skittered to and fro. He was on edge, wondering how he could move this relationship forward. Every time he met her, he thought it would be the only chance he'd get and that they might drift along as they were doing until she took up with someone else.

'You always seem to be alone,' he said.

'I'm training.'

'For what?'

She paused and looked down at her hands; a strand of hair slid across her cheek and she brushed it back.

'Just some swimming I want to do. I knew I'd probably see you down there,' she said, and smiled.

Her telling him she wanted to find him pleased him.

But when his eye fell on his watch he realized that if he

didn't go home, Sharon and Emma would arrive back and questions would be asked. 'I'd better go,' he said, rising. 'Ta for that – it was great.'

They stood up together and there was a moment when they faced each other. He didn't know what to say to her. In that curious, edgy pause, they came together.

Afterwards, when he tried to analyse it, he thought he acted purely out of desperation. Their eyes met, he could see from the heavy passivity in her face that she wanted him, but he knew he couldn't stay. Even now, even if he left immediately, a big row was bound to break out with Sharon.

'Lyn,' he said, stepping back from her, 'I've got to go – I don't want to – but I must.' He thought she looked disappointed, and he was glad.

As he drove home across the city, he sang and tapped his fingers on the steering wheel; though when he reached the entrance to the estate, the tune faltered and died.

19

When Lyn opened the passenger door, she found Dave singing a Garth Brooks number.

'Morning. All set and on your mark, are you? So, we've had the one day of summer.'

'Yes, looks like it.' Lyn felt half asleep. She'd been awake in the night, worrying about the dock. The night before training was always the same.

'Not burned off, then?'

'No, I've told you I'm going to keep on.' She thought her voice sounded snappy, but he didn't seem to notice. She didn't dare say, 'Swim the Humber Mouth.' The thought made her heart pound and her pulse race. It was a test, and she normally ducked out of testing situations. Fear of failure held her back every time, though she'd never admitted it before. She'd dropped out of competitive swimming, passed up opportunities, for reasons that were nothing but excuses. Now it was all coming at her.

'It'll be coolish today,' he said.

'Well, at least there won't be the contrast, will there? It's worse when the weather's boiling.'

She entered the dock as before, by edging down the wooden slipway. The freezing water gripped her legs, made her gasp as it hit her middle, and when she ducked her face under, it was as though all the air in her body gusted out. Her skin smarted with cold, but she struck out, telling herself that she'd feel warmer if she swam. Her head at least felt snug in her swimming cap.

The recurrent thought of the dark impenetrable depths below her, that bottomless pit in Youlgreave, stirred her to panic. Panic that lasted only a second, because she chanted in her head: *Get it together, you're in charge here – you don't want to look a stupid fool who can't hack it.* The jitters subsided. She watched the patterns her arms cut through the water, looked up now and then at the sky, a marbled moving mass. Seen from the water, and through her blue-tinted goggles, it was as though the sky opened up to become a living substance.

Swimming outdoors like this was a totally different experience. Outdoors you seemed to become part of the landscape, moving in it and not watching it from a distance. Your size shrank; you belonged to the dark water and the drifting clouds. A tantalizing freedom spread out. She touched it and then it retreated before the deadening chill of the water.

She began to swim back to the slipway, her legs heavy and the two middle toes on her left foot starting to cramp. It was all very well Dave telling her to keep on increasing the distance she swam and the length of time she could hold out in the water – but if she got cramp in the process, she'd have to quit.

'It's all about endurance,' he said. Endurance – but could she endure? She wondered what it was that caused some people to hang on long after others would have quit. Fred's dad must have had extraordinary powers of endurance to survive three days and nights alone in the sea. In your head the siren voices muttered away, telling you to give up, it didn't matter and why put yourself through it – this wasn't something that you *had* to do, no matter of life and death. But then Fred's sea-blue eyes fixed on her and the other voice whispered that it was a challenge, a trial, and she needed to do it. *You're doing it for your mother; it's a way of finding her, of showing her what you're made of . . . Doing it because you don't want to let Fred down, and you want to prove to Dave that you're serious.*

When she was at work she'd catch herself thinking of the swim with a longing tinged with fear. It was as though for a brief space of time she was part of a wider world where a freedom beckoned that she'd always dreamed of but had been too afraid ever to know.

On the way back in the car Dave noticed her shivering and put the heater on full blast. Rain pelted the windscreen and greyness closed in.

'More like December than summer,' Lyn said.

'Down in the mouth, are you?'

'Oh, no,' she lied, and listened to him rattle on.

'Sometimes I've seen grown men cry because they can't go on. I once saw this chap trying to swim on Windermere – he was doing fine and then one and a half miles before the end, he had to give up, really couldn't quite manage the last bit. It's no big deal, but . . .'

'But what?'

'But it makes you even more determined that it's not going to beat you. Mind you, there are some who don't try again if they've failed once. Depends on the person, whether they've got bottle or not.'

Lyn thought of the North Sea slamming on the beach at Spurn. You couldn't swim against that. All those huge concrete gun emplacements from the Second World War hadn't been able to withstand the force of the waves' belting, and lay crumbling on the shore.

She compared this to the smooth, rippling sheet of water on the other side of Spurn, the estuary, lying there so inviting. You would never believe that one side of the promontory would be so different from the other. But that wasn't what it seemed, either. Powerful currents criss-crossed it and you wouldn't stand a chance against them.

She hadn't told anybody about her visits to the Alexandra dock. They'd all think her mad and wouldn't be able to understand why she needed to make the swim. And maybe they were right. Looking out at the rain, she wondered why she was putting herself through this anxiety and strain when she could be somewhere warm instead of being half frozen and scared stiff. But set against it there was the feeling of a quest spurring her on . . .

Somewhere, tangled in her thoughts, was a memory of last night's dream. She was wading into the Humber and beneath her feet the mud felt smooth and soft, but the squelchy texture between her toes unnerved her. She felt she was wading into a quicksand that could swallow her, suck her down and suffocate her. She panicked, expecting her feet to be stuck fast. Then, to her amazement, the water shrivelled before her until all that remained was a trickle in the centre of the sandbanks. Sunlight filtering through a chink in the curtains had woken her and left her feeling confused.

The rain now looked as though it had set in for the day, and a wind had sprung up, lashing the trees.

'Did you ever think you'd give up?' she said into the intimacy of the muggy car.

'No. The first time I tried the Humber Mouth, I went from Cleethorpes instead of Spurn. I was into the swim, about halfway across, then a storm blew up. The boat was having a job keeping afloat, never mind me. I knew I couldn't do it that day. I was annoyed, but it wasn't going to stop me. A couple of days later I went from Spurn. I knew I had to.'

Fred had recognized this urge in her, she realized. He knew that you had to keep on for whatever it was that gave you your own sense of pride in who you were.

After Dave dropped her home, Lyn took a shower, luxuriating in its warmth for a long time. Swimming in the dock had prevented her from dwelling on thoughts of Eddie, but now with the relaxation of tension, he was back in her head.

On a weekend he'd be taken up with his wife and daughter. She tried to imagine what his wife would be like – pretty, that was for sure, if Emma looked like her. He never mentioned her, but she was shadowing them all the time. She'd be the one who bought his clothes, chose his sports gear – no bit of him would be untouched by her.

How could he keep on pursuing her? She needed to remember that she was just a diversion for him, perhaps because he wasn't satisfied with his life . . .

Some days she thought she didn't care: it was all the same to her whether or not she saw him again. Then at other times, like this Sunday, with the rain pinging against the windows and summer feeling as though it was over, she was plagued by the desire to be with him. She felt she must see him and tried to visualize what he might be doing at this moment, but she couldn't. Almost crying with frustration, she told herself that she must forget him.

20

Eddie didn't know how he survived the holiday. Being with Sharon full time afforded him no bolt-holes. The apartment was somewhere to sleep and eat, but it was cramped and the lavatory reluctant to flush. Sharon had discovered some strange black bugs, which scared her.

On the beach Sharon accused him of staring at girls, said he was insulting her. Her new bikini irritated her; she was convinced it exposed her cellulite. Did it look bad?

'You're fine,' he said. She wouldn't believe him. He hated these interrogations; he knew he was bound to say the wrong thing, because Sharon had impeccable standards – people always exclaimed at her appearance. She wanted perfection, whereas he had begun to feel that imperfections were what made the rest more compelling. He couldn't tell Sharon that, though.

Sharon stumbled along in her mules with Emma trotting along next to her.

'Daddy, are we going in the sea?'

'Course we are – come on.'

Sharon arranged herself on a towel and opened her holiday novel, a doorstopping paperback with fancy script and four glossy young women on the cover.

Eddie took Emma's hand and they jogged down the beach, picking their way between hundreds of immobile bodies soaking up the sun. The world was bursting with people. Most of these sun-worshippers were just kids. And Eddie was conscious of his age – the place made him feel old and done for. The previous evening when they'd walked through the streets, they'd run into hordes of youngsters, all jostling towards the clubs, all on the pull – girls in the skimpiest of tops and tiny shorts and lads already lurching with booze.

He knew Sharon felt intimidated too. Emma's eyes were everywhere, and he didn't feel easy with her seeing the blatant sexuality on show, but there wasn't an alternative. Behind everything lay boredom. He was bored, hot, didn't like the crowds, the foreign language clappering away, and his skin itched from mosquito bites. Sharon had dropped dark hints about malaria and how many millions died of it. The whole thing put him in a melancholy mood.

'Daddy,' Emma said, 'why do you and Mum argue such a lot?'

He hadn't expected this question in the middle of a crowded beach, and it took him aback.

'Don't know – I expect lots of mums and dads argue.'

'You aren't going to get divorced, then?'

'Oh, no, love, nothing like that.' This was his fault – he was responsible for his daughter feeling insecure.

Emma was diverted then by her footprints on the sand and the wash of the incoming tide.

Once he was in the sea he felt better, but glancing back at the beach with its rows of bodies, his edginess returned. Emma delighted him as she played in the waves, jumping into them and giggling. He must make an effort to avoid confrontations with Sharon – maybe if he didn't bark back at her then she wouldn't sulk.

Midway into the fortnight Sharon went down with a stomach bug and took to her bed. She dosed herself with some stomach tablets she'd brought and sent Eddie out in search of bottled water. Then he had to entertain Emma with tours of the resort and sessions in the swimming pool and on the beach.

One night at two a.m. when Sharon was asleep, Eddie let himself out of the apartment and went for a walk in the streets. Everywhere throbbed with the thump of music and voices from bars and clubs. The night smelled of perfume, beer and drains. It excited him, and he breathed in deeply with the relief of being outdoors and away from the atmosphere of the apartment.

Down on the beach it was quieter. He listened to the sea washing on the sand. The moon had come up, and everywhere was silver-spangled. Couples lay on the sand; the pale hillocks of a man's buttocks worked rhythmically. A girl sighed with pleasure. He walked down to the water's edge and was shocked by the craving he felt for Lyn. All week he hadn't allowed himself to think of her because he had to respond to questions from Emma, keep her happy and amused, nurse Sharon, and prevent himself from falling into daydreams.

Now Lyn was in his head; he could almost see her face – but he couldn't touch her. He let himself float into a moment in her front room. She stood at the window with sunlight burnishing her hair. He was caught up in a shocking wave of sweetness, longing for the feel of her skin, the smell of her . . . a way she had of pausing and looking at him. Oh, I can't bear this, he thought. I have to be with her.

He carried on up the beach, gazing at the waves frothing on the dark sand and falling back, only to re-form and billow forward once more. Couples whispered, panted, called out, and he scarcely heard them.

An arm knocking him backwards and catching him across the throat wrenched him out of his dream. He staggered, almost losing his balance. Someone had seized him from behind and was trying to throttle him. Eddie jerked into self-defence mode. He'd done personal safety courses often enough to respond automatically. Spinning round, he threw his assailant off, bent the fellow's arm back and tossed him on to the sand, where he fell with a thwack. Eddie stared down at him. In the gloom the kid was difficult to make out, but to Eddie he seemed like any young smack addict – nimble, raw and wiry, but not very powerful.

The lad clearly expected Eddie to kick him or worse, and he'd rolled himself into a ball. Eddie, now shaking with fear and adrenalin, looked hard at him, then turned away and began retracing his steps up the beach. The allure of the night-time beach had vanished in a threatening tackiness.

Eddie didn't relax until he reached the main road. He let himself into the apartment and paused in the silence, listening, and tiptoed into the bathroom, where he looked in the mirror at his bruised eye and scratched cheek. His neck ached from the tussle. He put his head under the tap and the stinging cold water brought relief.

A while later he slid into the twin bed next to Sharon's. He listened to her breathing and the occasional snort of a snore, and his pulse slowed, his neck muscles eased out. He thought he'd fall asleep straight away, but instead he relived the impact of the man's arm striking his throat and delved again into his moment of indecision and fear – and he came out in a burst of sweating and shaking. What he hated about the attack was the way it had crashed through his dream of Lyn, caught him at his most vulnerable.

21

Lyn was in the Linnet and Lark with Andy and the rest of the baths crowd when her mobile rang.

'It's my phone,' she said, and hurried out into the street. Andy shouted after her, 'It'll wait.'

She stood on the pavement, listening to Eddie's voice. At last he'd rung. She didn't want to appear too eager, not after his silence.

'Any chance of you coming out with me for a drive – say, tomorrow evening?'

His disembodied voice sounded contained, vigorous and husky in a strange way. She became so absorbed listening that she forgot to speak, and a silence stretched until she heard, 'You there, Lyn?' If only he would say her name again! But she said yes, of course she was there. 'Well, would you like to, then?'

'All right,' she said. They fixed it for eight. She remained outside for a moment, imagining him sneaking out somewhere to phone, or perhaps he was in the house alone.

'An admirer?' Andy asked.

'Wouldn't you like to know,' she said, grinning back.

Ben shuffled up, bearing another round of drinks. Andy drummed his fingers on the table and Shelly giggled like a maniac. She'd guzzled five martini lemons and two gins and lime that Lyn had counted. Ben's face had taken on a pink blancmange look. Wes concentrated on his pint.

'Ta, mate,' Andy said. 'Lyn's got a lover and she won't tell who it is.'

'Go on, Lyn,' they chorused.

Lyn blushed. 'You're just being silly.'

'See, she's gone red.' Andy wouldn't let the matter drop. 'You haven't been out with us for ages and as soon as you do, he gets on the phone. Think I don't know?'

'Andy, you've got it completely wrong. It's not like that at all.'

They all lived in the same area and so rang for a taxi to drop them off. Lyn and Andy were the last to leave, and as soon as they were alone together in the back of the taxi, Andy leaned over and pressed himself against her. He was clumsy with drink and very strong.

'Hey, Andy, you're smothering me. Back off.'

He didn't seem to be taking any notice, but then the taxi driver called out that they'd reached Lyn's street.

'I'm getting out,' she said. He made an attempt to come with her, but she pushed him back into the taxi and slammed the door shut. She only began to feel safe when she was in her own hall with the security lock snapped to.

The next evening Eddie arrived dead on eight. All day she'd been wondering whether he might fail to turn up or ring to say he'd have to put it off, and she was almost amazed to see him on the doorstep.

'Hi,' she said, trying to sound cool and pleasant.

'Lovely evening,' he said.

They started heading out of town in the direction of the coast. 'Have you had a nice holiday?' she said.

'All right,' he said, and then he glanced across at her. 'Well, dreadful.'

She couldn't ask why, but had to fill in the silence after the admission and so burbled on with, 'I don't go for holidays abroad much myself.' Safer ground, this.

'How's that?'

'Too expensive.'

He didn't take that up, and for a while they sat in silence as the countryside drifted by. The evening lay motionless and mysterious beyond the windows. The coast opened up before them and they reached Spurn. This time he didn't halt but drove on down the promontory. The Humber rippled under a high milky-blue sky shot through with washes of rose – a summer sky – and the air was still warm. When they climbed out of the car by the lighthouse, it seemed to Lyn they had entered an enchanted kingdom. The only sounds scratching the silence were the cries of seabirds and the rustling of waves on sand.

They struck out up the bushy incline that housed the old wartime installations hidden amid gorse thickets and marram grass. She knew he must have brought her here because he wanted things to go further.

'I've pictured us being here together so many times,' he said. He had put his arm round her waist.

'Where does your wife think you are?'

'Lyn, can't we just be us and leave her out of it?'

'But she's in it – she can't not be.'

'What can I say?'

She twisted out of his grasp. They faced each other in the hollow. A smell of urine and sea rocket rose from where the bunkers lurked in the gorse.

'Lyn, don't you understand? I want you – I can't stop thinking about you.'

She had to look away before the raw longing in his face.

'I can't just be turned on and off,' she said at last.

'I don't want you to be, and I'd hate it if you could be. Don't look so fierce – I'm not some mad rapist.'

She found herself laughing then. He began to smile too.

'Come on,' she said, 'let's at least find somewhere that doesn't smell of pee.'

They stood for a moment gazing down over the dunes. Here you couldn't see the lighthouse; it belonged to the smooth side of the peninsula. Lyn took a deep breath as she focused on the North Sea breakers slamming the shingle. Away in the distance the dark ghosts of ships hovered.

They turned towards each other and he kissed her, and there on the dunes they lay down together. Their kisses burned into panting breaths. He slid his hand down her bare midriff and opened her jeans. She thought of Max – he'd known how to pleasure her. With most of the men before him, she'd felt nothing. Do men think about their last lover whenever they embark on a new relationship? she wondered. This seemed like a betrayal.

As he eased her out of her jeans and unzipped his fly, she lost herself in awkwardness and desire. He knelt over her with his legs astride her and then his mouth came down on hers. She felt his penis thrusting against her, bumping and ramming, but it was as though she'd closed up. Then he convulsed and a sharp ammoniacal smell hit her nostrils. Wetness spread on her thigh.

'Hell, Lyn,' he muttered, 'I'm sorry. I've wanted you so much.'

She didn't say anything for a while but sat up and tried to wipe off his semen with a tissue and struggled back into her jeans. 'It doesn't matter.'

'Not a brilliant showing.'

'Never mind,' she said, now managing to smile. 'I don't expect I've helped very much either.'

He looked rueful, and that touched her. 'I never meant it to be like this,' he said.

They walked along by the breakers holding hands. It had grown very late but they didn't start to drive back until twilight had settled everywhere and big dark birds swooped off across the salt marshes. Trees cut black shapes on the paleness and the estuary lay on their left, a breathing presence, like some gigantic eel under the moon. He was very tender with her on the drive home.

After he dropped her off, Lyn made herself a mug of tea, unlocked the kitchen door, dragged a cane chair out and sat in her yard smelling the drifts of honeysuckle and roses and the night-scented stocks she'd grown from a packet of seeds. She still carried Spurn's wild intoxication with her and she could see the estuary, almost black and vibrating, returned at night to its mystery. She followed Eddie and herself wandering on the dunes and her body felt hot and heavy.

Looking back she realized she'd been hooked the first time she'd met Eddie on the foreshore. It had just happened. Of course, he looked good – but it wasn't only that. After the failure on the beach he'd actually apologized. She tried to imagine Andy in the same situation – he'd have been bombastic, made out she was to blame. Eddie seemed genuinely interested if she rattled on to him about work and the baths people. When she thought back, a lot of the time that evening, they'd been silent and she hadn't felt uneasy with him. Somehow they fitted together.

She finished her tea and yawned. She was tired now but still alert. Eddie seemed to be everywhere . . . and tonight she was being swept along with him.

22

Tomorrow he'd be forty. Sharon had been getting into corners about it for weeks with Di and Marie. He guessed he was in line for some sort of surprise party, and he was bound to find it gruelling, though he would have to pretend to enjoy every moment and call it 'overwhelming'.

Driving to work, Ed tried to forget about his birthday and instead thought of Lyn. Since the evening at Spurn he'd spoken to her several times on the phone but had been unable to see her. He was always planning how he could be with her. Today was a training day so he should be able to get away early. As soon as he parked the car, he would phone her.

She'd just arrived at work. 'Oh, hi,' she said.

He wanted to leap about at the sound of her voice. 'It's me.' How wonderful to be able to say that and for her to realize who it was without his telling her. 'Any chance of us meeting up? Like late afternoon?'

They arranged it for down by the pier. Soon he was whistling to himself and on his way to draw his keys. A training day shouldn't be too exacting. Well, it didn't matter what it would be like.

'Hiya,' Mal grunted when they ran into each other as they waited for their keys to come clanging down the chute.

'All right?' Eddie shot a sardonic glance at the other man.

'Nah, had a few too many last night. Could do without this, fucking Control and Restraint.' He chuntered on about how crap he felt, and Eddie tried to look sympathetic.

The session was to take place in the gym, and twelve of them gathered there to wait for the guys running it. Today it was Colin in charge. He was in his navy tracksuit and bounced up and down on the balls of his feet and grinned a lot. Eddie didn't think his grin denoted good humour – it was more the snapping of a crocodile.

The exercises got under way and they worked for some time in pairs, one being the aggressor, the other the victim. Colin and his sidekick, a younger guy, Darren, gave demonstrations of handholds and methods of overpowering a recalcitrant prisoner.

'You can do a lot of damage with this,' Colin syruped. 'Be careful about it – the law says you can only do this if it's really necessary.' This time he guffawed.

Eddie hadn't been listening very much because he was trying to decide where he should take Lyn when they met. He now saw that this exercise was a group effort.

'You're the con,' Jim, an officer in his twenties, told Eddie, 'so we're going to restrain you.'

Eddie had never liked role-plays – they made him feel ridiculous. But looking at the faces of the group surrounding him, the whole thing seemed to have become a trial of strength. He was supposed to be resisting the four guys who'd closed in on him. They were all youngsters and he was only on nodding acquaintance with them. He wished Mal were in the same group, or some of his friends from the wing. No time to do anything, because without warning they pounced. He instinctively tried to fight back. He was on that beach at night with the hand grabbing his throat. This wasn't funny – it was threatening, it was for real. Somebody had him in a headlock; another had bent his right arm back. They tripped him. He thwacked down hard on the mat and his neck hurt. They crowded him as though they were in a rugby scrum. A heavy chap tried to kneel on his chest. The one with the arm across his neck glared into his face.

Eddie choked. He couldn't breathe. Rage and fear boiled up in him. 'If you don't fucking get off me, I'll kill you,' he yelled.

Colin, standing back watching the groups, walked across. 'Great,' he said. 'Got some real action there.'

For the rest of the time Eddie thought the others were looking at him. He felt unmanned by their superior strength and the ferocity inside them that was let loose when they set on him. He understood that for them it was a game without rules; they were set on his humiliation. They were all in their twenties and here was he – forty. Al, the guy who'd been on his chest, gave him searching glances at times, as though he couldn't be sure what happened back there on the mat. Eddie knew they weren't playing; they wanted a victim and they got one. He continued on automatic pilot for the rest of the day, just waiting to knock off.

As he drove back down the long straight road into the town centre, he went back over that moment pinned to the ground, and a wave of heat gushed over him. His heart thundered, his fingers sweated on the steering wheel. He sucked in air, trying to take it to the bottom of his lungs, and stared out at the road and the jigging dust. Soon he'd see Lyn – it would be all right.

He parked in his usual position, as he did when he and Mal decided on a pint. Before him the estuary bucked and rocked. The smell of tar and saltiness and the sinuous undertone of bladderwrack blew in on the breeze.

'Hi.'

He swung round at the sound of her voice. 'Hello there, Lyn.'

She smiled at him, and he loved the way a dimple formed by her mouth. Her skin had taken on a honey colour from the sun. He liked her beaky nose and the way her hair was pulled back from her face with just a single lock falling across her cheek. She had that slightly crumpled look of someone who'd come straight from work.

'Would you like a walk along by the estuary first, or shall we go into the pub?'

'Perhaps a bit of fresh air first – I need it after being penned up all day. It's been just like a steam bath.'

He wanted to take her hand, touch her, but anybody could see them, and what could he say he was doing?

They cut along over the new Millennium Bridge and turned into a walkway running behind a private housing estate. The houses stood on reclaimed land where once ships were anchored in a dock. High fences and a border of flowering shrubs shielded the houses from the public gaze. On their right lay the estuary, leaping on its way to the North Sea. In this secluded paved area the sun brought out the sweetness of the flowering shrubs. Eddie took her hand and drew her to face him.

'God, I've missed you so much, Lyn.'

'You seem to grow on me,' she said, smiling – but that slipped into seriousness.

He kissed her then, holding her against him, blind and deaf to everything else. Eventually they drew apart and began to walk on, still holding hands. She talked about her day: the kids on free swims; a girl being sick in the pool; a gang of lads rushing in off the street and causing a fight in the water – just the usual stuff. He didn't tell her about the moment on the floor with the man on his chest and the others gathered round.

'It's my birthday tomorrow,' he said. 'I wish I could spend it with you.'

'Ed, you should have said before. At least I could have

sent you a card then.' She paused for a moment, looking away over the water. 'Good job I didn't know – the card wouldn't have been a good idea.'

That was the truth, he knew – she couldn't send him anything.

'What will you be doing?' she asked.

'I have an awful feeling that Sharon will have arranged something, some surprise thing that I'll hate.' It was the first time he'd pronounced Sharon's name in front of Lyn, and it made him uncomfortable.

'She must think that's what you'd like.'

'I don't know about that – it's more what she'd like. Anyway, don't let's waste time talking about it.' Guilt mustn't devour this lovely moment, but he saw Sharon's hurt face – after all, she was arranging this party because she wanted to please him and it was her way of showing it.

He threaded his fingers through Lyn's and kept his eyes fixed on the path ahead. Here on this day, with the sun warm on his face and the glitter skidding off the water into his eyes and a crazy thread shooting from her fingers up his arm, he felt an elation unknown to him before. 'We could walk all the way to the oil terminal along here I think, but it would take too long. What about a drink?'

'Let's go back to mine and celebrate your birthday.'

At Lyn's house he sat on her sofa with a can of lager in his hand, and she placed a plate of toasted cheese sandwiches before him on the coffee table.

'To the birthday boy,' Lyn chanted, holding up a glass of lager.

What started as a kiss ended upstairs in Lyn's sun-flower-coloured bedroom. Standing in the doorway with his arms about her, he looked round at the teddy bear and the panda and smiled.

She opened the windows and warm air rushed in. Children were playing down below in the street and a dog barked. He went to stand by her at the window and somehow they jumbled themselves into a long embrace. Her mouth tasted of mint gum.

He forgot everything as they wrestled out of their clothes. He hadn't seen her completely naked before and loved the unexpectedness of her reddish pubic hair. It bushed in a discreet mound and seemed very intimate, and alive. As he sucked her nipples, she trembled and her face took on a tranced look – as though she weren't really conscious. He meandered along, wanting to tease her open. As he stroked and kissed and licked, he felt her body grow limp and he had to keep counting in his head. He played with the little flap of skin within the fleshy lips and it seemed to stiffen; between her legs was creamy as the tip of his middle finger stroked the plushy folds.

With precision he managed the moment: he manoeuvred his way in and heard her sigh and then they were at one another – plunging, pushing, writhing. She called out; he groaned and then lay spent beside her. He turned his head to look at her and saw how her face was flushed and the strands of blond hair about her cheeks and forehead had turned dark with sweat. She smiled at him and he squeezed her hand.

They lay there a long time. He didn't want to leave her, get up and drive home. In the end it was Lyn who broke the spell by sliding off the bed, pulling on a robe and disappearing into the bathroom.

'Eddie,' she said on her return, 'I'm going to make some tea and then hadn't you better be going home? They'll wonder where you are, won't they?'

'Yes,' he said, 'I suppose I'd better – but by hell, I don't want to.'

In a dream he drove home. As he reached the estate, he

tried to become the person who arrived back every day from a shift at the prison. The fact that he was still in his prison officer's uniform should allay any suspicions Sharon might entertain.

'Daddy, Daddy, where have you been?' Emma said, rushing out from the kitchen.

'Work, love,' he said, now experiencing the familiar twinges of guilt as he hugged her.

'We've got a secret,' she said, 'but I shan't tell you. It's somebody's birthday tomorrow – I wonder whose it is.'

He joined in the game. 'Yours?'

'No. Guess again.'

'Mummy's?'

'No, silly, Mummy's is later on. Can't you guess? It's somebody in this house.'

'Blue teddy?'

'No, silly, you've got to try harder.'

'Could it be mine?'

'Yes!' She buried her face in his abdomen and hugged him.

'I wonder if we'll have jelly and ice cream.'

'We might.'

Sharon came through from the kitchen, where she and Di had been in a huddle. 'Oh,' she said, 'there you are.' She was smiling. Eddie saw Emma in her face and he was shunted back over twenty-five years – she was a teenager lingering outside her gate, not wanting to go in. But he saw too that she looked thin and overstrung. Guilt pressed his chest. Oh, God, he was such a bastard.

'You know what it's like,' he said. 'There was a bit of bother.'

'Wow,' Di said. 'What sort of bother?'

'Oh, somebody kicked off, you know. Can happen at any time. You never know when there's going to be an emergency.'

Di wanted more, he could see. Sharon liked the idea that Di was intrigued and so was diverted from any cross-questioning herself. Both women had jolted on to a higher key with excitement. He knew it was all about his birthday and the plans they'd hatched, and his feeling of unease deepened.

Eddie sat in the kitchen and, while the women discussed something in the lounge, ploughed through a ham salad that Sharon had left for him. Emma, given special dispensation to stay up late because today was Friday, sat opposite him and chattered on about her drama class. He tried to keep up a steady line of banter. Her guilelessness overwhelmed him. She automatically assumed that he was telling the truth.

He managed to keep up the jolly front until Sharon clopped into the kitchen and said, 'Time for bed, madam,' and Emma, though protesting, had to go upstairs. Eddie promised to come up in a few minutes and read a story.

The women had now taken themselves to the patio with a bottle of wine, and Di called through that he should join them. He said he'd just have a shower first and change, then he'd be down. This was his usual pattern and he knew he mustn't deviate from it. Besides, he feared Sharon might smell Lyn on him – Lyn had her own smell that reminded him of pine trees in strong sunlight.

He read Emma a story about a girl who discovered she had magic powers, enabling her to make nasty people vanish. Later, dressed in jeans and a T-shirt, he wandered down to the patio with a glass in his hand and another bottle of wine.

'Oh, good, you've brought some more,' Di said. 'We were just feeling like cracking another open, weren't we, Shaz?'

'That's right.'

He could see that Sharon was fairly drunk, because she

couldn't stop grinning, and again he glimpsed Emma's look of delight in her face. It was as though he'd received a blow to his chest like he had that morning in the prison. Before all those phantom babies had become ghosts in their lives, they could be at ease together. He seemed to be staring down the years at how they used to be, and he wanted to cry.

He poured more wine into their glasses. They gossiped on, and he was thankful for some long-running tale about the unreliability of tradespeople, how you couldn't get a plumber. Di had decided on a new bathroom suite but couldn't get anyone to install it. And the prices they asked for their labour were exorbitant.

He kept quiet and swallowed his wine in preparation for another glass. The muggy warmth made him think of the tropics, and it returned him to his walk with Lyn along by the new estate. In one first-floor window, he'd noticed a mounted telescope. Someone must sit there peering out over the water. Would it be a woman watching for her husband's ship? That must be fanciful. Or perhaps an old sea dog now grounded? His mouth remembered the softness of Lyn's lips and his nose the smell of mint on her breath and the fishiness between her thighs. He plunged down a ravine of arousal and had to make a determined effort to join in the conversation.

By the time Di left, it had grown dark and a moon, like a silver penny, flipped in and out of moving cloud banks. He collected the empty wine bottles and Sharon the glasses and they re-entered the house. Sharon flirted herself against him in the kitchen, and he realized that the wine and Di's having been there had stirred up a desire in her. Or was it that she could feel vibrations of the late afternoon coming off him? Or had she momentarily remembered the two of them as they were, those kids at school, parting, finding each other again and finally losing each other?

As he entered the bedroom he could make out Sharon waiting for him in the darkness. Her naked flesh felt hot and dry. She strained herself against him, running her fingers down his chest, sliding them into his boxers. Of course he responded. Lyn had given him an overpowering sexual need. But when it was over and Sharon had turned on her side, he was left tense, as though he'd not climaxed. For years sex between him and Sharon had been mechanical – first they'd been trying for a baby. When the miscarriages started everything changed. Sex might be dangerous, so better refrain. As Sharon became more and more discouraged, she no longer wanted it at all.

He lay on his back, wide awake, and felt his heart thumping with agitation. He was sweating and afraid. The crowd of faces stared down at him. The fellow's knee constricted his chest. He made himself take a deep breath. Gradually his heartbeat returned to normal and he relaxed with relief, but was still unable to sleep.

The next morning he lingered for a while, registering that it was a Saturday, that there was no need to hurry, that it was his fortieth birthday. Yesterday he'd made love to Lyn – he couldn't quite believe it had really happened. Already he was desperate to be with her again. He wished he could leapfrog this day and land down on a working day, on such days there was more chance of being able to see her.

'Happy birthday to you, happy birthday to you! Happy birthday, dear Daddy, happy birthday to you,' Emma carolled, leaping on to the bed and flinging her arms round his neck.

He nuzzled his face in her hair and pretended to be a wild beast. She chortled and shrieked. Sharon's eyes flicked open. 'Emma, this is a bit early,' she said.

'But Mummy, it's Daddy's birthday and he has to have his presents.'

Eddie got the idea that Sharon probably had a mighty hangover.

The day churned by. 'We're taking you out for a meal,' Sharon told him at about six o'clock, 'but you aren't to know where – that's a surprise.'

'Oh,' he said, trying to look pleased and as though he'd no idea where this was heading. He had an urge to phone or text Lyn; thought maybe he could sneak out for a run and meet her somewhere. He dismissed the idea as too dangerous and Sharon would be upset. He had been made to feel that since this was his birthday he must remain exclusively at home, so he sat an age planted before the TV, hardly aware of the images floating before his eyes.

At seven, when he'd put on his suit and a shirt and tie, Sharon emerged in a new long black dress. 'Well?' She posed in the lounge doorway.

'Stunning,' he said. 'Absolutely stunning.' She seemed to be satisfied with that.

Emma, fiercely excited, raced back and forth in her pink party dress. 'Isn't it time to go, Mummy?' she kept on asking. Sharon shushed her and told her the taxi would be arriving soon.

Sharon had booked a trendy venue (obviously nudged in that direction by Di and Barry), an old warehouse now converted into a bar. It operated on three floors and looked out on to what was once a dock but now was reduced to a decorative strip of water behind a shopping precinct.

Already guests milled about in the entrance and taxis swerved up on the old dockside, decanting people. Eddie saw Di and Barry giving their practised smiles. Sharon rushed over to them. Emma, made shy by all the grinning faces, hung on to his hand. His parents sat at a downstairs table in a corner, looking uneasy. His father had buttoned himself into an old suit, which had seen service at weddings and funerals and now spent all its time in a plastic bag at the back of a wardrobe. Eddie felt sorry for them and went over.

'Amazing,' he said. 'Truly amazing. No idea Sharon had arranged all this – fantastic.' He spoke in a loud gushing voice so that Sharon might hear. This was what was expected of him, and although he wanted to act his most churlish, he restrained himself.

'It's very posh, love,' his mother said, pleating the strap of her handbag like she did when she was agitated. Eddie knew the signs.

Sharon appeared at his side. 'I've invited all your old friends,' she said. He could see a good number of her workmates and the neighbours from the new estate and a couple of their old neighbours. Marie and Nigel came up, and Marie gave him a full-on-the-lips kiss. 'Happy birthday, birthday boy,' she cooed, and handed him a gift-wrapped parcel. All manner of packages had already been mounded up on a table. Sharon and Di wandered about, telling the guests that the buffet spread out on a line of tables would open soon and then they could enjoy themselves. Meanwhile slick young women, wearing navel-revealing tops and trousers that coated their bottoms and legs like black gloss, flitted round with trays of drinks.

Mal hove up out of the press. Eddie was amazed that Sharon had asked him. He was unaccompanied, a fact Sharon spotted immediately.

'Sally not with you, Malcolm?' she asked in a prim, accusatory tone.

'No, Sharon,' he said. 'We've split up.'

Sharon didn't seem to know what to do with this information and limited herself to, 'Oh, dear.' Eddie knew he'd hear more on the subject from her later.

'Surprise party, eh, Ed?' Mal said, slapping Eddie on the shoulder.

Something about Mal's expression bordered on the foxy:

a certain complicity, as though they both shared a secret. Eddie waited for the other man to betray whatever it was, but he didn't.

'How're things?' he asked, glancing at Mal.

Emma tugged at Eddie's hand. 'Are we having a drink, Daddy?'

'Yes, in a minute – go and find Mummy, she'll get you one.' Emma hesitated and needed persuading to cross to where Sharon and Di chortled away with Barry. *Nerd*, Eddie registered, trying to get a glimpse of Barry's shoes. Pointed black lace-ups tonight. Sly bastard. Barry would sit behind his bank manager's desk and tell people how to run their lives; lecture them on their expenditure levels. Eddie watched Nigel threading his way across to the Barry acolytes. All he needed now was for Marie to come fumbling and it would be quite an evening.

'Bet you weren't expecting this lot,' Mal said.

'No, mate, I wasn't.'

'It'll have cost, will this,' Mal said.

'Yes, I bet it has.' This thought had occurred to Eddie, and he'd wondered how much overtime he'd have to do to pay it off, because sure as death the bill would eventually become his responsibility.

'Who's a dark horse, then?'

'What are you on about?' With a shock Eddie realized that his dad had made his way over and was by his shoulder. Before Mal could say any more, Eddie jumped in with introductions.

'Very pleased to meet you,' his dad said, shaking Mal's hand. 'Nice to meet Eddie's colleagues – grand do this, isn't it?'

More wine circulated. Mal knocked the glasses back at a phenomenal rate and Eddie found his own hand reaching for more.

Sharon, after banging a knife handle on a glass, managed to still the chatter and declared the buffet open. The more timorous hung back and Eddie had to lead Emma to the tables and give her a plate. Mal was busy chatting up a young waitress and so Eddie escaped him for a while.

Upstairs a DJ had started playing and some guests dived off to investigate. Everywhere vibrated with the thump of music. Balloons drifted through the air.

Eddie stared up at a gold 40 hanging from a streamer that shimmied above his head.

Chewing a samosa, he slipped away upstairs, nodding and smiling at people and muttering 'brilliant's and 'fantastic's and 'thank you's as he went.

Mal lumbered up with Di. They started off dancing opposite each other, separate and yet with their eyes locked like a fox and a cat having a stand-off. Eddie watched until a couple of colleagues whom Sharon must have recruited through Mal joined him and insisted on fetching him another drink.

But Eddie was in Lyn's bedroom, standing by the window, dreaming of hot, wet places. His mouth was on her neck. Everything was going fast and slow at the same time. They were both panting. She looked, he looked. Looking, touching, stroking, and moisture starting in a sticky ooze. He longed to drown in all that magic silt. He could cry with longing – wanted to go downstairs, call a taxi and be at her place; have her in the hall, on the steep little staircase, bend her over chairs, know every crevice of her.

More people arrived in the dancing area. Marie showed up, as he knew she would.

'Enjoying your birthday, then?'

'Yer, great – couldn't be better.' His colleagues stood beside him and smiled at Marie, no doubt unimpressed by her staid appearance.

By the time Sharon and Barry & Co. galumphed on to the scene, grinning and chattering, Eddie had decided that he had to escape outside. He felt constricted and a bit sick. Just as he was about to make a move, he saw Barry reclaiming his wife from Mal, who was entwined with her in a corner. Mal, red in the face, threatening to become bellicose, was the perfect excuse. Eddie strode across and seized his arm.

'Let's have a breather,' he said.

'The cunt's dragged her off of me, man.'

'He's her husband.'

'Oh, right.' Mal was momentarily disconcerted.

They descended the stairs and Eddie saw that several of his colleagues had grouped themselves in the stairwell, pint glasses in their hands. It disturbed him to see how their shaven heads gleamed under the hall lights and their faces had taken on a hectic pink. The older ones who were balding anyway had turned an even deeper shade of salmon. They slapped his shoulders, congratulating him.

'Great party, Ed!' someone shouted. 'Here's to the next forty!' They raised their pints. He grinned back at them.

'Just taking a breath of air,' he said, leading Mal away.

Out in the narrow cobbled street, Eddie gazed across at the black water.

'That bird was all right,' Mal slurred. 'She'd got some fucking amazing tits – didn't mind showing them, either.'

'But she's married to that geeky bank manager.'

'What geeky bank manager?'

'That dude who came across.'

'Well – she was coming on to me.'

'Yes, she'd think you were her bit of rough, but it still doesn't mean you can maul her. Anyway, she's a coquette.'

'A what? You needn't try that high and mighty stuff with me, Ed. Oh, yer, and all the time you were on at me before about Sal finding out – you'd got something nice sorted for yourself, hadn't you? I saw you with that young lass. How long you been knocking her off?'

'That's not true – I haven't a clue what you're on about. You've no need to take it out on me, Mal, because you've messed up.'

'Who said I'd messed up?'

Mal's eyes bulged with rage. Eddie glared at him in exasperation, relieved that this rant wasn't taking place at the party, where everyone could have heard it. The night air, though warm, had cleared his head. He just wanted Mal to go home; his presence at the party was a liability.

'You're just like all the rest,' Mal grunted, staring in front of him.

'What do you mean?'

'The fuckers say I hit the kid. I never. Well, if I did, he deserved it – but I never. Suspension. Suspension, that's what it looks like. You don't care. Thought you was a mate.'

'Mal, look, I am a mate. I didn't know about this lot. I'm sorry.'

'Oh, don't tell me that one!' Mal shrugged free of the arm Eddie tried to put round his shoulders and staggered off down the cobbles into the night. Eddie started to go after him but didn't get far – some of the departing guests wanted to say their goodbyes, and he was drawn back into the building.

He went to the bar and bought a whisky. As he waited for the barman to pour it, he was back again with Lyn on that first day out at Spurn.

The barman plonked the drink on the counter top. Eddie put coins in his hand. He lost Lyn in the memory of Mal's engorged face. Sal didn't deserve this – she'd done nothing to cause it, but Mal couldn't stop. He wanted to be twenty again, nerves jangling with the excitement of the chase. Only he was middle-aged and his adventures had brought misery on his family. This was how it would go for him too. Did Sharon deserve this? What would Delphine think if she knew? They counted on him . . .

'Not still drinking?' Sharon tapped him on the shoulder and he jumped. 'We must go home. Emma's exhausted.'

'All right,' he said, dispatching the drink at a swallow, feeling his throat tight with tears he mustn't shed.

23

Lyn, up on the chair near the baby pool, didn't hear or see the commotion and it was only the sight of Ben kicking off his trainers about to leap into the water that shocked her into action. In a single movement she was down from her chair and along the poolside to the deep end. Ben was in the water battling to separate an elderly woman and a thin, dark man whose hands were clawing at her and propelling them both under. Lyn had a moment of panic. Should she jump in too? You were supposed to be able to control things from the side and avoid going into the water.

Before she could reach a decision, the woman climbed up the steps out of the pool, coughing and gasping. Ben had a hold on the drowning man and was bringing him to the side.

'Oh, God,' the woman spluttered, 'I tried to help him, but he dragged me under.'

They sat in the staff room at lunch, gobbling crisps and pasties. Ben slugged back his Coke, belched and narrated.

'Thought the feller was going to drown both of 'em,' he said. 'He had that woman round the neck. Throttled her. She should have left him – would have been easier.'

'But you can't leave people like that,' Lyn said. She'd been dithering inside ever since seeing the three of them in the water.

'So would you, if you thought he might pull you under?'

'Ben, she wouldn't have known that.'

'The public should leave well alone,' Andy came in, not looking at Lyn. Things had been strained since she pushed him off in the taxi.

'I said to him, "Don't you go jumping in again – keep at the shallow end." Them asylum-seekers can't understand what you're telling 'em.'

Lyn stopped listening. She'd got a headache and her eyes smarted; the chlorine seemed to be getting to her. She could smell it everywhere. It inflamed the inside of her nostrils and made her sneeze and her eyes run.

An hour before the start of the free kids' session sharp-faced lads swarmed about on the steps in front of the baths, some trying to squirm their way on to a window ledge to peer inside. A constant jostling blocked the swimmers exiting from the last session. Lyn heard the shouts and laughter, which formed a barrage of sound outside the building.

'Fucking hell, listen to 'em,' Andy said.

'Drown the lot,' Ben gurgled, halfway down another can of Coke.

It would be brilliant to be driving out to Spurn now instead of this – or driving out anywhere. Lyn stared at the traffic outside snarled up bumper to bumper before the traffic lights. Druggies lurched by on the other side of the road, up to no good.

The afternoon passed in a wall of sound: screams, shouts, laughter, splashing reverberated under the domed roof. Before her bodies wrestled and leaped, water fountained, showering on the poolside in a white spray. Bodies hit the water and rocked it into Atlantic breakers. Kids zoomed underwater. She stared until her eyes watered. If you missed a kid in difficulties – if somebody drowned – you'd never forgive yourself. It was more than a job; it was a responsibility, a pressure.

At last it was four o'clock and they were leaving. Lyn had to chase a group of girls out of the shower. They liked to stand there under the jets nattering to one another or arguing – 'You said he looked at you.' 'He never – he snogged me.' 'Liar, liar, your bum's on fire.'

They dragged out, clothes damp and faces red, wet hair dripping down their backs, still bickering.

Now the parents started arriving with their children. Lyn took a deep breath. Here came the lessons, her favourite part of the week. Around her were scurryings as they helped the little ones change. She kept a lookout for Eddie. If he didn't show, she'd find herself distracted, struggling to shut out disappointment – it made her realize how little she knew about his everyday life. From there a feeling of hopelessness could creep up on her.

Most of the children had changed and were ready to start, and she'd given up any hope of seeing Eddie, when Emma pushed through the swing doors with her father behind her. She met his eyes and a shock travelled down her body – she had to look away. She heard him telling Emma to hurry up and change.

'I'm sorry we're a bit late,' he said.

'Oh, that's all right.' She studied her trainers and couldn't look at him. This not being able to touch each other or say anything personal was strangely arousing, and she struggled to keep her concentration on what she was doing.

When he left with Emma at the end of the lesson, she stared after them, engulfed by a sense of loss. The threads that had begun to link them seemed so tenuous. If anything happened to him, she would never know, because for his family she didn't exist. At the door he turned and she wanted to call out to him but knew she mustn't. The door swung to behind him. That was it now until he phoned.

She cycled home in no mood for training in the dock. Images of the man and woman sinking in the pool returned to her. She remembered that other occasion when she knelt by the boy's side and placed her mouth on his, all with a knot of terror in her stomach. His face was what had burrowed in her head: the blue eyes wide open and unseeing and his skin almost translucent. Perhaps her mother's skin too would have had that marble whiteness when they found her . . . But she was kidding herself – after so long in the water, most likely her mother would have been almost unrecognizable.

Her skin froze as she thought again how easy it was to drown. Water could take so much, overpower you in an instant, sucking you under, bursting your lungs . . . but it was a life force too, mesmerizing – it could caress you like smooth fingers. There had never been a time when she hadn't been under its spell, though sometimes, like tonight, she hated it.

On arriving home she made a mug of tea; watered the spider plants on the windowsill and put off ringing Dave Jamieson. She fluttered back and forth: she was going to train – no, she couldn't bear it, not this time. In the end she told him that she had to work – someone had foisted an extra shift on her. He laughed and she knew he didn't believe her; he thought she was backing out because she couldn't hack it. His last words were, 'Let me know if you're still up for it on Sunday.' She thought of Fred's dad alone in the middle of an ocean. Shame tempted her to ring Dave back and say it was all right, that she'd changed the shift at the last minute. But she couldn't face lying again, and she really didn't want to swim. The dock was not a place to go when your head was crammed with images of drowning people. No, she wanted to chill out and forget.

But now that she had escaped training, she didn't feel relieved, only at a loose end, and she phoned Aunty Mags.

'Come round, love. I'm just going to pop out for a drink – come with me.'

Quick change into clean jeans and a vest and Lyn biked round to her aunt's house, midway in that long terrace where the kids had to play ball around parked cars and speed bumps.

The 'Greensleeves' chimes trilled, and Aunty Mags appeared in white trousers, a plunging top and gypsy earings. Her perfume started Lyn sneezing.

'Hello, love. Better lock your bike up and shove it under that privet. You never can tell . . . Let's get off directly.'

Aunty Mags's local was several streets away. Lyn always found it a bit blowsy. It wasn't of the theme pub variety, and yet they'd built a new extension on to the original structure and it squatted beside it, incongruous with its sloping glass roof that drew to a point. The bar was hedged about by men with builders' bums and trousers resting under their pumpkin stomachs.

On their arrival the men's heads swivelled round.

'Evenin' Mags,' several voices craked. Lyn could feel them staring at her.

'Hiya, boys,' Mags purred, her voice taking on the throaty timbre that Lyn remembered from the past and those holidays with boyfriends. In those days she sounded as though she had perpetual laryngitis.

Somebody produced a line of gins for Mags, and Lyn found a chap with bleeding-steak cheeks at her elbow. 'What's your tipple, love?' he asked, spraying her with curried breath.

She'd have preferred to say it didn't matter, but she didn't want to upset Aunty Mags, so she said she'd have a Bacardi Breezer, ta very much.

This pub, Lyn mused, belonged to another age. Whole families were encamped. The kids had to sit outside on benches drinking Coke or lemonade and watch the traffic shooting by on the road beyond a low wall. Serious drinkers with puce faces never budged from the bar, but other equally intent groups smoked in corners, coughing and hawking as the fug intensified.

Aunty Mags sipped her drink and poked her scarlet nails into a bag of salted peanuts.

'So how's things, Mags?' a man asked, flopping down next to her.

'Grand,' she said.

'You never look no different to me – you allus was a looker and you don't change.'

'Go on, Trev!' Aunty Mags purred with coyness. Lyn knocked back her drink and watched.

'Who's this, then?' he asked, indicating Lyn.

'That's my niece Lyn – she's my brother's daughter. Lyn, this is Trev who was at school with me. We've not seen each other in a long while.'

'Oh, right,' Lyn muttered, trying to smile in the man's direction. He had a withered Elvis look about him, and his hair, which must have been black at one time, bulged in a greying quiff above his forehead and straggled almost to his shoulders. His powder-blue suit and blue suede lace-ups with soles like car tyres had stepped straight out of the nineteen fifties. Aunty Mags leaned forward as he flicked open a gold-coloured lighter.

'I shouldn't be having a ciggy,' she told him, 'but I'm a weak-willed woman,' and she gave a throaty gargle of laughter. Lyn wondered what had happened to Aunty Mags's toyboy but knew she had to wait to hear about that.

'I've had to go steady on the weed myself,' Trev said, sucking down the smoke from his own cig like a vacuum cleaner gulping down dirt. 'My heart – had a bypass.'

'Crikey,' Aunty Mags said, and Lyn knew she didn't like this information. She wasn't good on illnesses and dodged away from people who were beginning to cave in. Lyn saw her aunt flinch.

'Said it'll kill us if I don't quit, like.'

'Trev, I think that lady over there's trying to attract your attention.' And indeed a stooping, washed-out blonde had drawn near their table. At this Trev made off.

As soon as he was out of earshot Mags turned to Lyn. 'Do you know who that one is?'

'Not really.'

'It's that Trev who two-timed me – you was a little girl then. Thought he was Mr Universe, and look at him now – nothing on him. And look who he's got with him! That skirt's right up her backside – proper mutton dressed up.'

Lyn tried to reconstruct the raven-haired lover from the cadaverous creature now reeled in by the equally stringy blonde. 'Now you come to mention it, he does look vaguely familiar.'

Aunty Mags threw down a good number of the drinks and didn't speak for a while. 'That bugger nearly broke my heart,' she said at last. 'Oh, yes, he was going to buy me this and that – of course he never.'

The mood that had prevented Lyn from training earlier wouldn't lift and forced her now to focus on Aunty Mags. 'Aunty,' she said, 'why do you really think my mother killed herself?'

The question seemed to get lost in the pub hubbub and the pop tune blasting along in the background. Lyn couldn't bring herself to repeat it and was shocked when Aunty Mags spoke.

'Well, Jim, your dad, being a looker and everything, had the girls swarming round him – I'm not trying to make excuses.' She took a gulp of gin and stared at her cigarette, which was almost down to the butt. A pause stretched between them, and Lyn feared Aunty Mags would leave the conversation stranded at this point. 'He was going with your mam, Elaine. She was a nice girl – seems a long time ago – well, it is. But there was this other lass, Jackie.

Now she was a goer. She looked like Marilyn Monroe – the blond hair, big bust, lips and everything. Well, your dad was besotted. They'd been out before he met your mam, and then she went off with someone else, but she got back with your dad. Of course your mam didn't know.'

Lyn sat holding her glass, but feeling the goose bumps starting on her back and arms as though she'd just emerged from the dock.

'But when your mam got pregnant with you, he married her. They'd only just got wed when I ran into him one evening – I was out with Trev – and he'd got Jackie with him. They were in this clinch outside the back of the pub. I'd gone out to use the toilet and there they were. Afterwards I said to him, "You know you can't go on like this, Jim, you've got a wife." But your dad goes his own way. He took no notice. Then your mam found out he was canoodling with that Jackie. She told him she'd leave him. She was about seven months gone by this time. They had a big reconciliation and he promised it was over. But it wasn't, was it? No, they were at it again a couple of weeks later, only your mam didn't find out until you were a few months old. She'd been staying with a friend of hers for a couple of days in the country because she'd got anaemic and tired all the time. She gets back early, thinking he'd be that pleased; was he, heck! Him and Jackie were upstairs in bed, weren't they – your mam goes up and catches 'em at it. You know what happened after that.'

Lyn could hear nothing but the thudding in her ears of the annihilating wave. It reared up and she watched it, seeming to be inside it and apart from it in the same moment.

'When your mam went and drowned herself, it couldn't go on – they was too guilty.' Aunty Mags drooped into herself, stubbed out her cig and stared into her drink. 'It did for your dad, really – never been the same since.'

'How could he have carried on with another woman like that? Her pregnant as well . . .' Lyn felt stunned, as though she'd been booted in the stomach. And this baby, the baby was herself, a baby born into deception – she had been there all the time the tragedy was ripening. She wanted to vomit. Her dad had done this. She couldn't link this greedy sexual predator with the person she'd always called Dad. He was elderly, rigid in his thinking, but kindly enough and predictable in his behaviour. The lies took her breath away.

'He's a monster,' she said. 'I just can't believe he'd do something so callous.' For her mother to have left her baby, she must have felt unendurably sad, desperate, friendless . . . To think of her walking into the mud at night because of all that lying . . . the quicksand of their lies and their uncaring had devoured her. 'Oh, this lot makes me want to scream. I can't handle it. I've never known my dad – had no idea. I've got to go back over my whole life now trying to make sense of it. There's been so much dodging about, always to keep me from really knowing what happened. So I've had to be lied to because he can't face what he's done – he *killed* my mother – and that's why he's had to keep me at a distance . . .'

'Shush – steady!' Aunty Mags muttered. Lyn became aware that people round about were casting curious glances.

'But how could he?'

'It's sex,' Aunty Mags said. 'Sex can make you mad.'

'Surely to God it must have been more than that?'

Aunty Mags's usual zing had disappeared in the pleatings of her upper lip and the smudging of her lipstick and her panda-eyed make-up. She downed her last drink with determination. 'Let's be making tracks, love,' she said. 'Seeing that Trev has really put me off. We can have a nightcap at mine.'

*

An hour or so later Lyn wobbled home on her bike. She wanted to rush round to her dad's house and force him to face the truth. She was trying to understand who this person she called Dad really was. Behind all that dull booziness was this wilful, uncaring man who wasn't prepared to curb his impulses. He'd let his lust stamp on the feelings of his pregnant wife. Everything whizzed about in her head; she couldn't think straight. Oh, but she was going to make him pay. Let him look at himself, how he was responsible for her lack of a mother. Her hands trembled on the handlebars. Her bike threatened to keel over. What chance had her mother stood against Jackie's curves, her allure – how could they have done this to her? The photo of the lost young woman floated in her head. She was reeling back through the years, searching for clues. All she saw, though, was the shambling figure, just home from work and washing in the sink; collapsed in an armchair before his evening pub visits – so ordinary. And yet behind that behaviour lurked the betrayer. He must have spent his whole life since then hiding from his own guilt.

She wanted to stand before him, yell at him – she, this nice, biddable girl. For once she intended to force him to accept what he'd done; look at the lives he'd ruined. Rage shook her like a buffet of wind. She saw herself in his house – why couldn't she hit him with a sledgehammer, grind him to pulp? He'd caused her years of loneliness and frustration. She wanted to be there that instant . . .

But you can't go there tonight, the cool voice in her head said. *You're in no fit state.*

24

Lunch hour. He was out on the road, running, with dust swirling under his trainers. A wind swept in off the estuary and cooled his face. Lorries blundered by. The disused cemetery was on his left; now a wood yard; the white hospital sign flashed up, the maternity hospital where Emma was born.

The weather had been very cold then, frosty, with gaunt trees, empty flower-beds and long windows projecting oblongs of orange light on to the asphalt at night. Time dragged, everything was in slow motion. Sharon lay huge on a bed and he sat beside her hour after hour and held her hand, though occasionally he would escape outside for a breath of air. She had carried a baby to full term – but what if even here a disaster were to happen? He'd sensed she couldn't escape her anxiety and it never lessened. Women still died in childbirth, and babies too. And then the miracle: Emma's birth. He had loved Sharon for presenting him with this tiny perfect being.

He ran on, sweating and panting, forcing down stirrings of guilt, but exhilarated to feel the wind on his legs and face. When the shift finished he'd meet Lyn, drive round to her house. The whole day was but a preparation for this. The intervening time since they were last together was a blank. He wanted to phone her constantly; texting wasn't enough, he longed for the sound of her voice, the slight hesitancy when the conversation started and then her laugh, the feeling that it was all right, they had reached an intimacy that was real and not some imagined bubble of his own creation.

Three-quarters of an hour later, pouring with sweat and gasping, he arrived back at the prison gates, drew his keys, showered and changed back into his uniform.

On the wing he ran into Mal, whom he hadn't seen since the night of his party.

'Hiya,' Mal grunted. Eddie noticed how red his face seemed. He'd taken on the look of an old soak. 'Up for a drink when we finish?' Mal screwed his face up and squinted at Eddie.

'Sorry, mate, can't this time. Got an appointment.'

'Pussy, eh?'

'No,' Eddie said, cringing, 'nothing like that – Sharon, actually.'

'Who're you kidding? I wasn't born yesterday. Take a bit of your own advice. Women are poison, keep clear of 'em. Sharon'll not let you get away with it. She'll take you for all you've got.'

Eddie couldn't find a retort and limited himself to grinning at Mal, wishing he could erase the other man's comments from his mind.

At last he was on his way to Lyn and he couldn't wait. All the time he was tense with the fear that something might prevent their meeting. He'd turned off his mobile in case Sharon should ring. He wanted nothing to stop him.

She met him at the door, smiling. He could only smile back because he'd made it and nothing catastrophic had intervened. Just seeing her was enough. He must ease himself back into the glow of being with her.

'I bet you're hungry?' she said.

'I'm just so glad to be here,' he said.

'I take it that means yes?'

They sat in her kitchen eating lasagne and salad and drinking red wine. She had put a candle on the middle of the table, and he looked at her across a yellow-and-purple cone of flame. He liked to watch the way she chewed and wiped her mouth on a paper napkin. Tonight it was a denim miniskirt, and he glimpsed soft inner thigh. The arch of her feet in their high-heeled mules made him want to stroke her insteps and kiss the lovely curve. Her maroon toenails peeped through the open fronts of the mules.

'So tell me – what's been happening to you?' he said.

'Usual routine,' she said, and then she looked serious.

'Not quite, eh?'

'Yes – I got to know something from my aunty that I didn't know before.'

'Oh, yes?'

'Why my mother drowned herself.'

He waited. She looked as though she might cry.

'I haven't had time to think it through properly yet.' She didn't say any more and he dared not probe.

A while later they were up in her bedroom, caught in a frenzy of kissing, stroking, panting. The palms of his hands felt the slight prickle of her pubic bush, then they travelled round her waist. He knelt on the bed, she facing him. He held the swell of her buttocks in his hands, trailed a finger into her anus and she shivered. Their mouths turned on each other. The anticipation of the moment stretched tighter. But he wanted to prolong this hovering on the verge of climaxing. Every particle of his day had been jostling to this point. She looked pale in the tea light of that room, and her blond hair might have been dark brown. Her lips, bruised from so much kissing and almost puffy, had the plushy bulge of velvet orchid flowers.

The end exploded in a frantic falling together. He was in her, over her, and yet felt enveloped by her. He held on, moving in the hot dampness of her. They groaned and sighed at each other, and then there was a long silence. Everything had ebbed out of him, and he lay with her head resting on his arm.

When he woke, he looked over at her and saw how the pillowcase near her mouth was darkened by a small patch of moisture from her parted lips, and he stroked her hair back from her forehead and then her eyelids flicked open. 'I'd like to waken beside you for the rest of my life,' he said. This was something over and beyond the physical; it was an emotion that he sensed would cause them both suffering. He didn't think he'd ever felt this tender before about anybody.

His eye fell on Lyn's alarm clock, and he jerked upright. 'Oh, God,' he said, 'I'd no idea it was this time – there'll be hell to pay.' Stunned, he started to pull on his uniform. There wasn't time to shower. Lyn had got out of bed and was watching him. She didn't say anything.

'I'm so sorry,' he muttered, kissing her on his way out. 'I'll give you a bell.'

He drove home in a daze, trying to plan how he could present some coherent reason for his lateness. Should he say a lock-down at the prison caused by a missing prisoner? A hostage-taking? A riot? They all seemed a bit too extreme. Perhaps the best idea was his first one – a lockdown. He must stick to one. When you started giving a number of excuses, you'd lost.

His hope was that Sharon would have gone to bed. But no, as he drove up to the house, he saw that lights blazed in the downstairs windows. He wanted to turn round and drive back to Lyn, but he couldn't.

No sooner had he unlocked the front door and entered the hall than he came face to face with Sharon.

'Where the hell have you been? You are never here when there's an emergency. You've had your mobile switched off all evening.'

'At work.'

'I don't believe you. Your daughter's very ill and where are you?'

'What's the matter? What's happened?'

'Emma's got a terrible headache and she's been vomiting. I've rung for the emergency doctor. It could be meningitis. You just don't care, do you?'

He was already making for the stairs. She continued to upbraid him. 'It's all right now when I've been worried out of my mind for hours – now you think you can just walk in and take over and it'll be all right.'

Eddie stood by Emma's bed, looking down at her. 'Daddy, you've been ages – I feel awful and I wanted to see you.'

'I know, sweetie. I couldn't help it – trouble at work. Sometimes you can't just down tools and come home.'

Eddie heard a car engine, then a door shutting and he crossed to the window in time to see the doctor arriving. Sharon spoke with him in the hall and then they mounted the stairs. Eddie only once remembered a doctor visiting at night and it seemed unreal, dramatic, somehow menacing. He took a deep breath.

The emergency doctor nodded at Eddie and approached Emma's bed, where he stood looking down at her and smiling. 'So how are you, dear?' he asked. Emma's answer was a burst of tears. The doctor placed a hand on Emma's forehead. 'Hm,' he said, and then palpated her neck. She flinched. He shone a light into her eyes. Eddie stopped watching; his shoulders ached with tension.

While the doctor washed his hands in the bathroom, Sharon started hurrying oddments of clothing into a holdall.

'What's happening, Daddy?' Emma wanted to know.

'The doctor's seeing what he can do to make you better.'

When the doctor returned, he told them he'd rung for an ambulance. Sharon elbowed Eddie out of the way. His nerves rattled with the animosity hitting him and his fear at Emma's illness. He hadn't expected anything like this, not for a minute. Sharon obviously held him responsible.

The ambulance swooping up, lights flashing, seemed to Eddie like a huge nurse snooping along on rubber soles down silent wards. The paramedics placed Emma on a stretcher. Under the white sheets her body seemed small as a doll's. He wanted to push them all away and put his arms round her, protect her from them.

'Are you both coming?' one of the men asked.

'You'd better stay here,' Sharon said, without looking at Eddie. She was shrivelled and rigid with hurt. Oh, where have we gone wrong, what the hell has happened to us? he thought. Those schoolkid lovers, who'd chalked their names on walls intertwined in a heart and couldn't wait to be grown up, they wouldn't rest until they'd destroyed each other. And now their only child might be taken from them.

Before he could make a rejoinder, they'd left. He stood outside the house with his head throbbing. The ache radiated from above his eyes.

When he went back inside, the house felt alien and huge. It echoed as he cleared his throat and walked across the kitchen tiles. The lights in every room increased the sensation of weirdness. He wanted to be at the hospital with Emma; he ought to have insisted on being there. She was his daughter too. How could Sharon exclude him? He remembered Mal ranting on about not being able to see his children. This was how it would be. Sharon would prevent him seeing Emma – and suppose she was so ill that she didn't survive? Just passing through those automatic hospital doors might be enough to pull her into the force field of killer germs. He had an urge to open the drinks cabinet and pour a whisky, but stopped himself. He must drive down to the hospital and see what was happening. He wouldn't let Sharon push him away.

All the way there he battled with the fear that gurgled in his bowels. He kept imagining Emma dead before he could reach her. He felt light-headed, a fragment of grit rattling in the container of his body.

Parking the car and trudging across acres of tarmac in the shifting amber lights was wading through thick mud. Every step held him back. Through the revolving doors and into the reception area he went, avoiding knots of bemused-looking people. A small stout woman in a red leisure suit, with matching lipsticked mouth and raddled cheeks, bumped into him. Mad bruiser-faced men stinking of booze got in his way. He wanted to yell at them all and kick them from the building, but he pressed on through more doors.

At last he reached a room where people waited on chairs and stretchers – lads with bleeding faces and blackened eyes – and all seemed in some way shocked, disorientated and odd.

'They've just brought my daughter in,' he told the woman on reception.

'What name is it?'

'Emma,' he said.

'What's her surname?' The woman gave him a funny look. He told her. 'They've gone through; they'll be in a cubicle down there.'

He made his way past stretchers all lined up with their supine cargo. Even glancing at them made him uncomfortable – it seemed indecent to stare at people in such stages of disintegration. This must be the NHS running down, he thought. Nurses scurried about and people with stethoscopes slung round their necks slotted cards into index boxes and padded off. Where were they? His heart hopped with agitation.

At last he saw them through a half-open door leading into a small room. A doctor was with them. Eddie pushed the door open.

'Hello,' he said. Sharon and the doctor turned round.

'Daddy,' Emma said.

'My husband,' Sharon said, then dismissed him by continuing with the conversation. 'So what do you think it is, doctor?'

'We'd need to do a lumbar puncture to be sure.'

'No,' Eddie said. 'No, I won't sanction that.'

Both Sharon and the doctor swivelled to look at him. 'You've got to think of what will be in Emma's best interests,' Sharon said in her Human Resources Manager voice. Eddie's hands shook with anxiety and anger. Didn't she know how bastardly painful lumbar punctures were?

'Would you deny your daughter life-saving treatment?' the doctor asked.

'You don't even know whether it's necessary. Why put Emma through something that she doesn't need?'

'We need to find out what the problem is.' The doctor had begun to look sour and as though Eddie was a time waster. 'Anyway, we shall admit Emma on to a ward and monitor her progress. I trust you have no objection to that?'

'Not at all. I just don't want her put through unnecessary procedures.' He wouldn't mention the word 'pain' because he was aware of Emma lying there with big distraught eyes.

A few minutes later a nurse appeared and wheeled Emma off, accompanied by Sharon. Eddie didn't know what to do.

'Go home.' Sharon's look in his direction was a poison dart. He could tell how she felt on the high moral ground because she was siding with the omnipotent doctor. But what did the doctor really know about anything? He wasn't the one getting the lumbar puncture. The thought of them plunging a needle into Emma's spine made Eddie sick.

*

A long time later he heard a taxi draw up and Sharon letting herself in. He had lain in bed, alert to the slightest sound. The day had been going on forever. How could it be the same day that he'd held Lyn naked in his arms? And now there was this new terrifying sequence of hospitals, of the nearness of death. Emma's face was in his head: her straight black hair flying about her cheeks in silky skeins, the white line of her parting, her smile, the feel of her hand in his. Her enthusiasm always thrilled him, linked him with a spontaneity he no longer possessed. When she found she'd been picked for the chorus at her drama class, her pleasure burst from her in her skipping legs, pink cheeks and sparkling eyes.

Sharon entered the bedroom and started to undress. 'What on earth did you start sticking your oar in for?' she said.

'What do you mean?'

'About the lumbar puncture. You were countermanding the doctor's orders.'

'Have you got any idea of the pain of a thing like that? It's only a diagnostic tool and they're prepared to put our daughter through that just because it *might* reveal something.'

'Eddie, how can you talk such stuff? You don't know. Are you trying to say that you know better than the doctor?'

'The doctor isn't fucking God.'

'Eddie, stop swearing. You always think you know better than anyone else, you've always been the same.'

'But how is Emma?'

'She was asleep when I left. I'll go back first thing in the morning.'

'We'll both go.'

'No, there's no point both of us going – anyway, you've got your precious work that kept you out half the night.'

She turned her back to him and burrowed into bed. He

lay there with everything churning through his head – Lyn, the ecstasy; guilt that he was betraying his family, the ones he should put first and support; and now this: Emma's illness. Again he saw the tiny body on the stretcher, the scared dark eyes staring up at him from the hospital bed.

25

Sunday morning loomed up. Lyn rattled around in herself. She hadn't slept well, and when she breathed in, she was convinced her chest creaked – it was bound to be an infection. Immersion in all that black freezing water, heart bobbing, breath strangling – that was the last thing she needed. It wouldn't be a good idea to go training.

Late Saturday afternoon when she'd returned home from work, she'd tried to decide whether she was ill. Having missed Wednesday training, and with Dave Jamieson's honk of disbelief still reverberating in her head, she knew she ought to ring him and say she'd train on Sunday, but she still hovered by the phone. Did she really want to go? Wouldn't it be simpler to forget all about it? As Dave asked her so frequently, why didn't she confine her swimming to the baths as she'd always done before? She pictured those brawny men with big powerful lungs – they were the types who swam estuaries and lakes. Fred's dad, standing there with his baseball-bat arms folded on his huge chest – he had the resilience not to be overcome by the sea. But then there was Fred – Fred's steady voice on the phone. She couldn't let him down.

She fiddled about making coffee, listened to a new CD, pondered whether she should go out with the crowd from work for a drink – but she didn't phone.

The phone call to Dave would go: 'Hi, er, Dave, I'm

actually not well, chest infection.' He could make what he liked of it. She bristled with antagonism. Her hand reached for the phone.

'Yes, it's me, Lyn . . . Yes, I'm up for it tomorrow . . . Don't sound so surprised . . . Yes, see you.' A few jokey platitudes and she hung up. If he'd been matter-of-fact, she might have muttered on about feeling ill, but his surprise that she intended to train had stirred her stubbornness. She would go after all.

With this in mind she decided she wouldn't have a night out, she'd stay in and go to bed early. The trouble with early nights, though, was she mulled over her life. Ed wound in and out all the time. She followed him into his new house on the smart estate. Sharon ran everything according to a timetable. Ed would be stripping wallpaper and then rushing out to take Emma to some class, helping his mother-in-law, the neighbour, friends . . . Sharon was maybe having guests round. You saw those open-plan houses in the evenings at the weekends with cars jammed in the drive and people milling around with wine glasses in their hands. And when the guests went, did they have sex? When she reached that point she began to feel a choking jealousy. But why shouldn't Eddie have sex with his wife?

'Sex,' Aunty Mags had said, 'sex . . .' She still hadn't been round to confront her dad. Just thinking about it made her stomach lurch. Once she'd had her say, there'd be no going back, and she was frightened of what she might uncover. Moiling away in the background was Aunty Mags's voice: 'Oh, yes, I saw your dad and Jackie, and I said . . .' The pictures came of the lonely figure, the girl – she wasn't a woman – wading out in the darkness, feeling the chill rising higher and the soft black mud beginning to draw her under. At home the baby slept. Andy at work must be like her dad – he didn't think of his wife and kids. No, sex turned his brain . . . Was Eddie like that too?

Sunday morning she waited outside the house for Dave to arrive. Although the sun shone, a coldness in the wind made her shiver and think of autumn. The sky seemed very high today. Did she really want to be doing this? The steaming shower back home afterwards would be a reward, and then she'd warm up the thick soup she'd made yesterday and have two crusty rolls with a hunk of mature cheddar. After such a swim you were ravenous.

Dave's car slowed to a halt. She smiled at him.

'Hiya,' he said. 'Thought you might have quit.'

'Come on, I told you I had to work a shift – couldn't help it.'

'All right. I'll let you off this time. It was a good night Wednesday, as it so happens. Quite warm – as warm as it ever can be in there.'

'Don't lay it on, then,' she said, grinning.

'So what are you planning on doing this morning? Is it just the usual dip in and out, or are you going to be a bit more adventurous?'

'You'll have to wait and see.' She gave him a coy smile but realized he'd laid down a challenge.

As usual she gazed out over the estuary while the car glided across the Humber Bridge. You could see for miles on the left, away heading up towards the oil terminal and the Humber Mouth and the North Sea. When her grandfather had gone to sea, her grandmother would have watched for his trawler swaying and rocking on its way back to the fish dock. The women were never allowed to see the men off – it was unlucky. In her dad's album she used to stare at a photograph of Grandad and his mates posing before the camera, and Nan had kept a framed wedding photo of the two of them on her mantelpiece. The estuary had taken him just like it had her mother. Now she understood why no wedding photos stood on her dad's dresser – he couldn't bear to be reminded of the bride he'd killed.

Dave was rambling on about golf – he seemed to play all manner of sports – but she didn't listen and he didn't appear to need any response from her. His muscularity filled the car. From time to time she nodded and beamed.

Grimsby poked up. She loved the shape of the old red brick Alexandra Flour Mill warehouse, made over now into classy flats. The rows of little windows intrigued her. When she spotted it, she knew they'd arrived.

'Don't forget,' Dave was saying, 'the times for outdoor swimming are about fifteen per cent slower than similar distances in indoor pools. You'll not be zipping along at the mouth like you are in the pool – you only need a bit of wind on the water and you're slowed down no end.' He tended to come up with vital pieces of information when you least expected them and you had to squirrel them away for future use. Was he trying to put her off? she wondered.

They left the car and made for the hut. Lyn turned her back to Dave, and he whistled to himself and flung his clothes on top of his sports bag. Two other regulars joined him and also started disrobing. Lyn waited until the men had sprinted towards the dock and splashed into the water. They yelled as the chill gripped them and then they were off, all three doing crawl, steadily gliding through the water on a circuit.

For a second she stood on the slipway psyching herself up for her entry into the dock. She took in its blackness, its fathomlessness, breathed in to the bottom of her lungs and trotted down the slippery planking into the water. The chill paralysed her feet and ankles and moved up to her thighs, hit her solar plexus and she gasped. Her breath pumped in quick bursts – her breathing was shallow and at the top of her lungs. She kicked out and gulped in air. She wouldn't think of bronchioles narrowing to choke her.

She forced her breathing lower and dipped her head into the water, thankful for her cap. Her goggles sealed off her eyes from contact with the water. She didn't like to dwell on the filth or the dead things that might be floating there. Whenever an object drifted by, she worried about what it might be. She couldn't cope with a bird or any other creature. There might even be rats – in fact, that was a definite possibility. Their distended bodies might rise to the surface and bob towards her. What if her hand should encounter one? Ugh! A violent shiver shook her. She dipped her head, then looked at the sky and watched the clouds turning. Head down. Her arms pushed the water back; her legs kicked out, propelling her forward in a long slow sweep. She tried to glide through the water and imagined herself as a dolphin. Her fishy body glissaded down the waves. She concentrated on the smoothness of her stroke and shut out dead rats, decomposing birds and drowned insects.

By this time she couldn't feel her body. It was just there, and she knew it was because it obeyed the messages her brain kept sending. She wouldn't let herself give up, not yet. She must complete a circuit no matter what. When she got home, she'd eat, get into bed and watch a DVD, something nice and soppy. She imagined the warmth and softness of being under her duvet and having a mug of tea at her elbow – she might even take her lunch up there on a tray and eat it while she watched the film. By concentrating on future delights she managed to keep going a while longer, but she knew she was flagging. What if she should find that she hadn't the strength to return to the slipway? She pushed back from the precipice of that thought and struck out for the wooden planking. Of course she'd make it, that simply wasn't in doubt.

Seconds later she was in the hut, standing under the cold shower, which felt almost warm at first. Then she groped into her thermal vest and her tracksuit, anorak and scarf. Next she unscrewed her flask of coffee and poured herself a cupful, sighing with relief. She hoped Dave wouldn't be long, and he wasn't.

'Better today,' he muttered as he made for the shower. She heard him gasping and sighing. The next thing his pink body was naked and jerking with cold as he scrubbed his towel over his skin and fought his way into his clothes.

He was right, she realized, you didn't bother who saw you naked; that didn't seem to matter. Dave was just Dave, a thickset, sinewy man with a swimming obsession.

'You did all right, didn't you?' he said on the way back, over the roar of the car heater.

This was praise, she thought. Usually he seemed surprised that she was still there at all.

'See you Wednesday,' he called as he dropped her off. She nodded and smiled, still thinking she could detect a note of jocularity in his tone.

It was over; she'd done it. She needn't think about it again for almost three days. In the shower she stood for a while just letting the water cascade down her and the tension ease from her shoulders and thighs. Her breathing slowed and she wasn't coughing or clearing her throat. She was so relaxed and so tired, she could barely wash herself and scoot downstairs to fetch up her tray of food.

Today she'd had a breakthrough. Even Dave had seen it. The exhilaration of having managed to keep going longer in the dock gave her courage and made her want to press forward, target this new-found energy on something that haunted her: her relationship with her dad.

She looked at her bedside clock: four. She'd not seen him since she'd told him she knew about her mother's suicide. If she'd gone there earlier she'd have battered him with a hammer, so she'd had to leave it until she felt more in control.

The image of her mother leaving home at night to wade into the water played over and over before her eyes. The figure staggered in the mud. Moonlight drizzled on the black satin of the water. The figure halted a moment and then continued.

That he could have caused this sorrow made her insides boil with rage, and the pity of it forced tears to her eyes.

Her dad would have arrived home from the pub by now and might be snoozing in his chair. If she biked round, she should be able to catch him before he made off to his evening pub session. Nothing was ever allowed to alter his routines. But tonight was going to be different.

You've got to confront him, she told herself halfway to her dad's house. *You owe it to your mother.* But she could hardly say, 'Why did you put my mum through hell because of that cow Jackie?' Or: 'You killed my mother. Why did you do it?' No, it would be too much – besides, he might deny all of it. And if he did, she'd flare up. She couldn't stand any more pretence and lying.

But what if Aunty Mags had made it up? She wouldn't have – she seemed so sure about it. She was drunk, near enough, and that was when the truth came out.

She locked up her bike and rang the doorbell before opening the front door with her key.

'Oh, it's you,' he said, tortoising from his springless armchair and blinking. 'All right?'

'Yes, fine. I'll just put the kettle on.'

'Aye, that'd be a good idea.' He yawned and stretched. 'Must have dropped off.'

He was behaving as though nothing had happened last time. She found she couldn't look at him and was relieved to be in the kitchenette. The TV burbled away to itself. All of her was snagged in a mesh of tension. She could feel the pattering of her heart. It was going to happen: she must force him to admit what he'd done.

Cringing, she dropped a tea bag into her dad's huge white mug, which was brown inside with layers of accumulated tannin. In the past she'd made efforts to remove the stuff with a pan scrubber, but it was hard to shift. He had to have that particular mug; she knew he'd just leave the tea to go cold and throw it out if she attempted to use a clean one.

She came through with the mugs, trying to hide the shaking of her fingers. Tea slopped over. 'Steady up!' her dad said. 'You've made a right mess there, lass.'

'If you had a decent tray it would be easier. Where's that one I got you?' She wasn't going to apologize – she could feel the anger burning in her chest.

'It's about somewhere – anyway, I'm not geared up for visitors . . . There's some biscuits in the cupboard, Lyn.'

'I am not a visitor, I'm your daughter, and I'd like to have been able to use the tray.' She fumbled about among the tins and unearthed a packet of chocolate-chip cookies. 'You don't want these,' she said, 'they're old – I'm chucking them out.' She shot a glance at him, but his face looked as it normally did: red, coarse-skinned, giving nothing away. I've never known you, she thought. I've no idea who you are.

'Waste not, want not. Give 'em here!'

'No, you'll get poisoned.' Part of her thought, Let him eat them, then; let him choke on them. To hell with him! She knew his stubbornness; once he'd taken up a position he wouldn't change. 'Half the tins in your cupboard want slinging in the bin.'

'They've never done me any harm.'

Now she wished she'd never said anything about the wretched tea and biscuits. The moment was drifting away. They'd just sit there in a silence punctuated by some remark he might make about telly and that would be it. *You must say it now*, she commanded herself.

'Dad . . . Dad.' Her breathing stuttered. She floundered. She was fighting that quiet girl who did what she was told and was always fobbed off: 'Go to your aunty's,' it had been. Go anywhere, just so that he didn't have to listen to her. No, she couldn't let him get away with it.

'Look, lass, I've got to get off,' he said, rising. 'Meeting a chap.'

She was thrown by this sudden announcement. 'I need to have a talk with you, Dad . . .'

'Yes, Lyn, but leave it for now.'

'Don't you even care what it's about?'

But she knew he wouldn't ask any questions – he'd make sure he wouldn't get trapped that way.

'All right,' she said, 'I'm going as well.' She left her untouched tea stranded on the table. 'See you.' She went out without giving him her customary kiss. In the yard she hurled the biscuits into his bin, where they landed with a satisfying thud. She wouldn't put it past him to retrieve them.

Raging, she made a wide detour into the city centre. She couldn't go home yet. She had to give herself time to calm down. The Sunday family groups had moved off for tea and the pubbers weren't yet under way, so that all she heard down by the marina was the creaking of masts and rigging as yachts swayed on ripples whipped up by the wind off the estuary. She marvelled that this stretch of water crowded with luxury craft should have transformed the disused dock into a new world.

She stared at the old lightship from Spurn, moored alongside the expensive vessels. Its presence there seemed symbolic, reminding her of her way forward. She wheeled her bike along by the water until she emerged by the former pier, where she stood gazing out over the shiny mass. How different it appeared from this angle. That morning, when

Dave drove over the Humber Bridge and she looked down at it, the estuary shone blue with shifting sandy undertones. Now it was slate-grey, merciless. This was where Fred's dad hauled himself up after swimming across from Lincolnshire. She imagined him powering through those miles of heaving sea, leading, not looking back. She heard Fred's voice narrating.

It came to her then as she stood gazing across the estuary: I'm in a chain of swimmers – first there was Fred's dad, next Fred, then Dave and now me. To hell with my dad! I'm not going to pass up this challenge.

'It isn't only physical stamina you need,' Dave's voice rang in her ears. 'No, you need mental stamina as well – real toughness.'

Fred's dad, a young kid racing through those waves, must have learned that early on, so that when the real trial came – the sea out at Alexandria in the midst of a war – he wasn't broken by all those hours of isolation and terror. Inside him, sustaining him, must have been a core of certainty, a belief in himself. She wished she could be like that, but she knew how fragile her nerves seemed. She had a fear of illness, of looking stupid, of being alone, of rejection, of dying. Out there on the water she wouldn't have anybody else to rely on – like it was at the beginning and would be at the end of her life. So whatever was it in her head, amid all the jittering and jumble, that could hold her together? She hadn't found the still centre yet, but perhaps now she had glimmerings of it.

26

Next morning they both rang into work and said they had to go to the hospital. Sharon didn't have any breakfast, only black coffee. Eddie was glad she spent so long upstairs putting on her make-up, because that allowed him to eat his bowl of cornflakes and his two slices of toast and marmalade in silence. He'd been awake most of the night. What if it was meningitis? What if he should have said yes to the lumbar puncture? He saw Emma's elfin face, her scared dark eyes staring at him. Her skin burned under his fingers and tendrils of hair lay damply against her forehead and cheeks.

'I hope you aren't going to be long,' Sharon said. She'd appeared in one of her black suits.

'No,' he said, 'I just have to clean my teeth.'

They sat in his car in silence. As he saw the glass fang of the hospital rising before him, Eddie wrestled with a vice-like cramp in his stomach. He turned into the car park and had to jolt along through potholes for some distance before he discovered a space. Sharon made no attempt to go to the machine and buy a ticket.

'You needn't have come,' she said just as they were about to slide through the revolving doors. Knowing his retort and her counter-charge by heart, he didn't bother to answer.

The hospital bulged with visitors and the afflicted, and

nurses frisked to and fro with sheaves of brown envelopes. Sometimes an important figure in a white overall plus stethoscope flitted in and out.

Sharon called out to a nurse in an office by the ward. Emma, yes, they could go and see her. She'd had an unsettled night, temperature still up and they were keeping her under observation.

Emma had been placed in a single room, and her bed was by a window. She looked very small, lying there propped up against white pillows that seemed to leach the colour from her cheeks. In the moment before she caught sight of them, Eddie had time to take in how alone and defenceless she looked, and he fought back tears. What if Sharon was right and he hadn't cared enough? Was this God's punishment? But he didn't believe in God. God was just a word used by other people. The last time he'd entered a church was when Benson, a colleague, died of a heart attack and all the officers who knew him went along for the funeral service. Before that it must have been when he and Sharon got married. Sharon had wanted to 'do things properly' and so insisted on a church, a white dress and all the trimmings. But these events had nothing to do with God. They were just a way of gluing life together.

Sharon bent over the bed and kissed Emma. 'How are you, love?' she asked. Eddie found himself blocked out and retreated to the other side of the bed. Emma turned her head to look at him.

'Daddy, why aren't you at work?'

That caught him in the gut, but he managed to smile. 'Thought I'd come and see you instead.'

'When can I go home?'

'As soon as you're better,' Sharon said.

'I don't like being in hospital.'

'You won't be in for long.' Sharon came in with bland assurances, but her forehead was fretted with anxiety.

They were asked to leave for a while because a ward round was in progress, and they sat in a room where several easy chairs had been grouped round a coffee table as in some doctor's waiting room. Down below, traffic pelted along the road and pedestrians hurried by, dwarfed now by the distance.

'I want to speak to the doctors,' Eddie said.

'No, you don't. You'll only start alienating them.'

'You carry on as though doctors have got supernatural powers. If you bothered to read the newspapers, you'd know that doctors need watching. I don't want my daughter's life put at risk because of some stupid doctor.'

'For God's sake, Eddie, there you go again.'

They glared at each other across the room. 'What is wrong with her, then? Do you know? Has anybody told us?'

'They said they're watching her – of course, we would have known already had you not opened your big mouth.'

'That's right – blame everything on me.'

'Eddie, you're shouting.'

'I am not – but the only time you ever pay any attention to me is if I shout.' He sat blazing at Sharon's black stilettos, because he couldn't bear to look at her face. She had put on her usual work gear, he realized – her Human Resources regalia.

The morning dragged by. Eddie tried to find out from the nurse whether the doctors had reached a diagnosis. Nobody seemed to know. They just had to wait and see. Eddie was irritated by the nurse's brush-off. It was as though medical information was a big secret that could not be divulged to ordinary individuals.

Right through the afternoon they took turns in trying to divert Emma. Eddie read from an old Enid Blyton book about the Famous Five going on an adventure, and Sharon tried to interest her in her PlayStation, but Emma said her head ached too much. Sharon went down to the kiosk outside the hospital and returned with an armful of assorted comics, but Emma remained white-faced and listless.

Eddie caught an expression of blankness on Sharon's face at some point in the course of that afternoon, and he sensed the depth of her suffering: she'd be back with those miscarriages, the blood, the griping pains, the feeling of total despair. He wanted to put his arms round her, find some way of comforting her – if only he could make things right with her . . . He looked for concrete solutions to problems, but here there was nothing to be done.

'I'm just slipping out for a bit,' Eddie said at five o'clock, unable to bear another minute sitting by the bed feeling impotent. Sharon merely nodded and carried on with a puzzle she'd laid out on the bedside table.

He walked down the eight flights to the ground floor, glad to be able to move his legs again after a day of sitting still. The heat and the airlessness on the ward had made his head ache too.

Down in the street he took in lungfuls of air and looked about him. The sun glinted on the hospital windows. He slid his phone from his jacket pocket but didn't use it until he was well away from the hospital. He longed to hear Lyn's voice. For the last hour he'd watched every minute, waiting for the moment when he could leave the ward and ring.

Her phone was turned off. Perhaps if he walked on to the train station, went into the buffet and bought a coffee, it might give her time to reach home and then he could dial again.

He stood in the yard behind the station and tapped in Lyn's number, but he couldn't even get her voice mail. No response. Where could she be? She might still be at work. But the baths must be closed by now – or perhaps they were having a late session. She'd mentioned those.

A cool pint with the froth foaming on it would slide down his throat, taking away the hospital claustrophobia.

He could walk into the hotel round the corner, spend no longer than ten minutes and then hurry back to the hospital. No, Sharon would smell the beer on him and that would lead to another battle.

Sharon glanced across as he entered the room. Her face, he noticed, looked tight with strain, and shadows ran from her nostrils to the corners of her mouth. The tropical tan on her cheeks made her look more weary.

'Go and get a drink downstairs,' he said, smiling at her.

'All right,' she said. 'I'll be right back, sweetie,' she told Emma, whose white face pulled into a pale smile.

'Daddy, when am I going home?'

'When you're feeling better,' Eddie said.

Outside in the corridor trolleys squeaked as a woman collected the cups and plates from teatime. She put her head round the door. 'Can't you manage anything, pet?' she asked, looking across at Emma's untouched sandwich and glass of milk. Emma's answer was a shake of her head. The woman removed the glass and plate and the trolley trundled away on to the main ward.

'Shall we play I-spy?' Eddie suggested.

'I can't think,' Emma said. 'My head hurts.'

'Okay, you just rest, Em.' Eddie stared down at the road, where the traffic had started to thin now that the evening rush hour was over. In hospitals the future seemed to be suspended – he couldn't imagine taking up his life again, going to work, locking and unlocking doors; all that belonged to another time. What if Emma had to lie here for months?

'I'm back, sweetie,' Sharon said, bringing a gust of the outside world into the room. 'How are you feeling?'

They remained until late evening, when Emma had fallen asleep. The nurse told them that Sharon could stay overnight, but they thought perhaps it would be best to go home and return first thing. The hospital would phone if

Emma's condition changed, but there was no indication that anything dramatic would happen.

What did she mean, 'dramatic'? Eddie pondered as they clattered down the stairs to the ground floor. The hospital had taken on its night-time freakiness and in the foyer Eddie noticed staggering drunks, one man with a savage gash over his left eye and two girls with the white faces of zombies.

'I don't know what we're going to do,' she said as they ploughed across the car park to find Eddie's car. He heard the despair in her voice, and he took her hand and squeezed it. When he unlocked his car and they climbed in, he saw in the interior light that Sharon's face shone with tears. He seemed to find himself inside her suffering again – the child she'd managed to have after all those long spells in hospital, this much-loved child, was in danger, and she couldn't do anything about it except watch and wait while her heart churned with terror.

He leaned across and put his arms round her, and she sobbed into his collar. 'Oh, Eddie,' she said, 'I can't bear this, it's breaking my heart.'

'I know, love,' he said into her hair. For a long time they continued to sit there, with him holding her.

'I'm so sorry, love,' he said, when they finally drew apart. 'It's awful. Come on, let's go and find something to eat before we go home.'

'Why don't we get a takeaway?' Sharon said. He agreed; he was really in no mood to sit in a restaurant.

'Let's have a look at what they've got in that Thai place,' Eddie said. 'I think they do takeaways.'

Eddie was already out in the street with Sharon beside him when he caught sight of Lyn. She was with a group of men and one girl. He met her eyes and for a fraction of a second they looked at each other, then she turned her head away and they entered a wine bar across the road.

He wanted to rush over and be with her, explain about Emma and how he'd been trying to contact her. But he found himself in the Thai restaurant, standing before the counter. Sharon studied the menu and picked something. He followed suit. They sat on a padded bench by the window, waiting for their meal. Eddie was able in this position to keep an eye on the street. He could see through the front window of the wine bar, even make out the contours of people's heads and shoulders, although he couldn't distinguish Lyn. He played back the view of the group – a big dark-haired chap seemed to be fooling about with her and trying to capture her hand. How dared the bastard do that! To see it all and not be able to do anything – to be left imagining but knowing nothing – it hurt, wouldn't go away, the picture kept on nudging its way back as though it had got stuck. Smithson in his pad must have imagined these things; thought of her with boys on the out. It was what all cons dreaded – the thing that broke men, sent them mad.

The meal was ready. The girl handed Sharon a plastic carrier bag and Eddie paid. Soon they were back in the car and he drove home.

They sat in the kitchen eating the takeaway and drinking wine from the fridge. Sharon's make-up was streaked with grief.

'You go back to work tomorrow,' she said on her way up to bed. 'There's no point in both of us being off.'

Pity and exhaustion hit him. He nodded, but didn't reply.

27

They'd been about to head into the wine bar when Lyn had turned and caught sight of Eddie. Her skin had gone cold. She'd wanted to call out, but then she'd seen the woman beside him – must be Sharon. They were going into the Thai restaurant for an evening out. He hadn't been in touch, not a word, and here he was taking Sharon for a meal. Where before her skin froze, now a fierce heat exploded in her chest and made her face flame. She couldn't bear the sight of Sharon – in fact, once installed in the wine bar with the drinks before them, she'd no idea what Sharon looked like because the shock of seeing Eddie took away her ability to be aware of details. The only impression she retained was of a brunette, somebody small and neat in a smart black business suit. She'd probably go to one of those private gyms and she'd buy classic clothes that were all beautifully lined. Not trendy, just classic.

They must have got a babysitter for Emma so that they could have this meal out. It might be a special anniversary – though perhaps they ate out regularly. She really had no idea what happened in Eddie's private life, and yet she had never felt that until the moment of seeing him and Sharon together. Perhaps she'd been a light diversion, a bit on the side – people always said 'a bit on the side' and then laughed.

'You aren't here, are you?' Andy said, wafting his hand before her eyes. 'Come in, Lyn, are you at home?' He pretended to be speaking through a megaphone. 'Anyone in there, Lyn?'

'Are you buying me another drink, lover boy?' she asked, now smiling into his face.

'Oh, right, a red wine? Bacardi Breezer?'

'Red wine should do me, ta.'

They called a taxi after an hour or so in the wine bar and asked the driver to drop them outside Pizza Hut. Lyn had begun to feel slightly drunk and couldn't stop laughing. Scrunched in the taxi with their thighs jammed up against one another, and Ben saying he thought he might fart any minute if anybody pressed his stomach any harder, she saw them all as a weird family – they spent so many hours together. Being in that building with its tropical heat and its semi-naked bodies preening and showing off, fighting and posturing, welded you together – you couldn't avoid it. You watched the idiocy going on, saw the tricks being played, and then you found yourself repeating them once you'd escaped the baths.

'Remember when we pushed old Kenny in on his last day?' Ben said.

'Yes,' Wes came in, 'and he didn't like it – he says to me before you did it like, "If they try to have me in, they'll find they're going in as well. Nobody's shoving me in."'

'Yer, but I got him in.'

'Aye, but he gave you a clatter afterwards.'

In the restaurant, while the others studied the shiny menus, Lyn followed Eddie into the Thai place. They'd still be sitting opposite each other, he and Sharon. Eddie must carry his emotional life in two quite separate compartments: Sharon in one, herself in the other. It was easy to see how somebody like Eddie could end up in a situation like the one she'd just read about in Aunty Mags's *True*

Life Stories about the couple who'd been married thirty years and then the wife discovered her husband was a bigamist. All those years she'd had no clue about his other family – granted, he had to travel for his job, but even then she would never have supposed that he had someone else stashed away and some more children. And there'd be girls falling in love with their brothers; women being taken advantage of by con men. Her favourites were those about women who went on holiday to the Gambia or other far-flung places, fell in love with handsome fishermen half their age and set up home there on the beach with them. They were followed by pictures of grinning black men, their arms round middle-aged, lumpy white women. The caption would read: 'I love him, but my children think I'm mad.' At least in such cases everything was unambiguous – that was perhaps why the women's kids were so disgusted.

'Hey, come on, Lyn, we've all ordered. What are you having, then?' Lyn picked the plainest pizza she could see and pretended she'd been studying the menu, unable to make her mind up.

After the pizza-gobbling they lurched into a city centre pub. Andy got started on his divorce and what a cow his ex was; Shelly could hardly keep her eyes focused; Wes hoovered down pints .

In the next pub a fight broke out – glasses zipped through the air and splintered. Some shaven-headed blokes laid into one another. Tables crashed over and beer fizzed. Bouncers muscled their way in. Shelly started screaming and Wes tried to comfort her.

They ended up outside in the street, waiting for a taxi.

'I'm proper bladdered,' Ben mused, grinning. 'Well, we did get to see a bit of action, didn't we?'

'I could have done without that. Don't know what these young 'uns are coming to. No respect – they've got no respect. I blame the parents.'

'Yer, go on, Wes, you blame the parents,' Andy chimed in, slapping Wes on the shoulder. 'How's our Lyn?' He switched his attention to Lyn and tried to put his arm round her.

'All right, thank you very much.'

'No need to snap. Your problem is, you're not getting enough.'

'Speak for yourself.'

The taxi swerved up and they all piled in.

'I'm your knight in shining armour, your prince on a white horse,' Andy crooned.

'Why don't you say that to me, And?' Shelly went in her most pleading voice.

'Because I don't want to.'

She howled on Wes's shoulder and he patted her as though she were a horse or a Labrador. Lyn felt too tired to listen to any more. Andy shoved his hand on her knee and she pushed it off.

'Behave yourself, Andy.'

'It's my birthday and you've not sung "Happy Birthday" to me,' Shelly whined.

'Come on, then! Happy birthday to Shelly, happy birthday to Shelly,' Ben warbled in a drunken, raucous voice. Nobody else sang. The taxi driver asked who wanted dropping off first, and that ended Ben's singing.

In a short time only Lyn and Andy were left. 'Don't even think of it,' Lyn said as Andy made to follow her.

'Well, I had to try,' he said, and she saw he was smiling, which was an improvement.

She couldn't shake off the picture of Eddie and Sharon together – of course, it was an encounter just waiting to happen, but that didn't make it any easier. Why should she spend her life waiting for some man? Being with Max had been the same – there he was with years of prison in front of him, meaning they could never be together. Now she was involved with Eddie and again she had to wait until he could see her. She couldn't phone him, must keep it all secret. In fact, she felt just the same as she had with Max. At this time in the morning everything seemed clear to her.

Once in bed her head began to whirl as though she'd been on the big wheel at the fair. Really, she'd have to tell Eddie next time he bestirred himself to get in touch that it was over – they couldn't go on like this.

28

Eddie woke again from the dream where he was running, his pursuer gaining ground on him, but he couldn't move forward because something unseen held him back. Damp with terror, he stared at the curtains. It was all right, he knew he was at home in bed, but the dream took some time to dissolve. When the men had pinned him down during the Restraint and Control training, that same fear had got him in the guts.

After a while he decided he might as well get ready for work. As he showered and dressed, he centred on Emma. Part of him thought he ought to spend the day at the hospital with Sharon, but he couldn't really see the sense in that. Sharon didn't want him there, which created a tense atmosphere. Emma would only be upset.

He hoped Sharon wouldn't come downstairs before he left. He had to be able to phone Lyn today. She was always around. He caught sight of her in the street, but the girl turned and it was someone unknown. At that very moment she'd be skidding to and fro in her little house with Galaxy going full belt as she downed her cornflakes, hair pulled back in a ponytail and her nose beaking.

He didn't wake Sharon, but left her a note: 'Sharon, gone to work. Will phone you later. Eddie.' Only when he'd done that did he remember that mobile phones had to be switched off in the hospital.

Once in his car, he began to wonder why he couldn't write 'Love, Eddie'. With the biro poised in his hand, he'd hesitated over the paper, wanting to end the note some-how – not 'Best wishes' or 'Yours sincerely', that would be mad. This was, after all, just a note. Yet he simply could not write 'Love'. He felt he'd discovered something he hadn't known before and couldn't bear to explore now.

In the car park he came across Mal. 'Hiya,' he said. 'How's tricks?'

'Don't ask.' Mal grimaced.

'Oh, it's like that, is it?'

Staff briefing was just about to start and Bri had taken up position behind his desk. He always liked to play the leader. Eddie hoped he'd get to the point sometime. Bri used twelve words where two would suffice.

'Don't forget to look in the Obs. book. Brown on the twos has been threatening self-harm – we can't ignore it. And there's another kid whose mother has died.' Bri rabbited on. Eddie kept shutting off. How would Emma be this morn-ing? He ought to have gone to the hospital instead of the prison. What if it was meningitis? If she really had got meningitis, then he would have held back her treatment. It would kill Sharon. He began to sweat. Bri was addressing him.

'Eddie, I'm having to ask you to go on escort duty, be-cause three people have rung in sick, and something's cropped up. Nettleton's got to be shipped out ASAP to Lincoln. We've agreed to take one of theirs, Cotter, in exchange. Nettleton's been making threats and he's too well known around here, so he has to go. A taxi'll be here in ten minutes. We've no transport, so taxi it has to be. Mal, can you go with him?'

Eddie saw Mal nod. This was not going to be a bundle of laughs. Eddie tried to readjust his expectations of the day. He hated to have his routine disrupted, and he really disliked escort duty – though he hadn't had to do it very often because Group 4 would normally be responsible.

Down in reception Eddie, still battling with the thought of Emma in hospital, found himself cuffed to Nettleton, a massive baggy-faced chap whom he distrusted. Nettleton's wrist rubbed against Eddie's, and the other man's flesh felt hot and bony. Being shackled to a stranger, someone notorious and unpredictable, was not calculated to make a person feel relaxed. With Nettleton sandwiched between him and Mal, Eddie tried to think of something to say. He could hardly open a conversation with Mal and ignore Nettleton. On the other hand, if nobody spoke the atmosphere would be even weirder.

The taxi was waiting in the forecourt and they climbed into the back. Eddie couldn't seem to escape Nettleton's hunking thighs, and his body wedged against him. Inside, he shuddered with revulsion. He loathed the enforced intimacy of being manacled to this man.

As the taxi driver sped along, Eddie moved into the scenario of Nettleton kicking off. He saw how it would go: Nettleton would raise his cuffed arm and bash the cuff against the back of the seat in an attempt to break it – or he would try to strike Eddie with his left hand. Stop thinking about it, he instructed himself, or you'll make it happen. But what if he did kick off? He often did over nothing – being shipped out could easily spark it off.

The taxi bumped along the scarred road. Eddie felt his shirt sticking to his back. He had to break the silence.

'You all right, mate?' he asked.

Nettleton grunted. 'Gor a smoke, boss, have yer?'

'Sorry, mate, I don't smoke.' If Nettleton lit up he would choke everybody – though if he couldn't smoke, he might kick off, and anything would be preferable to that.

'Here.' Mal lit a cigarette for him.

'Ta, boss,' Nettleton said, and he squinted across at Mal, giving the semblance of a grin.

Cigarette smoke hitting Eddie directly in the face made him feel nauseous, and he had an almost irresistible urge to tell the driver to stop, unshackle himself from Nettleton and walk away. His head boomed. His shoulders tensed. Then, looking across at Mal, he noticed the glum droop of his mouth, the slump of his shoulders. If he escaped, Mal would be stranded.

He forced himself to gaze out at the day. The car drew up at the tollbooth before the Humber Bridge and soon they began to cross it. Eddie stared down at the tea-coloured water, scrawled with currents. He saw the hotel where a long time ago he'd taken Sharon and Emma for Sunday lunch; the viewing area where he and Lyn often met; the track up which they'd run and walked. Every bit of that way was part of his breathing, his moving – it had become an extension of his body. He'd been on that track in all weathers, knew how quickly it could change. The day they got caught in the storm returned to him, when Lyn ran with her hair plastered about her cheeks and her T-shirt moulded against her skin, showing the clear outline of her breasts and the bumps of her nipples. For a while he lost himself in that moment and felt again his intense excitement.

'What they shipping us out for, then?' Nettleton grunted.

'Dunno, mate,' Mal said. 'They don't tell us anything – they just issue instructions.'

'I don't want to go to fuckin' Lincoln.'

'It's only the same as where you're coming from.'

Eddie wished Mal wouldn't argue with the chap – better to say yes and leave it at that. The more Mal struggled to reason with him the more Nettleton would argue. He tried to catch Mal's eye but didn't succeed.

'These old nicks are all the same.'

'Yer, but some's worse than others.'

They jolted past farmers' fields. Crows hopped about on the roadside, pecking. Now and then a tractor rumbled into view. Nettleton peered out.

'There's nowt here, is there,' he remarked.

'Too right,' Eddie agreed.

'Been in Lincoln before – had enough of it. Don't want to go back there. They're cunts – the lot of 'em.'

Nettleton had fired up, and Eddie expected the worst. Any second there was bound to be an explosion. Just let Mal feed Nettleton fags and that might hold the lid on for a bit. Nettleton seemed to be growing restive, shifting his legs about.

'Want another smoke?' Mal came in at last.

'Go on, then. Ta.'

While Nettleton sucked the smoke down inside him like a boa constrictor swallowing a piglet, Eddie relaxed and waited for the next onrush of bile.

At last they arrived in Lincoln, and inside the prison compound, they stumbled out of the taxi. Once Eddie had been unlocked from Nettleton, he yawned with exhaustion. Never had an hour passed so slowly. Nettleton nodded at them as he was led away to be processed.

When Smithson was moved from his dispersal nick on visits, he'd have been cuffed to officers. Eddie imagined them trying to close the cuffs on Smithson's powerful wrists and having problems snapping them shut. The wearing of hand-cuffs really made you understand what imprisonment was. You couldn't move your arms unimpeded – but it wasn't just the physical restraint; the emotional impact was worse. The Americans used leg irons – shackles round your ankles – and now he could see how demeaning that might be.

The morning seemed interminable. They had to hang about waiting for the prisoner to be fetched. As soon as he could, he would phone Lyn, tell her about Emma. Not being able to hear her voice was a deprivation.

At last they were on the return journey. This time he was cuffed to a weaselly, hyperactive little man named Cotter, who wanted to talk all the time.

'Nice to get on the out,' he said, staring out of the taxi windows. 'Haven't been out in a long while. Looks real bright. Can't be doing with them big black birds. They say them – crows, they'll be – mean a death.'

He rambled on, but Eddie was snagged on 'mean a death'. What if Emma were to die? He wished he'd stayed at the hospital – anything could be happening.

'I'm not suspicious like – but I mean, you hear all these things – oh, there's loads. Would either of you two officers have a burn?' His eyes squinnied up at Eddie and then across at Mal.

'Here,' Mal said, lighting him a cigarette and passing it across.

'Ta, sir.'

For most of the journey Cotter rabbited on about his case and how he was taking the prison to court, and how his rights had been infringed and he'd got his lawyer on it. Eddie sat back, thankful that nothing was required of him other than a periodic nod, or a 'Right', or a limited expression of sympathy.

Eddie tried to make plans. His shift finished at five. If he phoned Lyn in the lunch hour, he'd be able to discover whether there was any chance of their catching a few minutes together before he drove down to the hospital. He couldn't rest until he saw her again. The glimpse of her entering the wine bar had made his longing even worse.

As soon as Cotter had been deposited and Eddie could go for lunch, instead of making for the canteen, he told Mal he was off for a run. This time he ran in the opposite direction from his normal route, and pounded towards the city centre. He dodged by pedestrians and parked cars;

turned along by a dry dock lined with mud the colour of bitter chocolate.

Panting, he paused and dialled Lyn's mobile. No response. He tried to text her but couldn't. This inability to communicate could send you mad – he'd seen it too many times among the cons, who kept buying phone cards, getting on their bells in desperation to phone, but when they did get the chance nobody answered except a mocking BT answerphone voice. Three-quarters of the men in the nick were going crazy to contact someone on the out who wouldn't speak to them – wives, partners, girlfriends. In their misery they tore their cells apart.

Eddie ran back, lumbering now with anxiety, not wanting to contemplate what this silence could mean.

29

I'm not going to think about him, she told herself – but over and over she replayed his voice in her head, imagining the tone, both warm and cold, intimate – as though he were in the room with her and in the middle of a conversation that had been broken off. He hadn't been in touch – but of course when her mobile gave out, it had been a while before she could receive calls again.

'You all right?' Dave Jamieson asked just as they were about to enter the changing hut for a Sunday morning swim.

'Yes, course – why do you ask?'

'You just seemed a bit quiet, that's all.'

She was surprised he'd noticed anything. Normally he talked and she listened and he didn't look at her or seem to take anything in about her at all. She accepted that and was relieved at his apparent casualness. Invariably, his probing gaze centred only on any signs of weakening in her. She was growing to value this rigorousness in him because in an odd way it spurred her on – she suspected he adopted this attitude on purpose to make her work harder. Fred was quite different. Whenever she spoke to him on the phone he'd listen and ask the odd question, but in between washed vast stretches of sea and then he'd say, 'Aye, well, keep it up . . . let me know how it's going. Just keep at it.'

'Well, we'll get another few weeks out of this and then we'll have to pack up until next May,' Dave said.

'Why?'

'Lyn, you ask me why.' Dave gave a great bray of laughter. 'Because, basically, it'll be too bastard cold.'

'Oh, right.'

'You'll have to intensify your training or it'll be like starting again from dot one.'

The usual shock gripped her as soon as she immersed herself in the dock, but she struck out, peering at drowned insects through her goggles. She was used to them now that she realized they couldn't float into her eyes or stick in her hair and the dock would wash anything off her skin.

She glided forward, trying to sleek through the water like a porpoise. Sometimes she was a fish, at other times a gull floating on air currents, as she rested on a glide before moving into a kick that thrust her forward. For moments together she was absorbed in the rhythm of gliding and kicking and being part of the water. It occurred to her then that she was in herself, secure in the centre and not crumbling and crying out for help. Fred's dad out in the sea floated into view. He had taken up residence in her head and his sheer determination inspired her. She was swimming in the sea by Alexandria. A war boomed and cracked, and torpedoed ships sank. She swam on.

At last, when she ached with cold and tiredness, she made for the slipway, staggered out and rushed to the hut jittery with cold. Then she was into the usual routine: cold shower to slough off the dirt, a vigorous towelling and a fumble into tracksuit and fleece and a swallow of coffee from her flask.

'You're not doing bad,' Dave said on the way back. This meant of course that she'd made progress.

'You're a tight git with the compliments,' she said.

'Don't want you getting too confident. Wouldn't like you to think it's a walkover.'

'No chance.'

As she sat beside him in the car, her life scrolled back to being about twelve, on holiday at Withernsea with Aunty Mags and a soldier called Terry. She could smell the Calor gas in the caravan and the freshness of grass first thing in the morning when you stepped barefoot down the caravan steps. That was the time she'd left Aunty Mags sunning on the beach, entwined with Terry, and raced down into the sea. The cold hadn't bothered her, and she'd not realized how far out she'd swum until she'd looked back and seen Aunty Mags in the shallows, waving her arms about and shouting. Terry lumbered through the waves towards her. After that she'd been banned from swimming and told to play on the amusements.

Back home again, Lyn beat up eggs for an omelette. She willed Eddie to ring. But perhaps he was tired of her. He hadn't brought Emma for her swimming lesson – the last one until the new session started. Maybe he just didn't want the embarrassment of seeing her again.

She heated olive oil in her stainless steel pan and poured in the eggs. They began to crisp at the edges. She'd read in one of Aunty Mags's magazines that if you really focused your thoughts on somebody, you could send waves to them through the ether. But what if he rang up now, this minute? She'd have to say she'd decided it was over between them; that she couldn't carry on like this, not knowing where she was. It was all right for him – he could just pick her up or reject her like some old shoe. Only that sounded too much like whining. It'd make her seem desperate.

The omelette began to catch on the bottom of the pan. She whipped the pan off the gas and tried to flip the omelette on to her plate. It wouldn't budge. What if she ended up like Aunty Mags, with a head full of ex-partners and boyfriends? Well, at least Aunty Mags was still having fun; she never moped.

Her mobile chirped while she was scraping away at the

burned omelette. Here was the moment of truth: 'Eddie, hi, I'm afraid I can't talk to you any more. I've decided it's over.'

'Oh, Aunty Mags, I was just thinking of you. How are you doing? Come round? Yes, cool. Be there in about fifteen minutes.'

So he hadn't rung. But had she been too hasty in condemning him? After all, she'd known all the time about Sharon, so why had actually seeing them together made any difference? No, she wouldn't get back on that tack. If she did it would all start again – the waiting and wondering and hanging on and speculating. In the end you didn't feel you were alive at all.

'Just thought you'd maybe like to come out for a drink,' Aunty Mags greeted her at the door.

'Yes, I'm up for it.'

'Thought we'd pop round the corner have a little lunchtime bevvy?'

As soon as they entered the pub, the usual chorus of greeting rang out, which Mags answered with a wave of her hand as she tottered to the bar.

'Get sat down, Mags,' one of the bar-proppers said. And, as if magicked from the air, drinks plopped down before them.

Vintage pop blundered along in the background. Cheeks reddened. Smoke twined round the lights and laughter barked and wheezed. Lyn, after several drinks, began to feel spaced out. It was no good drinking like this after training – she'd have to stop it. But then, resurfacing, she focused on the conversation she'd had with Aunty Mags on their last pub outing. She suspected this invitation had arisen because of that explosive meeting, which had obviously unsettled her aunt.

'You know when I was asking you about my mother, Aunty Mags, and what happened, and you said that my dad was involved with that woman Jackie? Well, how come?'

'I told you, they were all after her. When you first saw her you wouldn't have known, like. She had the bust and the wiggle, but it was' – Aunty Mags screwed up her eyes – 'a way she had, real sly. I used to watch her. Some of 'em would say she didn't look owt special, then the next minute they'd have fell.'

Jackie with her sexy figure and sly ways slid in beside the handsome swarthy man and the pale lost girl. 'Haven't you got any pictures of Jackie?' Lyn asked.

'No way.' Aunty Mags sank her gin and stared into the distance. 'I tore 'em up, didn't I – after it happened, like. Wouldn't have been right to have kept 'em.'

'So did you know Jackie, then?'

'Know her? She was my best friend – that's how your dad met her.'

Another piece in the jigsaw. Lyn traced the coldness tingling along her arms and shoulders. Oh, yes, she hadn't finished with her dad yet – she'd force him to look at what he'd done.

'We was at school together, best mates,' Aunty Mags went on.

'Did she ever get married?'

'I told you, I don't know what happened to her – didn't care for her after she did that.'

'And you say my dad didn't meet her any more after my mum drowned?'

'That's right.'

'Because he felt guilty?'

'Well, he must have. Go and get us another one, love. Here, take the money. Get yourself one as well. Bring us some crisps and a packet of peanuts. Get what you want.'

Lyn stood at the bar surveying the snacks on offer and fell to thinking about how people saw her. Because she was tall, they assumed she was tough. She knew she seemed it on the outside, but then inside lurked this insecure person, scared stiff of everything. In and out of the crisps and peanuts flitted Jackie, Aunty Mags's one-time best friend. All these unseen people went bumping along in her head. Max was there too and now she supposed Eddie would join them.

'Did you know,' Aunty Mags said, when Lyn returned with the drinks, 'today was my mam's birthday?'

'No,' Lyn said. 'I'd forgotten it would have been Nana's birthday.'

'I always look at them cards in shops, you know, that say "Happy Birthday Mam" on 'em. Saw one this morning, real bonny, when I went for my paper, and I thought, Oh dear, I've nobody to buy for now.'

Lyn glanced at Aunty Mags and saw how her chin had sunk into its wattles. She didn't look at Lyn but kept her eyes down on her glass.

'Yes,' Lyn said.

The mention of cards and mothers brought back her own pain at being without a mother. The time at primary school had been the worst, when Miss Wilks said they would all make Mother's Day cards. Lyn didn't like to say anything, so she kept quiet and stuck pieces of coloured tissue paper on thin pink card and wrote a message in wobbly handwriting inside: 'Happy Mother's Day to my Mum *xxx*'. When the class took the cards home on Friday, Lyn didn't know where she could put hers. In the end she left it on her desk, but Miss Wilks came after her. 'Fancy forgetting your card, Lyn,' she said. Lyn told her then about not having a mother. Miss Wilks just said, 'Oh dear,' and the card was left where it was on the desk and Lyn went home wishing she were just like everyone else.

She supposed she could have given that card to Aunty Mags, or Nana, but neither of them was her mother and so she couldn't pretend they were. Now she wished she'd given it to Aunty Mags. She squeezed her aunt's arm and smiled at her.

When they finally tottered out of the pub, Lyn's head thumped and she felt she'd begun to float down the street. The trouble with drinking in the afternoon was that you had a sense of anticlimax; you wanted to do something else, but what? Aunty Mags seemed to have arranged some outing with her toyboy for the evening, so Lyn mounted her bike and wobbled off home.

Exhausted, she went up to bed and fell asleep, only to be awakened in the early hours by the sound of something hard striking the bedroom windows. She was yanked upright and breathless. Somebody was out there, trying to get her attention. She hesitated, listening. The pinging persisted as small stones struck the glass.

She slipped out of bed and stood by the window, not wanting to look down and see who might be there. She was in a world of police raids and guns, bodies falling and silence. By twitching a corner of the curtain aside, she could peer down into the street. In the darkness she made out the figure of Andy. She opened the window.

'What's the matter?' she called.

'Feel crap.'

'You'll wake up the whole street if you carry on like that.'

'Come on, let us in, then.'

She wanted to tell him to piss off and not bother her, but she got the idea he must be desperate. He was the sort who might jump from the Humber Bridge. He felt things, then acted, with no time lapse between his feelings and his reaction. She'd watched him often enough to know that. The first time you met him, you thought, 'Wow he's dynamic, exciting, sexy,' and then you saw him bombing from one mess into another and you realized – no, he's a disaster area.

'This is the middle of the night,' she said. He didn't appear to hear. She closed the window, pulled on her dressing gown and padded downstairs. Uneasiness settled in her chest. Why did he think he could turn up at two-thirty a.m. and expect to be let in?

As soon as she opened the door, she smelled the booze on him. 'You're drunk,' she pronounced, not bothering to hide her disgust.

'Straight up, Lyn, I'm not.'

'You could have fooled me.'

'God's honest truth – cross my throat and hope to die.'

At that she found herself grinning, reminded of how when they were at school they'd run a finger across their throat, chanting that line with great solemnity.

She led him into the front room, which at that hour had an unreal, prickly atmosphere. 'You'd better have some coffee,' she said. He flopped down on the sofa and didn't speak.

In the kitchen she made two coffees. Her eyes felt gritty. She'd be useless at work the next day. What on earth was the matter with him?

'Here,' she said, handing him a mug into which she'd stirred three heaped spoons of sugar. Perhaps he wouldn't be so hyperactive if he ate less sugar.

'What's the matter?' she asked. She jittered with tension, wished she hadn't let him in.

'Lonely,' he said, 'and pissed off.'

'You're off your head with booze. I'm surprised one of your girlfriends hasn't taken pity on you.'

'No need to be like that, Lyn babes. She's been a bitch to me. Whenever I say I'm coming to see the kids, she says they're going out and there isn't time. Gets up my fuckin' nose. You don't know what it's like. I've lost everything.'

Lyn saw he was on the point of crying. His face was red and meaty and his black hair gummed with sweat. As he sat there in his tight Levis and white vest that exposed his tattooed biceps, Lyn felt both sorry for him and appalled.

'I'm sorry, Andy, that you're in this mess, but I've got to get some sleep – I'm in for Early Birds and I'm going to be shattered.'

'Let us stay, Lyn, be a star – you can see I'm fucked.'

Her chest boiled with irritation and fear. Women got raped by men they knew, it was never by strangers. He was strong. When they'd had that wrestling match in the taxi that time, she'd had difficulty pushing him off. Nobody would hear if he set on her. She felt seriously spooked.

'No, Andy, I mean it. I just can't be doing with you here. Do you want me to call a taxi for you?'

He made to rise and come across to her, but tripped and coffee splattered on to the carpet.

'Now look what you've done – it'll stain.' Her annoyance halted him. She saw it was the way to go. 'I'm going to have to try to get this off now.'

'It'll come out,' he muttered. An inane grin creased his face.

'Look, am I phoning for a taxi or are you pushing off straight away?'

The taxi saved her.

'Come on, Andy.' He stumbled out of the house. She heard the taxi shoot away and she went to find a cloth to mop the carpet.

At four o'clock she finally got into bed once more. She thought she'd sleep immediately, but the moment she lay down, she began to worry that Andy would make a habit of dropping in late at night. And if he did, how would she get rid of him? Why wouldn't he leave her alone? She needed to make him know that she wouldn't stand for his behaviour – she needed to be stronger about it.

She lay staring at the ceiling, contemplating. Now it was Eddie who was in her head. Eddie, the caring family man, standing beside Sharon as they entered the Thai restaurant. But she knew he wasn't the perfect husband – perhaps he was used to having affairs, although he'd sworn it had never happened before. Really, when she thought about it, by getting involved with a married man she was no better than those pathetic women in her aunt's magazines, who let themselves be so easily duped, all in the name of love. The thought horrified her. *Don't be so spineless,* she admonished herself, *take control; you aren't that helpless.*

30

During the days with Emma in her little ward on her own, fear never left Eddie. Sharon's drawn face opposite him across the hospital bed, accentuated by her pale make-up and her red lipstick, was a skewer driving into his chest. This is going to break our hearts, he thought. The doctors and nurses dealt in platitudes. He felt his temper rising but bit it back. He couldn't afford to alienate them, as Sharon so frequently told him. She had yet to forgive him over the lumbar puncture and he knew she was poised to blame him, depending on the seriousness of Emma's illness. Guilt gnawed away. But it was more than that – he still felt surprised at how disillusioned and embittered he and Sharon had become.

Work was a release from the tension. Being in that glass tower – where it was always hot and airless and everything was impregnated with the odour of medicines, cleaning agents and dinners – paralysed his brain. Eddie rushed to the hospital after work and sat by Emma's side trying to be animated but finding his concentration slipping away.

They had paid to rent a telly, and that chattered away in the silences when they ran out of things to say, and helped hide the shrieking of sick babies nearby and the whining of young children wanting their mothers.

'Daddy, it is so boring in here,' Emma said. 'Really, really boring. It makes your head ache.'

On the day that the doctor decided that Emma could be discharged, they still had no clear idea what the illness had been.

'A virus,' the nurse said, and gave her 'Mummy knows best' smile.

'Give us a shout if you have any more problems,' the departing doctor said over his shoulder as he scurried off to attend a screaming child. Sharon had had an interview with that doctor. 'You let me handle this,' she'd told Eddie. 'You only alienate people.' But from what Eddie could see, she'd discovered nothing, had just been palmed off.

They drove home in the late afternoon. Eddie was silent with relief. He couldn't believe that Emma had recovered from whatever it was. Sharon clucked over her and began to plan the tea menu.

'What do you fancy, sweetie?' she wheedled.

Emma frowned. Hospital life had put a petulant note in her voice. 'I'm not sure – I don't want any *ordinary* things.'

'Like what, angel?'

'No beans or chips or anything like that. Chocolate gateau or chocolate mousse with cream on top or . . . or, I'm not sure.'

Eddie stopped listening. She was all right, that was the main thing. She was bound to lead Sharon a rare dance.

He hadn't been able to contact Lyn. While he was climbing up to the fours in the prison, or checking the locks, bolts and bars, she would slide into his head. She sent spirals of excitement zipping down his body. His mouth was on her throat. The insteps of her feet arched like bridges. She had practically no little toenail. Sitting with her legs crossed at the knee, she poised her dangling foot as she surveyed it. He loved the way she preened, satisfied, checking parts of herself.

They sat at the kitchen table eating a pasta dish. Emma picked at it, but Sharon had made having the chocolate gateau conditional on eating the main course. Eddie had the urge to say she needn't eat the pasta if she didn't want to, and he could feel Emma looking in his direction as she toyed with it. The shadows on Sharon's face stopped him. He smiled at Emma, said how wonderful it was they could all sit round the table at long last. Emma's fork continued to drive clumps of pasta about her plate. Without looking at her he knew what she was doing. If this went on much longer, he'd have to intervene. Couldn't Sharon be thankful Emma was back home and not dying from some frightful disease? Was her memory so short? The fork squeaked on the plate.

'Right,' Eddie said, 'I'll get the seconds. Pass your plate up, little 'un.' He held out his hand for Emma's plate.

'Don't rush her, Eddie. She hasn't finished yet.'

He heard the flatness of determination in Sharon's tone.

'She's had enough – got to save some room for the special cake.'

'Eddie, she needs the protein. You're always contradicting what I say. You never back me up.'

'For heaven's sake, woman, she's just come out of hospital – does it matter that she misses a spoonful of blessed pasta for once?' He found he was shouting, and his hands shook. Sharon retreated into stone. Emma's frightened eyes stared up at him, and he thought she'd burst into tears any minute.

Most of the time Emma had been in hospital a truce had reigned, but now, without warning, it was over. Eddie strode into the kitchen bearing the plates and opened the refuse bin. With a savage swipe he pushed in the contents of Emma's plate. Why must Sharon invariably make him feel a spoiler of home life, a person who had no idea about proper parenting? He wanted to surround Emma with love, make her happy, see her little face light up at some new treat. He didn't want her to grow up as he had, with a remote father and a mother who never dreamed of doing anything spontaneous or in any way unrestrained. The effect of this on him, he realized, was that he was scared of the unbounded, always looking over his shoulder. He watched himself being sensible, never overstepping the limit.

Funny how revelations could come to you when you shuffled food into the bin or got gateau out of the fridge.

He returned with the chocolate cake and some plates. Sharon didn't look at him. Emma studied his face. He noticed how her cheeks were the colour of bread and the shadows beneath her eyes mauve-tinged.

'I don't know whether I want any, Daddy,' she said. His irritation at Sharon made his stomach churn. Why couldn't she have kept her mouth shut? What a controller she was. Must she always be manipulating everybody?

In the end Emma ate a minuscule portion of gateau. Eddie couldn't face it. Sharon refused it too and continued to sit stone-faced opposite him.

Until Emma's bedtime, Eddie tried to amuse her by watching DVDs with her and playing board games. He could hear Sharon on the phone with work. He wished he could see Lyn, but there was no chance of slipping out. They had emerged from a nightmare and he mustn't tempt providence.

He sat by Emma's bed reading her favourite story, the one about the girl called Jinny who discovered she had super-natural powers. From downstairs came Sharon's voice, still on the phone. She laughed from time to time – she'd be on to one of her marathon sessions talking to Di now. No doubt Di and Barry knew all the intimate details of their life.

Eddie, on cleaning officer duties, had to supervise the cleaners as they swept the landings. The men shot about like dried peas on a tray. One minute he knew where they were, the next they'd nipped off somewhere and had to be rounded up. He discovered two of them fencing with brooms by the urinals.

'That'll do, lads,' he said. 'Come on, don't mess about.'

They seemed to regress in prison, and it was hard to think of them as grown men. He caught Mason skimbling off to the twos and yelled after him. The cleaners took this opportunity when everyone else was banged up to push things under doors and deliver secret items to other pads – it was all part of the wheeler-dealing that went on. He'd woken up with a headache and it was still there. Brain tumour? What if it was? Emma's unknown illness had made him nervous.

Lunchtime. Eddie supervised the trundling through of the meal trolleys to the servery. The men started thundering down the stairs with their trays. Some grimaced at the contents.

Once everybody was banged up again and the wing sank back into silence, he plodded over for a meal in the canteen. Mal waved a fork at him.

Eddie went over with his plate of lasagne. 'How's things?' he asked, sitting down.

'We're getting back together,' Mal said. 'Went round to see her, right – the kids have been real upset since I went, like. So anyway, I stayed over. It's going to be all right. I've told her it will.'

'Brilliant, glad about that. What about that case you'd got coming up?'

'Quashed. They've transferred the kid anyway, and they got him to withdraw charges.'

That's right, Eddie thought, everything nicely shoved under the carpet, no probs. And the reconciliation with Sally would last until Mal's eye started wandering again. Though he'd be a bit more careful next time for sure.

*

242

When he had got up that morning, Eddie knew that he would go round to Lyn's house at the end of his shift at eight-thirty. If she was out, he'd leave a note. All day he'd crammed this knowledge down, trying to lose it beneath the welter of routine tasks. The usual voice in his head warned: *You're playing with fire – you're going to regret this. You've seen what it does to other people.*

Pulling up outside Lyn's house, he saw a light in the hall. He ran a hand round inside the neck of his officer's shirt and found dampness on his fingers.

He rang the doorbell and stood back. A year seemed to pass before she opened the door. He'd begun to wonder if she really was at home, or whether she'd left the light on to confuse would-be burglars.

Then she was there. Her cheeks turned pink. He didn't know what to say. 'Oh, it's you,' she said. 'Come in.'

Who would she have been expecting? He followed her into the kitchen and was greeted by the lemony smell of her house. 'Why have you been turning your mobile off?'

She didn't answer. She was looking in the fridge when he went up behind her and put his arms round her. She turned to face him.

'Oh, God,' she said.

They grabbed at each other, gasping. The fridge door banged to behind them. Then she pulled off her jeans, and he shed his uniform trousers and boxer shorts. There they were, he still wearing his white shirt and his navy-blue socks and she her T-shirt. He manoeuvred her on to a chair and straddled it so he could ease into her, but it was too uncomfortable. They ended up on the kitchen floor, with her beneath him and him trying to shield the back of her head from the hard tiles. He groaned as sweetness surged up him, like the reverberation after the sounding of a chord on a piano. He heard her sighing and calling out.

In the silence afterwards, he lay beside her on the tiles.

It didn't seem strange to be staring at table legs and chairs and to have a fridge towering above him.

Later they sat in her front room. He explained about Emma's illness and the long hospital vigils. 'It's been hell,' he said. She said her phone had gone dead and then told him about the colleague at the swimming baths and his late-night call. 'I hate this,' he said, 'and there's nothing I can do.'

'I kept thinking we perhaps ought to call it a day,' she said. 'I mean, it all gets so difficult.'

'No,' he said, 'don't say that – it would be unbearable.'

'I know,' she said, 'but I don't know what the alternative is.'

'Let's take what we've got and have it, enjoy it to the full. There won't be anything like this again.' She was beside him on the sofa, and he put his arm round her and held her hand. She laid her head on his shoulder.

They sat talking, and he knew he'd have to pay for this intimacy. Sharon would freeze him out.

Just as he was about to leave, he noticed the evening paper lying on a chair. ANOTHER DRUG DEATH, the headline screamed, and below it was a picture of Wayne White. 'Oh,' he said, 'Whitey, the poor bastard.'

'What is it?' Lyn asked.

'I was at school with him. He was a heroin addict. Only released last week. That's what they do. They get out and have one mad binge and it kills them. He'll just have turned forty, and his son's in the prison as well.'

When they said goodbye at the door, he felt like crying. Everything was coming at him too fast, all the raw slippery edges of things: Emma's dark, scared eyes; Sharon in the straitjacket of past losses; Lyn with her uneasiness and bright bursts of laughter; Whitey in his Snorkel Parka and Docs and his son with a death sentence. He held her in the narrow hallway as though he could never part from her.

Driving through quiet night streets, he tried to imagine he was down by the estuary staring away at the rippling expanse. The water would go on and on, in an inevitable pattern of ebbing and flowing, whereas he was being tossed about, had no inner rhythm. He breathed in to a slow count, subduing his impatience to be at home in a flash. If he didn't force himself to get home, he had the suspicion that he'd never return.

No lights were on. Sharon had retired into her fortress of silence. The darkness and the frigidity were worse than an onslaught. He put on the burglar alarm, took off his shoes and crept up to bed.

The next day he was up early and she pretended to be asleep, but he knew she was awake because her eyelids quivered. He left for work without their having exchanged a single word. For days now she would ignore him, they'd edge round each other – he knew the pattern. Meals would be torture, but with his awkward shifts he'd miss most anyway. He'd plead with her to talk, but she'd stare at him with those wronged eyes and say what was there to talk about?

He started meeting Lyn in the lunch hours; sometimes driving to the baths and sitting in his car outside so that he could snatch a few minutes' conversation with her and hold her hand, sometimes calling by in the evenings when his shift finished. Being inside the bubble of their meetings helped him to waft through the days. He did the usual things with Emma, running her back and forth to her classes and to friends' houses. She was involved in a new set of auditions, this time for the Christmas production.

'They always take girls like Rosie Crawshaw and Laura Hardy,' she moaned, and Eddie had to console her.

'Well, they might not; it's no good giving up before you start.' They went through this conversation umpteen times.

One afternoon he met Lyn at five-thirty and they drove down to the old pier with the intention of taking their walk along by the new houses out towards the oil terminal.

'I miss you so much when I don't see you,' he said, and held her hand. He would have wanted to go home with her, make love and lie in her bed for hours just being together – but there wasn't time. They had to be two bodies in clothes; two people who'd been to work and must go home separately and spend the evening apart. He turned her to him and started a kiss out there by his parked car, with the autumn wind driving in from the estuary. He pressed his tongue between her lips, worked it round, stuck it against the soft inner sides of her mouth. It was his cock urging its way, parting the plushy lips between her legs, to reach the hot slithery zone beyond. His head spun. Their mouths ran with saliva.

'Oh, Ed,' she murmured, her face against his jacket.

He was home in time for dinner, but immediately he entered the house and saw Sharon, he knew that something was the matter. Emma had to be taken to her drama class after the meal, so he pretended he hadn't noticed anything.

'Daddy, you've not forgotten it's the audition?'

'No, love, of course I haven't.' He watched Sharon gouging at her ham and egg pie, and the point of her knife hovered above his chest. He could feel it ramming into his ribcage, slicing between his ribs. Something was pending. The explosion was bound to happen soon. He hoped she'd let him get out of the house with Emma first, because he didn't want to see Emma's terrified eyes gazing at them while they shrieked at each other. He pushed down a few mouthfuls of pie, but gave up, defeated.

'I'll be leaving the washing-up for you,' Sharon spat as he stood at the door, waiting for Emma to put on her anorak.

'Okay, Em?' he said. 'See you,' he said, but Sharon didn't answer.

'Wish me luck, Mummy,' Emma said.

All the time Eddie sat waiting for Emma at the audition, he struggled with a rising feeling of panic. Exhausted, he yawned repeatedly until his jaw clicked and he wondered if he'd dislocated it.

A series of boys and girls pirouetted across the stage, stood in the centre and sang snatches from musicals. Some forgot the words, blushed and dried up; others, particularly the girls, were like diminutive adults, but he found their knowing looks and the pert poising of their limbs disturbing and unattractive. He hoped they wouldn't be chosen over Emma.

When the auditions finished, Emma appeared. He thought she looked rather subdued and he hoped she hadn't been disappointed – he hated it when she bit her bottom lip and kept her head bent.

'Right, Em?' he said.

'Yes, Daddy – they haven't decided yet who they want. We've got to wait until next week.'

'Oh, right. Well, that's no big deal, is it?' He could see Emma thought it was. She must be trying to measure her chances against all those girls aping the body movements of adult women. Emma wasn't like that – she was a little girl still.

On arriving home Eddie went straight into the kitchen and started rinsing plates and loading the dishwasher. He told Emma to get ready for bed and he'd be up to read her a story.

'But it's early, Daddy. Can't I stay up a bit longer?'

'Not if we're having a story.' At that he heard her rushing upstairs. He hoped he could get Emma settled before Sharon turned up and started a row. He didn't think she was in the house and suspected she'd gone round to Di's. They'd be plying her with wine, and geeky Barry would be telling her about his golf swing or worse. She'd not been saying much about the conservatory lately, which might herald more ambitious projects.

He was at the sink when he heard the front door bang, and a gust of air whipped through the kitchen. Sharon was back. He kept going. Her heels clicked along the floor tiles behind him.

'There is something we have to talk about, Eddie,' she said, 'and you know what it is.'

His gut clenched. This was going to be big. She must have discovered – it couldn't be anything else. He kept his eyes down and continued slotting plates into the dishwasher.

'Sorry, I'm not with you, Sharon.'

'Don't give me that. How long has it been going on?'

'Has what been going on?'

'Don't play the innocent – you can't wriggle your way out of this. I said all along, birds of a feather – you and that Mal, and just see where that's got him. Don't give me any stupidity about you don't know. You do, because I saw you with that slag. I saw you in the middle of the town. You are a bastard, Eddie – I've always known you are. All these late nights – "I'm working." Were you, hell – you were knocking her off. Oh, I hate your guts. You are a liar and a cheat, and I've sat here night after night waiting for you to come back, and look what you were doing. You lying bastard. How dare you be so barefaced.'

'Daddy, you said if I was quick, you'd read a story. Daddy!'

'Not tonight, Emma,' Sharon screeched back upstairs.

'Look, Sharon, I promised – I have to.'

'How dare you! Typical, squirm out of the way when anything gets too hot for you, that's you all over. You have never put your daughter first when it hasn't suited you, so don't try to use that excuse tonight, because it won't wear.

Thought you'd string me along, like I'm somebody who doesn't matter. How long has this been going on?'

Eddie started the dishwasher and avoided looking at Sharon. 'I must go up and read to her.'

'Oh, no, you don't – you're going to tell me the truth. I want to know how long this has been going on.'

'Daddy! Daddy!'

'All right, Em.' He looked at Sharon then. She was white as the fridge and her face was working. It was bound in the end to come to this. He fought a choking sensation and became aware of the blundering of his heart. 'I'll be back in a few minutes.'

'Oh, no, not this time.' Sharon positioned herself in front of him in the kitchen doorway, vibrating with fury. To remove her he'd have to manhandle her, and he dared not trust himself.

'Sharon, for God's sake.'

'Just another of your tricks – tell me, tell me.'

'Daddy!'

'Emma, stop that,' Sharon bellowed. 'Go to sleep. I'll come up later.'

'You shouldn't have done that.'

'How dare you censor me. You are the last one on earth to do that – she is my daughter.'

'And mine.'

'And a fine father you've been.'

'Thanks for that.'

'Oh, no, you aren't going to divert me so easily. How long have you been screwing that slag?'

'I have not been screwing a slag.'

'Come on, it's too late for denials. You can't even leave my friends alone. Don't say you weren't shoving your tongue down poor Marie's throat. What is the matter with you? What a liar you are. Come on, I'm waiting.'

'That's not fair.'

'Fair! When did fair come into it? Is this fair, this lying and cheating?'

Eddie trembled with guilt and rage. She continued to block his way.

After a while she ran down – like a wind-up toy, Eddie thought – and they both fell silent. 'Well, say something, then. Say something. Why have you done this to me?' she asked after a minute or two.

'What can I say?'

'Oh, you have nothing to say? This is so typical of you. You turn the question back on me, make me do the talking. You've never had anything to say, have you?' At that she turned round abruptly and banged up the stairs sobbing. The lavatory flushed, then she moved across the landing and he heard the key turn in the bedroom door.

He slouched into the lounge, head whirling and the taste of acid indigestion sour in his mouth. A drink, that was what he needed, and he went to the cabinet, fetched the whisky bottle and poured himself half a tumbler.

The telly played before him as he slumped on the leather sofa, another of Sharon's credit buys. The whisky hit his chest in a burning stream. Everything had caved in. Emma would have heard their raised voices. As a child he'd heard his own parents rowing – mostly it would be his father in one of his morose moods raving at his mother. You rarely heard her voice; it was always Dad bellowing. He never knew why, and looking back he realized he hated his father for yelling at his mother. She was not allowed to express her own views on things – if she tried to, then his father said she was *arguing*. But she wasn't, she simply wanted to hold an opinion different from his.

He had hurt Sharon, and this whole thing would have terrified Emma. Sharon might want him to leave, and he wouldn't blame her. They seemed to have reached the stage where they had nothing to say to each other. Sharon had long since retreated into disappointment and her way out was her job – he knew she must be good at it, but by the time she'd finished listening to clients' problems, there was nothing left. He'd been unable to think any of this through – hadn't really accepted that one day Sharon would find out about Lyn. Everything now hung in limbo. But the burning sensation induced by the whisky comforted. An inane drama chirped away before him. The next thing it was two a.m. Automatically he set the alarm, snapped off the lights and staggered upstairs into the spare room.

This, he thought, as he lay on his back and stared at the ceiling, was what happened when you betrayed your family. *You don't get anything for free* – sayings of Mal. Of course, he was right. You had two choices: you weathered it out, like his mum and dad; or you made a break for it – that was what Smithson did by topping himself, and Whitey by overdosing.

But he couldn't let Lyn go. Smithson must have gone through hell making his decision, though it would have been worse for him if he hadn't. Eddie had often heard cons say, 'You don't miss a slice off of a sliced loaf.' But they would – they'd all be going insane thinking of their lover with someone else, however much bravado they had about it.

Sharon avoided him and didn't address him unless she had to. She spent a lot of time on the phone. Eddie was glad to be at work. He sneaked round to see Lyn at the end of a shift just after five o'clock two days following the awful scene.

He sat in her kitchen while she stirred eggs in a pan and slotted bread into her toaster. 'Shall I make a pot of tea?' he asked. She nodded. 'It's all kicked off,' he said. 'She must have seen us in town. She isn't speaking at the moment, and I don't know what to say.'

Lyn didn't reply.

They sat opposite each other eating the curly yellow scrambled egg. He'd not been feeling hungry of late, but now he noticed the distinct flavours of the toast and the egg and the tang of the tea, and it was as though his sense of taste had been restored. Neither of them said very much. He couldn't bear to bring his own misery into her life. But he sensed that she knew the score, because now and then she gave him a deep look.

He gazed at her pale, smooth face and loved the runnel beneath her nose; the way in profile her beaky nose made her look plain and then she'd turn full face and smile and her face became devastatingly beautiful. He ached to be touching her all the time. To see her fully dressed, you would have no idea of the symmetry of her body. The long sweep of her thighs and the neat bones of her ankles demanded to be stroked.

'I'll have to get back,' he said, 'and it's the last thing I want to do.'

'Why,' she said, now staring down at her feet and not at him, 'do I have to get involved with people whose lives are so complicated? I hate it – it just tears me apart, Eddie.'

She must be thinking of Smithson, Eddie thought, Smithson in prison for a twenty-year stretch. He would have topped himself because she told him she couldn't carry on, that's what it would have been. Smithson wouldn't have pleaded, he would have accepted what she said but it would have been a deathblow.

'I'm sorry, Lyn. I'm so sorry.'

'Ed, I honestly think we shouldn't see each other again. It can't go on like this, can it? Half the time I've no idea what's happening. I daren't contact you. I should never have got involved with you.'

'Please don't do this, Lyn, please. I know it's what you must have done to Smithson.'

'What?' She pulled away from him and stared into his face.

'It's why he hanged himself. Because you finished with him.'

'What do you know about it?'

He heard the rasp of her breathing, and he couldn't bear the scene that had gathered momentum like some car careering down a slope out of control. Why in God's name had he brought Smithson into it?

'I opened his pad and found him, didn't I?'

Her eyes were wide open and the blue had vanished in the black of her engorged pupils. All he could read there was horror.

'I never finished with Max,' she said. 'Please go – just go. I never want to see you again.'

In a haze Eddie got up, shut the front door behind him and set off on the drive home.

3 1

Later Lyn made her mind up to go round to her dad's. As she biked there, she rehearsed her words. She wouldn't save him. He would get it from her straight: 'Dad, I know why my mother killed herself – Aunty Mags has told me all about it.' At this point he'd try to shut her up, saying it was pointless bringing up the past, but she would press on. She'd refuse to let him slope off to the pub – she'd see that he sat there and heard her out. *I won't leave his house until I've nailed him*, she swore to herself. *If I don't get the truth, I'll have betrayed my mother.*

She gave her customary blast on the doorbell and let herself in. As usual, her dad was sprottling in his armchair before the telly. She took in his mottled face and his general bleariness, and her skin broke out in clamminess. Whenever she went there, he invariably seemed to be waking from a snooze preparatory to taking off to the pub. She'd know her time with him was limited and that gagged her. Was he being even more elusive today than normal? Was he doing this because he couldn't cope? She didn't care. Why should she let him escape? He'd never wanted to listen to her – not ever. He'd ask her a question, just to divert her from cornering him.

'Oh, hiya . . . was asleep . . . must have dropped off.'

She'd ease the way in by making the usual tea and then she'd move in for the kill. 'Are you having a mug of tea?'

'Aye, go on, lass.'

Barely able to look at him, she handed him his hideous mug. This time her hand was steady.

'Ta,' he mumbled, guffling into it.

She couldn't seem to open the conversation. Words jammed in her throat. Oh, it had never been any different. Even when there'd been a special event, a competition and all the kids' dads turned up to support them, he wasn't there. She'd have put herself through hell trying to psych herself up to ask him in the first place, and then he'd never turn up. Nobody had cheered her on.

'Dad, I feel we've never been able to talk . . .' She found the words struggling out. She hadn't meant to start like this. Already she could feel herself getting bogged down. 'You've never really been interested in me and my feelings, have you? Even when I won that trophy – when I swam for the county, you couldn't be bothered to come and watch . . .' Why was she saying this now? Her chest felt tight. She wanted to scream, let it all out, things he was determined not to hear, and that she'd been bottling up inside all her life.

His face looked smooth with incomprehension. 'What's brought this lot on, then?'

'You,' she said. 'You . . . the way you are.'

'Look, I never went to them competitions because I'm not interested in swimming.'

'But didn't you understand what it meant to me? Couldn't you see it was so important to me?'

He stared at the TV screen. 'I haven't had it easy,' he said, still not looking at her.

'What, you mean having a daughter that you've had to bring up without a mother because of what you did?' Somehow she was in it now. The hard knot pressed up in her chest.

'I don't know what you're on about, Lyn.'

'Yes, you do – and I told you last time that we needed to talk about it.'

'Talk?' He looked bemused. 'What about?'

'My mother's death.' Lyn dug her nails into her palms.

'Lyn, we've been over this. I've told you, there's no point.'

'But there is. There is for *me*.'

His face had drawn into that blank, stubborn mask.

'The point is, I've had to grow up without a mother – and you sit there and say now how difficult it's been for you – even though you caused it. And yet it never seems to have occurred to you that I've suffered all my life because of her not being there.'

'What do you mean, I "caused" it? What is it you're trying to say, Lyn?'

'It was you who made her kill herself, wasn't it?' Now all the blood seemed to leave her heart.

His skin appeared to tighten and his eyes bulged. He was struggling to control himself. She saw how his right hand scrabbled on the chair arm, and how he wouldn't look at her.

'What is all this?'

'You and Jackie – Aunty Mags told me.'

Coldness trickled down her spine – it was like plunging into the icy dock. She had to press herself into the chair to keep still.

'This is not your business,' he said after an awful silence. 'You know nothing about it . . . I don't know why Mags has filled your head with this stuff.' His voice was so low it seemed almost theatrical, and she had to strain to hear it. Was this something he'd practised, his way of letting himself off the hook so he wouldn't have to take any responsibility for how he'd behaved?

'Because I asked her, because I'm sick of being lied to and kept in the dark about my own mother.' Her voice had risen and she could feel the hysteria throbbing in it. She couldn't stop blazing back now. He was staring at her. His face had turned from pale to a terrifying puce colour and a thick blue vein in his temples pulsed.

'Just leave it alone. I don't want to hear any more about it ever, and that's my last word, Lyn.'

'That's how you've always been. I've been fobbed off – "Go to your aunty's" – and there's been a quid pushed into my hand – "Buy yourself some goodies." Just to get me out of the way. You never wanted a daughter, did you?'

'You're saying I've not been a good dad? Is that it?'

'It's a lot more than that . . . you've taken my mother away from me.'

She couldn't stop watching the bumping of the blue vein. He might have a heart attack and she'd be at fault. Now suddenly he looked vulnerable, but his mouth was still set in a line. He wasn't going to admit anything. She could tell he'd just go on bluffing it out. He'd said all he was going to say. His apparent fragility was undermining her, and she was in the black waters of the dock, straining to move forward but not able to. A paralysis gripped her limbs . . . fear overwhelmed her. But she was fighting back.

'All right,' she said, 'if that's how it is . . .' She banged her mug down on the table and the tea slopped over. Out she stormed, slamming the door.

She was trembling as she got on her bike. He was impossible. She couldn't break through his defences. She'd never forgive him for this; she'd never go round to see him again. From now on she hadn't got a father.

II

Roll All Our Strength

32

Riding her bike to work on an April morning, Lyn noticed the mild air with surprise. It was around six months since she'd last seen Eddie; months of raw, damp weather. She found herself grinning now at ducks waddling down the avenue by the mermaid fountains. Soon the speckled mother ducks would trundle along with yolk-yellow chicks chirping behind them. Her spirits lifted. She seemed to have been living in a grey tunnel forever. New Year's Eve had been the worst time – out clubbing with the baths crowd and 'Auld Lang Syne' playing, Andy's arms round her and she'd glimpsed the back of someone's head and thought it was Eddie, but the disappointment when he'd turned had forced tears to her eyes. Missing him was a physical ache that had never left her. Aunty Mags's remark about it being sex that had drawn her dad and Jackie together couldn't possibly have been the whole story . . . no, but she understood now the sort of compulsion that could overpower you and go beyond reason, and it was driven by a feeling far stronger than sex. But even in acknowledging this, she couldn't forgive her father.

When Aunty Mags phoned and said her dad had been rushed into hospital, she'd thought: Well, he asked for it. She wasn't going to visit him. But then she'd woken in the night remembering his puce face and the throbbing vein. It could be the end. If she didn't visit him, she might regret it later . . .

Shocking to find him in blue striped pyjamas, clean-shaven, looking alert and drinking tea from hospital cups and not his tannin-encrusted mug. And the sentence was pronounced – either he gave up the booze and the fags or he'd die. No two ways about it, the doctor warned.

'Bring us some Quality Street in for these young lasses,' her dad had said. 'They'll do anything for you – hearts of gold.'

'How are you?' she'd asked.

'Fine and dandy.'

That was it. He'd said nothing about his real feelings, but the blankness in his eyes had killed her anger. He'd made no reference to their last meeting, and it was as though it had never happened. In hospital, contrary to what she'd feared, he'd seemed quite well behaved – chirpy, in fact, with the pretty nurses in attendance. Now, though, she worried about him . . . she mustn't let him slip back and sink into gloom, not with the sun shining and everything new.

Until Aunty Mags's message, she'd been totally absorbed in thinking about her grand plan: swimming the Humber Mouth. Just because there'd been no outdoor swimming since last October didn't mean she'd abandoned the idea. It was always flitting about in her thoughts.

She had trained right through the winter in the baths and the gym, always at the end of the day when they were closed to the general public. She'd swim for miles, alone in the empty pool. Being there by herself strengthened her, confirmed her in the feeling that this was something she was doing for herself, was part of who she was, her sinews, her beating heart, her nerve fibres. She let herself relax into the water, become part of it.

When she thought about it, this waiting for the warmer weather to arrive so that she could phone Dave and resume training over in Grimsby was giving her more time to prepare herself for the big swim. The nearer it got, though, the more she worried. She hated the memory of that first freezing assault as you entered the water, the blackness, the bottomlessness; the sensation of being a fragile object that could easily be swept away. That moment could resurface at any time when she wasn't expecting it. She would tingle with panic that spiralled out from her stomach and extended all over her body. It was up to her. She was creating her own destiny and she couldn't escape from this bundle of nerves and responses that made her who she was.

What had helped her had been the phone call from Fred. Perhaps if she'd got a space, she'd like to come and swim with him at the private pool he used. She met him there every Friday evening and forgot he was in his eighties as she watched him butterflying down the pool, water spangling from his arms and shoulders. She was caught up once more in the awe she'd felt in childhood. He showed the mystery and beauty of water and how a human being could develop a kinship with it. 'After all,' he'd said to her one time, 'we were rocked in the amniotic fluid in the womb – it's who we are.' Swimming for him was an art form. She felt the excitement flaring inside her and she knew she'd keep in her head that picture of him gliding down the pool like some great bird. She'd remember him when she was failing and discouraged.

After Early Birds there'd be staff training.

Lyn had a coffee in the staff room with Ben, who seemed quite downcast.

'What's up?' Lyn asked. She liked Ben. He was a funny, gangling youth, but sweet, with his *K* legs and uncoordinated body.

'Nowt.'

'Go on, tell Aunty Lyn.'

'Shelly – she says I piss her off.'

'How come?'

'I want to go out with her.'

Lyn wished she could tell him that he didn't stand a chance with Shelly; that Shelly thought she was too sophisticated to settle for someone like him. He was too nice, too young, too lacking in guile and tricks. Andy was more Shelly's type, but Andy had other ideas. She didn't have time to say anything, though, because the training session was about to start.

A warm spell came on towards the end of April, and one evening Dave Jamieson rang up. 'You still up for the big swim?'

'Yes, brilliant – of course I am.'

'Tomorrow night, then. Okay?'

It was the same scariness all over again, but not quite. Now she was a lot fitter than she had been way back in October – the muscles in her back and arms testified to that. When the familiar uneasiness tried to swill about inside her, she made herself picture the pool with Fred flying down it; she saw herself too, alone at the baths, storming down the lengths. She was going to crack this one.

'Don't meet things head on,' Fred's voice said. 'Relax into them.'

Still feeling claustrophobic, she decided to go for a bike ride down to the bridge, something she hadn't done for months.

She soon felt too warm in her hooded top, and she stopped to take it off and fasten the sleeves round her waist. Everywhere pink almond and cherry blossom drifted against the early evening sky. Up the dual carriageway she cycled, watching how the weeping willow fronds swayed like pea-green hair. Cars whooshed past, catching her in a buffet of air.

As so often before, she paused at the viewing point, gazing out at the water, taking in its continual slapping and frilling along the pebbles and chunks of rock.

When she heard Eddie's voice, she wasn't surprised. It was as though she'd gone there on that evening because she knew she'd find him.

'Hi,' he said. She turned to look at him. He seemed older, she thought, there was more grey in his hair. 'How are you?'

'Great. What about you?'

'Crap. I've missed you like I can't tell you.'

'Don't . . .'

'I've come down here so often looking for you. I kept thinking I'd bump into you, or see you in the town, but I never have. I've thought I spotted you and then the girl would turn, and it was never you.'

'Eddie, please, don't say this to me.'

Embarrassingly, her eyes filled with tears. He pulled her against him and she buried her nose in his T-shirt. She had his smell in her nostrils. That was a terrible thing, she thought. When somebody you loved died, you lost the smell of them – it could never return. Her tears formed a damp patch on the cotton.

'Shall we have a walk?' he said eventually. 'It's such a beautiful evening.'

They set off up the track, walking side by side, and then their hands came together. She scarcely saw anything around her; all of her was centred in the feel of his fingers inter-laced with hers and the way their arms touched. They didn't speak for a long time.

'I can't believe I've found you,' he said. 'I've really haunted this place hoping to see you.'

He put her bike on his roof rack and drove her home.

Outside Lyn's house he didn't turn off the ignition, but they continued to sit there, neither able to move.

'Come on, then,' she said, and he followed her into the hall and she could sense his nearness right up her spine. A kiss started there, a kiss that made a pulse throb between her legs. The kiss landed them in the front room on the carpet, dragging off their clothes.

She bit his throat and his shoulders and he licked her breasts, traced the faint line of down from her belly button to her triangle of reddish hair. He licked her there too, lapping between her legs, while she stretched on her back in a gasp of pleasure. Then he was up on his knees and she felt his cock on her belly, and the kiss started again as he lowered himself into her. All of her exploded in a shower of silver particles in her head. She gave a great shudder, and her scream and his groaning mingled.

Eventually they staggered up from the floor and struggled back into their clothes. 'Maybe we should have tea,' she told him.

They sat side by side on the sofa, eating toasted teacakes and drinking tea. 'I can't believe I'm sitting here with you,' he said.

'Same for me,' she said. 'It's like magic to be able to do something so ordinary together like scoffing toasted teacakes. Other people just take this for granted, but it feels really special.'

'They're the best teacakes I've ever tasted,' he said, kissing her.

She didn't tell him that she'd sometimes dreamed he was making love to her and on waking had been devastated to find it wasn't real. But the dream sensation would creep back into the day at work, tormenting her.

'I wish I could spend this night with you,' he said when he was about to leave, 'and wake in the morning to find you beside me.'

'Yes,' she said. 'I just feel as though you've been wrenched away.'

In the hall he kissed her goodbye. She didn't want to see him go and couldn't watch him drive away, but returned to the kitchen to wash up.

After months and months of yearning, it had suddenly happened. He'd been there, she'd smelled his flesh, tasted him, felt his arms round her, the pressure of his weight. And then they'd been like two married people drinking tea and chatting – only they weren't. And now, just as quickly, he'd gone – it was as though he'd never been there. Only he'd drunk from that mug, eaten from that plate.

There was, she thought, no point in resisting this – it was something that had to happen. During the months when they'd not seen each other, she'd asked herself why she was so attracted to him. Down by the estuary they'd sometimes walked in silence and it hadn't seemed awkward. He never needed to rattle on and make daft jokes. With Max she'd not been able to be quiet. That Eddie didn't criticize Sharon or complain about his marriage had shown her he was different from all those men she'd heard railing against their wives in the years before Max. She'd never been able to respect them because of their lack of loyalty.

From the start of course she'd been drawn to Eddie's body – not that it was flashy, in your face, like Andy with his weightlifter's strut. In fact, with his clothes on he was quite understated. Stripped, he was all lozenges of muscle, and seeing him naked always made her want to explore those firm contours with her fingers.

In one vital respect Eddie was quite different from how Max had been. Max had lived life on the hoof; ate fast, didn't have a lot of patience. Eddie, she suspected, was like her. He liked to take his time, wasn't the sprinting type, reacted more slowly to things but they stayed with him.

He didn't jab at life, he spread out into it and was thought-ful. Eddie had a steadfastness – he wouldn't be knocked off course. She could imagine herself growing old with him, which she'd never felt about Max.

Hugging herself, she went to sit outside the back door and sat gazing up at the night sky and the first early stars.

33

Caught up on a gust of euphoria, Eddie drove home. The miracle of having found Lyn didn't allow him to think of anything else. He went back over the moment when she'd turned to face him – she'd looked so ecstatic, and he'd caught that smile he'd first seen on the photograph. Not until he was about to enter his estate did tension pincer his chest. If Sharon suspected anything, it would be the end. He must think of an excuse – how come he was missing for more than two hours in his running gear? She was bound to accuse him of something. Why was he so craven? What the hell, so what if there was a row?

The car wouldn't start when he wanted to drive back. Then why didn't he use his mobile and tell her? He never took his mobile when he went running.

The lights were on and the curtains not closed, and he saw her sitting in the lounge with Di.

'Hi. Do you know, the bloody car wouldn't start.' He had to get it in first, before any accusations started flying about.

'Oh? What was it, then?' Sharon asked. He saw the tight set of her mouth.

'Not sure – it's done this to me once before. I'll have to have it into the garage. I had to get a chap to let me use his jump leads.'

He noticed they were well down a bottle of white wine. 'Hi, Eddie.'

He smiled at Di. 'I'll just have a shower, then I'll be with you.'

He'd escaped, but found it hard to sleep that night with a fear that everything would blow up all over again. At the same time, he couldn't contemplate a future without Lyn. She felt so dear to him, a part of him as he was of her . . .

Lying wakeful, he asked himself why he and Sharon couldn't leave each other. She, after all, was dissatisfied with him. He'd never advanced beyond basic pay, and then there was the rest – the niggling little things about him that she said got her down. And for him? He'd found himself living beside someone who had changed from a lively, hopeful girl into a joyless woman. He supposed what cemented them was their shared history. But the life they had together was strangling him and wouldn't release its grip. They'd outgrown each other, only they didn't want to admit that relationships did wear out. As it was, they were set to tear each other apart. He could see it coming.

All those months when he hadn't seen Lyn had been a waste of house-viewing, the aftermath of a gut-wrenching scene with Sharon where she'd broken down. 'Oh, what's wrong with us?' she'd cried, and they'd held each other, both sobbing. He'd been staring at a lost dream and he sensed she'd been doing likewise. He'd tried to tell her that all the debts were choking him, wanted to say that trying to keep up with Di and Barry was ruining them, but he didn't. Their names would have been a trigger. And so the time when they could have spoken honestly was lost and the moment passed. He'd promised they'd move; that he'd never see Lyn again. They were going to make another go of it.

Now, looking back, he could hardly believe that evening had taken place. He felt he had been bullied into making promises, while she carried on as before. And now there was the added strain of her mistrusting eyes always on him.

The prison had grown increasingly crowded, sharpening the atmosphere of tension. On the day following his evening with Lyn, Eddie ran into Mal as he drew his keys.

'Guess what,' Mal said, grinning.

'No idea.'

'Got some good news.'

'Oh, yer?'

'Sal's having another baby – it's a late one but, I mean, lots of women today have babies in their forties, don't they?'

'Congrats,' Eddie said. 'Tell Sally congratulations from me.'

It was so predictable. By the time Sally was far gone in pregnancy, Mal would be having another fling with someone, probably a colleague. There were umpteen chances on away-day sessions; it was all about propinquity. Mal with his ear jewel and his Harley-Davidson was signalling to any blonde young enough to be his daughter.

'It'll be great having a new baby around – makes you feel young.'

Eddie said nothing, remembering the broken nights and early mornings and the feeling of being disembodied through lack of sleep.

Mal and Sally. Eddie thought of himself and Sharon. The baby would shore up Mal's crumbling marriage until the next time. And he and Sharon? She was making him buy a new house.

Up on the fours it was stifling. He worked along the landing opening up the pads and checking the locks, bolts and bars. Some cells were in darkness and the inmates in bed. Everywhere smelled of sweaty trainers and unwashed feet. Sometimes inmates lounged on their beds staring at their chirping television screens. These were the men on basic, with twenty-three-hour bang-up and no privileges. Mostly they were familiar faces, druggies, most under thirty with a sprinkling of old lags thrown in. The relationship he had with them was peculiar – guarded and yet jocular, but at times he had to be the confessor. With people like Smithson, though, there could never be any bridging of the divide: cons from dispersal nicks had usually taken some punishment in the course of their prison existence, and it was only hatred that had stopped them losing their minds. For them, Eddie knew, he'd always be a fucking screw. He wondered if there was any other job entailing so much ambiguity, so much negative feeling. This could make you become a 'con hater' or a 'sympathizer'. He supposed he'd cultivated detachment, but now he felt vulnerable, his emotions too near the surface.

Way up on the fours, with the giant fans in the roof scudding humid air over him, he sweated with panic. His heart hammered – he wanted to be in the open, not penned up. He made himself stand at the landing rail and breathe in deeply. This was stupidity; he was getting worse than the cons – soon he'd be whingeing to everyone else if he didn't watch it. Oh, but he wanted a different life, to retrain, to be outside . . . and he'd never have that life now, not with the debts.

Going home was no escape – they were meant to be viewing a house this evening. Sharon had now decided that this was her all-time favourite. It meant that he couldn't get to see Lyn. The thought of not being with her made him feel hollow inside. They'd not said when they'd meet again, because he didn't know when he could get away.

The appointment was for seven, and six forty-five saw them sitting in Eddie's car, waiting for the estate agent to turn up with the keys. This was a modern brick semi, a neo-Georgian number with pillared front and a double garage, a stone's throw from where Di and Barry lived. The garden had been landscaped and was an arrangement of paved paths and small beds planted with all manner of dwarf conifers. Everything looked very neat and controlled.

The estate agent swerved up in his Merc and oiled his way along, with Sharon beaming and nodding. They progressed from room to room, with Sharon saying, 'Well, of course we'd have to decorate this – the paper's too dark as it is.' Eddie knew that this meant *he* had to decorate the rooms. He sighed, acknowledging that from this one there could be no way out. Emma danced from room to room. She liked the house because it meant she wouldn't have to change schools and it was near where her friends lived.

'We'll have to buy a new stair carpet – this is really garish,' Sharon said. Eddie pretended he hadn't heard. He wondered how on earth they could possibly manage to pay for all this. He thought of his father's advice: 'Always live within your means, lad.' They'd be up to their necks with this lot, and if the value of property dropped, they'd lose a lot of money.

When they left – with Sharon running on about how they must go into the estate agent's tomorrow and get things tied up because the owners wanted a quick sale and somebody else was after the property as well – Eddie had to say something.

'You know if we buy now, we're buying at the high point. There's every chance it'll devalue soon, and then we'll be lumbered with this massive mortgage. Basically, love, we can't afford it.'

'Barry says this is a good buy.'

Before he could prevent himself, the words were out of his mouth. 'Like those shares that are now worth about a quarter of what we paid?'

'Oh, just because it's Barry – you're always the same, Eddie. As soon as Barry gives us some advice you have to discredit it. Barry couldn't know that the shares would drop, could he?'

'Look, it's his job – he's dealing with money all the time. I sometimes think if Barry told you to jump off a cliff, you would.'

'Are we going to buy the house, then?' Emma asked.

Eddie glimpsed Emma in the rear-view mirror, twiddling a strand of hair round her finger like she did when she was feeling upset, and he tried to control himself.

'Yes, poppet,' Sharon said, defiance in her voice, 'we are going to buy the house.'

34

'So what have you been doing with yourself today?' Lyn asked, looking at her dad zonked in his saggy arm-chair, eyes trained on the TV screen. The jolt of his col-lapse had pushed the row to the back of her mind, though it remained there like a bruise. Some things you couldn't change, only accept. She'd decided that she must call on him daily after work to make sure he didn't slide back into his pub routine. All the time she was at the baths she thought of him ambling about, aimless, not having any-where to go. She knew he'd lost the centre of his life. The doctors could just dismiss it as an 'addiction', but that wasn't how her dad would see it. 'It's given him a shock,' Aunty Mags had said when he was in hospital. But now, a month or so later, the jar to his system might have worn off.

'Oh I went out for a walk, like . . .'

'Where to?'

'Round and about.'

'Dad, for goodness sake!'

'What?'

He did look at her then and a smile pulled at his lips. She examined his colour. Thank God he'd lost that awful bleeding-steak look. 'So where did you go?'

'This feller I know, old Spike, from two doors up, said as I should go and see him – so I walks up to his allotment.'

'What was he doing, then?'

'Planting stuff – looked like bloody hard work to me.'

She handed him a mug of tea and made further attempts to draw him into conversation. 'Did he give you those vegetables on the draining board?'

'Hm, what . . . ? Oh, yer. Says it's something called purple sprouting – you don't cook it much.'

'Do you a hell of a lot more good than all that tinned stuff.'

He didn't appear to be listening. She thought she'd have to go round one evening and make his dinner using old Spike's vegetables. She needed to look after him. When she'd seen him in the hospital and heard the doctor's ultimatum, her eyes had filled with tears. However dishonest and vague he'd always been, he was still her dad, her only really close blood relative – even the callousness he'd shown towards her mother couldn't change that. He'd been there all the years of her growing up, a fixed point, not listening then most of the time either, but there nevertheless.

'Why don't you ask if you can have a plot, Dad? I could just fancy some stuff that's not wilting and dried up.'

'Don't know about that.'

'Here. I've brought you some Hobnobs, and they aren't out of date.'

Momentarily roused, her dad smiled and nipped up several biscuits. 'Ta, lass. Can't stop eating since I quit the weed. My cough's only been worse since I stopped – can't see the point really.'

'Go on with you.' She left him soon afterwards, saying she'd be back the next day, and instead of her ministering to him, what about him making her some tea – not with tinned peas and potatoes, though. He didn't seem to register what she'd suggested, but then surprisingly he nodded.

'Maybe, but I don't want any complaints, right?'

*

Wednesday, and she was in Dave's car bound for Grimsby and training in the dock again. Radio 2 bumbled in the background and Dave crooned along to himself. The atmosphere was matey.

'Dave,' she said, when they were driving over the Humber Bridge, 'what really made you start swimming, then?'

He glanced at her, smiling. 'Oh, I'd have been about six, something like that. I was on a seaside holiday with my mum and dad and the tide was coming in and I kept going off down these steps and trying to dog-paddle a bit holding on. My dad was one of these guys used to taking important decisions – engineer, you know – he looked at my mother and he said, "That lad's ready for lessons with Fred" . . . and you know about Fred, don't you?'

'Yes,' she said, grinning. 'We both belong to Fred.'

'That's right.' He barked with laughter. 'Anyway, it just went from there – swimming at school but nothing in particular. Didn't really get involved again until I joined this sub-aqua club, must have been in my twenties – and it was that made me get into long-distance swimming. I was used to pacing myself over a distance. I liked feeling water, using it to my own advantage. I reckon it's like martial arts – you know, where you use the power of the other person to overcome him. You don't bash and thrash, it has to be smooth. Reminds me of what Fred used to say: "Look at 'em, they're like bloody egg whisks in the water – they could use all that energy to go forward faster." He'd be looking at these younger fellers bombing along and he'd know next minute they'd be finished, all their energy used up beating the water.'

Dave hadn't talked about himself before like this, and she found herself focusing intently on everything he was saying. The idea of using the water's power to overcome it stopped her in her tracks: yes, this was what she'd sensed already. You couldn't fight with water, you could only go with it, bend to its sinuous coiling . . . if only she could find a way to make that happen.

'When you watch Olympic sprint swimmers like Fred they're smooth until the last length and then they put everything into it – they just about die on the finishing line, don't they?'

She liked it when he talked about swimming; it made him light up. It had been the same when Fred delved into his stories about the Humber Estuary and his dad.

'You can tell, you know, from the way people move in the water, whether they're swimmers. You should have heard Fred when he used to get on about some of 'em – he called it "the Barmston drain kick" and the "Madeley Street roll". "Oh, there goes a Barmston kicker," he'd say. It's when they don't breathe in the water and their bodies roll. You see, in the nineteen thirties and forties kids couldn't afford to go to swimming baths so they swam in the drain, and they'd be kicking the weed off their legs.'

They'd crossed the Humber and were running through flat arable country when Lyn, staring straight before her at the road, said, 'Dave, I really want to try to make the swim this summer . . . I just feel I'm like all geared up for it.'

'When you can stay in the dock for three to four hours at a time, you'll be ready. You know what I've told you, you'll be going about fifteen per cent slower than in the pool and let's say the swim was three miles, you'd need to prepare to swim over three and a half. You have to take weather conditions into account, and of course you won't be swimming in a straight line. And, more important than anything, you must pace yourself – it's no good going all out at the start and then running out of steam.'

'Sure,' she said, 'but I reckon I can do it.'

'Okay,' he said, grinning, 'we'll see.'

Four solid hours in the dock – wow! It had been amazing

at first if she'd managed forty minutes. It was no use paying any attention to what the other swimmers said about the temperature – those brawny blokes always reckoned it 'wasn't bad', whereas for her it was like being locked in a fridge-freezer.

When Dave had parked up, he turned to her in the car. 'Just one thing, missy – don't force yourself beyond the limit your body can take. I know where my limits are because I've learnt 'em. I pack it in just before I get the warning signals. You've got to learn when to stop. If you go on too long, you can't hold a cup or speak and your teeth are rattling like castanets. Mind you, when you first climb out the water you feel marvellous, got a rosy glow – but it doesn't last – and then it's payback time. You never, ever go into a hot bath straight after to warm up – that can do your internal organs in. So watch it.'

That day she stayed in the water one and three-quarter hours and felt dissatisfied with herself. She ought to have gone on longer, but she'd scared herself stiff when she hadn't been able to feel her feet and hands and she could see her flesh had turned plum coloured. She'd let Dave's warnings get to her.

When she got out she walked up and down fast for a couple of minutes, as Dave had told her, before making for the hut.

'I disgust myself sometimes,' she confessed to him on the homeward run.

'How come?' He swivelled an amused eye at her.

'I could have gone on longer today, but I let myself get frightened so I got out.'

He laughed. 'That's not bad,' he said.

Now she wished she'd not said anything. Dave giving her instructions was fine up to a point, but sometimes all the dos and don'ts had a paralysing effect – instead of listening to what her body was saying, she was centring on

Dave's words. You needed to plough on, despite all the dire possibilities.

'See you Sunday,' Dave said, and he was gone.

One afternoon getting towards the end of the session she was on the poolside with Andy, and only a couple of swimmers were threshing up and down. Installed on the observation chair, Lyn had retreated into a run out to Spurn with Eddie two evenings ago. Sunset, and it had been raining earlier on; now the sky was washed with rose quartz and opal. They walked along the beach on the estuary side, his arm round her waist. She saw them pausing in a kiss, felt the surge of desire. It'd seemed to her the most perfect moment ever – as though they were part of that landscape, that vanishing kingdom. 'They say it'll have disappeared in five years,' Eddie said. 'The sea will have washed it away.' It's like us, she thought, and she could have wept at the fragility and strangeness.

'What you dreaming about?' Andy said at her elbow.

'Spurn,' she said, trying to cover up her shock at being returned to the present.

'Pull the other one!'

'Well, what's so weird about that?'

'There's nowt out there.'

'There's the sea and the birds and the rocks and the lighthouse and all those rare plants.'

'You're a bit in the head, you are – who wants to go and look at the fucking sea? I see enough water here and I'm pig sick of it.'

She'd been on the point of telling him about her plan to swim the Humber Mouth, but now she knew she wouldn't. There was no point – he couldn't understand and he'd be belittling as well, trying to undermine her, as though there weren't enough negatives to struggle against in her life.

Even after that he pestered her again, wanting her to go

for a drink, but she said she must visit her dad, which was the truth. Staggering how he could imagine she'd be interested in him after he'd told her all the guff about his love life. He couldn't grasp that she might find it a turn-off. With him it was all about the chase, not about *her* at all.

In bed one Wednesday night after a swim in the Alexandra dock – when she'd been jubilant but exhausted, having pushed her time in the water up to two and a half hours – her sleep was disturbed by a persistent cough. First she turned on one side, then on the other, but still she coughed and her throat felt like sandpaper. If this developed into a major attack it would be too annoying.

Unable to sleep, she found herself going through the swim again and wondering how she'd ever manage to reach her target time in the dock. Then her dad and Jackie flitted back to haunt her, and the poor young woman, her mother, walking out into the silt and sinking all alone with nobody to care. She tried to remember herself at the age her mother was when she died – she knew she'd been desperate to find someone to love her, but already she'd got no illusions.

For her mother it must have been different. She'd fallen in love with that older man, his pencil moustache and his ease with women. She must have believed in love, felt it to be once and for all. He'd married her and then she'd discovered the betrayal. She was an innocent, had invested everything in handsome Jim and couldn't cope with finding out how love might include deception. In her grief she'd walked into that streaming and flowing, giving herself to it, joining her tears with it.

But what about her dad? He and Jackie were a pair – earthy, excitement-grabbing, people who enjoyed life on the surface – whereas her mother, Elaine, was the slim, introverted orphan, caught up in a passion that had sapped her life. Only her dad wasn't really this extrovert he'd seemed with Jackie. Dad didn't let people behind the façade, or had his guilt driven him in on himself?

For hours Lyn lay awake examining a past that wasn't her own and she didn't fall asleep until a few minutes before her alarm clock rang.

Next day she cycled to work still coughing and feeling breathless. By evening she was feverish and went straight to bed, but coughed so hard she couldn't breathe. They'd find her dead in bed – maybe she'd lie there for days before anybody discovered her. And she didn't want to die now, just when she was going to swim the Humber . . .

In the end she had to phone Aunty Mags, who came puffing round and rang for the emergency doctor, who prescribed antibiotics and steroids. Aunty Mags stayed the rest of the night, trotting upstairs next morning with a mug of tea and a jug of lemonade.

'How are you, our Lyn?' she twittered. Without her usual warpaint she looked strangely rubbed out, and her panda eyes had smudged into lopsided bruises down the sides of her face.

For a week she could do very little except sleep, and when she finally came downstairs she sat in an armchair. She'd phoned into work to tell them she'd be off for a while. When she rang Dave she was almost despairing. 'It's really knocked me out,' she said. 'It'll take me ages to get back on track . . . I'm so weak. I couldn't do a width at the moment.'

'Well, kid, you'll have to leave it for a bit. Take it easy, just forget about swimming. Ring me when you feel able. Sorry, Lyn.'

Being stranded like this made her tearful. One afternoon, much to her surprise, her dad ambled round. 'Your aunty said as you was badly, so I've come to have a look at you,' he said. 'Let me make us a brew – I'll find the stuff.'

The tea when it came tasted stewed, but she said how good it was. He'd discovered the biscuits and she watched him dunking a digestive into his mug. Was he still keeping off the bottle? He was much paler – a good sign.

'How are you, then, lass?'

Lyn pulled a face. 'Don't ask.'

He was obviously making an attempt to cheer her up, and he launched into allotment politics. 'We have a brew-up, you know, in the shed, mid-morning like, when we've been having a dig.' He rumbled about vandalism, and shows in the autumn his mate wanted to enter.

The next evening Eddie came by after work. He brought bunches of grapes and a box of mangos. 'I've been worrying about you,' he said. 'How've you been?'

'I just feel so weak,' she said, 'and like breathless all the time.'

'You'll have to stay off work until you're properly better. They aren't hassling you, are they?'

'Oh, no, it's nothing like that – no, it's something else.' She saw he was looking at her curiously. 'You see, you'll probably think I'm mad, but I want to swim the Humber Mouth. I've been training for ages in the dock in Grimsby. It's like a major thing. Now I wonder if I'll ever do it. I bet Dave Jamieson, this swimmer who's been helping me, thinks I've chickened out. I'll feel I've let Fred, the Olympic gold-medallist, down too. I daren't ring him.'

'Oh Lyn, you're amazing! You've really surprised me. It's terrific. You'll not let this setback get you down – I've known you long enough to see that. You're an awesome girl, and I love you for it.' He hugged her to him and she told him how it had all started.

After Eddie's visit, the next day her self-doubts began to drift away. Every day she got up for longer and pottered about, walked to the shops, did a few exercises at home, tried to eat more.

The first day back at work she felt wobbly and knew she couldn't chance the dock yet. It took a further two weeks before she rang Dave and said she was ready for training. 'Some of the lads at the club asked me if you'd got fed up,' Dave said on her first day back, 'but I knew you'd be back – you're too keen to pull out now.'

'Too right,' she said. 'I've told you, whatever happens, I'll do that swim.'

'Well, missy, you know the score. But you're a toughie, I can see that.' He was smiling at her and she thought she detected a slight change in his attitude to her. He seemed involved with it too now, wanting her to succeed.

Dave had told her everything for the swim was being arranged by the club. She didn't have to do anything, just be there and swim. He thought she'd be pleased, and she was, but the more she pondered about it, the more she wanted to have a stake in those arrangements. On a blazing Tuesday afternoon Lyn decided she'd cycle out to Port House to see a chap in the hydrographic office. She'd heard about it from Dave and knew that the club had been in touch with them.

All the way there it was really hot and dusty with the lorries churning up the mud from some roadworks, but going into Port House she got wafted in the face by the air-conditioning and everything seemed refrigerated. She kept wondering if she was doing the right thing, and then an obstinate voice in her head insisted it was her swim and she ought to know the exact details of it.

Inside, the imposing décor made her think she'd entered a strange land. The plants in troughs had been polished to a high gloss. The walls were studded with photos of coast-guard vessels. Even the lines of chairs with their high backs looked important. She was told to go through and speak to the men in an inner office. A collection of antique men sat peering at huge maps. You would never think that a piece of water could employ so many people. They were very polite, and one of them fetched her a chair.

When she said what she'd come for the man looked at her as though she were insane. 'Oh,' he said, 'far too dangerous, far too dangerous – you wouldn't do anything like that – nobody does that nowadays, more sense.'

'But they do. I mean, I know this chap, Dave Jamieson, and he's swum it a few times.'

'Well, I haven't heard of it and I really advise against it. You don't know how dangerous the estuary is. And you'd be risking not only your life but other people's as well. There's enough problems without this sort of thing. Thank you for your enquiries, but I really don't think we can help.'

So he was giving her the brush-off. She stood up, muttered thanks and left, shivering in the air-conditioned chill. *Stupid idiot*, she upbraided herself. And you thanked him too! You just took it all meekly, let him tell you what to do . . . That's you all over, let yourself be pushed around. Get in there, say you've got to know.

With flaming cheeks, she made herself walk back through to the office where the men sat studying the maps. She expected any minute to hear someone asking her what she was doing. The man who'd shooed her off surveyed her over his half-glasses in surprise.

'Yes?' he said, his face puckered with irritation.

Don't start apologizing, she told herself. Firm but pleasant.

'I really meant what I said earlier. I need to know some details about the Humber Mouth crossing.'

'I've already told you, you're making a big mistake thinking of such a thing, madam.' His expression became peevish and cold, and he turned back to the map he was studying, clearly wanting rid of her, but she stood her ground. His next tactic was to try to blind her with a lot of technical stuff and measurements she couldn't follow. This was worse than a complete refusal to give information.

'You'll have to spell it out for me,' she said at last. 'Just tell me simply, please.' She drenched him in a sweet smile. He didn't know how to react, but seemed to decide that the easiest way to shake her off was to tell her baldly.

'All right – be it on your own head. You want a neap tide, that's when the high and low water are somewhat near each other. Spring tides are once per fortnight. You want the least tide you can get. The lower neap tide is once a month, and we know exactly how high it'll be.' He fiddled with a paper clip and wouldn't look at her.

'Thanks for that. So, when would be the best time to make the swim, then?' she asked, pressing home her advantage.

'It's five hours before high water at Immingham and it'll be slack water at Spurn – the tide flows down the coast into the river. When the water's going up the channel it's at its most dangerous because it's flowing so fast. You can't swim against the tide. You have to angle across it – you swim across, not against.'

While he talked, he kept staring at a map, pointing with a pencil, and he only brought his head up now and again, just like a tortoise glancing about. She felt the waves of his disapproval hitting her.

'You'd be swimming due west, but swinging south – that way you wouldn't be fighting the tide. The tide takes you up the river,' he said, staring at her over his specs like some professor in a TV drama. 'The temperature would be about eleven degrees. But I'm not encouraging you. This is a foolhardy enterprise.'

'It's a pity you look at it that way,' she said, and for a second their eyes met. That was when he told her there was only one time she could make the crossing – and that turned the whole thing into a mission, brought it into immediate focus. She had to be sure to swim at that particular time or she couldn't do it this year. The date was August the second, at five in the evening.

In a bound the swim was upon her. For ages it had been in the distance, an aim, something to be striven for. Looking back, she realized the catalyst had been that newspaper cutting she'd found at Aunty Mags's. From then on she'd been driven, her energies centred on it. All that training had changed her, given her an edge and opened up the world for her. She felt this new confidence supporting her as she faced the man.

'I hope we won't be dragging you out of the Humber,' the chap said as she was leaving, and he even gave her a tight smile.

'Oh, no,' she said, smiling back, 'you'll not be doing that.' She sensed he was revising his opinion of her. She was buoyed up by the realization that she hadn't let herself be fobbed off this time, and she was on her way.

35

'We should be getting the keys next week,' Sharon said. 'I can't wait to get in there. We seem to have been messing about for so long.'

Eddie was thinking about Lyn. How could he wangle it to come home late tomorrow? He could say he'd been asked to work another shift. Sharon didn't seem to suspect anything if he told her in advance that he'd be late. The worst was when he turned up at nine or ten and should have appeared at eight.

'Eddie, you haven't heard a word I said, have you?'

He became aware of Sharon staring at him in irritation. 'Sorry, I was just thinking.'

'What about?' She centred on him now, and he felt the curiosity in her scrutiny.

'Just about work, really – some kid we got in last week.'

'Oh – well, anyway, you'll have to take time off for the move. We need to get this properly planned. So don't start swanning off anywhere. I've told Mum we're up to our eyes so you can't help her this week, and I've told next door you can't help with their concreting.'

'But Sharon, I promised . . .'

'Ed, you can't expect me to do everything. Once we get the keys, you could start the decorating, couldn't you? I mean, we need to have some rooms decent before we move in.'

'It'll be difficult,' he said.

'I don't see why.'

'Work. And I promised your mum I'd help with the tiling.'

'You've no need to now – I've told her. Ed, you're always running around for someone else – what about us? And if it's not that, you're drinking with that ghastly Mal.'

Eddie felt an immense bubble of rage expanding inside him. He didn't want to wallpaper and paint stinking hard gloss. He loathed the fumes and they never seemed to disperse. And when they'd sorted the new house, what then? What would be the next goal?

At least Emma was thrilled at the move. Perhaps he just had to keep quiet for her sake. If only there weren't all these things – the house, the furniture, the mortgage, stuff on credit cards – things Sharon tired of way before they'd been paid for.

'Okay, but I told my mum and dad I'd pop up there this evening – they need some heavy stuff shifted in the garden and I can't get out of it.'

'What stuff? I'm sure they don't need you. We've got loads of work to do here – we ought to start packing, and I wanted to pop round to see Di.'

'Can't you take Emma with you?'

'I don't want to make her late for bed.'

'I've simply got to go. I promised.'

'You're always making promises without any consultation. You don't take us into account, Eddie, and you never have.'

'I shan't be too long.' He kissed her cheek and smiled.

He was backing his car out into the road before she could make a rejoinder. His shoulders had knotted up with tension. He felt like an escapee. At any moment he expected an Alsatian to be sinking its fangs into his legs. He hadn't had time to phone Lyn and tell her he'd be round. If she wasn't there, he knew he'd be gutted. He must see her, hold her, smell her skin, her hair, get into the essence of her. Not being able to touch her hurt. Since their reunion the thought of not being with her was driving him crazy.

What if Sharon should ring his mum and dad and discover he hadn't gone there? If that happened the game would be up. He tried to examine the consequences, but all he could think of was Lyn. He was prepared to gamble everything on an hour with her.

No light shone in her front room – but then again, it was still daylight. Just let her be there. He rushed to climb out of the car and dropped his keys, groped to retrieve them. Standing before the front door, he took a long breath and pressed the bell. He listened to its ring inside the house. Perhaps she was working. Her shift pattern was about as erratic as his was. Why hadn't he phoned before he set off? But he couldn't, not with Sharon in the house. He shouldn't have assumed that she would be in. Unable to accept that she wasn't at home, he rang again and then he heard someone approaching the door. Lyn stood before him in cut-off jeans and a T-shirt.

'Oh, Ed, good job I heard you – I was out at the back watering my plants. They get dried out in this weather.'

'I'm so glad you're in – thought you weren't – was just leaving. Got away, didn't expect to. Oh, come here!' He caught hold of her and pressed her against him.

'Ed, I've got earth on my hands – you'll get messed up.'

'Bugger that!'

'Come and see what I've been doing.'

He followed her through the hall, into the kitchen and out into the yard at the back of the house. He stood at the door, staring out in delight and surprise. Here was no garden, but she'd transformed a mean oblong yard into a green wilderness, with shrubs twining from bowls and creepers swarming up the walls on trellises. Eddie compared this with the elaborately landscaped gardens beloved of Sharon and Di. They were the work of professionals and were controlled and tamed. This had been looked after with a tenderness and an eye to detail that amazed him. He hadn't seen this side of Lyn before.

'Do you like it?' she asked.

'I think it's paradise.'

She fetched them both a drink and they sat in basket chairs at the back door as dusk fell. He started to tell her about the looming packing and the move. Normally he rarely spoke of his life with Sharon, but on this evening he found himself unable to keep silent. She listened for some time and then she spoke in a very low voice.

'Eddie, you know you'll never leave Sharon – sometimes I've thought you would, but now I know you won't. You're in it too deep. It's too late.'

'What, you mean because of this bastard house? I never wanted to move; I've been manoeuvred into it.' He thought how weak he sounded, how defeatist. 'But I shall leave her – it's just a matter of time, of letting Emma grow up a bit.' He listened to himself, despising the way his life seesawed back and forth. When he was at home with Sharon all he could think about was avoiding detection, protecting himself from her anger. But on the other hand he couldn't live without Lyn. Only the thought of her enabled him to get through life with Sharon. Without Lyn, he knew now, his life would be a wasteland.

'Eddie, I've gone into this with my eyes open – I knew you were married from the start – I've only got myself to blame.' She sat beside him, twisting the end of her ponytail, and he saw a fat tear fall on her bare leg.

'Oh, love, I am so sorry. Oh, God, please don't cry. I never wanted to do this to you.'

'No, but this is what's happened. I've never felt able to

talk about it before, but tonight it all seemed to come into focus. You know my mother drowned herself when I was a baby – well, later I discovered she did it because my dad was having an affair with a woman called Jackie. When I heard about it, I went to my dad and accused him of killing my mum. It was awful. But now I'm just like that Jackie, no different. I couldn't understand how my dad could have carried on seeing her once my mum found out and he promised never to see Jackie again. It's like I've known in my head that I must stop our relationship, but I can't – I've been in it too deep. When we split up before, we should never have got back together.'

'Lyn, I'd no idea about your mum and dad. Finding out must have shattered you. I don't know what to say. And your mother's suicide, that's almost too harrowing to bear.'

'That's just how it is – I go cold every time I think about it.'

'Love, I can understand your feelings, but please don't talk about us splitting up.'

'We always seem to reach this point . . .'

'Don't you love me? Is that what you're telling me?'

'Eddie, love doesn't come into it.'

'It does. This is not some sordid affair. I've never felt like this about anybody.'

The twilight lay in blue drifts over the green wilderness, and he took her hand and held it fast. He thought that if he tried to speak he would cry. Her mother's story reproached him; it explained the sadness lying behind her smile. She was brave, a person with a deep seriousness – the Humber swim was more than just a swim . . . He couldn't help but admire her determination to swim that hazardous stretch of water no matter what. Never before had he felt how inextricably connected to him she was. A blackbird perched on a brick wall and sang, and the notes seemed more rounded and clearer in the dusk than in daylight.

'I'd better go,' he said, and they both rose and went into the kitchen, fingers still entwined. In the hall they started to kiss. He strained her against him, lost in the softness of her lips, the satin of her mouth.

In the bedroom they clung to each other. The wetness of her mouth was on his neck. He slid his fingers down her back, reached her waist and travelled lower, pressing her buttocks so that her thighs rubbed his. They were molten. Her breathing was ragged. He had to control his frenzy and the longing to be in her and voyaging in the wet warm fishy place that would suck him down and pleasure him. He dallied with her, though the force of the moment outside, the thought of separation and parting, made him want to grasp every last vestige of now and hold it fast. And woven into that too was her mother's story. Lyn had shared with him a terrible thing – he had looked with her over the edge of a precipice, and the sorrow bound them together in a way he hadn't thought possible.

He yearned to fall asleep with her in his arms, hold her safe, but he dared not. Already it was late and he sped home, dreading the confrontation that he expected. But the house was deserted and Sharon gone with Emma to visit Di. He exhaled with relief and went to wander in the dark garden.

About him he still felt the ecstasy of that scene in the bedroom – it was almost within reach, but not quite, and he was still insulated from the tensions in his own house by the atmosphere he'd carried with him. But there was also a sadness. He couldn't shake off the mother's death, nor dismiss the burden that it placed on Lyn. He felt he wanted to be alone to think it all through – life was rushing at him too fast.

He jumped at the sound of Sharon's voice calling. 'Eddie, what are you doing?'

'Coming,' he shouted back, now tensed against a new attack.

'What on earth were you doing in the dark?'

'Getting a breath of air.' Not a good idea to say 'nothing'.

'You could have got on with some packing. Emma's gone up to bed. It's too late for a story now, and it's no use her complaining. Your dad's not sent any tomatoes, then?'

'Oh, yes, he did. But I forgot to pick them up.'

The phone in the hall started to ping. Eddie made for it. 'Oh, hello, Mum,' he said. Sharon was almost at his elbow. 'Yes, yes, everything's fine – yes.'

'Tell her about the tomatoes?' Sharon hissed.

Eddie ignored her and carried on talking. 'Did you want anything in particular?' He realized this conversation didn't sound like that of someone who'd been at the house that very evening. Sharon hovered in the vicinity. 'I think I can hear Emma calling for you,' he said, turning to her.

As she mounted the stairs he continued to speak with his mother, weak now with the relief of having averted a crisis. 'I'll pop round tomorrow,' he said, 'see if I can pinch a few of Dad's toms.'

'Oh, they're not doing very well, love – he says they've got something called black spot.'

Eddie's head whirled. He'd have to clear off and buy some tomatoes tomorrow, but Sharon wasn't daft. She could tell the difference between supermarket and home grown.

How could he possibly carry on living like this, with Sharon policing his every move, and him having to be so careful to cover his tracks?

36

'Now, Lyn love, with the weather being so nice and you having been badly, why don't me and you have an away day to Scarborough?'

Lyn could hear the enthusiasm burring in her aunt's voice. 'Be lovely,' she said. So that was how on a Tuesday morning, instead of sweating it out at the baths, she was climbing into a black cab organized by Aunty Mags. 'We'll do it in style,' she'd told Lyn. 'Make it a proper day out.'

Aunty Mags, already ensconced in the back seat, chortled at Lyn as they were decanted at the station, 'This is the life, our Lyn!'

The train buzzed along, calling at every little station en route. Lyn peered into gardens and at double-glazed conservatories tacked on to houses. She loved this unimpeded view into other people's lives. Aunty Mags divided her attention between her magazine and anything that caught her eye through the window. 'Some of these lasses show everything they've got,' she remarked as a girl passed in a pair of jeans clinging to the lower reaches of her backside. 'If she bends down, they'll drop off ... and I mean to say ...'

In between the villages stretched fields, and Lyn watched shadows chasing across them, cows flicking their tails as they munched. At Bridlington passengers with rucksacks strapped to their backs staggered out lugging suitcases. By

Bempton she sensed a change – the sea seemed nearer although invisible. Scabious and fuchsias grew in a border by the track, and purple-headed teasels poked up over a wall. The nearness of the sea brought a new excitement to the air, a suspense, as though they were waiting for an event.

'It's a long while since I've been out here,' Aunty Mags said, touching up her ruby lips in her compact mirror, attacking Lyn with the pungency of her perfume as Scarborough station loomed up.

They clattered out in a straggle of holidaymakers, day-trippers and students.

'I remember going to that cinema once,' Aunty Mags said, pointing across the road at the Stephen Joseph. 'Fancy, it says "theatre" now. Who was I with? Oh, yes . . .' Lyn saw her trying to draw back from saying any more.

'Was it a boyfriend, then?' she prompted.

'No – no, it wasn't – it was that Jackie. We had a day out, her and me, summer holidays it was. We'd have been fifteen, just about leaving school. Went to a matinee and then down to the beach, like – there was a fair on. She got off with this gypsy.'

By this time they were crossing a main road. Aunty Mags tottered alarmingly on her strappy gold sandals, and Lyn had to hold on to her. 'That bugger nearly took me leg off,' Aunty Mags yelled as a four-by-four shot past with a man brandishing his middle finger at her. They were stranded in the centre, with cars zooming in both directions. 'I can't run, you know.'

'You don't have to, Aunty. We just stand here until it clears.' Lyn wished she could have heard more about the long-ago Scarborough visit, but for the moment that topic seemed to have closed down.

They reached the pedestrian precinct and joined the crowds making for the sea. 'Look, some caffs down there,'

Aunty Mags trilled, restored by the sight. They turned off down a side street and Lyn traipsed after her aunt into a café promising morning coffee and lunches.

Aunty Mags stared round at the clientele, mostly grey-haired, genteel ladies. She snorted but pressed forward to the glass counter. 'I'm going to forget my diet today, love. I'll have one of them cream cakes; what are you having?' Lyn restricted herself to a cappuccino and a biscuit.

'Have you seen your dad lately?' Aunty Mags asked as fluffy peaks of whipped cream engulfed her mouth. 'I've been too busy to get round there.'

'Yes. I'm just hoping he'll not slide back into pubbing again.'

'He's drunk all his life, Lyn.'

Lyn guessed Aunty Mags had only asked her about her dad because she wanted to know whether they'd made up after the awful scene. She didn't seem to realize that things with her dad weren't like that. Life just rolled on and you didn't analyse what had happened.

Getting down the road to the seafront proved to be hard work. Aunty Mags swayed and lurched, almost keeling over. They passed a William Hill's, an arcade of junk shops, charity outlets, a joke shop, dark-looking cafés, tatteries.

A blind chap thundered away on a keyboard while a dog slumbered at his feet by an empty tin. He struck up 'Teddy Bear' and Aunty Mags insisted on ferreting in her handbag. 'Lyn, love, put that in his tin,' she said, doling out a pound coin.

It was hot. Dogs yapped, children yowled and music blasted from the amusements and the few fairground rides. Behind them was the harbour, where boats chugged to and fro. Everywhere reeked of hot fat frying. Gulls mewed like babies. Lyn gazed at the sea, blue and glassy before her. This was what made the day worthwhile. Families were encamped on the beach and one or two children had ventured to where the waves were breaking. Nobody seemed to be in the water.

'Let's have a paddle,' Aunty Mags said, taking off her sandals. 'They've bloody crippled me, have these.'

They stumbled along until they reached the damp sand where the sea had washed. 'Oh, it's cold,' Aunty Mags said as the waves met her toes. 'No wonder they're not swimming. Eh, but it makes me feel six again!'

Wandering along beside her aunt by the water's edge, Lyn felt happy. Aunty Mags had an uncomplicated way of enjoying everyday things, and her pleasure seemed to spread out and rub off on Lyn. Wavelets on her ankles, sand between her toes and a breeze on her cheeks; the headland, blue ahead of them; and far out at sea, the ghost of a vessel – what more could she ask for? This sea was benign, caressing. It returned her to childhood day trips with Aunty Mags and the thrill of seeing all that enticing water frothing away before her, fizzy drinks, ice cream that dribbled down your fingers, deck chairs, a new plastic bucket and spade . . .

Later, when they were sitting in a fish-and-chip café with white pot plates of mighty haddock and chips steaming before them and a metal teapot in the centre of the table, Lyn smiled across at her aunt. 'This was a great idea.'

'Nice bit of fish,' Aunty Mags ruminated, smiling.

'What happened with that fairground lad and Jackie?' Lyn asked.

'She had a big snog with him and he wanted her to join the fair and stay with him. Thought I'd never get her back home – was last train at the finish. She'd no sense. I liked lads, course I did, but I knew what would happen to her if she stayed. It'd have been bare feet, no knickers and a load of kids in a stinking caravan to boot.'

They finished the day in the station buffet, where Aunty Mags dispatched several gins and lemon and Lyn treated herself to a glass of red wine. All the way back Aunty Mags snoozed and Lyn read her aunt's *True Life* magazine and luxuriated in the fascinating stories about the sixty-five-year-old widow who fell for a twenty-one-year-old Iraqi asylum seeker. Then there was the forty-year-old woman's discovery that her husband led another life as transvestite Annie, and looked ravishing in high heels and a miniskirt.

The following evening Lyn swam in the dock as usual, but on the way back from training, Dave suddenly turned to her. 'Look, Lyn, don't get into that state of mind where you think if you don't get to swim the mouth on the allotted day, that's it. I went three times to Spurn expecting to swim, but I couldn't do it – weather was too bad, winds too high, massive waves. Just had to come away.'

'I hope that doesn't happen – I'd be heartbroken.'

'Okay, it might not, but you have to be prepared. That's what they mean when they say the Humber's tricky.'

'I suppose . . . oh, but I just want to get on and do it.'

'I know you do – you're determined, kid,' he said, turning to smile at her. 'I've seen that.'

The car interior swam in a pleasant fugginess and Lyn relaxed, staring out at the summer evening until Dave, letting his thoughts run on aloud, jerked her out of her lethargy.

'I've wondered all along why you were up for this – at the start I did, anyway. Thought perhaps you were a bit of a dreamer. Then I got to see you were like me – you've sensed a challenge, you're competing against yourself, and you can't rest until you've conquered it.'

Lyn laughed. She wanted to tell him he was only partly right about her – this wasn't just about proving to herself she could do it; this was for her mother, and for him and most of all for Fred and his dad, a line of swimmers extending into the past. But she couldn't explain it. In the end she didn't even try. Perhaps it was better to let Dave believe what he wanted.

'Remember what I've told you – never thrash the water, because water's hard. Enter the water with your arms, keep it smooth; use the water, never fight it. And don't give it your all at the start.'

'Yes,' she said, 'I reckon I've come to feel that. I got the idea the first time I ever saw Fred swim – I was a little kid and he swooped up the pool like this great bird and he hardly caused a ripple on the water. He can still do that even now; it takes my breath away. But having seen how it ought to be didn't always help me. I used to get really frustrated because I wanted to fly like that and I couldn't.'

It came to her then that the most valuable thing she'd learned through all those months of training was not to run away when she was scared, because if you ran once, you'd keep on running. If you turned and faced whatever it was, at least you'd have a chance of overcoming your fear. You wouldn't like it at first, but you'd master it. She'd done a lot of running in her life and she'd been fighting this really brittle person who did things to be liked and accepted, was scared stiff of being rejected. She'd tried to please rather than dared to follow her own inclination.

Yes, she thought, I shall go through with this because the water's my world and I have to find out . . . go beyond what I know and what other people expect of me.

Two evenings later Lyn met Eddie down by the foreshore. It was quite late, and only a few dog walkers were about. They strolled along by the water, beige now and shot through with silver, as it squirmed and rippled along the silt and pebbles. Stones and chunks of rock glistened blue-black in the evening light. He didn't seem to want to talk, just to hold her hand and listen to her speaking now and then about swimming and her dad's slow recovery.

'He's getting quite excited about things he's grown from seed – broccoli and peas – and he looks like a piece of mahogany.' They both laughed.

As it grew later a stillness fell and all they could hear were the occasional squawks of seabirds and the boom of cars like North Sea breakers away on the Humber Bridge.

He looked at his watch. 'We'd better go back,' he said.

It was then that they saw an owl flying out of the trees. The reeds stood motionless, the estuary gleamed pewter and the waves washing on the shingle were scribbled with silver.

He caught hold of her and held her against him. They were enveloped by the strange hush everywhere. She felt his warm mouth kissing her and his body pressing against her.

'Tonight's been one in a million. Thank you,' he said as he dropped her outside her door. She turned and went into the house, still caught in the evening's enchantment.

The next evening Lyn received a surprising phone call from her dad.

'Hello, lass – want to come round? Thought as you might like to have your tea with me, like?'

She took a roundabout route, reaching the yellow-brick terrace where she'd grown up about fifteen minutes later. A savoury smell greeted her.

'Come on then, lass, get sat down.'

To her amazement, Lyn saw that he'd actually laid two places at the table. Normally he'd eat his meals balanced on his knee in front of the telly. He didn't belong to the sort of family or generation where men cooked, and now here he was with a meal all freshly prepared.

New potatoes, emerald-green broccoli and roast chicken steamed on her plate, over which her dad poured some dishwater-thin gravy.

'Now then, what about that, our Lyn? Admittedly I haven't sussed this gravy business out yet, but . . .'

'Fantastic!'

'That broccoli and them tatties are from the allotment.'

'Dad, this is fantastic – everything tastes loads better than shop . . .'

'Aye, I'll have some runners ready soon. Slugs have been a bugger. A lot of 'em on the allotments don't like pelletin' 'em because of the birds. It's mostly younger end, ones with kiddies – teachers, you know, them sort of people, who go on about it. Old 'uns like me and Spike hear 'em rabbitin' on about environmental this and that, and he just winks at me.'

'Dad,' Lyn said when they were washing up, 'I've got something to tell you.'

'Oh aye?'

She thought she heard apprehension in his voice – he'd be expecting her to come out with some sort of tirade against him.

'I'm going to do this open-water swim – the length of the Humber Mouth. It's all fixed up.'

'Eh, what's that, then?' He stood at the sink, his hands in the sudsy water, and twisted round to look at her. Lyn studied the side of his face, waiting.

'I'm swimming the Humber Mouth.'

'Bloody hell,' he said, 'fancy that! I thought you'd broadened out a bit when you first came in. Got some rare shoulder on you now, lass. Yer, you always was a bugger for water . . .' He didn't seem to know what to say next, and he turned and was beaming at her. Then it tumbled out. 'As it happens, lass, I'm very proud of you.'

She didn't have to force herself to hug him. Spontaneously her arms went round him, and they stood together holding each other.

She cycled home, trying to fit together all these different

people who were her dad: the one who let her mother die; the boozed-up joker of her childhood and teenage years; the lathe operator who came home in a boilersuit with grease-smudged hands and washed at the kitchen sink, making wushing noises as the water sprayed off him; the pensioned-off dad falling into dereliction; and now this man who spent hours in the open air and had just discovered fresh vegetables. They were all Dad, and she had to accept him – even the way he'd lied to her mother.

That moment in the kitchen before he spoke had brought the tears to her eyes; she'd felt him reaching out to her, wanting to show he valued what she was doing. He couldn't ever have spelled it out. It came to her then as she pushed her Yale key into the lock – he had to make his jokes and keep everything bobbing along or else he wouldn't survive. And now he was trying to find ways to redeem himself from the past.

In the same thoughtful mood, she wandered round her flowering tubs in the dusk, enjoying the scent of honeysuckle and rambling roses. She and Ed couldn't seem to let each other go. If her mother hadn't found out about her dad and Jackie they'd have carried on for years – but she did and she couldn't bear it. Would she, Lyn, act any differently from Jackie if Eddie said Sharon was having another child? She didn't know and could only hope she'd say goodbye and mean it.

Next day in the staff room at closing time, after a hectic afternoon of kids' free swims, Lyn decided to break the news about her swim.

'Don't forget, next Tuesday I'll not be in all day.'

'So is he taking you on an away day, then?' Andy asked. She could tell he really wanted to know. He must have somehow sensed that she was seeing someone again, and she wondered how she'd betrayed herself. Shelly's ears were flapping because she never liked Andy to show any interest in Lyn's affairs. Wes sank a mug of tea and looked on.

'You off out, then?' Ben asked.

'For anybody who wants to know, I'm going to swim the Humber Mouth.'

'Fucking hell, I always knew you were a bit in the head, Lyn, and now I'm sure,' Andy spluttered as Coke splattered his T-shirt. 'You're a nutcase.'

'What you doing that for?' Shelly asked.

'Because I want to.'

'Bonkers,' Andy said again. He couldn't seem to leave it. 'Thought you'd have had enough water here without going after some more.'

'Channel next, is it, Lyn?' Wes asked.

'Wow!' Ben breathed. 'That'll be well cold.'

Heartened, Lyn rode home. Now she knew she could go her own way and it didn't matter that none of them understood. In the past she would never have dared. She would have said what they expected to hear; gone with them on nights out and done nothing different or original. But now her future would be what she made it.

37

Today was the day of Lyn's swim, and he wished he were off work. If only he could drive to Spurn to see her start and then across to Cleethorpes to be there at the finish. But he would never make it in time – his shift finished too late. He would be with her throughout the day, though, imagining the moment when she'd enter the water at Spurn – five o'clock. The thought of her battling through that wide, deceptive expanse of water made him feel uneasy; she was strong, but the currents could be tricky and the waves powerful enough to sink a craft. He found himself wrestling with surges of emotion.

The drawing of keys, the crossing of the yard and the locking and unlocking, the stair climbing, all happened without his thinking about it. Even at seven-thirty in the morning, the sweat stood out on his face. The wing gagged with an intimate reek – a smell you'd not find anywhere else.

Bri was in his office, ready to conduct staff briefing. Mal joshed with a young female officer who had just joined the wing staff. Eddie decided to slip out of the prison at lunchtime and phone Lyn from his car. She would most likely be at home until she set off for Spurn in the late afternoon. Thank God Bri looked as though he'd shut up soon. Eddie vaguely caught something about some dodgy type on the fours but didn't register it. Then there was a security briefing about making sure you didn't walk in front of inmates when you were moving them, and not flourishing your keys. The security supremo had complained about various lapses he had observed and it wouldn't do.

'Never forget, these fellows aren't stupid. There are one or two very cunning characters amongst them.' Lecture over. Now, exercise.

Lyn would perhaps be relaxing in one of her cane chairs at the back door. Her yard was a suntrap. You could sit there letting your eyes wander over the honeysuckle and the passion flowers, the palm growing in a fan shape, the lavender overflowing a wooden barrel, the laurel bush and the rambling rose. He'd memorized that green wilderness so that he could take himself there and sit on that back doorstep staring out with her.

The morning hiccuped along. What would Lyn be doing now? Was she afraid? Of course she must be nervous. It was a trial, a challenge she'd laid down for herself – but there were the other elements too: her mother's death; her need to explore her own limits. She was so much more complicated than he'd ever thought when he first met her. He found concentrating on his work difficult – his thoughts kept straying back to Lyn. Was she feeling anxious; were her preparations going well? He wanted to be there, share it all with her.

The cons clattered back from the workshops and had to be banged up. That seemed to take an age; then roll call; then open up for lunch.

Finally he'd dropped his keys down the metal chute, clipped his tally back on his key ring and was making for the car park. He heard Mal shouting, 'Where you off to, Ed?' and pretended not to notice.

He climbed into his car. It was stifling, and he rushed the windows down. He took his mobile out of the glove compartment, tapped in Lyn's number and waited.

'Thought it might be you,' she said. 'How are things?'

'I was wondering how you're feeling.'

'Just psyching myself up.'

'Bet you're sitting on your chair at the back door.'

'Got it in one.'

He heard her laugh. 'I'll be with you all the way,' he said.

They talked for a while longer and then he said he'd have to go. He sat with his eyes closed, feeling the breeze on his face. Eventually he forced himself to plod round to the staff canteen.

'So there you are,' Mal said. 'Thought you was ignoring me just now.'

'Would I do that?'

'Yes,' Mal guffawed, 'you would.'

They smiled at each other and Eddie bit into his cheese and pickle sandwich. He didn't fancy the hearty brown dinner Mal forked between gravy-glossed lips.

Back to the wing. The pads had to be unlocked for the movement to the workshops at two p.m., and Eddie was up on the fours now beginning to unlock the cells of those going to work. The usual thunder of feet on stairs followed. The wing was at its hottest. His head ached over his eyes.

Lyn would be setting out for Spurn soon. Dave, the swimmer, would be driving her and they'd meet the chap with the boat who'd go with her when she swam. He saw the dunes, remembered that first visit: the shimmer over everything, the heat up on the headland, the longing, holding her near that military bunker among the blackthorn bushes and the gorse. That day had such a clarity about it, a simplicity marking it out. She ran down to the waves and stood there looking out to sea. At the time he was in the trance of her body moving so close by him but so separate. He burned to discover her, was tense at the idea of what her clothes kept secret. He didn't know then the story of her mother's drowning. Even on that glorious day, unbeknown to him, she must have been battling with the dark knowledge, viewing the estuary through that lens, but not betraying it.

The last of the inmates banged down the stairs on his way to the workshops. Eddie remained for a moment at the rail, gazing at the ceiling fans high up under the roof. They lurched round to little effect, like the wings of some huge blind beetle. Down below in the stairwell the working party crowded together, preparing for their saunter across the yard to the workshops. They wouldn't want to come back indoors once they'd been out in the sun.

She'd got to make it – he knew now how this swim was a quest. He wished he were going there to be with her, driving through those country roads where the hedgerows barred the way with shadow and the fields stretched to the blue horizon.

Someone had got on his bell, and the persistent shrilling sliced through Eddie's musings. The buzzer belonged to pad 18. Eddie crossed the landing, not in the mood for some complicated problem. He was tempted to turn the sound off, pretend he hadn't heard, because he had innumerable jobs to do and wanted to leave work dead on the dot at the end of his shift. But he stifled the thought and approached pad 18. Its single occupant was a chap called Griffin, who had only been in the prison a day or two. Eddie decided he'd simply push his face in, keep things very brisk, and back out straight away.

'Now then, mate, what's the matter?' Eddie said, moving forward.

Griffin didn't answer, and before Eddie could react, Griffin had caught him in a chokehold. A sharp kick behind his knee felled him. He gasped with pain and shock. The pad door crashed shut and he realized he'd made a cardinal mistake: he'd not shot the bolt. Griffin was no

308

youth on a Spanish beach. This was the attack of a practised fighter.

Eddie felt the blood hot in his face and his body drenched in clamminess. Inside the pad the air was thick. The walls were closing in. He was caged, no escape. Griffin would do for him. Panic made him breathless. *Don't be a fucking coward*, he told himself, trying to fight down the surge of terror. He was speechless, aware only of the mad blundering of his heart. He forced himself to take a long slow breath, wondering what Griffin's next move would be. Flat on his back on the floor, Eddie chanced a look at the man bending over him.

'You didn't expect that, did you?' Griffin said.

Eddie tried to keep his expression easy, knowing that he must not challenge Griffin in any way. Griffin had glacial eyes and curly grey hair and a tattooed beauty spot on his left cheekbone. He was no local druggie, but had the build of someone who'd spent years in a dispersal prison – such men always bore the stamp of obsessive weight-training.

'Too right,' Eddie said.

'Yer, well don't try anything. Take your belt off.'

Eddie gingered himself up into a sitting position. His back hurt and his neck felt as though it had been dislocated. Griffin fixed him with a strange blank look. Eddie hesitated and Griffin's tone became darker. 'Look, matey, I don't fuckin' mess about. See this!' He brandished a razor blade. 'You try anything and I'll slit your fuckin' throat, be sure of that.'

'Okay,' Eddie said, fumbling to unfasten his belt, remove the radio and hand over his keys. From his position on the floor he could see no way of tackling Griffin, and Griffin, as though sensing the direction of Eddie's thoughts, never let his gaze slip from Eddie's face.

'You stay where you fucking are.' Griffin went to stand by the door. 'Don't fuck about with me and you'll be all right. I know you screws, you're a two-faced lot, get your kicks out of watching cons suffer. You wouldn't be doing this job if you weren't twisted. Well, why are you fuckin' doing it, then?'

'The short answer is, I don't know.'

'Don't know! Don't know! What do you know, then?'

'Thought maybe I was helping people.'

'That's a laugh – that is a fuckin' laugh.'

Griffin propped his back against the pad door and lined a cig paper with threads of tobacco, then lowered his head to lick the adhesive, watching Eddie all the while. Eddie wanted to rub the back of his neck, which stung and throbbed, but didn't dare move his hand in case Griffin kicked off.

'Just tell me what you get out of it, then.'

'If you really want to know, I often wish I didn't have to do it. I find it very depressing.'

Griffin lit up and smoke pooled in the turgid air. 'Did you want a burn?' he said as an afterthought.

'No, ta, don't smoke.'

You had to keep them talking; try to set up some kind of dialogue. As long as they talked, you were communicating. Eddie delved in his head for personal security info to be used in the event of being taken hostage. The smoke irritated the back of his throat and he coughed until his eyes watered.

'You aren't used to pad conditions, are you, matey?' Griffin said in his low, controlled voice.

Eddie was most disconcerted by Griffin's voice and his eyes. His gaze drenched you in an Icelandic beam that froze you rigid.

'No,' Eddie said, 'I'm not, but I've always known they were pretty hellish. Look, mate, had you anything in mind for this?' Eddie didn't know what to call it. If he used the expression 'hostage-taking', that would set the thing in stone, whereas at the moment it remained untitled, just something that had happened. He had come across murderers who said, 'Well, of course I'm not a murderer' – as though their action were free-floating and had no name.

'You're here because I don't want to be held in this piss hole – it's shite through and through. I want a move to a civilized nick, right. I am sick of being pissed about. They're cunts here, I'm telling you. They want to fill the cons with methadone so they'll keep quiet: "You've got a headache? Oh, give the fucker methadone."'

Eddie, watching the other man, saw how the colour flamed into his cheeks. He vibrated with damped-down fury. Better let him talk it out, let the adrenalin wind down. At the moment the cold drill of his rage seemed unfocused.

If only someone would notice what had happened – but nobody would until roll check at four-thirty. The guys on twenty-three-hour bang-up didn't get monitored until then. What if they didn't notice? But they were bound to. There wouldn't be any chance of reaching Spurn or even Clee-thorpes in time now.

'You don't know what it's like, do you? What's your name, then?'

'Eddie.'

'Yer, Eddie, you've had a nice happy life, haven't you? No hassle, no probs. Everything fine and dandy. Nice house, wife, kids, the lot. Big car – screws always have big cars. Is it one of them people carriers? Range Rover? Eh? Merc? Big black shiny job?'

'Yes, I know I'm lucky compared with a lot of people. What's your first name, mate?'

'Yer, you see, you don't know, do you? To you I'm just Griffin and a number. I don't have a first name, so we might as well keep it at that, no change.'

'Okay, Griffin, if that's how you want it.'

'No need to try to come on smart with me.' Griffin moved

his foot and Eddie thought he was about to kick him or worse, but he tried to sit quite still as though relaxed.

Eddie received an icy dart from Griffin's eyes and suppressed a shudder. Griffin had sunk down to a squat on the floor, his back supported by the door, but his eyes never left Eddie's face. Squatting like this, Griffin was level with Eddie, and to Eddie this felt like another effort to dominate him.

'I've taken some punishment from screws like you over the years, Eddie. You don't need me to tell you about my life – you know it, same as the lives of loads of cons. You could make a fuckin' pattern out of it: fuck-hopeless parents, children's home, abuse, YPs, bullying, nicks. And all the fuckin' time it's batter or be battered.'

As Griffin's low voice narrated, Eddie's chest felt tight and light. It was as though Griffin wanted to make him responsible for all the failures of the prison system and all the inequalities in society.

So Griffin thought he had a privileged life – Sharon and the bastard new house; the constant scurrying to wallpaper, paint, keep the structure perfect, keep up with Di and Barry and their circle; placate the bank manager; take on more overtime to pay up; fight down his guilt about Lyn; the abandoning of his dreams of a new career.

And soon, out at Spurn, Lyn would be entering the water, wading through mud perhaps before she started . . . but he'd miss it; miss seeing her walk up that beach at the end. Only there'd be the interminable distance in between that moment on the beach and her setting off – the struggle all the way across with heavy waves ploughing at her. Another surge of panic crashed over him. He made himself count in his head: *breathe in one, two, three, four, out* – and he counted to eight.

'You don't know about any of this, do you, Eddie?' Griffin ranted.

'What can I say?' Eddie muttered. 'I know what you mean, but I can't change it.' He knew how the job could sour you, how your idealism shrivelled – it happened without your ever having realized it. You began to fit the stereotype other people had of you: the warder. You see-sawed between fear of what men blown to hell with coke and smack might be capable of unleashing in unsuspecting moments, and the repugnance you felt when your colleagues treated all prisoners like druggie scum.

'You wouldn't change it if you could, would you?'

'How do you know?'

'The government's got a whole fuckin' industry running on the backs of cons – all them screws' wages, probation, drugs workers, teachers – there's too much money invested for it to close down. Cons are stupid cunts – they never see it. Never saw it myself. You do the same thing again and again; you never learn.'

Griffin was well launched on the subject of the penal system, and Eddie nodded periodically, wondering absently when he might be sliced. When he didn't arrive home at the appointed time Sharon would start fulminating about his lateness – Eddie could hear her muttering on about Mal and going to the pub and giving no thought to his family. Part of her would be moiling over suspicions. Now she always suspected him of an affair. *When something's dead, it's dead,* he thought. The words leaped up in his head like a neon sign.

Griffin's marble stare forced him back to the cell. 'You with me, matey?'

'There's a lot of truth in what you're saying, Griffin – and it's true that if all of you in here decided to go straight we'd none of us have any jobs.' What now? This dialogue couldn't go on indefinitely. He must try to think of a way to get Griffin to decide that holding him hostage was a pointless idea. 'In view of what you've just said – I mean, about learning from actions and not repeating the same mistakes – don't you think it'd be a good idea if you decided not to carry on with this, and then we could get someone to open the pad door?'

'You would say that, wouldn't you, Eddie? Just because you're finding yourself a tad inconvenienced, eh?'

'Just a suggestion, nothing more.'

Griffin fashioned another roll-up. 'Sure you don't want some burn?'

'Positive, ta.'

'What will your wife say to you being held up in here, eh?'

Eddie detected some *Schadenfreude* in Griffin's twisted smile.

'She'll just think I'm out having a bevvy, and she'll be mad. Then if she does find out the truth she'll be annoyed because it's nothing but a nuisance to her.'

For some reason this seemed to tickle Griffin, and he shook with laughter. 'Fuckin' hell, man, she doesn't sound like a bundle of laughs.' The beam seemed to soften a little. 'Women, there's some diabolical fuckers. Got a couple of kids by this mare, right – but would she let me see 'em? Would she, fuck. They're teenagers now, don't even know where they are. She fucked off with my best mate. In here you have to put all that behind you. There's no point; it's all too much aggro. But sometimes I get to thinking about those kids – boy and girl, Kylie and Kirk – and I think what a waste, what a fuckin' waste. What have I done with my life? Where has it gone? Yer, there's times when you start to wonder at the total fuck-up of it.'

'I know what you mean,' Eddie said. 'Don't get the idea that I've not fucked up as well, because I have.' He found himself staring across at Griffin, but he felt as if he was no longer catapulting into the centre of a mad vortex.

Eddie imagined Lyn might be entering the estuary at

Spurn – or she could be standing on the beach there, gazing out towards Cleethorpes. *Please, God, let it be calm, let her swoop through the water.* If he could only keep his thoughts fixed on her, she would succeed.

Griffin lit up again. The pad drifted in an acrid haze. A pigeon had perched on the windowsill outside and gave a shadowy cooing call. 'They become your friends,' Griffin said, noticing that Eddie had turned his head to look at the bird. 'You get to see the little things. Spent a long time in solitary – you get like you don't know how to behave with other people.'

Eddie nodded. 'Mind you, the loneliest place on earth can be in the middle of your family.'

Griffin's laughter honked. 'Looks like you should be making changes, mate.'

'Yes,' Eddie said, 'I think you're right.'

'Well, do you want me to slit your throat or what?'

'Be grateful if you didn't.'

Feet pounded up the stairs. 'Workshops must be coming back,' Griffin said. The flap on the door flipped back and a face peered in, someone gesticulated. 'He wants some burn,' Griffin said. He had shot to his feet and shook his head. The flap banged to. Men shouted to one another; heavy doors slammed shut; keys rattled. An officer's face appeared behind the flap. He was obviously shocked. Eddie braced himself for what would happen. It wouldn't be pleasant. He breathed in deeply.

'Here we go,' Griffin said. 'Here we go.' He shot a glance at Eddie. 'You needn't worry, mate, I shall go gently.'

'Thank you,' Eddie said.

The officer, Smythe, one of the hefty brigade who'd sat on Eddie during staff training, had summoned a serious backup. They waited outside, and when the door jerked open, Eddie glimpsed their faces. He knew they were poised to manhandle Griffin, and he heard his voice cutting in

315

first. 'It's okay – Griffin's giving you the razor blade; there's no problem.'

He could see Smythe wanted to come on heavy and felt cheated. Griffin had dropped the blade on the floor. For the length of a heartbeat they all stared at one another, and then Smythe led a rush on Griffin. 'Come on you fucker,' he growled, and they dragged Griffin away, but not before he'd sent a sardonic glance in Eddie's direction.

The PO and the SO moved up to Eddie and both talked at him, but Eddie couldn't concentrate on what they were saying. He could only peer after the group disappearing with Griffin in the direction of the segregation unit. Damp with sweat, impregnated with smoke, his spine and neck aching, he stood there frowning. He would get clear of this diabolical place. *Things*, he heard in his head, *have got to change.*

'You all right, Eddie?' Bri, the SO, asked. Eddie knew that Bri had said exactly the same words to him when he'd found Smithson strung up in his cell. 'Are you all right?' – as though you could be when you had witnessed despair of such magnitude. They expected him to say yes and he did.

The governor and deputies crowded round. Officials talked. Somebody rumbled on about statements, debriefing and counselling. Eddie was led off the wing. In the governor's office he sat with a mug of tea before him.

'Eddie, I'm sure you'd like to phone your wife?' the governor said, gesturing at his phone.

'No thanks – it's okay.'

'Well, later, I expect, when you've got over the shock . . .'

'No,' Eddie repeated, 'I don't think so.' Experiencing an unaccustomed feeling of release, he grinned across at the governor.

38

If only the night would end. At times she was unsure whether she was asleep or awake, her stomach knotted with anxiety. What if the water was freezing? Suppose she found she couldn't make it? . . . Stupid to be wittering on about it now – of course she was going to do it. She ought to have been resting properly, saving her energy, instead of worrying.

She caught the weather forecast at seven o'clock on her kitchen radio. It would be a fine day. She slobbed out in her pyjamas to the back door, hauled a basket chair to the open doorway and fetched a bowl of cornflakes. Sitting there with the early sun warming her face, she let herself enjoy the jade and sage green of her secret garden. A white rambling rose twined up a trellis on the wall and in the sunlight its scent perfumed everywhere with a heady sweetness. Later on she would have to do some watering – but by that time she'd have undergone the trial. Her stomach muscles tensed; she shivered in the warmth, chomped the cornflakes down fast, and slotted two slices of bread into the toaster. The toast popped up and she worked butter into it and spread a thick layer of honey on top. She wanted to keep moving about because that seemed to drive out her night-time fears.

'Give up doubt,' Dave had told her. 'It's all here in your mind. You're going to swim the Humber Mouth. You can do it. I know you can. I've watched you – you've put me in my place. Believe in yourself. Go with the water, not against it.'

But at the same time he'd said: 'I've seen grown men cry because they couldn't go on. Often it's because they don't believe they can.' She had a sudden vision of the men in the hydrographic office peering at their maps. 'Oh, you'll not do that, it's too dangerous – nobody does that.' In an instant she could see the estuary at Spurn stretching before her with the misty crane arms away over in Grimsby and the water in between bucking and swirling endlessly. Those waves could slam her under, fill her lungs . . .

Stop it! she yelled inside her head. Don't be such an idiot. You aren't going to let Fred and Dave down, or yourself. You've been getting ready for this day for a long time – you're prepared for it. You know that core of certainty inside you; you know your own strength, and it'll carry you through. There's no reason why you shouldn't try to enjoy the journey too.

Fred believed in being inside life's challenges and taking pleasure in them. And it was a wonderful day for a swim. Something else he'd said returned to her now: 'We're born alone and we die alone, but there's the stretch in the middle where you show what you're made of . . .' Show what she was made of, that's what she had to do.

She was steady now, but buzzing with energy. After showering she wandered about in her tracky bottoms and a vest, then decided the pots needed water after all and took herself to the backdoor step, where she surveyed the green arbour. Each plant was special, and she'd studied it, watching how it developed. Now was full flowering time and the air was crazy with perfumes. A bee buzzed on the rambling rose. Next door's marmalade cat picked its way along the top of the wall, stepping over creepers and peering down at Lyn with its slitty lemon eyes.

She tilted the spout of the watering can into a pot of red geraniums. Moisture pearled on leaves and a herby scent hit her nostrils. She gushed water on the ferns whose fronds drooped from a long trough. The baths would be steamy. Andy and Ben were on first thing. She smiled picturing Andy pacing the poolside, rolling his shoulders, and Ben lounging on the high chair, face blank with heat and boredom. They'd be expecting her to mess up – well, Ben wouldn't, but Andy was bound to. But what did Andy's sour grapes matter? She was set on her adventure . . .

Lunchtime. She was sitting drinking a glass of apple juice and letting her gaze drift over the mass of shining foliage when her mobile rang and she heard Eddie's voice.

'I'll be thinking of you all the time,' he said, 'so when you're out there, you know I'm with you. Love you.' He was gone. She rubbed away the tears starting to trickle from her eye corners and set about brewing a pot of tea and making a big fry-up of egg, bacon, mushrooms, tomatoes, hash browns and toast.

Eating that huge meal proved harder than she'd thought. As she broke off from consuming it, she ran through the day's arrangements again. Dave would come for her at three and drive out to Spurn. He'd booked a day's holiday, as he'd volunteered to be with her. 'You're an angel,' she'd said giving him a hug. 'Thanks ever so.' He'd looked pleased. When she'd come back after that really bad chest infection and flu, his attitude to her had changed. From then on he understood that she wouldn't give up and he'd become as keen for her to succeed as she was.

As she cut up her egg and bacon, she thought about what she ought to take – she'd need flip-flops for the beach, fleece, towels, Thermos, goggles, toilet bag, Vaseline to stop chafing. 'Whatever you do, don't get grease on your arms and hands,' Dave had instructed. 'If they have to pull you out, you don't want to be slipping through their fingers.'

After she'd washed up, she took the stairs two at a time. She was going to wear her favourite scarlet cossie; she liked the cut of the back and it hadn't let her down so far. Pleased with the spread of her shoulders and the length of her thighs, she grinned at herself in the mirror, then slipped into her tracksuit. Time to pack her bag with the gear she'd laid out. After that she toured the house, checking to make sure she hadn't forgotten anything she needed. When she returned, everything would be different. She was bound for a life-changing event. Now she just wanted Dave Jamieson to arrive and to be on her way.

That was when the phone rang, and it was Fred. 'Enjoy your swim. You'll show what you're made of,' he said. She could tell he was smiling, and the warmth of his voice brought the tears to her eyes once more.

Dave pipped the horn and Lyn belted to the front door, sports bag in hand, rucksack on her back.

'Hi. Got everything?' he called through the window. She nodded. 'Dump your gear in the boot.'

Radio 2 crooned away as usual, and Dave sang along to Johnny Cash, then took off Elvis with a big warble in his voice. Lyn couldn't stop grinning.

'So, missy, you didn't know I was a singer, did you?'

'No, Dave, I didn't.'

'Well, then, you've learned something.'

'Fred's just rung,' she said.

'Yes, he would . . .' Dave said, and grinned back at her. 'He's on your side, lass – we all are.'

They flew along out of the city, leaving the snailing traffic and the swaying buses behind. The lines of brick houses subsided into a patchy area of bungalows and two-storey buildings scattered among smallholdings and petrol stations, car repair places, rusting piles of machinery, and nurseries. These were just places on the way to somewhere else, haphazard collections of buildings and small enterprises lining the twisty road away to the coast.

It was like the day when Lyn first went with Eddie to Spurn. The sun blazed and the sky stretched blue into the distance. From time to time clouds bowled across. The hedgerows stood high and speckled with dog roses and purple cranesbill.

'All set for it?' Dave asked.

'You bet.'

'You should be all right today. The water shouldn't be too bad either. The boat'll meet us there – it's a fishing boat with a diesel engine. With Gerry on board you'll be fine. Remember what I said – you'll go in a V for about forty minutes and after about an hour and a half you come back in another V. The boat plots the course – the pilot knows where you should be heading and you just swim by the boat.'

Past Kilnsea, and they reached Spurn. Dave turned right along the winding, deserted washboard track. Lyn stared at the salt marshes and the mudflats where seabirds balanced on one leg. The pools and viridian pads of weed dotting the mud lent everything an eerie subtropical atmosphere, so that she imagined they were entering a region of mangrove swamps like she'd seen on telly.

Here it comes, she thought. *It's now, it's what I've been waiting for.* And she felt how all of her was focused in on the feel of the day and what she was about to do. She was no longer afraid, but was letting each minute unfold.

Dave parked. She could see the boat drawn up on the beach and three men beside it chatting. She knew one of them from the swimming club. They had stopped and were looking in Lyn's direction.

'There you are – Gerry and Ken are all set.' Dave made off towards them and Lyn followed. She stared out over the expanse of water scrawled with wavelets running into the misty distance. The crane arms of Grimsby reared up way ahead. When she'd been training at the dock in Grimsby, she'd often thought of Spurn over on the other side, and now here she was gazing back from it.

'This is Lyn,' Dave said, and two men extended their hands to her. Gerry's handshake was so firm it hurt, but Lyn found it reassuring. Ken's hand by comparison seemed dried up and slack. Nick from the club contented himself with giving her an encouraging grin.

'You'll be fine,' he said. She was glad to see him. He'd watched her from her first day training in the dock and had always supported her from the boat.

'So you're the swimmer,' Gerry said. 'You've picked a good day. Looks like a settled afternoon, though we could get a bit of wind later. You never can tell. I've rung the coastguard, so he knows what's happening. You just take it easy – we'll be with you all the time, and if you want a drink or anything, just say. If you get so you don't want to go on or you can't – whatever it is, give us a shout and we'll have you out of the water in two shakes. You don't need to worry about direction, we know where we're going. I know the Humber like the lines on my face.'

If you get so you don't want to go on or can't. Why had he said that? Did he think she was incapable, that she'd soon be whining for help? Why would he offer her an escape route unless he thought she'd need one? Am I getting paranoid? she thought. Of course he has to tell me all the safety stuff – it's his job.

'Well,' Dave said, 'I'll watch you set off and then I'm going to drive round to Cleethorpes and I'll be waiting for you there.'

'That's really good of you, Dave,' Lyn said. She slipped out of her tracksuit, stuffed it into her sports bag, and turned to him.

322

'Good luck, kiddo, I know you'll do it,' Dave said, giving her a bear hug. 'See you on the other side.'

'You're a star, Dave,' she said, feeling tears welling up again.

She handed Gerry her rucksack, and Dave took her sports bag. Then Gerry and Ken shoved the boat, *Sea Sprite*, into the water, and the engine ticked over as they waited for Lyn. After a last drink from her water bottle, she eased on her cap, making sure her hair couldn't escape. Next she put on her goggles and settled them on her nose. She took a deep steadying breath. Dave stood by his car looking over at her. She waved and walked down the sandy strip towards the water, taking care not to step on any pebbles.

This was the moment, this was what she had trained for. All that time in preparation, and now the swim itself seemed to have stolen up on her unobserved.

The chill of the water in comparison to the heat of the sun on her shoulders shocked her as she began to wade in. On the horizon the grey tankers dithered, lying low in the water. A gull screeched overhead, balancing on air currents. Mud rose past her ankles, her feet squelched in the soft-ness rising up her legs. She sank into the sensation of the mud on the foreshore and her mother wading into it, sinking deeper and deeper. Coldness hit her legs. She wanted to turn back. But she lifted up her feet and floated off.

Now she struggled with the chill striking her chest. Her breathing stuttered. She forced it lower. This was no different from being in the dock – why was she making such a big deal of it? She dipped her head and brought it up – standard dock training. She breathed in and pulled.

She was off, swooping through the water. Her body vibrated with euphoria and dread. The boat throbbed nearby on her right. She heard Gerry say, 'There you go, you're away now.' The coastguard station was on her left and the black-and-white-striped 'Dynamite' tower on her right. She wouldn't let herself get snagged in that moment at the start. It was going to be all right. Remember what Fred said: 'Enjoy your swim.'

'You'll swim diagonal to the middle of the river,' Dave had told her, 'and come back diagonal on the other side.' Now that it was starting to happen, she could feel herself losing any sense of direction. But she stayed with the boat, trying to keep fifteen to twenty feet away from it.

As she swam out of the shelter of Spurn, the weight of the water drove at her in more powerful eddies, knocking the breath out of her. The tide was on the ebb, and she could feel it dragging her away from the Humber. She remembered the hydrographic office man talking about whirlpools and how at times even small boats couldn't make this crossing. She let the thought sink away because that wouldn't happen today, not with the sun shining and in the middle of summer. All she had to do was let herself be carried forward by the drift. Not against, but with . . . 'Never fight it,' Dave had said.

She imagined she was pulling out by the Spurn Bight, another landmark on the map, when she began to pass three anchored cargo vessels waiting for the tide to lift them off. They lay low-slung and massive in the water, seeming to dwarf her, and through her goggles she caught vague glimpses of crewmen leaning over the side, grinning down at her and calling out. Their nearness amazed her – they couldn't have been further than twenty-five feet away – and she was relieved when she'd passed them.

After that encounter she settled down into the swim. Gerry's voice punctuating the constant throb of the engine, and the sound of the waves hitting the boat's side, formed a steady background music. She heard herself inhaling and exhaling, and the whispering of breath established a pattern.

She couldn't see above the water, and the external world retreated, hovering at a distance. Now there was only the flipping of her feet and the curving of her arms, water flying in sparkling veils from elbows and the wailing of sea-birds. She had experienced this at times in the dock too: a sensation of becoming part of the whole, of moving into a rhythm greater than your own and being permeated by it. Try to resist it and you'd be crushed, but relax and go with it and you'd be swept forward. She felt a conscious power in the sensation of gliding down and through the onrush of waves.

She seemed to hear Fred's quiet voice speaking to her, urging her on. 'You can do it,' he said. 'It's all in your head; you're in charge.' The terrors that had eaten away at her at the thought of the swim, of being out alone on this vast open stretch, vanished in the movement of her arms and legs and the even thread of her breathing. Even the sound, smell and thrust of the waves were comforting.

'You all right, love? Want a drink?' Gerry shouted.

'No thanks,' she yelled back.

Gerry's question had wrenched her out of her inner composure, and she began to worry that she might be getting too near Bull Fort. She hoped Ken and Gerry were watching out for it. She knew from the map that she ought to pass the fort on her right side. According to what she'd read, the fort was a gigantic concrete-and-metal structure dating back to the First World War. Dave had told her that during the Second World War anti-aircraft guns had been mounted there to protect Hull from attack.

Whether or not she'd passed the gigantic structure she couldn't tell, because her head was buried in the crests and sucked down in hollows. She ploughed on, aware now that a stiff wind had sprung up. The waves were rearing up higher, so she couldn't time her breathing. Lurching hard to her left, she tried to gulp in air but was pushed under by a mountainous sea. She tasted salt. Her shoulders ached. Impossible to breathe – she must have her head up. But changing to breaststroke could give her cramp. No choice, she was gasping. Even swimming breaststroke seemed impossible. As a tower of water slammed at her, she was driven to arch her back into a bow.

At times disappearing into the stinging brown depths, she lost sight of the boat. The first time the boat disappeared, she faltered, plunging into a quicksand of panic, but just when she thought the worst, another surge caught her up and brought the boat into view. That boat needs painting – must tell Ken, she thought. The only way to survive in these two-foot waves was to drop to side stroke, but that was dodgy as well. Try as she might to anticipate the force driving at her, she was continually being knocked under by it. Don't get too near *Sea Sprite*, she kept telling herself. The next minute she'd lose sight of the boat and terror made her heart bang. She managed side stroke for an endless half hour. Respite – they were coming into the lee of the land and she was able to change back to breaststroke and then crawl.

In and out of the tussling Eddie wove. She replayed his last message: 'I'll be thinking of you all the time . . . you know I'm with you.' She thought of him as she breathed in, kicked and glided down the shining mountains and shot into troughs.

The waves came in long rolling lines, but sometimes there was a slackening and she coasted along until she was caught off guard on an even stretch. A wall of water heaved up, slamming at her head on, flattening her. She was swept under, lost sight of the boat again, had her nose and mouth full of the muddy, stinking Humber, gasped and fought for breath. Her chest felt tight. She was back in that bottomless pool, tentacles dragging her under. The intense chill weighed her limbs down. Leaden, she was sinking, suffocating. All she had to do was shout to Gerry that she was flagging. If she didn't, she'd drown. She must do it now while she could.

Another flurry swept her under. Bright pinpricks of light, like bubbles in stale water, swam before her eyes. This was drowning. She wasn't strong enough. She was beaten, defeated. It was all too much . . . easier to let go.

The voice inside her challenged: *Okay, go on, go on, panic, choke! Get on with it, panic as much as you like.* The battering knocked her under again. She came up, choking and treading water. Coasting, she took long slow breaths and tried to exhale evenly while she struggled to get control. She was at the end of herself and had to focus on what was in her head. 'Don't fight the water,' she heard Dave's voice chirping at her. 'Go with it.'

A smaller flurry brought respite.

She realized that she'd look an idiot if she dropped out now . . . She'd trained, the boat was out, Dave was wasting his holiday driving round to Cleethorpes. Fred was expecting her to make it . . . She couldn't take the easy way out.

'Everything all right there?' Gerry bellowed.

'Fine,' she called, trying to make herself believe it, but she knew she was done for; couldn't imagine continuing.

If only she could stop now. The battering of the waves exhausted her. Her heart blundered, she felt too fragile to move forward. It wasn't a matter of swimming the distance, it was having the toughness to withstand the hammering of the water and its coldness. Every stroke demanded so much more effort than it would in a swimming pool.

Into her head came Dave's words: 'I've seen grown men cry because they can't finish the swim.' She knew now what made them cry. But she wouldn't be reduced to tears. She hasn't got this far to be beaten back now. No, however bad it got, she was going to finish.

In one way she'd been heading towards this all her life – right from the time when she'd struck out to sea and left Aunty Mags screaming at her on the shore. She must be strong enough. Even the thing she'd feared most all her life – isolation, being alone – now she was facing it, was in it, but it didn't matter. The sky wasn't falling down, the water wasn't sucking her under. It was a vast sprung mattress beneath her. *You're just part of it, let it support you*, she told herself. *You don't need somebody else to hold you up*.

Just a bit further, if she could do the next ten strokes. Yes, she'd carry on until she'd completed those. She counted in her head, reached ten and started another ten, focusing on the numbers. Tens rolled in her head, one ten following another and she thought of nothing else.

The counting ate the distance, devoured the time. She fixed on it, so that she didn't let the agony in her shoulder muscles, the stabbing in her lower back and the niggling cramp in her feet overwhelm her.

And as she counted, she began to feel that instead of battling against a suffocating onrush, she was being swept forward on it. Her body was no longer tensed against the battering, but easing with the forward motion.

'The tide's taking you in now,' Gerry called, confirming it.

Peering down, Lyn glimpsed sandy shore beneath her. She realized she was swimming in much shallower water. With delight she felt how the current was lifting her and carrying her towards Cleethorpes. As she swam, a great surge of exhilaration buoyed her up, and with long even strokes she glided along, able to take pleasure in the dazzle and spuming of the waves and the strength of her body moving through them.

'You're doing grand,' Gerry's smoke-roughened voice shouted.

'Thanks,' she called back. Weary but triumphant, she swam on, seeing through her goggles at last the amber glow of sunshine weaving over the way ahead. Seabirds boated, but at her approach rose in a flurry of wings to soar into the air. She gave herself up to the drive of the current bearing her homewards, and she relaxed into the sway and rhythm of it, aware of the fragments of weed and driftwood floating near her, all part of this estuary. She thought of rivers, oceans, the North Sea around the headland at Spurn, and she realized she'd never felt the wonder of it so keenly before. Now she could glimpse a fragment of it: she was in it, part of it, being led along by it.

The day at Scarborough with Aunty Mags returned to her, and the feeling she'd had as she'd stared at the sea that it did have a softer face. Would her mother, wading out and being swept away on the outgoing tide, have seen the Humber like that? She could never know. The tight thread of tension and of grief began to slacken, and she was swooping into a calmer place in herself.

Land beckoned, and when she bobbed up, she could glimpse the vertical stacks of chimneys at Killingham, and the tops of other buildings. She struck out towards them, driven by a burning elation. She wanted to yell out with joy, because she knew that instead of caving in, she'd finish.

About the Author

Photo: Sarah Jane Daniels

Daphne Glazer is the author of three other novels and her stories have been broadcast on BBC Radio 4. Born in Sheffield, she has lived in Hull for many years, where she works as a Quaker Visiting Minister to several prisons and as a creative writing tutor. Tindal Street Press published her *Goodbye, Hessle Road* in 2005. This 'bold and compassionate' novel won much praise for its immediacy, authenticity and vigour; for its candid exploration of 'the nature of human evil'; and for its intimate evocation of Hull as a place 'haunted by its proud, seafaring history and almost eerie with menace' (Linda Anderson).

Acknowledgements

I would like to thank Mike Sawdon, long-distance swimmer, for his valuable advice on all matters pertaining to open air swimming and for giving up his time to read the manuscript.

My thanks go to Jack Hale, Olympic gold medallist, for sharing his father's story, and swimming lore, with me.

Thanks also to lifeguard Gareth Hopkins, who read the manuscript and advised on details of indoor swimming, as did lifeguard Simon Fenton.

My friends, Jean Hartley, Margo and Noel O'Sullivan, helped me as always along the way, reading and offering useful comments.

I owe particular thanks to Emma, Alan and Luke at Tindal Street Press for their imaginative guidance and wise advice.

Thanks, too, to Sarah Daniels for her evocative photography and to swimmer Leanne Stacey for being our cover model.

Also available from Tindal Street Press

GOODBYE, HESSLE ROAD

Daphne Glazer

'A tough and tender story
about a tough and tender city'
Alan Plater

Donna, with her flamboyant hair and intricate tattoos, likes to hide behind an upfront attitude. When she strikes up with Shane, the joy she feels is clouded by his lawless past and her own anguish over a friend's death. But as grandmother Ruby shares memories of wartime romances and goes dancing in her silver shoes she offers her family a lesson in passion and survival.

'*Goodbye, Hessle Road* captures the struggling and disenfranchised underbelly of a hard-working city in all its shabby grace and faded colours; in its past glories, and in the evaporating dreams and unravelling hopes of its present occupants; and in all its vibrant, determined, blowsy, spirited splendour' *Robert Edric*

'It is the subject matter which makes this novel so important, putting me in mind of Pat Barker. Daphne deals with the nature of human evil with unflinching candour'
Linda Anderson

'Three women of different generations who poignantly convey strength, sadness, love and joy in abundance, yet without a trace of sentimentality. An enriching read'
Valerie Wood

ISBN 978 0 95479 131 5
www.tindalstreet.co.uk